THE IMPOSTERS

Also by Tom Rachman

The Imperfectionists
The Rise & Fall of Great Powers
The Italian Teacher

THE
IMPOSTERS
A NOVEL

Tom Rachman

Little, Brown and Company
New York • Boston • London

Little, Brown and Company
Hachette Book Group
1290 Avenue of the Americas, New York, NY 10104
littlebrown.com

First North American Edition: June 2023
Originally published in the UK by Quercus Books, 2023

Little, Brown and Company is a division of Hachette Book Group, Inc.
The Little, Brown name and logo are trademarks of Hachette Book Group, Inc.

The publisher is not responsible for websites (or their content) that are not owned by the publisher.

The Hachette Speakers Bureau provides a wide range of authors for speaking events. To find out more, go to hachettespeakersbureau.com or email HachetteSpeakers@hbgusa.com.

Little, Brown and Company books may be purchased in bulk for business, educational, or promotional use. For information, please contact your local bookseller or the Hachette Book Group Special Markets Department at special.markets@hbgusa.com.

ISBN 9780316552851
LCCN 2022947009

Printing 1, 2023

LSC-C

Printed in the United States of America

To Ian Martin, for food and friendship

Contents

Chapter 1   The novelist   1

Chapter 2   The novelist's missing brother   17

Chapter 3   The novelist's estranged daughter   60

Chapter 4   The man who took the books away   100

Chapter 5   A writer from the festival   127

Chapter 6   The deliveryman who stood in the rain   176

Chapter 7   The novelist's last remaining friend   215

Chapter 8   The novelist's former lover   257

Chapter 9   The novelist   285

Acknowledgments   *341*

THE IMPOSTERS

The novelist

(DORA FRENHOFER)

HER HUSBAND IS CHATTING, his comments interrupted by potato salad. Democracy is in crisis. Another bite. Someone's friend said populism. Chewing. A woman on the radio worried.

Dora – seated opposite at the kitchen table – responds only with 'Mm', a noise of such ambiguity that Barry worries he's talking nonsense, so talks more, an abundance of words that might include something clever eventually.

On the one hand, he says.

'Mm.'

On the other?

'Mm.'

'What time did we say for them to get here?' He knows, so the question can be understood as marital sonar, probing the mood of a spouse, registering what bounces back.

Dora, who is seventy-three, spent most of her decades without a husband, intentionally so. But that preference changed when she plotted the last chapter of her life: once feeble, she'd end it. The plan presented a problem. Act too soon, and you annihilate a worthy part of your life. Act too late, and you never act at all.

So she found her solution: a younger husband (nine years her junior) to monitor her, and tell her when to act. Dora refers to Barry as her 'ageing assistant' – the kind of joke one repeats too often, which is how one knows it's not quite a joke. Someday, he'll hesitate in the next room, plucking up the courage, then will march in, declaring sorrowfully, 'It's now; probably now.' But lately, it's his physical changes that startle Dora: a stooped grey man joins her at every meal, whereas the tall craggy woman appears only in mirrors.

Barry swallows a last mouthful of lunch, and fetches his little tin of sugar-dusted French candies. He flings a purple sweet into his mouth, cheeks caving as he sucks, the bags under his eyes rising effortfully, a melancholy man posing as a chipper one, still exuding the lonely English childhood, an engineer father who wept once, undergraduate studies hiding at a Cambridge library, followed by a series of enchantments with the charismatic, who mastered him.

Barry began as research for one of Dora's late-career novels, a melodrama involving divorce. She sought authenticity, and someone provided the number of a family lawyer. Before their first meeting, Barry read several of her books, and worried that she might convert him into a character. When she arrived, he praised her memoir above all. Everyone prefers the memoir, so she likes it least. A novel is what you make; a memoir, what's made of you. Put another way, novels are her inner life, even if her inner life rarely sells more than eighty-six copies worldwide.

Still, Dora has managed to keep barging her volumes into stores over the years, a succession of small novels about small men in small crises. As for Barry, he never did become a character in that book – he loses his temper too rarely for fiction. Instead, he morphed into an endearing companion at her elbow during classical concerts, such as those recent Bach cello suites at Wigmore Hall, when Dora enquired during the performance if he was alright, and he leaned to her ear, first clearing his throat, causing her to rear back, then: 'Scientifically, men are more likely to be moved to tears by music,' he mumbled. 'According to studies.' She pulled his arm closer, placing his hand on her thigh, causing him to look up shyly, meeting her green eyes.

Dora checks her watch – they should be here. Who are they again? She clasps her hands, arthritis-knobbled knuckles, blue veins under translucent skin. Barry leaps to his feet, and hammer-punches the table, causing the candy tin to leap in fright. Irritated, Dora looks up.

He's yanking his tweed-jacket lapel, tongue sticking out.

'What are you doing?!' she asks.

He jerks about, silent but for the squeak of his rubber soles on the kitchen tiles.

She realizes: he inhaled that purple candy. It's lodged in his windpipe.

'Barry?' She stands. 'What do you want me to do?' She grasps the cuff of his sleeve but he pulls away, both hands to his throat, thumbs pushing either side of his Adam's apple, to dislodge the blockage. He stares, wide-eyed, desperate.

Dora almost speaks. But nothing. She stands motionless before him. Finally, she turns, and walks stiffly up the hall.

Dora passes the staircase, and finds herself in the living room before tall bookcases that run down the wall. When younger, Dora stole a volume from each man she slept with: ancient intercourse flashes on the shelves among scolding classics, her own novels loitering sheepishly at the margins.

From down the hall, she hears a thud – it's Barry, lurching around in the kitchen, his shoe banging into a cupboard. A gasp follows, and loud coughs.

If coughing, he must be breathing.

The back of Barry's tweed jacket rises and sinks, his arms planted on either side of the kitchen sink, into which he spat out the candy. He twists on the cold-water tap, hoisting the purple dot slowly toward him.

'You're okay now,' she affirms.

He sits at the kitchen table, a sheen of sweat on his face, shoulders shivering with each breath. 'Well.' Another long hacking cough. 'I almost.'

'You almost what?' When Dora worked as a young office typist, she once saw a German businessman suffer a stroke. Nobody did mouth-to-mouth because his beard was flecked with pumpkin soup, still warm from lunch. He ended up with brian damage. Not 'brian' damage. That looks wrong. How do you spell it?

'Gate.'

'Pardon?'

'They just opened the gate,' Barry says. He calls to the front door a strangled, 'Coming!'

Barry, who devoted his legal career to divorces, only found his true passion in recent years, after enrolling in a part-time counselling course. On Dora's encouragement, he abandoned law, and posted an ad in their North West London community magazine: 'Couples Therapist.' At first, his clients never returned more than twice. Barry didn't help his cause by never insisting on payment – it gave an impression of amateurishness, which was the correct impression. Then, Dora crossed paths with an outgoing couple, and they lingered to gab, and the woman phoned back, asking if Barry's wife might sit in on the next session 'just to make it an even number of boys and girls'. Dora agreed: she needed fresh characters.

This afternoon's clients are still outside the closed front door, whisper-bickering before they knock.

On the inside, Barry tells Dora softly, 'I could've *died*.'

'Look, cancel the session, if you want.'

'Coming!' Barry repeats to the door, and opens it.

The male client is a frosty-sideburned Glaswegian ad exec who dresses like a hipster in his thirties, which he was twenty years ago. His wife – a plump pharmaceuticals rep of Lebanese origin in an overtight suit – wants to rekindle their romance. He prefers training for ultramarathons.

As it's sunny, Barry set up chairs in the back garden. Even before his clients sit, they've resumed their dispute from the drive over: 'You just proved my point.'

'You. Are seriously. Insane.'

'*I* am?!'

As they summarize their past week to Dora, Barry leans over his yellow legal pad, writing nothing. Clients always address Dora, for the same reason that she has often attracted people: she takes an interest, but doesn't mind if they leave. At an ill-timed juncture, Barry points out that there's a drizzle, and should they move to the living room? The ad exec is busy talking, and refuses to budge – he's fine! So Barry steps inside for umbrellas, and Dora joins to help. In the front hall, Barry blocks her. 'Do I even need to be here?' he says. 'I feel so expendable. You just walked out of the kitchen, Dora! And now we're sitting there as if nothing happened, listening to these people's sex life.'

'Or lack thereof.'

'Don't miss my point.'

'Then don't be absurd.'

He heaps three umbrellas on her arms, and opens the front door. Raindrops slice inward. He steps out, closing the door after himself. The metal gate tinkles open.

Down residential streets, he strides, wavering after a few steps – then hurrying along, knowing this is out of character, which impels him to defy character. Barry wipes his forehead, an ironed hand-kerchief over thinning damp hair. Humiliated: that's how he feels.

He reaches the park, formerly the grounds of an aristocrat's palace. Whenever upset, Barry fast-walks a loupe around it. But 'loupe' is wrong. Is it 'loup'? Anyway, he tries to outpace his thoughts, which keep circling back to Dora as ever, a constancy of interpretation that exhausts him.

By the duck pond, a beagle strains toward brown water, held back by the commands of its barking owner: 'No, Wally, I forgot the towel. Wally, no!' Barry presses his palm to a chain-link fence, and considers the criss-cross imprint. As a boy, he played with toy soldiers, though never on war manoeuvres; they held talks. A sense of time overcomes him, and the face of his mother, and a plunging span from then to this.

'I won't charge them for today.'

'You were in the park?' Dora asks.

'No, no – just around.'

'I pictured you by the duck pond.'

'You pictured wrong.' Pause. 'Are you going to ask where?'

'I'll keep you at the pond,' she says. 'You *could* charge them – they had the full hour.'

'It's reasonably strange, what happened.' His voice tightens.

'Exactly what, Barry?' She's suddenly ferocious, such that he'd take back everything if he could. '*What* was strange?'

He looks around the kitchen as if for a dishtowel, instead opening the fridge simply for somewhere to direct his gaze. 'Was there anything more from those two?'

She presents her page of handwritten notes, the paper blistered where raindrops landed. Barry carries the sheet upstairs to the attic office, to deposit her latest contribution in a filing cabinet. He never reads Dora's notes on his clients because he fears discovering insights more acute than his own. But he can't ignore her views this time; he missed most of that session.

He holds her page almost too far to view, giving a perfunctory scan. But his expression shifts, and the page nears his face. Barry hastens back to the filing cabinet, riffling in there for Dora's notes on previous clients. Reading, he holds still, his stomach falling.

In all those sessions, he finds, Dora never once wrote of the clients. Each page tells of the same person: an ageing man in tweed, seated beside her, posing as a therapist. Her observations are all alike, with sentences that wander, words illegible, and spelling mistakes, as she never used to make.

He slides all her notes back into the hanging file and locks the cabinet, needing those pages far from view. He sits at Dora's writing desk, his gaze flitting around her attic office. She's malfunctioning. He knows it.

An image from the Bach concert comes to him. When the musicians were performing a piece that he knew Dora adored, Barry glanced over. She was just staring at the seatback before her. He touched her thigh, and she turned, looked up. He scarcely knew those dimmed eyes.

Before, Dora had instant opinions on everything. She knew what she thought, what you ought to think, what everyone else should. Yet lately, when overwhelmed, she just stalls, or walks from a room, returning later as if nothing happened, and indignant if Barry suggests otherwise.

She talks of writing another novel. There will be none.

Barry tucks his chin down, breathes in and holds it, exhaling slowly. He glances at the ledge of photos behind Dora's writing desk: her daughter long before the girl grew up and ran far from her mother to Los Angeles; a faded snapshot of Dora's hippie brother in the mid-1970s with a beer in hand; a black-and-white portrait of her parents in the Netherlands after the war.

Barry has met none of these faces, yet will eventually be left here with them, he the last resident of this home, only creaking floorboards and his mutters, imagining her retorts, which made him laugh or hurt him, or both, and he'd take either, just for her voice in the room. He blinks fast, a flutter of eyelashes; he swallows. He must talk to her this instant.

In the darkened hallway downstairs, Dora awaits his footfalls, which will be sturdy until Barry reaches one step from the bottom, where – avoiding eye contact – he'll announce: 'I'm your ageing assistant, Dora. I'll tell you when. But it's *not* now.'

'Something's the matter,' she'll reply. 'With my brian.'

'Your brian is fine!'

Nobody comes downstairs. Nobody is upstairs, or anywhere else in this house. Only Dora, pondering a fictional character, this husband Barry, based on someone she met in passing once, and written into a story that isn't quite working, as none of her stories quite work anymore.

When younger, Dora populated her novels with bumblers, and depicted them with affection. Yet this story regards an unsympathetic character, a failing novelist, based on herself. It's a punishing self-portrait.

Dora regrets much about herself: that, while she wrote kind characters, she was too impatient for kindness herself; that she always spoke with honesty, no matter whom it wounded; that she rummaged through everyone to extract literary characters, who had the advantage of behaving as *she* wished, the disadvantage of being unlike anyone she met. Either she was a poor writer, or humans were poor characters.

'I need to finish this life of mine pretty soon. Don't you think?' she asks the staircase, as if interrupting Barry's descent, as if pulling him down from that last step, pressing her cheek against his brow, and spying his wrinkled closed eyelids, thus finding an ending to her story: the fading woman no longer wants an ageing assistant, only to age with this man. She does long for such a companion. Yet she'd have struggled to endure a week with him in her house.

Dora climbs the staircase toward her attic office, wincing at each impact on her sore knee. At the landing, she refuses to pause and catch her breath, proceeding straight to her desk, tense, wondering if she has anything more to do, knowing the answer.

DIARY: DECEMBER 2019

I'm jittery, this screen before me. What if the book I'm trying to write comes to nothing?

I look out my office window at other narrow London houses, populated by families growing up and down over the years. A small child appears in a distant pane. This far away, my vision is blurred: just a momentary girl, under a roof pronged with obsolete aerials.

I revert to the correct view, my desk. A computer screen, keyboard, the cursor blinking aggressively at me.

These sentences are fact. I'm writing as myself, Dora Frenhofer, not pretending to be anyone else for a change. But every other chapter will describe a different character. And this presents a problem. Readers want a book to add up to something, not to some things. So I must tie these people together. Maybe the manuscript could be about writing itself? Or about writers?

For a half-century, I've survived as one of those. I consider myself both fortunate and a failure. At the start, I had a spell of luck, and mistook it for a career.

'Maybe I need to retire,' I remarked a few years ago, walking with an old man I was then seeing.

'Retire as a writer?' he said, smirking. 'Who do you tell?'

He was right. You just stop. Nobody notices. But I panic to imagine that step. It feels dangerous even to mention. I should change the subject fast. So:

I needed glasses, and ended up with a black eye. Early for a work lunch, I was wandering down the covered arcades off Jermyn Street, puzzling over the idea of men, as depicted in displays of gents' boutiques: handmade shoes for bankers; spotted silk neckties; the hatter's yellow homburgs.

An optician's storefront presented no nameplate, just a hanging sign of a metal nose with spectacles and a magnificent moustache. I checked my wrist, near, then far, bulging and shrinking numbers: I probably had time, even if I couldn't quite see it. A clerk — unaware that I peeped through the window — removed his glasses, licked each lens in turn, and wiped them on his shirt.

'How may I help you?'

An optometrist could test me right now, though she was startled when the clerk opened the backroom door, causing her to toss aside a travel magazine as if it were smut. She trundled out a metal apparatus, half-medieval, half-futuristic, and pressed my forehead toward the battery of lenses.

'Clearer now?' she asked, as I studied the eye-chart pyramid, topped with a triumphal 'E' and descending toward a fuzz that might've been 'P H U N T D Z'. She flipped lenses. 'Or clearer now?'

I couldn't say, but felt that I must, or I'd fail somehow. 'The second one. Definitely.' Pride, it seemed, would cause me to squint for the next few years.

For much of my life, I'd navigated without optical correction, excepting a pair of reading glasses that I own primarily to lose everywhere. But in recent years, objects beyond my reach have started dissolving. How much, I asked myself, did I really need to see everything? By now, I already know what most things look like.

'As I tell clients,' the optometrist informed me, 'bifocals are like wisdom: you're finally of an age where you can see far away and near at once.'

'Isn't the problem that I can't see either?'

In silence, she rendered judgement on my miscalculating eyeballs, inputting a prescription to her database while I considered the upside-down headline of her discarded travel magazine: 'MYSTERY ON THE HIPPIE TRAIL', featuring a blurry (to me) photo of a young man among prayer flags in the Himalayas. I recall those days, when many of my friends trekked east with spiritual intent, returning with slides of Buddhist monasteries. This was when travel was still a form of disappearance, and nobody knew quite what had become of you till the handwritten letter fell through a mail slot back home, bearing a fragmentary report from your past. When my brother travelled overland to India in 1974, I gave him a copy of War and Peace *for the trip. I still dreamed of becoming an important writer.*

When young, I pictured writers as an intellectual tribe, toiling in Parisian garrets, frowning around New York bookshops, engaging in fiery spats in St Petersburg. Perhaps they'd invite me inside someday. Here and there, they did – and I wanted to run. When they chose not to have me back, I wondered why.

But before I get to all that, I must finish with my eye exam. For suddenly, I was late, hurrying from the optician's to my lunch on Dean Street, sidestepping the clamour of midday Soho, thronged by hipsters darting hither and thither, like a dance number involving portable coffees.

On the narrow pavement ahead, a google of media types jabbered in high-volume glee. Politely, I asked to slip through. (I want to keep these sections truthful, so must amend that. I was not polite.) 'It's not your personal street here!' I said. 'Can I get by?!'

A young woman laughed and I was ashamed, for I agreed with her. But I'd committed to indignation, so pushed by, only to misjudge the distance and stumble, my face bumping into the pole of a traffic sign. I heard gasps, and a few kind observers took half-steps forward. I refused their help, scowling up the pole as if for an explanation, and reading: 'SIGN NOT IN USE'.

One eye scrunched, I walked on, their chatter resuming behind me but not about me — I was dissolving from their consciousness, even if mine still throbbed with them. Humans everywhere, jammed together, demanding to speak. This included me. I had no case for myself over them. Why should they have moved?

Doubting yourself is no way to enter a restaurant. So I acted. Small talk followed. The menu moved back and forth.

'What happened?' my literary agent asked with concern, pointing to my eye.

I looked up from the threat of drizzled sea bass. 'A metal pole crept up on me.'

'Are you alright?'

'Actually,' I said, 'I wanted to ask your advice.'

'Get yourself a steak.'

'Oh. I'd been thinking fish.'

'For the eye, I mean.' She took a photo of mine, and handed over her phone: a swollen purple bar down my wrinkly profile, a whisp of white hair intruding into the frame.

She folded her menu, smiling in anticipation. 'Exciting: you have something new to tell me about?'

'No, the opposite. I just hoped for your thoughts.'

'Cool.'

I didn't want to say any more. But did. 'I wonder, honestly, can I justify another book? Battling with a manuscript for the next several years, and knowing there's every chance nobody will read it. At what point do I accept my situation?' My voice was jagged, for I was exposing myself.

'Wow.' She looked faintly irritated. I hadn't expected that. 'I do hate to see you dispirited like this, Dora. But ploughing ahead is part of the job. Don't you think? Unless you really can't bear to. In which case.'

'No, you're right. Fair enough.' Embarrassed, I switched to safer matters: the ugliness of politics, the prettiness of desserts.

We collected our coats. 'Look,' she said as we parted, 'what you need is to get back to work. Start a new novel!'

So I'm trying, fearful to begin, excited to: the emptiness of a page, the possibilities of a word. I could choose any of them. Come on then.

Only, I can't get the distance right, my face diminishing and growing in the screen reflection, recalling that metal nose hanging before the optician's, that sign with its magnificent walrus moustache.

So far, I have only a character in search of a story, seated at a desk, trying to type.

~~When the servant presented the newspaper and coffee at the door of his upstairs office, Mr Bhatt snarled her away.~~

Or

~~Everyone in the household leaves Mr Bhatt to steep in his rudeness.
Meals have passed, but he is too proud to march downstairs to the
kitchen.~~

Or

A grey cloud expands from Mr Bhatt's nostrils over his magnificent
walrus moustache, whose black bristles twitch with curiosity.

2

The novelist's missing brother

(THEO FRENHOFER)

A GREY CLOUD EXPANDS FROM Mr Bhatt's nostrils over his magnificent walrus moustache, whose black bristles twitch with curiosity. The overhead fan chops to a halt, the lazy blades slapping defeatedly at his cigarette smoke. Must be another power outage: a Hindi love song jangling in the kitchen has stopped too. For once, the Delhi electrical grid comes to his aid.

Able to concentrate at last, Mr Bhatt pushes aside spread-eagled library books and flicks empty packets of Panama cigarettes off his desk, exposing green baize where he pinions today's *Indian Express*, raising and depositing his thighs to circulate the air, his seersucker-suit trousers sighing.

Maddeningly, the newsprint has been defaced: pencil strokes under sentences, comments in the margins. Mr Bhatt propels his nose toward the page, but cannot decipher what his wife scrawled. If Meera, who rises long before he does, is going to read the news-paper first, she must leave all as it was. Or yesterday's events appear according to what *she* happens to believe important, much as when they visit the cinema, and Mr Bhatt is churning with emotion, only for her to whisper a scathing comment, and suddenly he sees all through her vinegar.

He removes his square-framed glasses, and licks the lenses, wiping each across the breast pocket of his pyjama top. With a sip of tepid instant coffee, he orients himself to the Tarzan comic strip. Next, he attempts the crossword, which he cannot complete, so curses the idiots who designed these clues. He advances – rather, regresses – through the newspaper of 13 May 1974, back to front: cricket results, business stories, lastly news. While reading, he unscrews and re-screws a jar of Brylcreem, taking distracted sniffs.

The front page is overrun with 17 lakh railwaymen on strike. Perhaps Mrs Gandhi went too far, arresting so many trade-union leaders. But she mustn't surrender now, lest another gang of rowdies rises up. Where would it end?

Mr Bhatt steps onto the balcony over Jor Bagh – by his estimation, the second-best neighbourhood in south Delhi. In the fenced park below, an ox stands with a plough fitted to its back. The caretaker – that peasant with paan-red teeth – has just left the beast stranded. The radio warbles again down in the kitchen below, and Mr Bhatt returns inside his office, pyjama lapels fluttering from the overhead fan.

While running the bath, he completes his morning jumping jacks, then enters the water with a slosh, shaving while seated, as recommended in the newspaper, for it steams your pores. What they failed to mention is that the bathwater becomes dotted with stubble. Mr Bhatt spends minutes pondering how to extricate himself without coating his torso in black specks.

He dresses for lunch: seersucker suit and a navy school tie that curls like a quizzical elephant trunk, owing to Mr Bhatt's habit of twisting it around a finger while considering his mission. He has much to tell Mrs Gandhi. Should he cram it into one letter? Or select a shocking fact, and place that before her?

First comes the problem of salutation. 'Madam Prime Minister'? Or 'Your Excellency'? Or just 'Mrs Gandhi'? She won't respect a man who kowtows. Madam Prime Minister, he thinks, we hurtle toward disaster! Are you aware of the work of Dr John B. Calhoun? This American scientist constructed a perfect habitat for mice, which mated and multiplied to their hearts' content with no predators or diseases; a mouse paradise. But soon, they swarmed by the thousands. The excess males lacked mates, and withdrew. Cannibalism spread, as did mouse perversity. Societal collapse next. Then extinction. That, Madam Prime Minister, is *our* future. At independence, we were three hundred million. A quarter-century later, we've nearly doubled. The density challenge will worsen this decade. By the 1980s, life will be bleak. As Delhi chapter leader of ZPG (Zero Population Growth Pvt Ltd), I propose the following simple, but firm, measures: a tax on new children; a surcharge on cribs; cash bonuses for the childless. Those who cannot resist mating should produce only one offspring, who shall be rewarded with reserved places in the better schools (provided such boys are bright). The national press must join the effort: no more news photographs of sweet babies, but denunciations of prolific parents with shaming pictures, along with a Worst Family of the Week.

Despite these cogitations, the typewriter page still contains only three words: 'Madam Prime Minister'. For inspiration, he opens a much-consulted copy of Dr Paul R. Ehrlich's *The Population Bomb*, folded on page 152, where Mr Bhatt underlined: 'The disease is so far advanced that only with radical surgery does the patient have a chance of survival.'

How, Mr Bhatt asks himself, can people amble into the future when this — famished humans swarming like locusts (or cannibal mice) — awaits us? He turns to the balcony door, his pulse quickening as if a mob clattered onto it now, sniffing at the window, crashing through, feasting on him. He flicks his lighter sideways, dragging the flame away from the cigarette, as in stylish movies. Exhaling, Mr Bhatt pictures himself not as an independent scholar but as the child of his father and mother, as if they were still in this world, and aware of the duty weighing on their son, R. A. S. Bhatt: to save India.

Suddenly, someone *is* rampaging up the outside stairs. Mr Bhatt snatches a fountain pen, and dots the nib on his fingers, the blue constellation proving that he has not been idle this morning. The office door swings open, and Ajay bursts in, giggling because he's not allowed here. The twelve-year-old bolts around and jumps, landing on his bottom, then back to his feet, attempting a cartwheel on the Persian rug, which slips, as does he. 'You'll break a bone, you fool,' Mr Bhatt warns, repressing a half-smile — until the boy grabs a book, and hurls it. This earns an angrier reproach: 'Hey! That's stupid now!'

Ajay pretends to study a battered cricket ball. He's got a runny nose.

'Where's your hankie, *meri jaan*?'

'I already blew my nose.'

'You wiped it on your sleeve. That's why they put buttons there, to stop backward boys wiping noses on sleeves. Did your mother not provide hankies? How hard can it be, no?'

Ajay is back from his first year at boarding school. Mr Bhatt was a Dosco boarder himself, unhappily so. But he believes that a young man worth his salt must endure, and Mr Bhatt is no more likely to recant a belief than to shave his moustache: he'd look like a child.

The boy is peeking at the page hanging from the typewriter, so Mr Bhatt swats his son away, then points to the mailing address in the upper corner, Safdarjung Road, residence of Mrs Gandhi. 'A correspondence we have going.'

The boy is not as impressed as he should be, so Mr Bhatt runs his knuckle up and down Ajay's ribs, which sends the boy twisting to the ground in laughter, and raises a smile on the man's face. In this room, at this desk, a monumental idea is taking shape. People will die because of Mr Bhatt. More will survive. 'Straight downstairs,' he orders. 'Enough of your nonsense.'

Ajay's wildness is a joy to Mr Bhatt but he never laughs, for it sets an example. He feels older than his years (thirty-one), and he welcomes that. What troubles him is when his son joins in Meera's condescension – the implication that a bumbling fool labours up here.

'How many minutes to cook you?' he asks Ajay. 'I want tender meat only.'

'One hour?'

'We can tell your mother to cook *naniji* instead,' he says, meaning Parvati, his mother-in-law, who is staying. 'But old meat is chewy. You would taste better.'

'What about we eat you, Baba? But my question,' Ajay adds, leaping topics as ever, 'is how does a brain think, do you think?'

Mr Bhatt takes off his glasses, licks the lenses, wiping them on his shirt, replacing them. 'A brain has an idea. How? From a pulse of blood that sends, that goes through cells,' he proceeds, with the gravity of a man who has no idea. 'And cells, they send these ideas from the senses. This is a bit complicated for you.' He escapes to the front balcony, spying a peasant in the park talking to friends – a bunch of layabouts, they are. 'How does a brain think, Ajay? I'll tell you.' He turns back. The boy is gone.

THE ENGLISH WORD 'ANCHOVY' is new to Theo Frenhofer. Even deducing it from his native Dutch – '*ansjovis*' – he struggles to visualize this fish, seeing only sea, silent on top, teeming beneath. In his imagination, the gull in this novel keeps swooping above a glossy surface, swooping and swooping, for Theo is stuck on the same sentence, distracted because the printed English words in his head are drowned out by English spoken at the adjacent table.

It's ridiculous: the guest-house courtyard is otherwise empty, but they took a table so close that he could touch that Swiss girl's shoulder or the Canadian boy's wrist. Should he move? Sun cuts between the overhead vines, roasting Theo – that could be his excuse.

The Swiss girl rests her legs on a rickety chair, bare feet inscribed with tan lines from her sandals, which lie unbuckled on the floor beneath. Her Canadian companion has a faint blond moustache and long blond hair, shirtless and fit, arms behind his head, hairy armpits on display and shoulders bulging, a belly-button hair trail disappearing into faded-denim shorts. On their table are two keys: not a couple.

Pretending to read, Theo eavesdrops, learning that they happened to check in at the same time. The Canadian boy invited her to 'take a weight off' in the courtyard café, where he crash-landed his giant yellow backpack, currently beached against Theo's ankle. On her lap, the Swiss girl cradles a purple Rajasthani sack, her slender arm atop, a beedi cigarette between her fingers.

The shirtless Canadian is asserting his travel credentials with disaster-bragging, though he has limited material – he only just arrived in India, so talks of flights, describing a con man at Delhi airport, and the drive here to Benares. The Swiss girl draws back her frizzy hair into a bun, jaw jutting, left cheek dotted with two small moles. She's a hardened trekker, six months since she and her friends left Geneva in a converted army truck, overland via Iran, across the salt desert, into Herat, watching tourists play chess on the giant board at Sigi's Hotel in Kabul, through the Khyber Pass to Pakistan, and onward.

Theo also reached India overland, though he saw little besides a bus window. His elder sister, Dora, prompted his voyage, deciding that he should leave behind his troubles in their Dutch hometown. She took the train from Munich, where she'd recently published a first novel, and she ordered her brother out of bed, telling him to come with her to Amsterdam. Theo feared contending with his sister, who suffered a common failing of the intelligent: able to dissect an animal, identify every organ, name its role – yet never wonder what the creature thought. In Amsterdam, she sought to stir her younger brother to action, assuring him that *she* knew what he must do. In a tour-company office, she forked over 299 guilders to a hippie seated at the desk, then folded more bills into Theo's breast pocket for spending money. 'But, Theodoor, I demand stories when you come back. Understood?' Her eyes shone as she slapped his hand affectionately.

When the bus pulled out, his fellow passengers roared with excitement. Theo only gripped his jeans, hands sweating. During the long ride, everyone else disembarked when possible, seeking hostels for the night and food and hashish. Theo slept in place on the bus, greasy hair over acne-starred face, large lips, large teeth. Only when the bus was empty did he get up to stretch, for he suspected that his sockless white sneakers stank. Even with nobody there, he had a shy boy's hunch.

Arriving finally at the Delhi terminus, the other passengers whooped in jubilation, and set off in groups. Alone, Theo found his way to the train station, fighting down terror: people everywhere. He bought a third-class ticket to the holy city of Benares, which Dora had mentioned, and he disembarked there, walking down shadowed lanes as bicycle bells tinkled around him, causing Theo to flatten himself against the nearest wall. The sunlight flickered on and off, causing him to look up: monkeys crossing electrical wires. He stepped on a vendor's basket, and handed over rupees in apology, ending up with an onion.

Signs pointed to Dharma Guest House, and he hurried to its entrance, climbing the stairs to the first vacant space he'd seen in a day: a courtyard café, adorned with a pink-yellow mural of the elephant god Ganesha before snow-hatted mountains. Wooden doors lined the outer courtyard, numbered and each shut with a padlock. The manager had refashioned this place for Westerners, and kept his elderly parents at a distance, though a bony old gent shuffled around, vermilion tika on his forehead, waistcoat over dhoti and slippers. In Room 9, Theo tried his lumpy cotton-stuffed mattress, and glanced around the single dwelling.

He remained there in Room 9, visiting the communal bathroom only during off-hours, and never risked the streets. His sister had convinced him that hope awaited halfway around the world. Instead, he woke in dread – within weeks, he'd have no money left. And then? Flipping between cold panic and denial, he distracted himself with paperbacks that departing guests had left by the check-in desk. Thrice daily, he was interrupted by room service: always jam toast, a metal pot of tea-leaves boiled in sweet milk, cardamom, cloves bobbing. Once, a servant grinned at him, and Theo became self-conscious, so paid his bill, and lugged his bag to the train station, intending to reach Calcutta, whence he'd venture into those holy mountains depicted in the guest-house mural. He'd find an edge of the world to peek over, and maybe lean forward.

But nobody would sell him a train ticket. An educated man hovered, and finally explained: the railwaymen were on strike. Theo retraced his steps to Dharma Guest House, and closed the door of Room 9, resuming his residency on that lumpy mattress. The other guests were always just passing through, and vacated their rooms by midday to sightsee. That was when Theo emerged, sitting under the vines, talking to himself, reading to hold back the present. He tried always to get back into Room 9 before any guests returned, but today an 'anchovy' distracted him.

'You'll get raped.'

She scoffs at this claim of the Canadian boy – already, the Swiss girl has hitchhiked around this country, and remains alive. She boasts of a plan to explore the Ganges tomorrow, taking photos at sunrise.

'How much is that?' the Canadian boy asks her.

'You find a man with a boat, and you pay him.'

'I'm up for that.'

'Good – this is cheaper with more. Maybe also this boy, who listens?' She turns to Theo, who is still pretending to read *Jonathan Livingston Seagull*. 'You?' she asks him. 'You will come?'

MR BHATT'S MOTHER-IN-LAW AND his wife stop chatting when he enters the kitchen, and they turn off the radio. He mooches about, glancing in cupboards. 'Why do you two sit at the servants' table?'

Parvati rises with difficulty, legs wide for stability, hands on hips, pushing herself upright. 'What is this on your face?' she asks Mr Bhatt, and reaches toward her son-in-law, causing him to flinch.

'What is what?' Walking into the hallway, he checks in the mirror: blue smears across his face. Before Ajay burst into his study, Mr Bhatt dotted pen ink on his hands, as proof of earnest endeavour. He must've touched his face after. Meera arrives with a wetted napkin, and cleans him. Between swipes across his face, he whispers to his wife: 'When is your mother going?' Parvati was to return to Bombay days before. Yet he already knows the answer, so gives it: 'This bloody strike.'

Whenever Mr Bhatt's mother-in-law is visiting, he gripes. Yet he is fond of her, and touched by her closeness with Ajay, which reminds him of the aunties and grannies who adored him in child-hood. 'She does no good for that boy,' he whispers, softly enough that Parvati – still in the kitchen – cannot hear. 'Does that woman know algebra? Does she know chess?'

'She raised nine children, including all her brothers,' Meera replies. 'Of course she knows how to occupy a boy. But Ajay should be back at school – you cannot keep him here forever. Jandhu can drive him to Dehradun. We are saying this for days now.'

'How I'm going to the library with no car? And what does it matter if the boy is here another few days?'

'Just now, you were saying he's a nuisance!'

'Leave me alone. And turn off the radio in daytime hours. And stop writing on my newspaper.'

'So many rules.'

As he stomps up the outside stairs to his office, the radio in the kitchen switches back on, warbling 'Chura Liya Hai Tumne Jo Dil Ko'. Mr Bhatt smiles, flushing with love for his wife – her defiance a flirt, like his grumpiness.

On the balcony, he watches faraway kites on faraway rooftops, each line swaying, leading down to another particular person. Every-where, humans eating and sleeping and multiplying. Ajay is far below, batting a cricket ball around the front garden, nattering to himself, a test match for one.

That night, Mr Bhatt meets his wife in the hallway, she leaving the bathroom, ready for bed. He was lurking, impatient about whatever she was up to in there – then restoring the best version of himself, for he will seduce Meera tonight, the first time in months. 'You and your mother were complaining about me?'

'Why is that your question?'

'It's my question.'

Abruptly, the flirt-squabbles feel stale. They've been this way forever, but Mr Bhatt is weary of it; she is too. But if either speaks sincerely, the other mocks. At the beginning, spats led to the bedroom. Lately, they lead him upstairs alone.

Mr Bhatt transforms his wife's lack of passion for being ambushed outside the bathroom into a rejection of his life's mission. Indignantly, he consoles himself with the notion that there are upper-class intellects and middle-class ones. To fail at commonplace activities is evidence of a loftier purpose. As he once told her, 'You imagine Albert Einstein driving badly, do you not?' But even the English language, Meera employs with more facility than he. Once, she had a short story published in a British literary journal, an achievement he praised with a curling smile: to scribble tales was a girlish hobby, almost vile when mankind stood at the precipice. If she writes again, he told her, use a pen name. Also, never a character who is him. 'Besides this, anything goes!' he said, to sound liberal.

'Even love scenes?'

'I already said, don't write about me.'

If she wanted, Meera could provide his breakthrough. She'd have words to address the prime minister, a declaration to propel this issue (and Mr Bhatt himself) to the upper echelons. But the propulsion wouldn't be his. So all that he expects – and what his wife is so stingy with – is admiration. Her praise infuses him like nothing else, much as her derision empties Mr Bhatt, a plug yanked from the basin of him. She has only herself to blame. And he has only her to blame too.

Mr Bhatt touches her shoulder, his hand sliding down her soft skin to the crook of her elbow.

'What are you doing now?' she asks.

'I have to explain?'

But the plug has been yanked. He waves her away, telling her to go to her room. 'Don't let the boy bother me in the morning – I have work!'

IN DAWN DARKNESS, ISABELLE photographs a bony-ribbed cow, its tail-swat frozen by the flash. Dazzled, a passing little girl with a badminton racket blinks and sidesteps them, surveying these three young foreigners.

'You know where is the Ganga?' Isabelle asks.

The girl wobbles her head 'yes' with an authority that contains the woman she'll become. 'Now with me,' she says, and strides ahead like a teacher on a school outing. 'Hallo hallo – with me now. With me.' Finally, she turns down what appears to be a dead end with an open window in the far wall. When Isabelle reaches it, she steps through. The two young men follow.

The horizon glows orange, rising into a navy haze above the Ganges, birds wheeling overhead, a whiff of sweet rot emanating from the sandstone steps that slope down to the ghat, where worshippers perform puja in the river. Isabelle widens her eyes at Theo, and squeezes the boy's arm, which affects his chest strangely. This outing – to his two companions, just sightseeing – is Theo's most important event in weeks.

'When we get on the boat,' Steve tells her, 'take pictures of the cremations.'

'It is not allowed, I think,' she says.

'Act like you don't know.'

At the edge of the river, Isabelle turns the aperture dial on her 35mm Olympus, eye to the viewfinder, a slow shutter clacking twice, capturing blurred pandits sinking under the black with a slop, resurrected in a burst, inhaling and brushing their fingers across their teeth. A mother and daughter in saris stand waist-deep and push out candles, then caress the river, stroking dripping fingers down their faces. A shirtless fat man – sacred white thread across his gut, palms together – clenches his eyes and bows pneumatically, splashing the water, garlands and debris bobbing.

A boatman leans on one oar, yessing distractedly to all that Isabelle asks. When she has exhausted her demands, he accepts a thin stack of rupees, and flattens his hand to the young men.

Over the next minutes, more passengers enter. The creaky wooden boat sinks lower with each person, water squashed down, then burping back, slapping Theo's hands, which clutch the edge of the vessel. Strangers talk in languages he can't understand, but he imagines their screams, as if the boat were to flip, everyone trapped, grabbing at him. He pivots about as if awaiting someone. He must get out. But standing could overturn the boat.

The boatman dips his oars and pushes off, water twirling away, its surface winking under the low sun. The overloaded vessel glides past the stepped terraces topped by Mughal forts, gold-roofed Hindu temples, ramparts holding back the caterwauling city. The opposite bank is a flood plain, empty compared with the architectural pandemonium on the near side. Theo looks from one bank to the other, picking at his blemished face, trying not to be sick. Is that mist? A log smoulders. Stray dogs pick at the pyre.

Isabelle rises to her feet, causing the boat to wobble and other passengers to gasp, though the boatman pays no mind. She's seeking an angle on the cremation ghats. In passing, she pinches Theo's shoulder. He tries to speak but no words come. She's nodding toward the water, and her face disappears behind the camera. She photographs a floating log. Until it's the floating limb of a goat. No, the arm of a creature. Rather, a dead child's body, threads of hair fanned across the surface.

THE PROTESTERS ARE BLOCKING Mr Bhatt's chauffeur-driven Ambassador. Two stray dogs stand on the roadside, surprised halfway through mating, still attached by the genitals. Mr Bhatt gives a violent tic of his head, his muttering amplified by the driver, Jandhu, who reaches out the window as far as possible, and thwacks a protester.

Mice warring for resources, Mr Bhatt thinks.

Jandhu holds down the klaxon, and lurches the Ambassador past the demonstrators, who are bumped aside.

'The life of a man is of no greater importance to the universe than that of an oyster,' Mr Bhatt remarks.

Jandhu wobbles his head in agreement, though he understands little English. Looking through a train window from Oxford to London, a young boy surveyed fields under a drowning sky, the land seamed with hedgerows, empty of humans, the boy unsure of any single verbalized thought, just a reservoir of sentiment. Why does Mr Bhatt remember that sight? He lived in England briefly as a child, his father an Indian High Court judge on a half-year fellowship.

The car stops before the Delhi Public Library.

'Is it locked?' Mr Bhatt asks, reverting to Hindi.

Jandhu runs over to check, rattling the doors with no effect. He asks a passing student, then jogs back. 'Railwaymen,' he says.

'They run the library now? How did our country fall so low?' Mr Bhatt talks as if already in politics – not holding office perhaps but a secret eminence behind the scenes, advising the mighty. The theme of Mr Bhatt's backseat speechifying is self-sacrifice: he evokes the gallantry of Indian forces at Bogura, and how we celebrated as brothers after giving the Paks a bloody nose in Bengal. 'Then what happened? We turned on each other, our own countrymen!'

Jandhu is rungs lower in status, but every man has an intuition as to every other man's violence, and both know that the driver would be dominant. Mr Bhatt offers him a cigarette, pretending it's the last in this packet, and that he merely prefers to open a fresh one. Jandhu accepts, sliding it into his breast pocket for later – to smoke with the boss would cross a border.

When it comes to population control, Mr Bhatt explains to Jandhu, our government does have policies: implant loops in the ladies and provide rubber sheaths for fellows. But that's not enough! Not nearly. Our young men run into battle, risking death for the nation. Why not the lesser act of controlling the fly on their trousers? The sexual urge, Mr Bhatt explains, is man's lowest instinct, like those dogs in the street attached by the genitals. Thus, if reproduction is our most base drive, depopulation is the pinnacle of reason.

He frowns, recalling something Meera said, how he'd provided only one child. They'd always agreed Ajay was the start and the finish. What does she imply? That he is less than productive? Annoyed, Mr Bhatt's rhetoric grows more combative. Simply limiting offspring won't do! We've left this too late. The brave must consider the greatest sacrifice: to voluntarily leave the human race.

'Your son? You'd want this of him?'

'What are you talking about, Jandhu? Not children,' Mr Bhatt snaps.

'But when Ajay is grown?'

This impertinence reminds Mr Bhatt why some men are drivers, and should be trusted with nothing more. But that raises a concern: how to persuade the common man? What stirs a lowly fellow like Jandhu to surrender his life for the sake of another? You crack that riddle, and you've solved all.

To do just that, Mr Bhatt frequents the library, reading books and articles on the mysteries of suicide, always in an isolated carrel, shoulders high and books at his belly, as if he were consulting pornographic material. In his satchel right now, he has Hume's justification of self-murder, Montaigne's defence of noble suicide, and a mimeographed publication of the Birmingham Coroner's Court, which transcribed hundreds of suicide notes.

Misery can lead to self-destruction, of course, but valour and intelligence are motives too. Now and then, Mr Bhatt bumps into his father's friends around Delhi, and they stiffly recall the man's accomplishments, and smile to recall his wit. He was the brightest man Mr Bhatt ever met. What had he known? Mr Bhatt's own moods lack action; he would never harm himself.

Most suicide notes, he discovers, are either instructions (so-and-so gets my suits); or sniping (they never cared); or apologies (I ruined your life). Some aim to wound the living (*you* did this); others to cause minimal impact (bye). But above all, Mr Bhatt finds, suicide notes are trivial. The answer is missing, a hollow within every note. His father left none at all. That is a larger hollow still.

On the drive home, Mr Bhatt gazes out the window, hardly noticing the protesting railwaymen this time. A plan is forming. He mutters a line, read so often that he can recite it almost verbatim. 'The operation will demand many apparently brutal and heartless decisions,' Dr Ehrlich wrote in *The Population Bomb*. 'The pain may be intense.'

THE BLOND CANADIAN GUY, Steve, turns out to be wealthy – his dad owns a mine in northern Alberta. When he flew to India, Steve travelled from Delhi airport directly to Benares in a taxi, a two-day drive. Now, he must return to the capital for his onward flight to Kathmandu, while Isabelle has a thousand-mile trek southwest to meet her friends in Goa. Without any trains running, it'll be a nightmare. So Steve has a proposal: drive to Delhi together, where she can find a bus south.

'But we have no car,' she notes.

'I'll buy one.'

Isabelle leans back, impressed, and agrees – provided that Theo joins. Although he says little, conversations fizzle when Theo steps away, prompting Steve to kiss her, kneading Isabelle's small chest as if to increase its volume, she waiting for the tall Dutch boy to return. As for Theo's travel plans, he mumbled something about seeing the mountains. Mostly, he dreads the departure of his acquaintances, with premonitions of solitude again in Room 9. But they want his presence on their roadtrip; they're insisting.

Two Swedish hippies accept traveller's cheques for a papaya-orange Volkswagen Beetle that they drove all the way here from Frankfurt. They warn that its clutch is erratic, the fan grinds, and the glove compartment falls open when you hit a pothole – but it goes. Theo takes the backseat, noticing that his shirt flutters over his chest, heart pulsing. What will he do in Delhi once they all split up? On this ride, he must tell them: I'm lost – please, help me.

Isabelle wants to drive the first part. She has no licence, but her father always let her drive in the French countryside. When she sits at the wheel, Steve – in the front passenger seat – slips his hand under her backside. She calls his bluff, half-standing in the cramped VW to pull off her skirt, just underpants now.

Steve is dismayed. 'What if Indian guys see you like that, and run us off the road, and rape you?' he asks. 'How would you feel then?'

'Not so good.'

'Put some clothes on.'

'You can protect me, Steve.'

'Do you not shave your legs?'

Once they're beyond the outskirts of Benares, Steve demands a piss break, so she pulls over. Without Steve, she and Theo discuss nothing but Steve. 'He knows not very much about the world,' Isabelle comments. 'But he is a beautiful man.'

'Is this why you like him?' Theo asks.

'Is this why you do?'

She points out that there are little curtains on the side windows of this car, but not much privacy. And where would Theo go, if she and Steve made love in this Beetle?

He's back, looking suspiciously at each of them. Steve tells Theo that it's his turn to drive, and pulls Isabelle into the backseat with him.

'I can't see anything from here,' she protests.

'You know what they say: no one rides for free.'

The windscreen magnifies the sun on Theo's face. He turns the key. The wheel shudders in his sweaty hands, and he blinks hard to look more directly at the road ahead: people crossing, motorbikes veering from nowhere, trucks bulldozing by. He could make a mistake.

'Let's move, man!'

Theo pulls out, foot hard on the gas to catch up with other cars, which snaps his neck back. He slows, swallowing, and glances in the rearview. They're writhing, Isabelle whispering for Steve to wait one second. Theo watches the cracked road rush under the car. I am a pointless human. A pink lorry baps its horn. His armpits prickle, mouth parched.

'You kill us almost!' Isabelle cries, red-cheeked and laughing. She clambers over the rattling gearbox, scooching into the front passenger seat.

At nightfall, they're still hours from the capital, so they park on a dirt road, the hissing of nature all around, punctuated by distant car horns. Lit by the VW dome light, they consume leftover samosas and bottles of warm Coca-Cola mixed with Old Monk rum, which spills on the car seats.

They must've all fallen asleep, for it's abruptly bright, their surroundings transformed: not the cobra-infested jungle of last night's fantasy but a public footpath fringed with bushes that they rudely parked on. Locals keep peeping through the car windows at these hairy zoo animals behind glass.

Steve drives the last stretch, speaking only to propose places to stop and have sex with her.

'You are crazy?' she replies. 'That is a village, Steve!'

The villages grow into towns, then suburbs, then a metropolis, people crouched at roadsides, sledge-hammering rocks, swatting flies at food stalls. They've reached the edge of Delhi, hemmed in by other vehicles, yet Steve keeps searching, turning his irritation against the traffic, punching the horn, holding it down. Nearing the city centre, he veers off the road, halting on the soft-shoulder, pedestrians bounding aside, looking at him with bemusement. 'Here. Right here.'

'I don't understand,' she says.

'Nobody cares! This whole fucking country's on strike! Come on!' He's out of the car, and pulls open her door, yanking her arm; she resists. 'Under that bridge.'

'But there are people!' she exclaims. 'They are everywhere!'

He marches all the way to a stony outcrop at the water's edge that is strewn with wet laundry, washermen standing around, observing Steve with perplexity. After a moment, he turns back, shouting to Theo: 'You take lookout!'

Isabelle is shaking her head. 'It is not possible.'

Jogging ahead, Steve prowls around for a secluded space, unwilling to quit, ending up faraway – before turning back, sprinting toward them, full-speed, so fast that Isabelle tenses for impact, her shoulder turned protectively. At the last instant, he stops, crouches to level his face and hers, both hands on her shoulders. He looks to the sky. He screams. And he strips to his underpants.

'Steve? What you are doing?'

Leaving a pile of clothes at her feet, he turns and sprints back down the stony outcrop, dodging washermen and barking at ragged children, who dart aside.

'Steve!'

He leaps, appearing to levitate for two seconds – before the river crashes, an explosion of brown that bursts up, and swallows him. Isabelle and Theo watch where he plunged, the empty surface swaying, lapping against itself.

IF YOU MUST, YOU'LL kill to protect yourself. 'The threat,' Mr Bhatt mutters to his cluttered desk, 'the threat is us.'

A shiver passes through him, for he senses something potent in that phrase. He tries stating it aloud with varying emphases, finger jabbing at a different word each time: 'The *threat* is us.' Or: 'The threat is *us*.' Or: 'The threat *is* us.' Lastly: '*The* threat is us' – by which point, he has sapped the phrase of sense.

We in government (to whom Mr Bhatt addresses his thoughts), we in government are not cruel. We do *not* propose hurting anyone. The opposite. Consider this like conscription during a military invasion. And make no mistake: we *are* invaded. In this conflict, self-elimination is not cowardice but courage. Therefore, Madam Prime Minister, therefore –

He reaches an edge, the confines of his imagination. Mr Bhatt leafs through the library book of suicide notes, seeking a breakthrough, a clue, the key to what inspired such acts. But most of the notes were, frankly, written when drunk.

He drags from the typewriter roller his incomplete letter to Mrs

Gandhi, and threads in a fresh piece of paper, which wavers under the ceiling fan while he summons eloquence to match that of his freedom-fighter grandfather, who composed historic missives at this very desk. At length, Mr Bhatt holds still, hands motionless above the keys, only the flicker of a baby finger, nothing to fling steel against paper. What is it that stirs the valiant to act? They long to escape smallness, to step from the pullulating crowd, to proclaim their true soul rather than the stammering botched version of daily life. In a stunning single act, they express all that they stood for. Thus what once made them cling to life is exactly what inspires them to surrender it. Yes, *that* is it!

He jumps to his feet, then hurriedly back to the chair. Type!

But what?

The notion is slipping away. What connects Mr Bhatt to his own life? What would *he* sacrifice everything for? He pictures his beloved, and how he'd want them to remember him. Suddenly, *clackety-clack* fills the room. Black words accumulate down the white page, preceding slightly his knowledge of what they'll be, so that Mr Bhatt is informed of his own beliefs by reading the page before him. He intended merely to list what men give their lives for. But the writing got away from him, becoming a citation of those he loved, then an apology to his wife and son for his failings, weaknesses he'd never admit aloud, least of all to those so dear. Mr Bhatt confesses that he hasn't done what he wanted in life; that he isn't as clever as they think. If they heard this, it'd murder their admiration of him. He squeezes his thigh to think it – then turns with a start. 'No!'

He pulls out the page, slapping it face-down on the desk. 'I told you! You are *not* allowed!'

Ajay looks down at his shoes, mumbling that Maa wants the maid to clean up here, that she says his office is a fire hazard.

'Did I ask for the maid? Can you not see I am working?!'

Ajay registers his father's face, the wet streaks downward, so Mr Bhatt brushes down his moustache, stamps his foot, then rises in a huff, clanging down the outside stairs, unsure of his destination, inflating the fury to hide that he has no reason for it. 'Chased from my own home!' He bangs on the roof of his empty Ambassador. 'Where are you, Jandhu?' His driver is chatting with the caretaker in the park, and jogs over.

In the backseat, Mr Bhatt jiggles his leg, wanting to return upstairs. He never knows how to ask pardon. Equally, he is poor at tyranny. So he bullies a cigarette, yanking it from the packet, scraping the match so violently across the box that it snaps. Jandhu asks where to.

'I'm thinking!' A terrible thought it is: that page, still up there, face-down on his desk. What if Ajay noticed him flipping it over, and turns it back, seeing his father's barest feelings? Or if Meera reads it?

He orders Jandhu to wait, and races back up the stairs, breathlessly barging into his office, causing the maid to gasp, and bow her head. He snatches the note off his desk — must eradicate it from all existence.

Once they're driving, Mr Bhatt winds down his squeaky car window, and is invaded by the beeps of motorists, the bleating of vendors. Uneven tarmac joggles his lighter flame till it kisses the cigarette tip, a burnt-toast smell supplanting the smog. He feels far more polluted by the folded page in his pocket, as if it contained a photograph of himself in an act of filth. Yet Mr Bhatt can't just fling this piece of paper from his car window into the gutter, full of dung and spittle and soggy newspaper pages; cannot dump his heartfelt feelings toward Meera and Ajay into that. He considers himself a modern man, unburdened by superstition. Yet he harbours certain convictions about cleanliness and dirt. To efface this embarrassing page, he should dispose of it in sacred waters. The closest point is Old Yamuna Bridge, where Mr Bhatt can roll down his window, and toss the note into the river below.

Vehicles are gridlocked as they feed onto the bridge, with a steady flow of pedestrians slogging along the verges. The baby-blue Ambassador lurches, stops, lurches, until they are gulped into the bridge's lower deck, sunlight blotted out. Mr Bhatt's eyes adjust, perceiving the spans of iron, a horse-drawn cart and a flatulent Rajdoot motorbike, cars and cars, people and people. If he threw the note from here, it'd never reach the side of the bridge. He must get out, and toss it directly down. When the car next idles in traffic, he opens the door. 'You go on,' he tells Jandhu. 'You go on!' He cannot have Jandhu witnessing this.

Mr Bhatt presses a handkerchief over his nose, moustache bristling at the exhaust stench. He pushes past scruffy pedestrians to reach the girders, and flicks his note through. The folded paper nose-dives on the other side, stuck there. He kicks his shoe at the fence. The page remains stuck.

Pulsing from the heat, Mr Bhatt tries again to reach it. Cannot. Nor can he leave his intimate self exposed there. A barefooted boy offers to fetch whatever precious object the rich man is seeking over the fence. Mr Bhatt refuses, but the boy is climbing regardless, so Mr Bhatt grabs his shirt, drags him back down, whereupon an unshaven uncle snatches the youth, slaps him, and leads him away. Mr Bhatt wipes his dirtied hands with the hankie. Shakily, he climbs up the fence himself, and lowers himself to the outside of the bridge, steadying himself by clutching huge bolts in the ironwork.

He smells the river below, the effluent of his city. Behind him, a couple of rowdies laugh, and he shouts back cutting remarks, then returns to his giddy view: placid blue above, gushing brown below.

On the riverbanks, dhobis scrub undershorts, flanked by heaps of linen drying under the sun. A washerman slaps a shirt against the rocks, slaps it again. This, Mr Bhatt thinks, is why mine miss all their buttons. He stoops – still holding onto an iron bolt – and retrieves the folded note. He scrunches it up, and reels his arm back to throw the balled-up paper.

But he hears splashing down there: a tourist boy has jumped into the river, and is hollering in English to his two friends, a skinny girl and a lanky fellow who stand on the rocks, mindless that the dhobis are trying to work there. The girl hollers at the swimmer, and hands her beedi to the tall boy, who takes a puff, exhaling fast.

So disappointing, the grade of young person who visits India. Mr Bhatt's ire doubles to realize something: he can't dispose of this page now. The river below is filthy with hippie. What if a breeze caught his writing, and the swimmer collected it? Those creeps, bandying his private feelings around! Bloody foreigners – they should go back where they came from.

Carefully, he shimmies along the outside ledge of the bridge, distancing himself from the swimmer. Mr Bhatt holds to girders as he goes, one hand on iron, the other on the scrunched page.

The sun is burning him but he won't wipe away the ticklish

sweat beads, lest he smears bridge dirt on himself, and how would he explain that when home? He chortles, contemplating himself up here, imagining what his nervous mother-in-law, Parvati, would make of such a sight! He will be sorry once the trains resume, and a first-class carriage rolls her home. Ajay will return to boarding school too. Mr Bhatt suffers a pang: the house empty again.

Throughout Ajay's sojourn, Mr Bhatt has sought to impress the boy, as his own father impressed him, an eminence at a writing desk — the same desk where his father took his life. When that happened, they rushed Mr Bhatt back to boarding school, forbade him to tell anyone, but he did, and forever regretted it, that people knew.

All that Mr Bhatt wants, he suddenly recognizes, is his son near. Why send Ajay to the boarding school that he himself hated? Why can't Ajay stay at home? Mr Bhatt will find activities for the boy — they can read the same books, discuss them. He'll show Ajay everything he knows, and Ajay will soon know more. He mustn't become like me. Mr Bhatt draws a shaky breath, sweat trickling, then is distracted by the riverbank: the sopping hippie getting out, shaking like a dog. The river below is clear, so Mr Bhatt can dispose of this letter. But with his free hand, he first struggles to open the crumpled page, wanting a last look.

He stares at the crinkled paper, perplexed, as if the victim of a cruel magician. This was his confession. But all it says is: 'Madam Prime Minister.'

Mr Bhatt searches his memory: rushing upstairs to his study, the maid there, she gasping in fright, looking submissively at her bare feet, he grabbing the page.

The wrong page. He took the wrong page. His confession is still there, beside the typewriter.

His stomach muscles tighten, innards clenched. He needs to get home *immediately*.

Something else, though: he must ask Meera what they should do. He is young still. She is too. And their greatest joy is that child.

THE DHOBIS ARE LOOKING at the bridge, talking to each other. Theo shades his eyes to see. A little man in a seersucker suit stands on the outside, edging slowly down the ledge, a piece of paper fluttering in his hand. Abruptly, he loses balance, and grabs for the bridge – but drops the page. He snatches at air. The paper floats lazily down, landing silently atop the water, seconds after the man's splash.

In nervous surprise, Isabelle laughs. The washermen call out.

Underwater, bubbles fizz around Mr Bhatt, his glasses lost, a shoe gone too, cheek and ribs buzzing where he hit the surface. Each time he opens his eyes, he sees only stinging darkness.

Whatever air remains in his lungs he leaks from pursed lips, flailing his arms and legs. He can't tell which direction is the surface, and opens his eyes in a frenzied search for brightness. Guess wrong, and he'll paddle toward the bottom.

His body howls for oxygen while his mind shouts back: Do *not* open your mouth. Veins swell in his neck. Another air bubble tickles his ear, drifting sideways.

Sideways! The air is rising that way! Sideways is up!

He attacks the water, which cedes and resists at once. But he *is* moving, his starved lungs excruciatingly tight, and he. He almost. Just. Brighter. Much brighter now.

He bursts into sunlight, hitting at the water surface with force, gasping, his vision fuzzed. The river is still pulling him from below. He tries to kick off his remaining shoe, which is inundated, like a stone laced around his foot. He can't rotate his arms in this suit jacket, so tries to slough it off, but his head goes under each time, and he gasps back to the surface, coughing and spitting. A soldier stands atop the bridge. Mr Bhatt shouts for help, swallowing water.

Isabelle turns to Steve, who wrings out his wet hair, then picks distractedly at a grey blister on his foot. 'He can drown!' she says, then shouts at the dhobis, who reply in Hindi. They are calling to the man, who keeps disappearing, then bobbing up in a churn of arms and froth.

'None of *them* is diving in,' Steve tells her.

'He is in trouble!'

'*You* go then,' he says. 'It reeks in there.'

'I cannot pull a man from a river! I am not so strong! Come on, Steve!' She cups her hands around her mouth, shouting: 'You are okay? You need help?'

The man in the water turns slightly, another cough-sputter.

'He can't understand you,' Steve says. 'He only speaks Indian.'

As Theo watches all this around him, a peculiar sensation overcomes him: that everything led to this instant. That this was supposed to happen. That, somehow, it's about him.

'What you are doing?' Isabelle asks.

Theo kicks off his sneakers, pulls down his filthy jeans. He doesn't care: not ashamed of himself, not worrying about the acne on his back, or the body odour. The coldness of water shortens his breath.

It's sharp underfoot and slippery. He pushes off, chin ploughing through white laundry foam, a chemical stench that causes him to close his lips, drawing a warm breath through his nose. Long hair covers his eyes, so he ducks under, then comes back up, flicking aside his soaking locks. He spits, swimming fast, strong and certain in the river.

After a minute, he treads water to orient himself, a momentary inner tremor at the nothingness below – then he resumes, swimming the crawl diagonally across the waterway because the current is dragging that man downriver. Theo's eyes close, his face dips under, head turning, oxygen again, face in the water, head turning, another breath, kicking.

Mr Bhatt takes another coughing gasp of air. The sky is a featureless blue without his glasses. Something occurs to him: he has nothing to tell Mrs Gandhi. He deserves no public role. All his countrymen, all the coming catastrophes – he has no power to avert anything. One man can't save mankind. Not a small man.

His body still fights. But his mind is detaching.

Then horror awakens him: if he dies, Meera and Ajay will read the note by his typewriter, and it won't look like a confession of love. They'll discover his satchel of library books, and see the topic.

But it's not *that*! He would never!

He pictures Ajay, informed by strangers, as Mr Bhatt once was, needing words from his father, who is an absence of words forever.

In terror, Mr Bhatt's energy surges, a greater drive than ever in his life. He simply *refuses* to leave Ajay and Meera. It's clothing that pulls him down. If he takes the largest breath possible, and allows himself to sink, he can pull off the seersucker jacket, next his shoe, lastly the trousers. After, he'll surface, be light enough to stay afloat, and can doggy-paddle to shore.

He can do it. Right now!

He doesn't.

Mr Bhatt tries to embolden himself. Ordering himself to act.

Now.

Now!

At last, he sinks under, eyes closed, all attention on touch: first, his right shoe (no, wait: wasn't removing the jacket supposed to come first? Too late – pull off that shoe). Bending his knee, he struggles with the laces underwater. Cannot get his fingernails in the knot. He's turning upside-down, and must be sinking, for the water darkens.

He yanks at the knot, his fingers stiff, as if arthritic. Leave the damn shoe! Get the jacket off. He shakes at it, only tangling his arms in the sleeves.

His chest is bursting from need of air. He must get back to the surface, and try again. His arms are trapped behind him.

Mr Bhatt – teeth grinding, grinding, lips spreading finally – takes a sniff. His mouth opens, inhaling, throat flooding. Reflexively, he coughs and inhales, water filling his chest. Legs jutting, fists clenched, Mr Bhatt widens his jaw. His tongue sticks out, eyes bulging. His ribs shudder. Mr Bhatt goes still, arms behind him in the jacket sleeves, eyes gaping at blackness.

Theo keeps searching for that man who fell. Treading water, he turns back toward Isabelle and Steve, those from the rearview mirror, now calling soundlessly, bobbing there on the riverbank. The deafness of water amplifies his pulse. Theo flips to his back, and floats to gather his wits, haze above, chest trembling, breath out of sync.

The fallen man is gone. Theo's acquaintances are gone. Everyone is absent. He's suddenly exhausted, too far from land, drifting fast.

He flips onto his stomach, momentarily forgetting how to swim, falling beneath the surface for an instant – then back up. His vision is specked. In swimming class, a school instructor told them not to expend strength by fighting a current. Redirect yourself gradually. 'Do not panic' is the first rule. One of the students replied, 'Isn't "Do not panic" the first rule of everything?'

A ripping sensation up Theo's back and right leg – he lets out a yowl, and reaches around, running his fingers up his spine, finding a trench in the flesh, a sliver of himself gone yet without pain. Did he hit a submerged rock? Is there an animal down there, attacking him?

He kicks downward, his breaths too fast to catch. He touches his back compulsively, fetid water splashing into his mouth, the metallic taste of blood. He floats past more washermen on the bank, banging clothes on rocks. A little boy waves, shouting, 'Hallo!' The child runs along the river's edge, then is gone.

Upstream, Isabelle speed-walks along the riverbank as Steve ambles behind, she frantic for any sight of Theo. They keep passing people, and she asks if anyone saw their friend. The search assumes an unreal quality: an emergency, but nobody knows. They reach a factory installation. Nowhere farther to go. They hurry back, she scanning the water, Steve saying how dumb that guy was to jump in, if he couldn't swim well.

Suddenly, Steve shouts, 'He had my fucking car keys!'

'In his jeans?'

'Fuck! Everything's in that car: my passport, my plane ticket, my traveller's cheques. Why didn't you bring his stuff, Isabelle?'

'Why did *you* not?'

They run back to the promontory under the bridge, praying to find Theo's belongings. They're still in a heap: the tennis shoes, shirt, bell-bottom jeans, including the car keys. 'It's a miracle none of these Indians stole my car,' Steve remarks, and continues to the VW, popping the front trunk. 'All accounted for.' He returns with Theo's backpack, telling her, 'The guy'll be *fine*.'

'We leave his things here, you are saying? You want to go?'

'Well, what's your plan?'

'That we don't leave.'

'Come on – we can't stay here the rest of our lives. We wait a bit longer, then put his stuff on a rock or something.'

'Be quiet! I cannot think.'

'Look, I need a shower. You didn't go in that water.'

'This is what you are thinking right now?'

'Why are you shouting at me?'

'I am not shouting!'

'I smell like I took a bath in dog shit, alright? I need to get to the downtown, and find a hotel, and grab a shower. I'm not catching cholera out here. My Kathmandu flight leaves in two days.'

'Steve, you are not make sense. We are waiting for him.'

'*You* wait.'

'Fine! I wait!' She swears in French, collects her belongings from the car, and returns to the river's edge alone, smoking fiercely, counting how many beedis she has left, faint-headed.

Steve returns with their friend's passport. 'I'm stuffing this in his backpack.'

'No! You take all this to the embassy of his country! Right now! You tell them this happens. They bring people to help. Okay?'

'How am I supposed to know where the Dutch Embassy is?'

'You find it!'

'I bet you anything it's closed right now.'

'There is a railway strike, not a strike for diplomats. Come on!'

Steve walks off, amid the *thwack* of laundry hitting rocks. He guns the Volkswagen engine, and drives away.

Isabelle keeps walking along the riverbank until the factory blocks her, then back again, studying the water, each time passing the same little boy who says, 'Hallo!' Eventually, he's gone. It's dark now, and eerie.

Where are the officials from the Dutch Embassy? She can't stay here alone. It's not safe. Shivering, she walks to the road, where a sleeping auto-rickshaw driver leaps at the sound of her voice.

Over the next two days, she wanders around Delhi, brushing off touts who want to sell her a sari or change her money. She keeps looking for Steve, but never sees him. Are people searching for their friend? In a guest house in Paharganj, she meets a group of French boys heading to Goa. They offer her a seat in their camper van, if she can make herself narrow.

She mentions her missing acquaintance, how worried she is. One boy notes that it's the consulate, not the embassy, that she needed – his father was in the foreign service, so he knows. It's tough, he says: she doesn't have that Dutch boy's full name, nor any of his documents. But rest assured, he tells her, the Dutch will do what's appropriate. If it makes her feel better, he'll see if there's a consular official in Goa to check with. You did everything possible, the French boy assures her.

She relaxes into her seat in the van. She has a good feeling about Theo – just *feels* that he's safe (because she has a good feeling about her new friends, soothed to speak her language again, after too long translating every thought).

YEARS LATER, ISABELLE IS concluding a long career in human resources for a French supermarket chain. She has lived well off her salary, and owns a spacious apartment in Boulogne-Billancourt. Her granddaughter is planning a trip to India, inspired by Isabelle's hippie travels. Does she have any recommendations? Isabelle laughs. 'Oh, but the country has changed since I was there!'

For a few years after that trip, Isabelle went around claiming to understand Indian culture, dropping half-understood phrases into conversation – '*Achcha, achcha. Theek hai.*' Her cartons of Koda-chrome never produced a single picture, though, due to an event that still upsets her. Upon returning from India, she couldn't afford to print hundreds of slides at once, so put the rolls of film away. Life scooped her up and deposited her in her most important love affair, a marriage, two children. In 1981, she scuffled with her husband, Charles (the French son of a diplomat, who'd enticed her to join his friends in their van to Goa). She hit him, then stormed out in fright at her act of violence. When she returned, he'd taken out all her Kodachrome from India, and stomped on every roll, pulling the black tongues of film out.

Isabelle goes online to help plan her granddaughter's trip, checking for reports of terrorism in South Asia. Gazing through bifocals at her iPad, she reads a review of a documentary by a Dutch filmmaker who went seeking a countryman who'd disappeared in India decades before. The missing youth's parents died awaiting his return. In the documentary, an Indian crook appears, variously claiming that a serial killer murdered him, or that he was kept confined for years – before the criminal admits that he knows nothing about the case. Isabelle pauses at the line, 'Nobody reported his disappearance at the time.'

What, she wonders, was the name of that boy she met in Benares? The name mentioned in this documentary doesn't ring a bell. It says he'd be in his mid-sixties, if alive. His older half-sister appears in the documentary, a minor Dutch novelist based in London, who explains that her brother had a depressive breakdown a year before his departure, and the trip was supposed to restore him. She wonders if he could be alive somewhere – not knowing has been agonizing. A photo of the teenage Dutchman accompanies the article; he's holding a beer bottle. The quality is poor, but the person looks unfamiliar to Isabelle.

At all the dinner parties of past decades, amid everyone's tut-tutting about conflict in the Islamic world, Isabelle bragged of her overland trip to India, which included a visit to Afghanistan. This was before the Taliban, she explained, before the Russian invasion even, before the mujahadeen. She saw men on mules with World War One rifles, and it was truly wild, and they smoked hash from conical pipes, and the women truly wore burkas – at the time, she'd only thought, *What beautiful fabric!* She recalled a grimy clinic in

Iran too, where she and a friend sold their blood for travel money, and girls in Tehran wore miniskirts back then – yes, in Tehran! Imagine! And an Indian rickshaw driver once picked her up near the river in Delhi, and she thought he was going to rape her, though he was merely pointing to a guest house, and this was a lesson about prejudice – an admission of humility that she declared proudly. Yet, at all those dinner parties, never once did she mention that Dutch boy whose name she can't remember.

Her granddaughter plans to roam freely in India, as Isabelle once did, not checking email or WhatsApp. She'll just post to Instagram now and then, and her family can follow her activities that way. Often, Isabelle has rhapsodized about travel before the internet. Nowadays, she says, people never really *go* to a place – abroad is imprisonment in the same packaged experience. (She herself hasn't travelled outside Europe this century, and frankly doesn't want to visit poor countries again.) In any case, she plans to set up an Instagram account as instructed, and hopes her granddaughter will be on the phone constantly.

Isabelle touches her iPad screen to see that article and the photo again. She recalls a ride down the Ganges, when they were rowed into the mist, the Dutch boy seated at the other end of the wooden boat, clutching onto the splintery sides, as if they might flip. She stood to take a photo of the cremation ghats, knowing this would impress everyone. That Canadian miner's son – what was his name? With the grey blister on his foot and the long blond hair. They didn't properly sleep together, did they? So much of her life has been forgotten.

On the bridge, there was that Indian man who fell. But was that definitely a person? Could it have been an object that looked like a person, as happened during the boat ride down the Ganges, when they agreed afterward that they'd seen a dead boy in the water, while the truthful ledger of her memory knew it was a charred log, or maybe a goat, though she talks to this day of once seeing a child's corpse floating in Benares?

The Indian on the bridge – he resembled an actor in a silent movie, a small man in a seersucker suit, tiptoeing along the girders, piece of paper flapping in his hand. A delay between splash and sound, then he vanished, the water shutting over him. And everything persisted, as if he never was.

DIARY: MARCH 2020

My taxi from Almería airport drives past arid landscape into a city that's charmless at first sight, with drab residential blocks and a concrete seaside walkway. I've rented an apartment here in the south of Spain because I'm nostalgic for how I wrote when younger. I'd go somewhere foreign, away from everyone I knew, accompanied by nothing but plot shards and character lumps. From these, I'd scrape out the contours of a book. For ten days here, I'll try again.

I open my old laptop at the dining table, sunlight glinting on silver keys. I typed fast once, but my fingers are less cooperative now, me pressing one letter, another appearing onscreen. I blame the machine. That's what machines are for.

Anyway, I'm coping, lenient about garbled words, persisting down my ramshackle sentences, a sharp turn at the end of each line, and on to the next. I'll tidy the chaos later.

Suddenly, I'm in darkness but for the glowing screen. Out on the balcony, I orient myself to the present again, the night below streaked with headlamps of mosquito-droning mopeds. During hours of concentration, I hardly noticed how crippling that kitchen chair was. I'm on a high: working and alone.

This solitary practice of mine started when I was around twenty, after an argument in Paris. I'd moved there less than a year earlier, and found a German sculptor, whose mattress I shared in a Rue Saint-Denis garret.

Klaus considered my body and my language mistakes endearing (I speak German, having grown up near the border), so he planned our summer in his native Bavaria, where we'd hike and eat indigestible sausages. But at the train station for our departure, I precipitated a row. I didn't believe my side of the argument, so grew more heated. In truth, my objection was unstated: that he wanted to stomp up pointy mountains in leather shorts within the long-lashed gaze of awkward cows, whereas I wanted nothing of the kind. I'd grown up among farms in the Netherlands, and the whiff of manure and the sight of land that went on endlessly — it felt like regression.

The result was that he boarded in a huff ('Don't come then!'), and I obliged, gone before the train whistled. All the way back from Gare de l'Est, I lugged my leather suitcase (always a strong young woman), and mounted his building's spiral staircase, its wooden steps groaning about me for six flights. Sweating, breathing hard, I closed the door after myself, and flung open the windows, wide enough to risk pigeons. All this oxygen, and it was mine alone.

But what to do? In that apartment, sloping ceilings precluded shelves, so his books were strewn across the floor. After stubbing my toes on the greats of German literature, I crouched to see what a few had to say. There I sat, cross-legged, reading. Eventually, I dragged a letter pad onto my lap, and attempted a story myself. Time lost count, replaced by utter focus. When I stopped, I held still but remained elsewhere, my cheeks hot, mind befogged.

I went slightly mad. For weeks, I produced pages and pages that I never read, fearful to break the spell. Otherwise, I walked the streets, and watched people, and ate bread. How long could I go without speaking to anyone but myself? But perhaps I was a writer – maybe an important one! Until, gradually, the isolation gnawed into me. My scrutiny of characters turned around, fixing on me now, noting how I was pitiful and devious and false. I found myself studying a plaster medallion where the light fixture hung. I imagined myself hanging there.

Nowadays, I repress dark thoughts by outstriding them in a London park, the same park every day. In the evenings, I titrate my mood with wine. Above all, I must work, or another plunge follows.

To avoid madness while in Spain, I conduct a daily outing, speed-thudding along the Almería seaside walkway toward the fish-scented port, under palm trees that have unclasped their dates, sticky beneath my functional shoes.

An Arab busker – bald and toothless, though barely thirty – is playing the musical saw, stroking a bow along the blade in a wavering rendition of 'Nessun Dorma', his tinny boombox swelling with orchestral accompaniment. A family of stray cats listens on a boulder at the sea's edge, a wave charging toward them, then changing its mind.

The busker notices me, this stiff old walker marching down the promenade. In tribute, he switches songs – 'Fools Rush In' by Elvis – and catches my smile, pleased with himself. He calls to me.

'Sorry,' I reply in passing, waving my hand, balled into a friendly fist, 'don't speak Spanish.'

On my return, he hails me again, this time in English: 'You! Coming here!' He asks my name, then makes a praying gesture, turning this finger-steeple downward, to a cup on the pavement. 'You can help me, Miss Dora?'

'I've got no coins on me.'

He shows me his smartphone: an app lets you send a contribution. He pings the details to my number, and I resume my walk, promising to register later — I'll donate then.

I'm back at the laptop, poking the wrong keys and some of the right ones, so near to the lines that they're places with people in them, hinting and scowling. Hours later, I stand, trying to rectify my bent spine by jutting my elbows backward. I'm tipsy from hope (could this book turn out well?), sobered by fact (few will care), and I want more, so sit again, knobbled hands on the keyboard, fading eyes on the screen.

Eventually, my time in Spain elapses, and I'm awaiting a flight home, seated at an outdoor patio in the airport. I wrote on a high, describing people with none around. Now I'm in a crowd again, watching an elderly Englishwoman with pink hair and befuddled gaze smoking a Marlboro, her white-haired husband toying with his nose ring. They have no reason to talk after all these years. The trip is over.

Why am I holding my phone right now? Oh, yes — that donation app. I was going to send the busker something. But a Twitter notification distracts me. My literary agent has told me I should start tweeting. Writers (we at the lower tiers) must cajole and beg the public to take an interest. But I've never yet wanted to blurt this way. Instead, I scroll past culture-war spatter, reading updates about this virus from China, which is spreading to other countries. A death was reported in Los Angeles, and a stand-up comic joked about it, and everyone is furious, except those who are furious at the furious. In northern Italy, entire cities are under quarantine, as during medieval plagues. An opera singer belts out an aria, and everyone looks irritably at me, for I'm struggling to lower the volume on this YouTube clip: a tenor serenading locked-down Italy from his window.

'. . . *those seated in rows sixteen to thirty-six are now invited to* . . .'

Before boarding, I drag my rolling bag to the toilets. Crammed in a tiny stall, I sit and urinate while finishing the clip, screen out of focus, which causes me to extend my phone arm, then draw it near, nearly fumbling the phone into the toilet.

'. . . *any remaining passengers for EasyJet 8164 to London Gatwick please proceed immediately* . . .'

Once in my window seat, I wake the laptop, considering my work of the past days. Instantly, I'm through an escape-hatch, that writerly privilege of elsewhere — till my stomach is hiked skyward, the plane's nose tilting upward, my warm shoulders pushed against the seatback.

Above a twinkling Spanish sea, the plane wheels around, turning toward England, and I peer down, insistently not falling through plexiglass, my gut fluttery from height and from hope, for I've figured out how this book could work.

I turn from clouds back to screen, and tinker with the opening of Chapter Three.

~~A car door slams. She cannot make out what they're saying outside.~~

Or

~~Her bare thighs are cold.~~

Or

She's on the toilet, reading Twitter.

3

The novelist's estranged daughter

(BECK FRENHOFER)

S HE'S ON THE TOILET, reading Twitter. Beck never tweets – it'd waste material or require her to stake a position. But she does follow 3,246 accounts, scrolling down an infinite ladder of pop-culture yammering and emotional spray.

Do men read their phones like this, given that they urinate standing? How could they look at the screen while avoiding the floor? Actually, they *don't* avoid the floor – but they were splashing it long before the Digital Age.

She wonders if this could work as a bit for one of her male stand-up comics: a middle-aged schlub at the bowl, checking notifications; he far-sightedly extends his smartphone, cutting the piss stream, which bounces back over him. He's drenched, and on a date.

She hears a bang outside. Beck holds still, listening. Nothing more.

What'd the guy be looking at on his phone to make it funnier? He urinates on the video for 'Baby Shark'? Nah, too cheap. What about an appeal for Afghan girls wounded in war, and he soaks them, and tries to explain it to his politically committed date? Goddamn it – she has the chorus of 'Baby Shark' stuck in her head now.

A car door slams. Men are speaking Spanish outside her house. What's that moaning?

The phone rings, and Beck fumbles it between her legs, slamming them closed just in time, pinning the iPhone, warm glass between her thighs. But she trapped only a corner. The rest dangles over yellow water.

It keeps ringing, trembling her thigh flab as she slides a hand under her legs. She raises her clenched knees, grunting, but lacks the stomach muscles. Her legs flop back down, followed by a plop-splash that chills her buttocks. The ringtone gargles.

Through wavy water, she reads caller ID – *Adam* – and snatches toilet paper: a mini-squat, swipe, unsure where to dispose of it. Not atop Adam. She chooses the basin, and yanks up her boxer briefs and sweatpants, the iPhone death-rattling against porcelain. Gotta do it: she sticks her hand in, the sleeve of her hoodie sopping. Beck wipes the phone across her chest. 'Hey, can you hear me?'

'Kinda. Where are you?'

'I soaked my phone. A toileting issue.'

'Don't wanna know,' her manager says. 'I'm just checking in with clients before we run screaming from the office. Everyone's home-working for the rest of this week – a test-run in case they lock us down.'

'They need to say this in iPhone ads, don't you think? "Takes a drippin', and keeps on clickin'." Should I rinse it?'

'What, you didn't? You're talking right now on a pissy phone?'

'I dab-dried. Can I put it under the tap?'

'What the hell, Beck! I work for Apple now? Ask a Genius. I'm calling about J.J.'

'Are you getting that crackling noise?'

'The special – we must discuss.'

'I can see my day unfolding at Verizon now.'

'Are they even open?'

'They better be. Phone people are essential workers.'

'I haven't decided if *I'm* essential,' Adam says.

'Everyone is unnecessary except the deliverymen.'

'Watch the J.J. special. Okay? We gotta discuss.'

The moaning outside is louder. Beck raises the bathroom blinds.

A gardening-company truck is parked on her street, cab doors open. Three workmen have got out, and are looking at something on the road, hands on hips. She reaches the landing window for a better view. On the tarmac, a body twitches. It's Rodney.

SHE BURSTS FROM HER house, and the gardeners take a step back. One climbs into the cab of the truck, and calls the others to join him.

Beck kneels before her bull-terrier, his hind leg kicking, as when he dreams on the couch. But the motion is off, a malfunctioning machine. His lower lip is slack, black gums bared, a thread of slobber pooling on the warm road.

The gardeners' truck grinds into reverse, backs around the corner.

Alone on her residential street in Venice Beach, she lifts Rodney onto the grass, consoling him, her voice shaking.

Minutes later, a burgundy Prius creeps up. The driver's window whirs down, and a middle-aged Persian woman unhooks her surgical mask, careful about the lipstick. 'Uber?'

'Could you open the door?'

'Where you are going?'

'I put it in the request. The animal hospital up Broadway. Open the door, please.'

'Yes, but you are not putting "animal" in request.'

'How do I put "animal" in getting an Uber?'

'You can put "animal".'

'I need to get him to the vet. This is urgent.'

'I take *you*, no problem. But not animal.'

Beck tries to control herself. 'You're out of your fucking mind!' That didn't go well. She needs this person. But something over-flowed, and she can't restore it. 'You want to take *me* to the vet, without my dog? Are you insane?!'

'You can cancel the ride, please?'

'Why, so you get a cancel payment? No fuckin' way. Take me to the hospital!'

'Do not call me words. Everyone is under pressure with everything.' The driver hooks the surgical mask back around her ear. 'You can work with me, please?' She steps from the Prius, takes the long way around it, pops the trunk, and finds a pink beach towel with the image of a cartoon princess and the logo *LOL Surprise!* 'Any blood on backseat, and you are paying holstery. Also money I am losing while not drive. Is okay?'

'Can we go please?' Beck wraps the pink towel around her dog, and gets into the back, Rodney on her lap, his eyes blinking slowly, though he is limp.

The driver takes Beck's phone, and reads aloud the animal hospital's new coronavirus directives on dropping off customers. She starts the car engine. 'Why your phone smells like toilet?'

ON THE SIDEWALK BEFORE the veterinary hospital, there's a queue: a ferret on a leash; a cat box; a lime parakeet in a cage. The owners watch Beck struggle from the Prius. 'He got hit by a car,' she tells them.

'Get in line,' the ferret owner says.

'It's an emergency.'

'Everything's an emergency if it's your emergency.'

'No. Some things are actual emergencies.'

The owners of the cat and parakeet move aside for her. The ferret owner just strokes his long ponytail. Beck's arms shake from the weight of Rodney. A sign on the clinic door says: *For safety of staff and customers during this time of global pandemic, we allow only one person in at a time! Thank you cooperation!*

In her frenzied state, she reads the sign over and over. She's still second in line when Rodney dies. Upon realizing, Beck draws a pained breath, then others, trying to calm herself. She won't rest him on the pavement. She can't see clearly, her eyes stinging. Soon, she's presenting a credit card, signing a form, giving them her friend, her arms still trembling from the weight, even after handing him over. The parakeet still waits outside, its owner averting her gaze.

Beck opens the door to her house only a crack – an outdated habit to prevent Rodney from bolting. Most evenings, they'd sit on the couch, she tickling his stomach, turning to meet his gaze. Why didn't she barge into that clinic instead of deferring to a ferret?

She turns on the TV for the distraction of noise: 'I *know*, Kelly! You're telling me, girl!' Clenching her hands, she keeps noticing objects: tattered leash, a squeaky rubber chicken. She walks down the back steps into her overgrown yard, finding a breach under the wooden fence where Rodney must've escaped. Beck wonders if there's something faulty about her, something repellent: he had food and affection, but scratched his way out of her presence.

She stamps down the dirt-fringed tunnel, but is running out of tasks. No distractions in a minute. She powers down her phone to rinse it in the downstairs bathroom, the pee still unflushed, three sheets of toilet paper in the basin. When she tries to restart her iPhone, it won't. She charges it. Nothing. It's neither living nor dead, everyone she knows locked inside.

Her only internet access is a thick old laptop. She hasn't used it in weeks, and finds herself logged off Instagram and Facebook and Twitter. The 'Forgot Your Password?' reminders go to Gmail – but this too has expelled her, and will admit her only through verification on the defunct phone. So Beck is stuck, banished to the outskirts of the internet, with access to nothing but news sites with their old-fashioned 'front pages', featuring Italian opera singers performing on balconies and angry Chinese waiting outside hospitals. California reported its first death.

She surveys the couch cushions, indented where Rodney lay, and raises the TV volume. Beck can't decide whether to tell everyone about Rodney tonight, or say nothing ever. She keeps hearing moans: looking out the landing window; oh God.

What she needs is work, the distraction of watching comics perform. At the club tonight, she'll waylay a Gen Z opener, and ask her to fix the iPhone. But there's a problem: no phone, no Uber. How to get anywhere? The only comedy showcase reachable by foot is a mediocre room in Santa Monica.

Beck assumes her public look: short hair gelled and mussed into hard little shark fins; nerd glasses; roomy blue jeans and green Fluevog shoes; a button-down men's dress shirt, neck size too large, which gives the inadvertent impression of a little head on huge shoulders. She lumbers up the street, skin cool and guts roasting. Few cars are out. The stores are all shut. At the barred entrance to the comedy theatre, she glimpses a barman inside, doing inventory. He opens the door for her.

'What happened?' she asks. 'One of you guys caught the plague?'

'Nah, they shut our shit down. Everyone's out now: the Improv, the Store, the Factory, Largo.'

There's nothing to add when not discussing line-ups. 'My dog just died,' she says.

'Shit. Why?'

'Mexican gardeners hit him.'

'What, with their fists?'

'Jesus! No. With a fuckin' truck.'

'On purpose?'

'This is not the conversation I expected when saying my dog just died.'

'Sorry, Beck. I suck at sympathy. Or is that empathy?'

'Both. You suck at both.'

Long ago, back in the days when Wall Street was (briefly) ashamed of the Financial Crash and comedians were just setting up social-media accounts, Beck still did stand-up in New York, shambling up to the microphone in white Reeboks, sidestepping tables, gazes of the late-late crowd stabbing her, she more conscious of her gait than since schooldays, realizing that she hadn't yet mastered walking. She can summon it still: the metallic smell of the mic, damp with that night's stand-up spittle; dust particles in the spotlight; her airway refusing to cooperate, as if the crowd were seated on her, jumping up and down to close an overstuffed suitcase.

She was hopeless, all flop-sweat and rushed material, so dry-mouthed that you could hardly make out the words. At her final open-mic, someone in the crowd was sniffing throughout. 'So, wait,' a comic asked years later, 'it was quiet enough to hear people *sniffing*?'

She hasn't faced a crowd in years, and is unknown to the public. Yet Beck Frenhofer is among the most influential comedians of her generation.

WHEN THE COMEDY CLUBS were still open, Beck killed her daylight hours at home, snacking and lurking online until someone switched the lights out over Los Angeles, and she found a bar stool in the vicinity of chlorinated toilets, sipping a screwdriver and flinging back salted peanuts as another untalent mugged the microphone.

Each set she disassembled in her head, noting the progressions from set-up to punchline to tag, judging each comic's stagecraft too. Beck experiences comedy as a mechanical object: punchlines to reverse-engineer, premises to screw down, misdirection to hammer in, callbacks to tighten. Rarely does she laugh; jokes don't have that effect on her. But she is addicted to watching defectives expose their worst experiences for the amusement of drunks. She studies audiences too, all those cackling faces – plus the few who can't laugh, so look around, flinching if they meet her gaze.

Comics arrive in generations, the same crew at the same open-mics and pay-to-play rooms; then hosting their own shows just to get stage time, shelling out for a rental space and a sound system and nobody comes, which might be the funniest part of the evening. Despite all that, the newbies – going up at ridiculous hours, throttling the mic stand, competing with an espresso machine – come offstage wild-eyed, abuzz from a mix of fame and shame, wanting to punch, to fuck, to go again. It's a battle against the public, and the comedian *must* prevail.

Those who endure lap up years of humiliation, which makes stand-up an art in purest form: one's inner life for the applause of strangers. Eventually, a member of each generation finds a manager, books commercials, pitches a sitcom, and that person coat-tails a couple of friends along with them, while the rest panic because nobody downloads their podcasts, and it's nearly a decade of this shit, and they've wrecked their lives, so can't stop now. They hate-hug in the parking lot outside the venue, gossip about who's banging which wait staff, and smile about the ex-headliner who crashed his electric scooter on Sunset.

Gradually, each generation thins out, retreating back through the stage curtain – those who return to designing webpages full-time, or finish the philosophy degree, or raise a kid someplace with lawn sprinklers, saying Beck should totally visit, meaning it not meaning it. A handful become hacky road comics, suddenly plump, gradually old. One guy's wife and infant perished in a fire while he performed out of town, and when he returned after the double funeral, a fellow stand-up quipped, 'Hey, folks – Mr Complain is back!' At the comics' table, everyone laughed. To say 'too much' is treason.

Other comedians envy her connections, her knowledge, her income. But none wants her career. If you search the name 'Beck Frenhofer' online, the credits are minimal: a year writing for a network sketch show at the turn of the millennium; a gig in the Oscars writers' room; producer of one movie, *Bad Baby*, which was panned but became a cult hit (buying her this house).

But non-disclosure agreements hide the reality of her career. Behind the scenes, Beck has written for many of the biggest comics, those too busy or too depressed to piece together a new set. What happens is that Netflix offers a stand-up star huge money for a special, but the comic can't expend months touring a new act, especially when any audience member could secretly film it, and upload to YouTube, deflating the product right there. So Beck – whose gift is writing material that mimics anyone's shtick – will compose their sets. She's a trick of the trade, like those script doctors whose names appear in no credits but who wrote half the movies in Hollywood.

She has a second role in comedy too, this one unpaid, as agony aunt to the ego-crushed. Her greatest gratification comes from helping newcomers. Yet more than a few comics dislike her presence, she sitting there at the bar, judging them. A few months back, she was advising a young female comic at The Comedy Store, when a male headliner walked past, saying, 'Hey, hey, hey – it's the lesbo casting couch.'

Recalling this, Beck picks up her phone, which is where she goes when wanting to feel worse. Only a black reflection. On her laptop, she reaches the Verizon chatbot, and requests a replacement phone, her messages brusquer than she'd be with a human. She wonders if there's a bit in that: how rude can you be to a robot?

She hates this habit of refashioning any brain blip into material. As a young comic, her routine was a patchwork of other stand-ups' styles. What she wanted was to be admired while revealing nothing. Her work now, impersonating the foibles of others, hearing crowds holler in adoration for a guy who wrote none of that – it has levied a cost, corroding Beck, turning her cynical: that the public are stupid; that her peers are deluded self-interest machines; that we'll never fix politics; that the climate is done; that everything ends badly. Whenever she felt a flicker of hope, Beck spoke of it to Rodney, that quizzical little face looking at hers, then a lick. She just paid to incinerate him. Beck tears up, and pinches her stomach hard. Is it too late to stop them? Could she bury him in her backyard?

She googles 'dog's body in garden'. The first result is an ad for Dogsbody, an online task marketplace connecting you with free-lancers who'll do household chores. Its homepage features a beautiful woman of indeterminate race holding a plunger and beaming because your plumber is a moral choice. Dogsbody also has moral carpenters and moral cleaners, each rated out of ten. Beck clicks a name with such an abundance of emojis that she wonders if 'ROSA 😊 😄 😊

😎😊😊🤗😇😇😌😊😋' is cognitively impaired. The person has ticked every skill possible – either the most capable human in history or the least.

Beck shuts the website, and seeks a contact form for the veterinary hospital. Yet ads for Dogsbody trail her around the internet. In an attempt to stop this, she clicks one. Minutes later, she finds herself sending a price enquiry.

hey there!!!! hows it goign! Rosa replies. **What douneed?**

four hrs housework, Beck types.

?4people?

four HOURS

tuesday good;'/??

Beck almost replies, **Are you having a stroke right now?** but deletes it, and forces herself to her feet, looking out the window over her backyard. After the break-up – after Laura left, to be exact – Beck picked a fight with the housekeeper, and dismissed the woman. Her home has become a dump since, the carpeting grey with dust where it abuts the walls, the garden a jungle.

Everywhere is decay, she thinks. The global pandemic is only the start. Why are people surprised? The shock is that humans never destroyed the planet with nuclear weapons. But there's time.

She waits on the front porch till a random dude passes, and offers him a Breville centrifugal juicer in exchange for using his phone.

'You jacked it?' he asks.

'Did I steal my juicer? No, I bought it on Amazon. My phone just died, and I need to call someone.'

Uncertainly, he pulls a banged-up phone from his back pocket. She dials her manager.

Adam is suspicious at the unrecognized number, then hears her voice. 'Hey, you hung up on me before,' he says. 'What's up with that?'

'I didn't hang up. I screamed, and the line dropped. You never even tried to get in touch. I could've been in three suitcases by now.'

'If I called the cops every time a client screamed and hung up on me . . .'

'Rodney died.'

'No way! I am *so* sorry, Beck. Did I ever meet Rodney?'

'My dog, you asshole. He got hit by a truck.'

'Ohmigod! What happened?'

'He fucking died. Didn't I open with that?'

It's a problem in the ha-ha business: transitioning from ironic to sincere. Few have solved this. Adam responds by messaging an intern (his whole team is home-working; a nightmare), and the kid is ordered to drive to Beck's with toilet paper, and transport her malfunctioning phone to Verizon.

'Why toilet paper?'

'Have you visited a store lately?'

'What, there's no toilet paper in greater Los Angeles, except in the possession of your interns?'

'Correct. CAA has cornered the market.'

'Could your intern possibly take my phone, and *not* bring it back? I feel I'm done with notifications; I feel notified.'

'Did you watch the J.J. Carmelo special I sent?'

'Not yet, no.'

'Beck!' Adam has pestered her about watching this for weeks, needing her notes on the rough edit. She loathed that writing gig, and has no contractual obligation to watch the result. Beck had known J.J. by nodding acquaintance before his Live+ special. The man cultivated a prickish air, onstage and off. Sometimes, prickish means shy. Sometimes, it means prick. Here, it meant prick.

He'd come from the Bronx, doing blue comedy in the 1980s, hef-Italian, hef-Puerto Rican, specializing in what used to be called 'ethnic material'. He chain-smoked, and swaggered through tales of snorting coke off Dominican hookers' backs, crashing his Trans-Am, and running from the scene of domestic assaults. In late career, he's come to resemble an ageing Leonard Cohen without the dignity, tufts of hair in his ears, tennis shorts, white tube socks, Air Jordans. He looks like a heart attack in a race-track toilet, unmissed till next Tuesday. Except that something happened: the era of unintended consequences.

Streaming-video channels need fresh content, and the cheapest was stand-up. You film a special in a night or two, the material comes audience-tested, with minimal production values, an intro of the performer plodding along a city street, entering the theatre, the crowd's hilarity filmed with three cameras, footage straight to the editing booth, PowerPoint marketing plan, release date, upload, done. In parallel, comedians' podcasts took off, hours of shop-talk that, mysteriously, fascinated civilians. Overnight, a once-seedy niche of showbiz turned hip. Plus, plenty of those podcasters grew up watching J.J., and now invited him on, providing 'Uncle Jay' with a young following for his old-guy vulgarity. A new streaming service, Live+, bought two of his classic videotaped hours, and commissioned the special. Which is where Beck came in.

J.J. Carmelo's act dried up years back, and he was filling the gap with crowd work, abusing the boozed-up for the amusement of the rest. That wouldn't work in a concert setting, where the audience couldn't see his targets. So Beck was employed to write jokes good enough for people to applaud this emotional derelict. He filmed at a small theatre in New Jersey, and Beck declined to attend. Last she heard, he'd bombed, and they weren't sure if it was even useable. Adam emailed her a screener link. Normally, she'd be professional, and watch. But it arrived just after Laura left.

'Here's the deal,' Adam tells her. 'I fix your phone, and you watch the effing special. Agreed ?'

Later, Adam's henchboy appears, bearing toilet paper. He takes her inoperative iPhone, and produces a pin, picking dust from the charging port and ignoring her questions, as if she were Mom. A minute later, he plugs in her phone. The screen illuminates; not dead after all.

That night, Beck gazes from her rooftop terrace over closed Santa Monica Pier, the beach empty, no planes in the sky, no helicopters. It's like a post-apocalypse movie, where the main character must reckon with her new reality: *I'm the only person who made it; not another solitary person.*

Adam said that all his comics are petrified, their performance income vanishing with the shutdown, and nowhere to work out fresh material. They're stuck indoors, separated from those whom they love to be loved by, societal collapse pending, their life's work more obviously frivolous than ever. On everyone's phones, the disease closes in, with national borders sealed, warnings about handwashing, families looking through windows at nurses in hazmat suits.

Already, Beck saw society as thinly protected, that optimism was disappointment postponed, that we'd run out of toilet paper. At last, everyone has figured out what she knew. Things *don't* get better in the end. You *can't* do anything that you set your mind to. Everything does *not* happen for a reason. Sometimes it happens because of a bat in China.

ROSA 😊😄😊😎😊😊🤕🤒😵😐😊🥴 rests her ten-speed bicycle on the bushes out front. Over the first month of lockdown, Beck dealt with nobody but delivery drivers. Can't recall how you do this, talking.

The words gush out: 'Move the bike round back if you want I guess there should be space though there's hardly anyone around to steal anything I don't think I don't know whatever you prefer is fine.'

'Hey!' Rosa says. 'You're Rebecca?'

'Beck, yup. You need water?'

'Would *love* some!'

Rosa is a small woman in a navy tanktop and orange Carhartt overalls, dressed as if trick-or-treating as the handyman. She rolls her shoulders, smiling, and wipes her forehead with a palm blackened from the handlebar wrap on her ten-speed. She downs half the glass of cold water, pauses for a gasp, then finishes the rest, a breathless thank you.

'You came all the way from Los Feliz?'

'Only took me an hour!'

Inside the house, Beck asks that they remain far enough apart to avoid murdering each other with micro-organisms. 'Needs a massive clean, plus some other tasks. I'll do a list.' She can't stop chattering with this weird intensity: isolation-mouth. Take it down a notch.

Rosa jots out the assigned tasks, and pulls her hair into a scrunchy, stubbly armpits on brief display.

Beck is distracted by something about this woman's features, which are oddly high-def. What *is* that? She realizes: a young person in daylight.

Technically, this gig is illegal; they're breaking lockdown. But Rosa is willing – productions are halted; even the fantasy of an audition is gone. Dogsbody earnings have fallen off a cliff too, and her other hustle – entertainer at kids' birthdays – is worse. Right now, anything is better than playing sardines with her six housemates, which is double the number she signed up for: three girls who actually pay rent plus three insignificant-others, dudes who moved in when Covid restrictions threatened to force them into celibacy. So Rosa's lockdown has been weeks of unemployed actors arguing over video games and smoking weed in her living room.

When showing Rosa around, Beck hears herself trying to impress the young woman. Because she's unexpectedly middle-class, white, and American-born? Beck wouldn't admit that, but it's so. To rebel against this fact, she acts curt, saying she has work to do, and carries her laptop to the upstairs bedroom, where she listens to Rosa singing over the lawnmower, tone-deaf but committed.

'You also do stuff like removals, right?' she calls down. 'Or you have associates for that?'

'All me.' She flexes her twig arm. 'Tougher than I look.'

'I hope so.' Beck explains what she needs removed, adding more as she goes, offering all the DVDs, the music system, various appliances in the kitchen.

Rosa proposes gathering it up, and returning later with a truck. 'I clear anything but dead bodies!'

'Could you put in the dog stuff especially? Mine just passed away.'

Rosa covers her mouth. 'I'm so sorry.'

'*You* didn't die.'

'What's her name?'

'Let's leave that out.'

'Oh. No prob. Sorry.' Rosa scours the house, gathering squeaky toys and bowls, plus the doghouse from the yard. Delicately, she approaches Beck's bedroom, speaking through the closed door. 'Did you want to see anything before it goes?'

'Just disappear it.' That came out rude, so she adds that Rosa should help herself to food from the fridge and cupboards – Adam's henchboy loaded her with bags of rice, plus other items now nearing expiration. 'Anything vegetable is yours.'

'You mean to eat right now?'

'To take, I meant. But, sure – eat it now, if you want.'

'I'm actually starving. I'll turn off the clock.'

'Keep it running. You're on a job.'

'Could I at least knock something up for you? My folks actually ran a restaurant back in Sacramento.'

'Are your folks coming to cook?'

'No, but I worked there one summer.'

'It was good, this restaurant?'

'It only lasted that summer.'

'Sounds great.'

'Take your chances, I guess!'

Before adding any ingredient, Rosa seeks permission, which gives Beck a reason to join her in the kitchen and watch, though she keeps telling her to do whatever.

They sit apart at the long dining table. Beck looks into her spoon, brilliant red with gazpacho. So strange having someone here again.

Rosa speaks of favourite food trucks around LA, and her former job assisting a culinary stylist in the Bay Area. She was a musical-theatre kid in school, so figured why not give it a try.

'Isn't New York where you break into musicals?'

'Oh, *now* they tell me.'

Rosa isn't obsessed with fame, which tells Beck that she'll get nowhere. When she babbles about showrunners she'd like to work with, Beck listens without comment, as when hearing the clumsy kid talk of the pro sports team he'll join.

Beck returns to her bedroom, lies on the floor, gazing sideways at a pillow on the carpet. For a couple of hours, thoughts float past. Should she call Laura, and tell her about Rodney, whom they adopted together? 'Liar,' she mumbles, imagining the conversation, how she'd speak, how false she'd be.

Rosa hollers up the stairs, and Beck notices the window: dark out. With effort, she climbs to her feet, knee sore, breathing from exertion.

'All done down here!' Rosa says. 'Unless you got anything left for me.'

'So I pay you how?' Beck asks, though she remembers.

'It's zapped off your card, which you entered online. So we're good.'

'What's the rate again?' All just to talk more.

'Forty smackers an hour.'

Beck would pay her just to stay longer. But you can't say that. 'And the receipt comes by email?'

'I can send it right now. Don't forget to rate me online!'

Beck asks Rosa to wait a second, and hastens to the roof terrace alone. Heart kicking, she places a call. 'Hey.'

'Hey there! You know I'm still downstairs, right?'

'I had a thought. I was just thinking. You're stuck at your place with all those people, which is not exactly healthy. I got extra bed-rooms here. It's just stupid.'

'Whoa, are you—'

'Hear the ground rule first.'

'Just one ground rule?'

'Only one. No assassinating me with coronavirus. Otherwise, you stay for free.'

BECK'S OLD SILVER LAPTOP is open, a galaxy screensaver awaiting instruction, unsure of its purpose on the kitchen table except to gather milk-spatter from her Froot Loops. 'You seen this?' she asks, playing a clip of President Trump saying doctors can treat the disease by injecting patients with bleach.

Rosa snorts, shakes her head. She's the rare smart person to exist as if the mad king of America didn't. Just a shiver if the president's name is spoken. She'd rather talk classic movies or mid-century furniture or tell wending anecdotes about growing up in Sacramento and her nutty jobs since.

She has the charisma of an enthusiast, speculating about improvements that one could do to this house ('. . . you knock down that wall, and add a skylight, and . . .'). They disagree vehemently on taste, speaking over each other, revelling in the make-believe. After all, Rosa moved to Los Angeles for make-believe: acting. Yet it's hard to imagine her as anyone else. She's always herself, an ability that Beck previously viewed as if through binoculars. She pictures Rosa thirty years from now, maybe owning a bric-a-brac store in New Mexico, brown from the sun, hydrating with cucumber-infused water, enthusing over a Shaker chair that just came in.

Neither will forget this shared refuge during the plague.

Beck's phone rings, and she declines the call.

'You never pick up, do you. Such a power move.'

'I'm here with you.' Shocked that she said that.

'You're not tempted to see who?'

'It's just my agent.' Actually, Adam is her manager, but people are more impressed by 'agent'. She hates hearing herself show off – but keeps on. 'He's bugging me for notes on this thing I did.'

Rosa seeks details but Beck is vague, both for legal reasons and to sound important. Rosa has heard of J.J. Carmelo. 'What's he like?'

On Skype calls, J.J. barely looked into his camera, forcing Beck to watch the brim of a Brooklyn Dodgers cap, staring at the stylized 'B', his black-coffee sighs smellable through the laptop screen. J.J. resented that a writer had been forced on him. His idea for this special was 'political correctness', which (as Beck didn't tell him) was so hacky by now. Who even called it 'PC' anymore? When he ran through material, he didn't even try to sell it, just read as if from a grocery list. 'Got this bit on the vagina museum, how it's closed each time I visit.' He paused. 'I don't hear laughing. Something wrong with Skype today?'

'I'm waiting to see where you take it.'

'The giant tampon.'

'That's part of the museum?'

'Jesus H. Christ. Google it, will ya?'

He had no interest in who Beck was, yet she heard herself cheering him along, playing her paid role. She says none of this to Rosa. Only that J.J. was as you'd expect.

'And you did what exactly?'

'I was like a consultant.'

'Why's your agent need you to watch the special so much? You must be a big deal.'

'I'll put it on, if you're curious.' Immediately, Beck regrets the proposal, her heart sinking to view that junk again, her old self, her comedy-world self. But Rosa is thrilled to watch an advanced screener.

The special, *J.J. Carmelo: Cancel This*, begins in darkness on a bare stage. An audience of a few hundred people stirs. Onstage, a man's silhouette appears, and that is sufficient: the crowd leaps up, roaring and clapping. A woman in the crowd shouts, 'Love you, J.J.!' Everyone cheers. Still in silhouette, he launches into his opening: 'I was thinking, people. What're we gonna do about all the morons?'

The crowd bursts into laughter.

Rosa turns to Beck, wondering if she's allowed to voice an opinion. 'Why's that funny?'

Beck shrugs, and sits forward – this opening is nothing she worked on. For the next five minutes, J.J. improvises a rant about how the most oppressed group in society are the stupid. They're banned from elite colleges, they get the worst jobs, they end up with shitty healthcare – all because of nothing more than who they were born. 'This, folks, is the last acceptable prejudice. And, thank fuckin' God,' he concludes. 'Because if we ain't gonna mess with dumbasses, who we got left? We, as a people, need to come together. We need to come together, and hate as one. It's a teaching moment, bitches.' At this, music kicks in, the brassy opening of 'Crazy in Love', with Jay-Z thundering about 'history in the making', spotlights spinning around the concert hall. The audience members are on their feet again, going wild. At last, the stage lights come up, and there he is: J.J. Carmelo, mic in one hand, middle finger to the rafters, a straight white male in blackface.

The crowd seems confused: a few chuckles, awkward ones. They retake their seats. J.J. lets it sink in, then tells the audience to get used to it – this is how he's doing the special.

'What the?' Beck murmurs. 'I never worked on *any* of this.'

'Uhm,' Rosa says, 'not sure I get the point.'

Beck is silent, gripped by the awfulness of this special. J.J. Carmelo makes no attempt to explain, just baits the audience. Every bit falls flat (including a few she wrote). Boos ring out; heckles too. Any night, you can see comics bombing at clubs, but not in a filmed special. These are hardcore fans – alienating this many people that fast is tough. Now J.J. is slamming individual audience members, telling them to scram if they don't like it. Some oblige, shouting down the aisles that they want their money back, with J.J. responding that they can keep their stinking shekels. Forty minutes in, hundreds of seats are empty. J.J. tells those still left to go fuck themselves, and he walks offstage. The stragglers are incredulous. More boos. Cut to credits.

'Well, okay,' Beck says, processing this. 'That is *not* what I worked on.' She doesn't add something that she couldn't explain to a non-comic: to eat it that badly – there's something legendary about it.

She phones Adam. 'What the actual fuck?'

'You watched J.J.'s masterpiece, I take it.'

'I won't get my on-release money, I'm assuming.'

'We should be so lucky! Those idiots at Live-Plus put it out.'

'Wait, what? They went out with that?'

'Are you not on social media? It went up Thursday, and is blowing up. Not blowing up in the good way. Blowing up in the Al-Qaeda way.'

Over the past weeks, Beck forgot the jangling power of hits and losers. Adam is shoving that cultural din back at her. 'The Live-Plus guys are Wall Street – they had no idea how this'd play,' he explains. 'They figured that, with lockdown, they'd get zero new content, and they only just launched, so wanted something hot. So they threw it up there.'

'Because blackface might slip through the cracks?'

'It gets worse. A bunch of old clips are circulating of J.J. doing routines about "fags". In 1983, to be fair. But, speaking as a fag, "fag" ain't a great look in 2020. Elite-level cringe.' Adam's voice tenses, approaching something that will bother her. During the powwow with the Live+ folks, J.J. Carmelo worsened matters, going all surly and uncommunicative, so they invited a lawyer onto the Zoom call, and informed J.J. that they were taking down his special *and* the old ones they'd bought. 'His life's work, kaput.'

'Tragedy.'

'Then you came into it.'

'Me?'

'J.J. was freaking out, saying how he's not a racist, how he doesn't need to defend himself.'

'While defending himself.'

'Right. And they come back with: "White guy in blackface – slam-dunk racism. End of story." Then J.J. goes, "Why'd you hire me, if I'm not allowed to be J.J. Carmelo?" And they go, "We can't be associated." At which point, J.J. drops the Beck bomb.'

'What are you talking about, Adam?'

'This special can't be bigoted, J.J. tells them, because an LGBT person of colour wrote it.'

She needs a second to understand. Beck doesn't think of herself that way, but is now tokenized retrospectively. 'Don't put my name on this dumpster fire!' she says. 'Like, does an NDA not go the other way?'

'Beck, deep breath.'

'*You* take a deep breath! This shit has nothing to do with me!'

'I had the same exact reaction. The guy's scum. We're ditching him. Almost definitely. But I had a thought.'

'There's no version of this that's okay, Adam.'

'Listen! Listen. "Beck Frenhofer" – who's heard of that name?'

'Thanks.'

'All those NDAs keep you in the shadows. *This* would give you a name.'

'A name covered in slime. I'd get cancelled before anyone knows who I am.'

As they argue, Beck is hating her shoulders. She left the living room, and stands before the bathroom mirror, where she has taken off her XXL black T-shirt, and is trying to find the most repulsive angle on her back. She took antidepressants once, and gained a hundred pounds she never lost. This morning, she emailed the tenants at the East Village apartment she owns, telling the two comics who rent it that they needn't pay till lockdown ends. They replied without thanks, just, 'So we'll have to pay all those months once lockdown's over???'

What happens when all this ends, and life returns to normal? She can't say it aloud, but the pandemic has been her best experience in years: no panic that she's falling behind everyone, no dejection that others are living her best life.

'We turn it around,' Adam tells her. 'This dude wants to tread on you? Well, we tread on him.'

SHE AND ROSA ARE drinking bourbon on the roof. How to tell someone – especially a young person who still believes in fame – that you want no more ratings, no more contests? Beck hears herself reminiscing about her adolescence, when she listened obsessively to her dad's comedy albums, and recounts her quirks growing up. She takes another mouth-burning slug of whiskey, uneasy, because she's telling herself to someone. She only does this once every few years, and should stop. But once begun, it's like swimming toward a speck of land – you must reach it, or you go under. 'Want to hear me violate a bunch of NDAs?'

'Yeah!'

She explains the true nature of her work, her role in the J.J. debacle, and how they're trying to drag her into it because her father was black, with the added bonus that she's not exactly straight. '*Your* personality is what I want,' Beck says. 'Calm.'

'Here's what I don't get. If you write awesome comedy, why not just become a massive name yourself?'

'Serious success isn't about writing ability. You need to be a person who people want to laugh with.' Beck is breaking all those non-disclosure agreements to raise her status with Rosa, yet is now denigrating herself. She pivots. 'Know how much these guys are offering me to take the fall? Two hundred grand. All I have to do is say I wrote the one thing that I *didn't* write.'

'Two hundred grand?! That is life-changing.'

Beck doesn't say that, for her, it's not. But she recalls being hungry when struggling in New York, her outer-borough basement, almost thin, stealing leftovers from club kitchens.

'You'd be amazing onstage,' Rosa insists. 'You have a way of seeing things and saying stuff. Not, like, funny ha-ha. But, like, super-dark. And getting right to it.'

'I never stopped writing my own act actually. I have tons of material.'

'So you have a routine?'

'Hours.'

'Do something for me!'

Beck leans forward, head in hands. 'No way.' Her temples are throbbing. Adam already held a video-conference with Live+ about what J.J. calls 'the lesbian-of-colour angle'. She's getting that queasy career feeling again, as if late for something, as if people are talking about her, as if she's let someone down. The prospect of standing before strangers, saying words – she wants Rosa to reverse herself: 'Actually, don't.' To say, 'We do our own thing.'

Instead, Rosa simplifies matters: 'They pay you. You get famous. Then be whatever you want.'

It would blow other comedians' minds if she did a set. Beck could get spots anywhere once LA clubs re-open. With a phone call, she'd have a Netflix scout there. Beck imagines an audience gawking at her; her mouth goes dry.

'Who cares if people neg you?' Rosa says. 'You're way above them.'

'You know what the late great Mitzi Shore said? "You only know you're succeeding when people hate you." '

'Totally!'

Beck's upper lip itches from sweat; she wipes it. For the first time in weeks, she has a crowd in her head again. 'I don't know.'

'*I* know.' Rosa gives her a side-hug, rubs her back.

Beck goes rigid. 'Social-distancing.'

'Oh, right. My bad.' Rosa steps away.

Beck reaches for the rail around the terrace, her eyes narrowing, as if distracted by something out there.

'When you *do* do your act,' Rosa says, 'you're gonna rock.' She heads down to her room.

Beck is left on the roof, leg jiggling, looking toward an ocean too dark to see.

FOR NIGHTS, SHE WORKS on her act, poring through old notebooks, alternating cold fear at how awful she is – and the possibility that she is amazing, that she'll reveal herself and people will get her.

She paces past her bed into the en-suite bathroom and back,

experimenting with the delivery of lines, shoulder pricked, eyes widening, trying to hear objectively, as if at the bar and watching herself, which jabs a shard of panic into her. She scrolls Twitter to find if people are raging yet about her role in the J.J. Carmelo special – it's frightening when the masses hate you unannounced; but provoke them knowingly, and it's a thrill. She wants Rosa to be around for this. Whenever her housemate leaves the room, Beck wants her back, even if she went only a minute earlier, and they'd exhausted the conversation, and Beck needs to sleep. Instantly, she's longing for more.

Play it out, though. After the scandal hits, comedy nerds will compile a spreadsheet on Reddit of all shows whose credits include 'Special thanks to Beck Frenhofer'. The *New York Times Magazine* profiles her, recounting the case as another sign of all that's wrong with all that's wrong. The scandal won't be J.J. in blackface. The scandal will be how comedy used her.

On Twitter, denunciations of J.J. Carmelo are plentiful, including a campaign to boycott Live+. But never a mention of Beck Frenhofer. These executives are paying to smear her name. So get on with it!

She goes downstairs. In the darkened doorway of Rosa's bedroom, Beck lets her eyes adjust, and enters softly. She stoops, her face near sleeping breaths, then retreats upstairs.

Back in her room, she's rehearsing again, downing slugs of Jack Daniels at dawn to fall asleep, then waking in her jogging pants, zipping up the hoodie, slipping on Havaianas, nearly tumbling on the stairs. Rosa left a note: *Out shopping!*

Beck herself hasn't left this house once since lockdown. She summons her image of Rosa in thirty years, running that antique store – Beck wants to be there then, not here now.

But this scandal *is* happening, right? She clicks her online-banking app, and the Live+ payment went through. All is official. Another payment catches her eye: $320 to Dogsbody LLC.

It's the same amount daily since Rosa moved in: $320 to Dogsbody. Each conversation they had, every meal, weekends included – that was paid.

'IF YOU'RE DISPUTING THE charges, I'll get you your money back,' Rosa says, hot-faced. 'Not sure how I'll do it. But fine.'

'I'm not asking for my money back.'

'I gotta make a call,' Rosa says, leaving for her bedroom. 'And don't worry,' she shouts back. 'I won't charge for today.'

'Can you wait one second?!'

For the rest of that day, Beck keeps hesitating on the upstairs landing, trying to make out whispered phone calls in the guest bedroom below.

The next morning, Beck pulls off her eye mask, and discovers a text message i left. take care.

The guest bed is stripped, towels stacked, keys atop.

Her phone rings.

'Well, how is *your* day?' Adam always talks like a stripogram when delivering good news. 'So, *I* was chatting with the Live-Plus folks.'

'Why aren't they leaking it? This is getting ridiculous.'

'Becky, my dear, something interesting's happened in that glorious place that I so fondly call the interweb: a backlash to the backlash. Before, everyone was saying J.J.'s a flaming racist, right? Which is obviously bullshit, but whatever. Then, Part Two: right-wing nutjobs start jumping in, by which I mean Trump country, all threatening to boycott Live-Plus if J.J. gets cancelled. And the free-speech folk got involved too.'

'Can you just tell me what's happening?'

'Viewer numbers for the J.J. special – exclusively on Live-Plus: hooray! – are through the roof. Half of America hates him, but who gives a shit? The other half of America is a fuckload of eyeballs,' he says. 'So, you ask: What's in it for me? That's the best part. *I* just negotiated for Live-Plus to not associate you with this hot mess – *and* you get to keep the payout. Two hundred grand of free dough, darlin', for doing fuck-all. But wait; I'm not done. Here is the best part, Beck. I. Got. You. A special.'

Her hands go cold. She puts the phone on speaker, rests it on the table. Suddenly, she wants this. Immensely. Years watching, resenting them, dying for her turn. *She* has something to say. The worst parts of herself. For everyone to laugh at. For Rosa to watch. For Rosa to know her.

'FYI,' Adam goes on, 'I'm not sitting still on the two hundred grand, either. We'll get separate terms for your director credit. Basically, nobody felt right putting you in the firing line on this, and J.J. needed to take ownership. Even he figured it was better to face the woke than to end up like Milli Vanilli. Right?'

'Wait. I'm confused. What you negotiated is for me to *direct* a special?'

'And you're most welcome, my dear.'

'Who says I want to direct for J.J. Carmelo? I thought the whole point was *my* career.'

He shifts tone, hard suddenly. 'Whoa. I don't deal with anger issues. Take that somewhere else. You don't want to direct a Live-Plus special? Send back the money. I'll give up my commission, if you want to go that route.' He means dropping her. 'What you need is to get with J.J., and work through ideas. That is what I'd seriously advise. His thinking was shooting the new special at a correctional facility: "J.J. Live at San Quentin." But who knows with Covid. I figured a selected audience on Zoom, and "crowd shots" of fans at home. You've seen his apartment in Brooklyn. It's – how to say? – characterful. Filming the intro there could work. Or a fake real apartment? Anyway, that's for you to figure out.'

'For me? Seems like everything's been decided.'

'I was expecting a bit more joy here, Beck. You keep the money *and* your reputation. You get how this works, right?' Regretfully, he must dash to another meeting, which is Hollywood for 'Fuck off'.

After they hang up, Beck finds herself staring at her list of recent iPhone calls. She presses the name, looking at this trilling object in her palm. It rings eight times, then voicemail. 'Hey, it's me. Let's not . . .' Beck begins. 'You know? I have all this space! And if I'm gonna socially isolate anyway. Right? Plus you need a place. It's crazy. Seriously.'

Some people never check voicemail. Beck follows up with a text, replying to Rosa's goodbye note, composing the longest message she's ever thumbed into a phone. She keeps adjusting wording, tweaking lines – until, by mistake, she sends it. Horrified, she reviews the note. Thank God: nothing bad, just typos and honesty. According to iMessage, *Rosa Dogsbody* is typing.

But the reply doesn't come.

So Beck messages an audio file, a few minutes of material – the most embarrassing events of her life rendered in punchlines.

She watches the blank screen.

Nothing is distributed fairly, she thinks, and forwards her entire J.J. Carmelo payment – after commissions, nearly $180,000 – to Rosa.

OVER THE NEXT WEEK, Beck limits herself to calling Rosa's number six times per day, and hangs up every time it goes to voice-mail. Adam sends details on the J.J. special, now planned for the Irvine drive-in. The Live+ team wants to crank up the edgy political material, and someone from the corporate side hatched a title that everyone loves: *J.J. Carmelo: The Great Awokening*.

Beck's phone is ringing. She snatches it, checks the screen. It's her mother in London. 'I was just listening to this radio programme on people trying to become teachers to their own kids in lockdown, and I thought of you,' Dora says.

'Thought of me?' Beck snaps. 'Why?'

'I was just remembering when I taught you to read.'

'What are you talking about? I learned to read at school.'

'No, you didn't. Sitting on my lap. You don't remember that?'

'Why are you calling?'

'Just, I keep wanting to talk with you, Beck. Have we spoken this whole time, this whole epidemic? I don't even know what you're up to. I keep imagining you there.'

Half-listening, Beck checks incoming messages. The banking app shows a new payment: Rosa returned the entire sum.

The doorbell bongs.

'I need to go,' Beck says.

A peppy guy stands before her, presenting an object. 'Don't recognize it?' he asks. 'Freshly laundered!' It's the pink beach towel, emblazoned with *LOL Surprise!* that the Persian driver gave her to cradle Rodney when he was dying. The guy gets back into the animal-hospital van, and drives away.

Beck stands in her open doorway. A trio of surfer dudes strut past her house, right down the middle of the road. They're heading toward the beach, shirts off – jogging there now, racing each other, shouting who's gonna get there first. They're the types she could never be: volleyball till sunset, beers on the sand, hooting at jokes.

For a while, everyone was hiding out, apart together, noticing how short their lives were, and that competition is a madness, and that you should probably eat too much. For a while, she felt human among humans.

But everything is returning to normal. They're running stand-up gigs on patios. She could call an Uber, and see who's performing. Her stomach drops.

Beck stands there in her front door, towel clasped. The cage is open. The animal stays in place.

DIARY: APRIL 2020

A long foreign number is blinking on my silenced phone. I wasted this morning reading upsetting news. At last, I started to work — then this number started calling.

The line crackles, a man speaking a language I can't understand.

'Wrong number,' I tell him.

His voice rises in urgency — then he screams. The call ends.

My screen remains lit for a few seconds. It dims. Something just happened to someone. I should report it. But what exactly? And to whom?

I return to my computer. I can't concentrate. I keep re-reading the same line.

I struggle to focus lately. We've been in Covid lockdown for weeks, with outdoor excursions only for food-shopping or exercise: you may gain weight or lose it, but not much else. Those with locked-down kids are in tatters. Those of us without dependants are supposedly baking sourdough and attempting yoga poses. I'm just trying to maintain my spirits, but my writing is stranded in mid-sentence.

At the start of all this, people spoke of meeting up 'on the other side'. But I can't see the pandemic ending in parades, only with a planet still hurtling toward catastrophe, a culture still ripping itself apart. Given that, what are the prospects for a manuscript like mine?

Then again, fretting about the future of the novel feels so trivial now, which is itself telling. The triumph of screens will be complete after this.

I watch the silent phone on my desk. It's blinking again, that same number, demanding me.

'Who is this?'

'Miss Dora?'

'Who is this?!'

In the background, I detect a second voice, also male but deeper, haranguing my caller, who moves away from the phone to plead in a language I don't recognize. There's a slapping, and my caller howls. 'Miss Dora?!'

'What do you want me to do?'

'You can help me? Please?'

Either my battery died, or the connection dropped, or I hung up. I'm unsure which to tell you, what each version will make you think of me. But I recognized his voice.

When I was renting that place in Almería, the busker showed me an app, allowing me to drop money in his cup digitally. He messaged me his number. But I never did donate.

I've read of scammers who target the elderly, acting as if in peril, abducted and brutalized – but they'd be spared if only someone paid the captors. Will you? What kind of person do you consider yourself?

That call must've been staged. After all, who – if truly endangered – would phone a stranger? Which is why I hung up.

I consider my phone, its invisible wires leading to almost everyone on the planet. How would I have managed this pandemic if Beck were a little girl, and still here, barging into my office as she did aged four, the door swinging open, banging into the wall, causing me to swivel from my big desktop computer. She was supposed to be in bed but giggled maniacally, running circles in her pyjamas, flinging herself to the carpet, then back to her feet.

'Way too late for this,' I told her. 'Anyway, playing in my office is a reward, Becky, and we never even did reading practice today.'

'Five minutes here? Just five, Mumma? Please?'

'I only just got you into bed! The answer is no. Go downstairs. Now.'

In those days, I was so bad-tempered. Not angry with Beck quite, but at a hole in myself that I only noticed because of her. I'd welcome such an intrusion now, so change my reply: 'Okay, how about this? You read me five pages of your book, then we play for five minutes. But immediately to bed afterward. Alright?'

The four-year-old's plump hand rests on the storybook, beside a pointing middle-aged forefinger (mine, still straight and slender then), which directs Beck to the next word. I can't recall who taught me to read, but I do recall paging through my mother's book collection, her favourite volumes spared from the fire when others were burned for heat during the war. Back then, I couldn't fathom print that small. By early adolescence, I admired books from a distance. Only in Paris did I read many. My interest was genuine but I also sought to impress, to be someone who knew all the references. I dipped into perplexing French philosophy, and noble Russian poetry, and irreverent American novels – a slow reader trying to catch up, to distance myself from a youth misspent in countryside. I never did read many works that I should have. Years later, when my first novel came out, I worried that literary types might quiz me about The Great Books, exposing me as an imposter. But they never asked; nobody knows.

When I myself had a daughter, I emphasized reading, so that she'd never feel as small as I had. Literature had become sacred to me – not only because it was my career, but because books contained many of the finest minds, offering insights into our species. Which raised a question.

Why were most children's books about animals? Another notable trait of kids' stories was comeuppance, though that was easier to understand. What preoccupied me, back when I was reading aloud from the animal-based justice system, was whether literature really could instill goodness. Wasn't one feature (moralizing) undermined by the other (animals)? We fill storytime with huggable creatures, then raise children in societies that treat animals as servants and lunch.

Another genre of children's tale, I discovered, involved the charming crook. These stories were always popular, which suggested something sinister in kids – or perhaps just the need for a breather after all that sermonizing about not thumping your little brother with a candelabra. When someone gave my daughter a picture book of a sneering fox who attended a fancy-dress party and, page by page, devoured the guests, I worried about creating a predator. On the other hand, children who dabbled in pirates and unicorns rarely became pirates and unicorns. And if they did, it was going to happen anyway; the stories appealed because Blackbeard was relatable.

Lately, a moral mission inflames culture for grown-ups too, based on the suspicion that adults themselves need educating, given the mess of our world; that hurtful words are close to violence; that oppression itself can be tackled by those who run the local theatre and the small press. If we had such sway – if novels disarmed the thugs – perhaps literature should attempt little else. But doesn't a story fizzle if proclaiming what people really ought? The jolt is seeing what people really are.

Either way, Beck never became bookish. Before lockdown, I saw reports of today's pushy parents enrolling their kids in 'Coding with Lego'. I'm unsure I'd have wanted a coder in the house. One discovery in raising a child is that a person whom you'd like is not necessarily one who'd thrive. For example, I always felt like an outsider, so encouraged my daughter to look sideways at crowds. Yet conformists seem far more fulfilled. Similarly, I wouldn't have wanted a kid who lived on a device. But the future will be.

I'm looking at my office carpet, seeing my four-year-old Beck there — before she bolts back downstairs to her bedroom. She sprinted everywhere when little. I'm alone again, and turn back to the computer.

Remind me: what was happening in this scene? I review partial drafts, suffering the gut-clenching realization that what I imagined was eloquent isn't. I mustn't fret about whether the writing is bad. Just put it onscreen, and judge it later. I'm trying.

But my phone glares at me. I check that number again, the long area code connecting to a possibility I'd rather not visualize. Even if those screams were fake, they're based in reality. Somewhere, right now, as I write and you read, people are dragged into a room to be hurt, and not just with offensive ideas.

I hit SEND on a donation, aware that I've been duped. At least I can return to work now, my bribe paid to morality. Soon, I'm lost in a scene. But something distracts me.

My silenced phone. It's flashing again.

A screen that you stamp on and it still works and stamp on again and it has a crack in the display but still works and then stamp on again and it works still and you stamp on it again and it never works again — a face is like that.

Or

~~Amir is placed into a cell the size of a wardrobe.~~

Or

He walks down a narrow corridor, staring at his feet, as ordered.

4

The man who took
the books away

(AMIR)

HE WALKS DOWN A narrow corridor, staring at his feet, as ordered. Amir's left shoulder – yanked back in this restraint – throbs, while his right knee is so swollen that it could give way. Still, he walks with full weight on both legs. Nobody should notice a weakness.

A meaty arm turns him to the wall, and a door opens. He's thrust into a confinement cell the size of a closet. Its floor is occupied by a large black duffel bag that he stumbles over, his arms shooting forward to brace himself on the cell wall. The duffel bag pushes back against his ankle. There's something in there.

The guard takes off his handcuffs, and commands Amir to enter the bag, which expands and contracts beneath him, the creature inside breathing. It's dark in this cell, so when Amir crouches, he feels for the closed zip, running his right hand across the bag contours, which jut at confusing angles.

The guard flicks a red Bic lighter, and holds it up for illumination, so close to Amir's face that he smells burnt eyebrows, the flame swerving, a shadow flickering over the bag, whose zip he finds. His left shoulder is too painful to help much — he uses that hand only to grip the canvas, gaining purchase, and he parts the zipper in a long black seam.

The face of the creature inside cannot be distinguished, only silver threads of beard hair. It seems impossible that Amir could fit, with another man already inside. The guard gives a push-kick to Amir's lower back, arching him forward, his inflamed knee landing on soft tissue of the man in the bag, who gasps, and says nothing.

Amir, suppressing grunts of exertion, folds himself inside. But he cannot close the bag from within. Impatient, the guard yanks up the zipper, needing to stamp down the bag's doubled contents with his police boot, hard-rubber treads on Amir's back and ear. The zipper teeth clench above his eyes. Inside, his bones press into someone else's. The guard clicks a padlock on the zip sliders; the two men are trapped inside. The rusted cell door clangs shut.

Only half-breaths are possible. Ownership of a limb isn't immediately clear, except by pain of impact against another. Amir gnaws his lips, realizing only from the taste of iron that they're bleeding.

When the other man exhales, it's a warm burst into Amir's nose. The smell repulses him. He wants to obliterate this person. The door opens again, and the bag is grasped. The guard stabs the bag with a ballpoint pen, struggling to breach the canvas, finally puncturing it, jabbing the other man, whose body flinches. By the fourth air hole, the fat guard is breathless, and he's lost the pen inside, so gives up. The cell door clangs shut again.

The infinite black is now spotted with cylinders of lighter darkness. Amir presses his mouth to one, torn canvas against torn lips, sucking in fresher air. Both men hold to their breathing holes. Once quenched, they remain quiet.

The other man jostles for space, which causes Amir to protect his own, pulse quickening from exertion, both of them wordless, pushing each other, crushed against the cell walls, pinching the other's flesh to make him stop. A fight conducted in silence is over. Both men lost, mashed into positions their bodies can neither sustain nor escape.

Amir has no breathing hole now. Terror swarms over him. He pushes the man, who drives back harder.

FATHER HAD A HEART attack. Amir's aunt phoned, claiming with booze-slurred insistence that he must fly out, for she could not cross the border to see her ailing older brother, owing to her medical fragility and the political danger she'd face back in her native country. She asked if he had called his father at the hospital yet. Amir intended to. Amir intended much.

At twenty-nine, he looked young to the old, old to the young. To his family, he merely looked evasive, once-bright eyes turning away. His aunt knew Amir could travel from London on short notice without professional consequences – he had no serious employment, working for a removals company that pledged to recycle but merely sifted for what its staff wanted, and dumped all the tape cassettes, filing cabinets and books at a landfill.

Upon touchdown in his aunt's city, Amir switched on his phone, and learned that his father had just died. Now he needed to rush, for the burial would be within a day. He took a cab to her place in the city centre, pressed her buzzer till his finger hurt, finally hustling into the building behind another resident, bounding up to her floor, and banging on the door. 'Where *were* you?' she asked him.

He sat in an armchair, out of breath. 'Can I even get there on time?' The quickest way was a bus. To save roaming charges, which were astronomical once you crossed the border, his aunt provided an ancient Nokia with a local SIM card, stuffing a charger into his luggage.

'Now,' she asked, 'would you like something to read?'

'What are you talking about? I have to go – I need to get there.'

Before lunchtime, he was in a packed coach, his back wet with sweat. Across the aisle, a young couple in surgical masks spoke loudly, sharing earbuds, a ticking beat audible each time the thrumming ceiling fan turned away. A little boy sat with shopping bags of used shoes. A wizened old woman scrolled a cracked-screen smartphone, rubbing her eyes. Amir told her of the reason for his trip because he sought the pity of strangers.

The bus crossed a border, entering the country of his birth, but Amir hardly saw his surroundings: talking, talking, then sleep. He opened his eyes only when the bus was stationary, the last few passengers stepping down the front stairs. A dusty road snaked around the hillside past a military checkpoint, with a barren valley below where a construction crew had abandoned digging equipment. This route would've been impassable months earlier during the fighting. But the government had 'reconciled' the area, and opened the road.

Amir exited the bus half-asleep and blinking at the daylight, landing on the road with a twist of his ankle. He massaged it as two young soldiers checked documents. His papers were in the hold of the bus, and he communicated this, but the soldiers told him to wait his turn. As they went down the line, they dismissed passengers, each filing back inside the bus. Only three passengers had issues to resolve, including Amir. The bus engine restarted, diesel fog from its tailpipe, heat radiating against his back. Urgently, Amir opened his daypack and rummaged inside to show them: nothing here. If they'd tell the driver to open the cargo door, he'd produce his documents. A soldier told him to be quiet, and disappeared with Amir's cheap phone into the makeshift office, its door wide open. A brawny moustachioed officer sat there, drinking maté, lips puckered around the metal straw, dimple in one cheek.

Amir and the other two remaining passengers waited, the sun scorching them. He could see into the office, and nobody was doing anything. Finally, a different young soldier emerged, and knocked on the bus doors, which opened. He ordered the driver to leave. The three remaining passengers shouted. An officer emerged from the office, and told them to shut up. The bus doors closed with a hiss. Amir was about to protest further, but waited because another excluded passenger – an old man whose young wife and little daughter remained aboard – was already bellowing objections. The officer swung something at this man's head. He fell sideways, arms extended rigidly, landing hard. The bus shifted into gear, turn-clicker blinking, though they were in the middle of nowhere. The officer held a hammer. The bus rolled gently up the road, around the corner.

On the ground, the old man bled from the side of his head, a dark pool expanding around pebbles, creeping toward Amir's dress shoes. The wounded man sat up, then stood, giddy, half his body yellowed from gravel dust, caked on the bloody side of his head. The officer with the hammer returned inside, joking with his moustachioed commander, whose legs were up on the desk. He changed channels with a remote control, growing annoyed with this uncooperative TV, aware that three civilians watched him as the sun watched them. He came out, remote in hand, and kicked the bleeding man in the behind, telling him to go. The man asked about the bus. A young soldier looked to the commanding officer, who gestured as if this were the stupidest request – how was he in charge of buses? The young soldier pushed the man, told him to run. Holding his wounded head, the man hurried up the winding road, parallel to tyre tracks of the long-departed vehicle.

The commanding officer pointed his TV remote at the professional woman beside Amir. She bowed her head, speaking too fast, fingers extending toward the officer, as if to reach through a cobweb without breaking its thread. As she pleaded, the officer elbowed Amir in the jaw, knocking him to the ground, his face buzzing, mind stalled. From that instant until now, another version of himself took over, as if the self-conscious surveillance camera on himself had turned off, just a body now, an insect programmed to keep existing while slowly swallowed by a lizard.

At the roadside, they put zip-ties on his wrists. He wondered whether to say these were too tight, but instead made his fingers into beaks, which alleviated the pressure. A meat van pulled up, and they slid up the metal door. Men sat on the floor, some in suits, some in shorts and flip-flops. He struggled to climb up there, arms behind him, and they shoved him in finally. He landed hard on his tailbone. Sprawled among other men, Amir watched the van door lower with a rattle of metal, daylight pushed down until only a horizontal thread remained. The van growled and advanced, the men seated around him banging into each other. It smelled of dried urine and bleach, like a locker-room toilet. Amir kept moving his jaw — it felt as if his teeth weren't aligned anymore. His phone was gone. His luggage and passport too. He'd miss his father's burial.

After a long drive, the meat van parked. The sound of shouting outside grew louder, deafening, until the metal door ripped up. In sudden brightness, Amir closed his eyes to slits, his face and clothing engulfed in grasping hands, his own still tied behind his back. Dragged out this way, he dropped off the lip of the van, hitting the ground, a cloud of dust rising, the surrounding shrieks even louder now, another prisoner from the truck landing atop him, and another. A baton struck his back repeatedly, and his mouth twice. He balled up, tucked his chin. If you cried out when struck, you were struck again. This was a lesson: don't scream. Those who couldn't stop would be stopped. Soon, the blows petered out. Only the attackers' shouts persisted. The attacked stayed silent.

In the first holding cell, Amir ran his tongue over the cracked-tooth stumps in his gums; couldn't stop jabbing at them. He pulsed variously, from jaw, hip, knee. The slightest movement of his left shoulder was excruciating. His long-restrained hands were swollen and stiff, as if arthritic. Summoned for check-in, he rose with difficulty, exerting himself not to limp. Prisoners had to wear blindfolds, but the guards had run out. So you were forbidden to look. 'If we see eyes, we take them out.'

In an office, a voice told Amir he could look now. He didn't. The voice insisted that it was fine – open your eyes! Amir found a little fellow with civilian clothing and an irresolute moustache, which matched that of the president pictured on the wall. He ordered the soldiers to remove Amir's zip-ties, and offered a chair. Amir sat, still not looking directly at the bureaucrat. He answered all questions honestly, interrupted only by sniffs, which caused the man to look up and see blood dripping from Amir's nose. The bureaucrat expressed disgust. When Amir said he was a French student but lived in London, the man appeared concerned, and asked to see a passport. It was on the bus. The man asked the destination of that bus, and noted it down. 'You *speak* like you're from here,' he said suspiciously.

'I was born here.'

The man left the office, absent for five hours, presumably checking into Amir's story. Contacting the French authorities could take a while, Amir assumed. Finally, the man returned. 'Did you fill it out?'

'Fill out what?'

The man had forgotten what Amir had said, had forgotten that he was even here. He dispatched him back to the cells. The soldiers had found a sweat-damp blindfold, and tied it around his head, knotting it with force. Amir angled his gaze down to watch his footsteps, lest they walk him down a flight of stairs for fun. He never saw the bureaucrat again.

To scare prisoners in the communal cell, the guards sneaked up to the door and crashed it open. Instantly, everyone had to assume the security position: facing the rear wall, on your knees, hands behind heads. Even when locked in the cell, prisoners were forbidden to advance closer than six tiles from the door.

The cell was built for four people but housed nearly forty, some clothed, some not, all emaciated except the newest, and silent until the guards left, whispering beneath the distant mumble of the guards' television. The cell walls were white at the top, dark at the bottom, where prisoners could touch. A neon light buzzed throughout the night.

Wake-up was 5:30 a.m., after hearing unseen birds and unseen branches rustling outside. As the sun moved across the sky, a rhomboid of daylight widened over one wall, too high to reach. On hot days, prisoners who had shirts took them off to flap and circulate air. Weeks passed, and a season changed, sunlight more and more briefly on the wall, its slant narrower, then gone one day. Each morning, blankets had to be piled in the middle of the cell. When unmonitored, prisoners stood on those blankets, straining to see over the outside bars. Mostly, they sat – you grew dizzy standing with so little food.

Once a day, the cell door opened for feeding, everyone scurrying into the security position. A guard foot-shoved an aluminium tureen of rice, olives and boiled eggs (less than one egg per man), the whole lot mixed together. They had to eat immediately – you couldn't save food, and were beaten if caught doing so. They swallowed the eggshells too and the olive pits. The cell toilet could be used once daily; you had a minute. On freezing days, guards threw buckets of cold water on them, so their clothes clung wetly as they slept. A few detainees recited religious passages. Others spoke of family. Mostly, they discussed recipes.

Amir grew alert to sounds: the 'welcoming committee' greeting another truckload of prisoners; water through old pipes, meaning it was time to use the toilet; the electronic *clack* of a digital camera to record a death.

The interrogations had no objective, except as a time-killer and workout for bored soldiers. Every room in the facility contained a photograph of the president, and they made detainees grovel before it, and call him their lord. They had to name their wives and mothers and children, and describe them, and beg the guards to fuck those family members.

The ways to hurt a body are age-old, part of a long human tradition. Much as teenagers smash a broken television, the guards were curious to see the components of a man. They rarely tortured to death. Fatigue stopped them; it was exhausting work.

You cannot remember pain itself. What terrorized Amir was its approach. Duration couldn't be understood either. He told himself just one minute more, and done, as with a medical procedure. During, he sweated more than he'd ever done, and saliva pooled in his mouth, as if about to vomit, or defecate. He wondered about saying aloud that this would kill him soon, or if that would provoke them to go harder, to show that *they* knew the endpoint, not he. He made himself boring by obedience.

During those interrogations, Amir learned why they had arrested him: on the Nokia that he'd borrowed from his aunt were satirical songs mocking the president, plus a video of ducks waddling down a dirt road, described as 'The biggest ever pro-government march'. He explained that the phone was borrowed, and named his aunt, giving her address in the adjacent country.

Under prison regulations, guards were supposed to wear surgical masks against the pandemic, but few did. Prisoners who caught the disease – that is, everyone who'd arrived without it – hid their symptoms. Amir had already suffered a mild case in London, and couldn't tell whether he was reinfected. If a prisoner was heard wheezing, or was denounced by fellow inmates, he was taken to 'quarantine', and did not return.

Some prisoners waited for relatives to pay bribes to free them. Sometimes, this happened. But Amir had purposely told nobody in London of his true destination, a country everyone associated with war and terrorism. As for his alcoholic aunt, she'd have heard that Amir never turned up for his father's funeral. She was always complaining of Amir's irresponsibility, and might assume he'd just returned to London, avoiding her again, as the rest of the family did. And even if she knew he was here, she had no way to help.

A few prisoners 'separated' – lost their minds. But Amir only stared at nothing, thought of nothing, living as if no places existed, just the tile floor. At night, everyone jockeyed for space. Waking was cruellest, the weight of not wanting this. Amir would keep his eyelids closed for as many extra seconds as possible, trying to vanquish self-pity, then distracting himself with the sight of their bodies and faces, overwritten with programmed drives: hunger, thirst, pain, hunger, fear, exhaustion, hunger, fear, hunger, hunger, hunger.

How long since he arrived here? He isn't sure. A country could've ended; he wouldn't know. Sometimes, he suffers a falling sensation, as if the floor is dropping beneath him. This place, he knows, has deformed him forever.

He swallows now, tasting thick plaque on his rotting broken teeth, the other man's breath mingling with his own. He doesn't understand why they're in this bag. You often don't know why; you just persist.

He tries to shift away, his pelvis scraping the canvas bag against the floor, his swollen knee in the other man's thigh. He can't twist around, and the effort infuriates him. The man's beard is raking his face. He wants to kill this creature. Amir's arteries swell, blood rushing around his body. The disgusting animal beside him parts those lips, leaning to Amir's ear. 'Are you hurt?' Amir recognizes that voice: his brother.

IT'S DANGEROUS TO DISCOVER relatives in this prison. They become leverage, the device of your torture, or you a tool in theirs. 'Why the fuck did you come back here?' Khaled asks.

They were born weeks apart but only met a few years later. Amir's mother – a French citizen who'd worked at an aid organization in the capital – raised him in affluence. By contrast, Khaled's mother was rearing three daughters besides him, all on the modest civil-service salary of their father. When Amir was seven, his mother moved them back to Paris, but wanted him to retain a link to his roots. So she sent him to this country every summer to stay with his bohemian aunt, a modern woman who worked on the radio, chain-smoked and drank wine imported from the next country (where she was to export herself once the war broke out).

On those childhood vacations, Amir's father turned up at least once per trip. He was proud of his French son; he was too proud in general. Shy to speak accented French, the man passed little time with Amir. The boy's aunt, when working at the radio station, deposited Amir in the courtyard of a nearby apartment block, where boys his age kicked balls and climbed walls and fell. She left him there to make friends, to figure out his meals, and she returned each evening. The first day, he was taunted by a bigger boy. Amir told his aunt, and this amused her, and she insisted that he should befriend the boy. Amir only understood later that she'd left him in that courtyard to dump her nephew at his father's feet – it was where he, his wife and other children lived, including that bigger boy, his half-brother Khaled.

At first, Amir had the impression that their family connection was secret. But everyone soon knew, including the half-sisters who came to meet Amir, inspecting him till he was dragged away like a teddy bear by Khaled. Previously, their father had been proud of his secret son. Now that it was known, he became aloof with Amir – and seemed to despise Khaled. Amir once witnessed their father kicking Khaled. The adults looked away.

On the outskirts of Paris, Amir attended a school for the children of bobos who worked at museums, in public relations, and academia. In this milieu, his non-French identity had status, so he accentuated the Arab side. But each summer vacation, this reversed. Khaled – who matured physically long before Amir – acted as guide and guardian throughout the holiday, announcing his brother wherever they went, then giving an expectant smile, as if Amir were to per-form Frenchly.

When Amir attended university, he lived in a slope-ceilinged garret in the 10th arrondissement, its hardwood floor populated by empty wine bottles whose mouths were choked with melted red can-dles. In the middle of the room was a raft: his unmade bed, with a crystal ashtray that kept tipping over when he read paperbacks there, causing much cursing and a shake of the sheets out the window, ash floating over the elderly prostitutes in Rue Saint-Denis.

When Khaled emailed that he was visiting Paris, Amir didn't respond immediately; he wanted a way out. Finally, Amir replied that he had tons of studying, and that it might not be easy for Khaled to manage without fluent French. When Amir went out with his half-brother, he phoned those in his social circle beforehand, apologizing. Khaled hit on every female friend of Amir – erudite feminists, all. To Amir's shock, they laughed with Khaled, entertained by this specimen, the crooked grin whose insincerity was sincere, and who didn't consider the rules of this country as serious rules.

The next summer, Khaled visited again. They walked around Paris, Amir telling Khaled of various neighbourhoods, citing great intellectual figures his brother didn't know. Khaled was distracted whenever young women passed, his gaze tracking them, which irritated Amir when he spoke of Foucault dying or where Derrida resided or what Houellebecq got wrong. The only topics that gripped Khaled were money and luxury. He photographed expensive sports cars on his phone, and entrusted his fate to the God of professional athletes, that holy goalscorer and trophy-giver. Khaled believed Muslims to be more humane than Christians; mistrusted Blacks; and had a distaste for Jews (but a respect for Israelis, for their military). Much of this jarred with those in Amir's circle who embraced ethnic authenticity – provided that it was the correct authenticity: anti-racist, pacifist, non-consumerist.

Amir ended up avoiding his half-brother by hiding at the library, then sneaking out to cafés for drinking sessions with friends. From guilt, he rescued Khaled's visit at the last, engineering a boozy final two nights out, so they could hug in a selfie, and mean it.

But neither kept up contact beyond the occasional forwarded meme, plus a heartfelt email a few years back, after Amir's mother died of cancer. By then, Khaled was married, and had a boy and a girl. Amir glanced at the pictures, but children all looked the same to him.

His own life hadn't proceeded to plan. A decent American college accepted his doctoral application, and he'd expected to teach there, and fantasized about female American students. Then, without much explanation, his visa application was rejected. Only lawyers could fight it, and he had no such funds. In haste, he found a third-rate university in London, where he frequented Francophone students, and spoke as little English as possible, except with shopkeepers who also spoke little English. On better days, he perceived himself as an up-and-coming intellectual; most days, just as a video-game-playing nobody whose glance caused women to study the ground. The immigrants he'd walked past in poor neighbourhoods of London and Paris (people ignorant of what was all the rage, what was all the outrage) – they always seemed uncultured, more like Khaled than himself. But they'd understood something that Amir only learned late: weakness and power.

He expected to see Khaled at their father's funeral, and planned to apologize for Paris, though his brother would deny knowing what he spoke of. He also wanted to admit aloud that his life hadn't turned out, how he'd quit his doctorate, how he worked low-paid jobs in London, clearing junk from rich people's homes, unsure what remained in his life.

Amir grabs Khaled, unsure whether he's holding skin or clothing, only that it's damp. 'You're here.'

THE GUARDS DISCOVERED THAT two inmates were brothers. So they arranged a fraternal event, Khaled explains. They are to fight tomorrow morning. The winner must beat the loser to death. The guards are bringing friends to watch. Amir is the smaller brother, and the weaker. He has never punched anyone. 'Can we not do it?' he says, knowing the answer. Resistance is just delay filled with suffering. However, the guards could be bluffing, waiting to see if two brothers would agree to fight – then calling them scum for doing so, spitting at and hurting them. 'Khaled, you'll destroy me.'

'We'll see.'

'No, it's obvious.'

This admission of brotherly inferiority, even now, is shaming. Amir moves about, wanting to escape himself, the point of his elbow digging into his brother, who pushes back. During his detention, Amir has sought to blame something for this: his mother's idealism, for example, which led to him keep up the language. Yet it was his hatred of work that led him to travel, hoping to inherit something from his late father. Instead, he inherits death this morning. Amir pushes his knuckles hard into the canvas bag, but runs out of energy. 'If I could have a strong drink right now, I actually don't think I would.' A wave of regret overcomes him for what he never did in his life. Queasy, he finds an air hole, the frayed canvas, his pulse too fast.

'You never said why you came to this shitty country,' Khaled remarks.

'For the funeral.'

'What funeral?'

Their father died in April. Khaled was arrested two months before – he's learning only now. It doesn't upset him. He falls quiet, but briefly. 'I was wondering why he didn't pay someone to get me out. Teaching me a lesson, I thought.' Their father claimed to disdain Khaled for his line of business – a guy who could get you stuff, electronics across the border, and more besides. Khaled had a reputation for working with anyone, regardless of their side in the war. Everyone liked him, nobody trusted him. But their father's distaste never provoked Khaled's hatred, just wore him into indifference: the dead man was just someone he'd known.

'You're going to fight back,' he orders Amir. 'I'm telling you to.'

Amir turns from his air hole. 'So that you don't get in trouble?'

'There are fights where you have a big guy, and everyone bets he'll win. But then the small guy can really fight.'

'I'm the small guy who really *can't* fight. Even in my mind, I have no idea how to punch someone.'

'We can spar right now,' Khaled jokes. 'Well, *I* am gonna try, so go fuck yourself.'

'Such an idiot, you are.' A pleasure in brotherly banter. Amir smiles, wipes his sweaty face against the interior of the bag.

Khaled asks if he's got a girlfriend.

'A girlfriend?' Amir says. 'Why don't you ask if I've got a wife?'

'You? No way are you married.'

'Why not?'

'You're too soft. She'd need to propose.'

'Move your elbow, you fuck.'

Khaled swears at him in French.

Amir does the same. Lovely to curse in his own language.

Since his arrest, Amir keeps recalling something from school. His class watched a documentary on the Drancy deportations, and an elderly female survivor of the Nazi camps told the television interviewer, 'They could do anything to our bodies, but they couldn't touch our minds.' That isn't true, Amir thinks. His mind is in charge of nothing.

He struggles to extricate an arm, needing to scratch his scalp, feeling bald patches there. He dreads a mirror. All three of them – mother, father, he – will be gone tomorrow, and forever. Three years back, they'd never have imagined their time was so short; they'd have wept. Khaled will remember us, Amir thinks. But what good is that? He's the kind who can't give a coherent account of this morning, let alone recount another's life. He wouldn't think to; he wouldn't know why.

Once, when led from cell to cell, Amir passed a heap of men, eyes open like fish, numbers scrawled in marker on their foreheads. Don't think ahead. Just this, just now.

He'll command Khaled not to tell people what happened, only that he'd seen Amir in prison, and he hadn't survived. Amir can't bring himself to give this instruction. Each time he nears the thought – his coming transformation, permanent blindness, deafness, loss of taste, touch, opinion, words, disappointment, possibility, memory: eliminated, for always – he's dizzy as if flipped backward over and over, opening his eyes, closing them. Somehow, he dozes for a few minutes to the background of his brother talking.

The day before he left England, Amir did a solo removals job, struggling to find parking on a leafy street of terraced houses in North West London. He left his van far from the location, meaning he was miffed by the time he knocked, rapping hard on a red front door. This was exhausting work that he hated, but he could take shifts when he pleased. Mostly, he stayed at his studio flat in Hounslow, kitchenette in the corner, a PlayStation, junk food from a nearby petrol station, cheap Australian wine, online porn, his phone. When he ran out of money, he'd call the removals company, and accept another job discarding the artifacts of a stranger's life.

Behind that red door, a tall old woman in dark jeans appeared, maroon jumper, knobbly hands clasped, one over the other. She looked at him from a height, cheekbones like a pushy man's elbows, an indent in her temples, dull green eyes. She didn't look away, so he did. 'You're here for the work.' She backed inside to admit him, wavering momentarily when either of her legs left the ground, then landing with hard certainty, as if towers strode.

She had many belongings to discard but was not moving out, just 'rationalizing', which struck Amir as the wrong word. She had an accent, so he doubted her language skills, as she doubted his – one of those metropolitan conversations where non-native speakers silently correct each other's English. She led him around three floors, initially pointing to specific items, then wearying, and just telling him to take what wasn't essential.

'I don't know what is essential for you,' he said.

'Downstairs, I'd say the fridge, the oven, the kitchen table are essential.'

'All the rest goes? This furniture also?'

'Why not.'

'They say to me this is a small job. I need more guys for this.'

'Not *everything*. The rubbish bits, I mean.'

'Which is rubbish?'

She pointed to the music player, which Amir approached, wondering if he could sell it: an old CD player with a stack of classical discs that'd be worth nothing. The bookshelves were half-empty, a few hundred volumes lying on their sides. No resale value.

'This?' he asked, of a large framed poster.

'The Bosch?'

The print itself was worthless, a picture with heaven on one side, hell on the other, with human depravity sandwiched between. But the frame had value.

How faraway that house feels, yet the red door must be there now, existing at this exact time.

The old woman boasted about her purge: shelf by shelf, week by week, she'd been throwing away all her books, most already dumped in the blue recycling bin. Sanitation workers rolled noisily up her street each Thursday morning, flinging into their ravenous truck another alphabetized section of her past. She pulled a fallen hardcover from her shelf. 'Recognize that person on the back?' He guessed before looking that it would be her. Author photos always struck him as pathetic: the soon-to-be-forgotten posing as the long-to-be-remembered, hand on chin, gazing soulfully from a remainder bin. He was embarrassed for her, that she found it necessary to assert her status to a bored stranger holding moving boxes. Dutifully, he looked at the photo on the dust jacket – she, Dora Frenhofer, pictured decades ago at a panel event, pin-striped suit jacket with padded shoulders, a handsome middle-aged woman, red lipstick, mahogany hair chopstick-impaled.

'You had a haircut,' he remarked. Hers was white now, and badly shorn.

'I did it myself, cut with fabric scissors during the first weeks of lockdown.'

He folded boxes. All her remaining books he placed inside slowly – slow not from caution but because she paid by the hour. In other boxes he placed knick-knacks. At first, he asked which to take. But she never declined, so he just went around, helping himself. Working away, Amir pondered his father, just hospitalized then, whom he'd fly to see the next day, and this stirred thoughts of his mother, wondering how those two ever got together, which prompted a harsh judgement of his own past few years, how unappealing he'd be to any woman now, the degradation of this work, and the oddness of removals during a pandemic.

She was eating lunch, and offered him egg salad. 'You can take off your mask. I'm not worried.'

They hardly spoke until she learned that he'd grown up in France, whereupon she switched to his language. Anything he mentioned about Paris triggered the old woman to recount something about her time there, from age nineteen and into her twenties, as if his life existed primarily as a conversation-starter. While she was going on about 1960s artistic Paris, he interrupted for a smoke and insisted on going outside, though she said he was welcome to light up here. On his return, she thanked him for the company, remarking that she hadn't known how much she had missed it during all these weeks. She'd not had a single meal with a person during that time.

'No family around?'

She had a daughter, Beck, who lived in Los Angeles. But the

old woman changed topics dismissively – not a matter she cared to delve into. He resumed filling boxes, and carried them to his van. Amir appeared a final time, asking if she needed anything further, presenting a form for her to sign.

'I must admit,' she confided. 'I suddenly feel ill that those books are going. Not so much my ones that I wrote. But there are books that came from my mother and father.' Amir was ready to leave, so made unloading sound impossible.

'Have you ever slept?' she asked Amir, signing and returning the pen. 'You look about the tiredest man I've ever met.'

He didn't like her. But he dreamed of that old woman, of being looked after, of sitting silently at meals, eating her food, lodging in one of her empty rooms upstairs.

'I need a piss,' Khaled says. 'I've been holding so long that I can't go now.'

'Why'd you ask me for permission if you already tried?'

'I wasn't asking permission. I told you I need a piss.'

Amir sputters with unintended laughter.

Khaled muffles laughter too, that of someone who doesn't know what was funny but wants to join in. He squeezes his brother's knee – the bad one, and Amir curses.

'My brother!' Khaled says. 'We had a good laugh.'

'More of that. Make me laugh again.'

'I don't know how I did it.'

A cell door clangs, not theirs. A guard is hacking and sniffing.

'Brother,' Khaled whispers. 'So sad to see you.'

THE GUARDS DRAG OUT the duffel bag, and pull at the padlock – none can recall the combination. They light cigarettes. Someone finds scissors, and the blades pierce the canvas just above Amir's face, snipping downward.

As ordered, he sits up. His fingers touch something: beneath him is that pen used to poke holes in the bag. They're told to stand. He does so. Trembling, he tries to focus on counting seconds. A guard complains that Amir is wet. Someone sniffs the air, and pretends to vomit.

More guards arrive, talking about a Dubai restaurant that sells steak dipped in gold. They push Amir and Khaled toward a larger cell, where spectators can watch. But they forgot the key, so someone must return to the guard station, and they argue over who should go. Amir's brain is not processing, just stuck on a repeating fact: it's now.

It's now It's now It's now It's now

The guards are complaining about the allocation of parking spaces. They unlock the large cell. Someone mentions 'the little faggot', meaning Amir. They bet on how many minutes this will last. Tension suffuses the room, violence approaching.

Amir notices that he's clutching that pen.

'Someone left this,' he says.

For an instant, the guards aren't sure what he's doing, and someone slaps his hand, and the pen hits a far wall, and someone else says that it was his pen, and makes Amir collect it, and hand it over. This interruption deflates the guards.

A loud man works them up again, shouting about the fight. He slaps Amir across the face. Amir – gaze still on the floor – says nothing. They shove him, and he stumbles, rights himself.

'Come on!' a guard tells him.

'Now!' another demands.

Amir tucks his head down, clenches his jaw, waiting for Khaled's first blow.

'Now!' the guard repeats, and shoves Amir, and twists his face to scream in his ear: a ringing deafness. Amir's body is just a vessel in which he huddles. His eyes are smarting from drips of sweat. Blinking, he glances at his brother across the cell.

Once an athlete, Khaled is a skeleton now, his shaved head nicked and notched, a thick greying beard. His arms are extended before him, fingers splayed, as if the lights were off. His eyelids resemble black slugs. But those aren't the lids. His eyes are open. The sockets are empty, plucked.

Arms outstretched, waiting for the first blow, Khaled is mumbling something.

Amir makes sense of it. It's not a prayer. It's a single word. It's French, and meant for him. His brother repeats it. *'Merci.'*

DIARY: MAY 2020

I check the time. My event is now. I need to stop writing, and start impersonating a novelist.

What I agreed to was a literary festival in the English countryside. They promised a night of glamping, though even this failed to dissuade me. My hope was to salvage my failing literary career through networking, which I'm awful at. But all looked promising, for I was to appear onstage with two prominent writers: a fashionable young Brooklynite known for dystopian fiction of such political obviousness that it wins awards; and an Irish ex-bouncer who wrote drizzly little novels for little readership before switching to television, where he scripted episodes of Succession, *thus succeeding in the successor medium. I fully intended to disgrace myself with backstage schmoozing.*

But, a global pandemic.

Now we're appearing via Zoom, neither here nor there, with a reputedly live audience of several dozen watching on devices. While the moderator makes the best of it, I fixate on the screen, how old I am compared with everyone else, and how my resting face — limp and absent — resembles a death mask. I must adopt an expression when my attention drifts, as it already has. A respectful half-smile perhaps? A pensive frown?

There's no point in my describing people as 'young' all the time. Nearly everyone is young now, except the 'eminent'. For those neither 'young' nor 'eminent' — just white-haired and worried — there's a different word: 'invisible'. Yet today, I'm notably visible in split-screen, nodding knowingly as the moderator lists my fellow guests' accolades and genius grants and movie deals, before citing my only almost-successful book (getting its name wrong, which is fine). Behind me in the video frame, I notice, are a pair of my dirty socks and yesterday's twisted underwear, at rest against the IKEA cupboard. I should've sat before IKEA bookshelves like everyone else.

After a reading by each of us, the audience is invited to message questions. These appear onscreen, and the moderator sifts through them, bypassing crackpot queries and selecting flattering ones, most for the Brooklynite, plus a few for the TV writer.

'Guys?' the moderator tells the online viewers. 'Let's not leave our other guest hanging. More questions, folks!'

A half-minute passes.

'Come on, people!'

The two other writers gaze down, eyes flitting side-to-side, apparently checking their phones.

'Well, lucky me,' the moderator proceeds. 'I get her to myself. So tell us,' she asks me, 'what's next for you, Nora?'

After we sign out, I'm faced with my onscreen reflection, which causes me to turn away, my attention halting at the pile of unread novels on my desk. How, I wonder, can this (literature) coexist with that (screens)?

I'm absurd to persist. Or perhaps I'm just a wasp-brained algorithm, completing the programmed task. Plus, quitting would stamp my life as a failure — that I didn't resign, but bookworld fired me.

What I need is to work. Yet I'm haunted by the phantom of people watching me on devices.

Stop worrying what others think! Then again, isn't that the subject of fiction: what other people think?

It's the act of writing that infatuates me. And others' books remain among my pleasures, that anticipation before opening a cover, and anything could be inside, and you'll never quite predict it. I'm still awed at others' craft, how they patch together words, and produce people.

But all these writers, all yearning to create something of moment despite its near-impossibility — do they too wonder where this fits anymore?

~~She rarely makes it through an hour of television, so he must watch every episode twice.~~

Or

~~He stops short at the entrance to their bedroom.~~

Or

He picks his beard in perplexity at the new bedside tables, which she must've formed by stacking copies of his latest novel.

5

A writer from the festival

(DANNY LEVITTAN)

'EPISODE ONE'

FADE IN:

INT. DANNY AND ZOEY'S BEDROOM – NIGHT

The messy Park Slope bedroom of author DANNY
LEVITTAN (around 40) and his financier wife,
ZOEY (also 40). She's resting on the mattress in a leisure-wear tracksuit, lit by
the television at the foot of their bed.
Danny stops short in the doorway, having
noticed something. She hits 'pause'.

                    ZOEY
    I'm watching. What?

HE PICKS HIS BEARD in perplexity at the new bedside tables, which she must've formed by stacking copies of his latest novel. On the bedroom wall, an episode of *Succession* is paused – Danny saw this one last night, but Zoey fell asleep. She can rarely stay awake through a late-night hour of television, so he must double-watch every show, his dreams haunted by character actors shouting, 'You can all go fuck yourselves!'

When they met two decades ago, Danny was majoring in English literature, Zoey in African studies, and neither seemed likely to own New York City property, let alone a four-bedroom in this desirable smug of Brooklyn, a short walk from Prospect Park. But upon graduating, Zoey – big-boned Irish-American soccer player with a conscience and a calculator – took a figuring-it-out job at the wealth-management firm of her best friend's dad. Seventeen years later, she's VP for social commitment, arriving daily at Connecticut headquarters with an ankh necklace under her business shirt and an endangered-turtle tattoo on her shoulder. It's *she* who can afford this place.

Danny's contribution is household chores, prompting her to remark that straight men are visually incapable of distinguishing between clean and wiped. Among his recent assignments was to find them bedside tables. But she is prone to pickiness and he prone to dithering, so Zoey took matters into her own hands, piling up those hardcover copies of his latest novel that long dwelled in Penguin Random House boxes down the hall.

'On the upside,' Danny says, 'you have twenty copies beside you every night, if the urge ever hits you to actually read it.'

'Don't you feel, at this point, that I'm pretty familiar with your writing? It's like you with your shirt off – I know how that looks. Do I need to see it again?'

'That's how you describe my fiction?'

'To be totally clear, I don't *mind* seeing your upper body.'

'This isn't what I need to hear right now.'

'Feed me lines then.'

'I thought you said dialogue wasn't my strong point.'

Her eyes remain on the frozen TV scene. 'Can I?' She un-pauses.

Danny's problem with her financial support is not pride; he swallows that with the weekly Zabar's delivery. The problem is they've lost their shared sense of mission. In their twenties, she shared in the tribulations of finding him a literary agent, and rallied Danny to keep at his writing. She was elated when he got a story in *Harper's*, leading to his debut novel, which she adored, then the second book, of which she remarked, 'I totally see what you're trying to say with this.' The third was a story collection that took her a year to get through, he watching in peripheral vision in bed each night as the pages sank toward her face. 'It's not that I'm *not* enjoying,' she said. 'I'm just exhausted.' Her exhaustion amounted to his lodgings, so he could not complain.

The next decade, Danny spent toiling at his novel-cum-bedside-table, *Babylon Lullaby*, a piece of writing more heartfelt than any he'd yet attempted. When conceiving the storyline, he watched scenes unfold behind his closed eyelids while falling asleep each night, and lurched awake in the small hours, scribbling notes, adjusting character names, fixing word choices. For years, he laboured this way, wringing scenes from everything he'd witnessed, each belief about humanity – a novel of which, if asked how long it took to write,

Danny could have pompously replied: 'My whole life.' *Babylon Lullaby* was his essence, distilled for posterity, and he daydreamed of his essence attracting a teaching position. When his agent shopped foreign rights, an Australian publisher snapped them up, and emailed him that *Babylon Lullaby* was 'sublime', and invited Danny to a book festival two years hence.

Since those thrilling days, nobody else found the sublime in his book. The *Babylon Lullaby* publication date didn't help: 19 January 2017, a day before Donald Trump's inauguration, when few cared about magical-realist historical fiction while magical-realist historical fiction unfolded on CNN. The novel was hardly reviewed – not in *The New York Times*, not *The Guardian*, only a lukewarm mention in the industry organ *Kirkus*. By the time jurors for literary awards met, they'd never heard of this novel, nor did Danny know them personally, so they saved time on the impossibly long reading lists by discarding *Babylon* without opening it. He'd once hoped that critical acclaim would compel Zoey to read what meant so much to him. At least they had furniture.

For Danny, accepting his book's death was akin to digesting a hardcover copy. He moped for months, then emailed Nell. She'd once described a literary agent's job as 'one-third contacts, one-third contracts, one-third therapy'. He required the third third, and she proposed lunch at a Midtown bistro. Her counsel was simple: stop writing seriously; write for profit. It doesn't have to be forever. Consider success a palate cleanser.

Before, such advice – to write what people wanted – would've offended him. But he was starting to suspect that the name 'Daniel Levittan' might never appear among The Great Authors. What hurt was that he'd never even infiltrated the top literary circles, where he could've made common cause with like-minded mediocrities. Instead, luck dribbled away, puddling in bags under his eyes and patching his beard white – effects that could've looked authorial in the era when he first sought glory, but that now looked nothing like a writer was supposed to look. Trapped in the right body at the wrong time, he articulated self-pity through excessive interest in the correct grinding of rare coffee beans, and by longing for the analogue past, much of which remained present if you weren't lazy. But he was: a man with a wind-up watch who checked the time on his phone.

Over that lunch, Danny and his agent brainstormed profitable plot points: the British upper class during World War Two; plucky refugee children; kinky sex; lighthouses were hot; speech impediments too. 'Endearing ones,' Nell specified. 'Not the weird kind, if that's not offensive to say.' In thirty minutes, between bites of balsamic-drizzled sea bass, they mapped out his write-by-numbers novel, which Danny composed in a five-month blur, producing a slab of brainrot so cringe that he suspected it could succeed. He emailed Nell the manuscript, *Gentlelady in the Lighthouse Window*.

She replied immediately: 'LOVE the title!' Weeks later, she read it, and raved even more, then took several more weeks prepping a submission package – she wanted to go wide on this one. They had the obstacle of his previous editor, Craig, who had a first-look deal on the next novel. But Craig was highbrow, so Nell expected he'd pass. If he did, she could stoke a multi-publisher bidding war, and Danny would feel mildly ashamed when the book came out, but able to support himself. 'Then you write anything you want!' she reminded him.

To writer friends, Danny was evasive about his current project. He planned to confess once he had the big advance. Then, as Nell was sending *Gentlelady in the Lighthouse Window* for consideration by his most-recent editor, a date on the calendar popped up: that festival.

The problem was, they had invited Danny as a serious literary author, a guise he'd spent months stripping from his soul, with much anguish. Now, he was expected to assume his former persona. Thankfully, he'd do so far from reality, Australia. But he's not sure how to feel about this, so distracts himself by checking his phone, packs stupidly early, and wanders from room to room in their apartment. 'Think I'm gonna head to the airport now.'

'Isn't your flight tomorrow?'

'I've decided to walk there.' He hoists his hiker's backpack.

'To Australia?'

'To JFK. It'll clear my head.'

A long ramble should resurrect the artist in him. Minor novelists drive; literary greats walk. (Why, he wonders, are famous authors always boasting about their walks? Do ideas come when in hiking boots? Or is it just that successful novelists own places in the country?)

His own hike – through Bed-Stuy, Cypress Hills, Woodhaven, Jamaica – proves less than pastoral, tramping for two hours over concrete, under traffic lights, past filthy vans. When not checking the Maps app on his phone, he contemplates authors whose careers he envies, and wonders if they were walkers. David Foster Wallace seemed more likely to spend hours thinking about going for a walk, then not. Zadie Smith would probably gaze down from a Manhattan window, free-associating about the quirkiness of pedestrians. Did

Kafka hike, or just pace? Virginia Woolf definitely walked: in the dim lamp of his college memory, she strides across London, and glimpses a dwarf. She walked right into the sea at the end, didn't she, rocks in her pockets.

Danny's hands are stuffed into his, numb from cold. The snowdrifts haven't melted in Queens. He's lost, turning in place. A police car bleeps once and pulls over, the officer asking if he's doin' good. Danny – round metal spectacles of a Victorian botanist, bushy beard, musty three-piece suit and neon backpack – babbles about urban hiking. Repeatedly, the cops call him 'sir', meaning it as an insult. Upon leaving, one of them mumbles, 'Fuckin' a-hole,' which shocks Danny. Did he act like a fuckin' a-hole? Was he fundamentally a fuckin' a-hole?

He reaches the outskirts of JFK, its misery hotels and anti-terror fences. An author in search of an entrance, he locates the terminal finally, takes a seat, and settles down to read. He brought *The Brothers Karamazov*, which he plans to start and finish during the estimated 34 hours, 45-minute travel time to Australia. It's a portly volume, whose cover he folds open, clearing his throat, as if about to narrate to gathered passengers the family history of Fyodor Pavlovitch Karamazov.

But the movement and voices of those passengers are a hand that slaps down the page: he must look up to see where they came from. The answer is: everywhere – twitchy humans trapped between fright and flights, primed both for a shout of 'Get to the ground!' and the shout of their names at Starbucks – the cost/benefit of the American airport. But New York doesn't equal America, as both sides are eager to confirm. Danny picks out a few venturers from Trump country: a guy wearing a T-shirt of an AR-15; a woman with confederate-flag kerchief hanging from her back pocket.

He returns to *The Brothers Karamazov*, page 3, then checks his phone, then the departures monitor. Zoey was right: stupidly early. He must kill hours more, and invokes the aid of snack food and internet. By the next morning, he has reached page 5 of *Karamazov*, and is wearily consuming a breakfast burrito when his flight appears on the monitors. At last, he can check in.

'Passport, please.'

'Wait. What?'

Suddenly, he's in a spinning clock, sprinting for the taxi stand, calling Zoey at work, telling her what an *idiot* he is. It's an oddly affectionate conversation, she explaining where his passport ought to be in their bedroom, rooting for him to still make the flight, urging him not to stress. He will get there. Festival folks will dote on him. Australian fans will swoon. 'Hanging out with book people will remind you of why you got into this.'

'Love you,' he says, reckoning with how much he owes Zoey, how she'd have wanted a family, how his moods held her back, how he wants the best for her life. He resolves that, when back in nine days, he will find an apartment of his own.

FADE OUT.

END OF EPISODE ONE

`EPISODE TWO`

FADE IN:

INT. HOTEL ROOM IN AUSTRALIA - NIGHT

An alarm clock shows 8:17. DANNY wakes, jet-
lagged. He parts the curtains, low sunlight
on the horizon. He calls the front desk.

> DANNY
>> (on phone)
> Hey. When's breakfast till this morning?

> HOTEL CLERK
> It starts at six.

> DANNY
> But till when?

> HOTEL CLERK
> You mean tomorrow?

> DANNY
> No, today. Right now.

> HOTEL CLERK
> Uhm, our breakfast is only served in
> the morning, sir.

DANNY CONSULTS THE WINDOW again, inverting day to night. He splashes water on his face. It's so hot in here. He left in winter and only arrived by summer. His luggage is full of wrinkled three-piece suits, corduroys, woollen socks.

He skims his tour itinerary: the first event is a bookshop reading tomorrow at 9 p.m. Checking his phone for messages, he finds an email from the Australian publicist, Nousha, wishing him luck tonight.

Tonight? He checks the date on his phone. He's onstage in forty minutes.

Danny sprints for the lift, unwashed, panicked. He jumps into a cab waiting outside the hotel, and scrambles out at the Broken Shelf, banging his shin into a sandwich board chained to the sidewalk: *Reading tonight! Daniel Levittan, author of* BABYLON LULLABY*! Come one, come all!*

All couldn't make it. Nor could one. He stands in what looks like a barn with a small library in it, fifty empty chairs before a lectern, no humans but the cashier.

'Hey,' he says, approaching her, 'I'm Daniel Levittan?'

'You don't sound so sure. Let me get the events person. Ronda!'

Awkward wait.

'You guys hold lots of readings here?'

'Ronda's coming. I've not read yours yet.'

'So many amazing books to get to, I bet!'

She dials an internal number, and shout-whispers: 'Not my job to babysit, okay?!'

Moments later, Ronda arrives, a twentysomething with dyed-grey hair, pink cat-eye glasses, and a floor-length dress with Harry Potter lightning bolts. 'Let's give everyone a few minutes to arrive.'

'Sounds like a plan!' Danny responds, hiding his disappointment behind exclamation points.

'When did you get in?'

'Just this morning actually!'

'Too soon for a bit of lubricant?'

'Sorry, what?'

She points to a table of fifty glasses of red. 'Help yourself.'

A couple enters the store, a rickety lady propping up her prehistoric husband. Ronda hastens over to them, pointing at the stacked display for *Babylon Lullaby*, then indicating Danny, who straightens his posture, as if in a police line-up. The elderly couple shuffles over to inspect him, and the tremulous wife takes a copy, considering both sides of the cover with interest – and places the book under her arm. They sit directly before the lectern.

'My Australian fanbase in full!'

'People turn up late in this city. Others'll be here soon.'

Soon arrives. Nobody else does.

Danny – to centre himself (thus avoiding the centre of himself) – refreshes email on his phone, and finds one from Nell, who reports having told his previous editor at PRH that her client probably prefers his trashy bestseller at a more commercial imprint. It's a win-win. If Craig wants *Gentlelady in the Lighthouse Window*, he'll need to pre-empt with decent money. If not, Nell goes wide, and prods her editorial friends into an auction. 'This could move fast!!' she emailed. 'Keep your ringer <u>ON</u>!'

Ronda asks if he's ready to start. He pretends to mute his phone, and pockets it, aflutter with the Nell plan. Yes, alright, it's the end of his highbrow hopes. But with middlebrow money and – above all – success at something, he's high. If only he'd always known corruption was so pleasant. A secondary benefit is that he is bulletproof tonight, viewing this absurd situation with amusement: his walk to the gallows, a bound copy of his past decade on the lectern, Ronda there behind rows of empty chairs, giving him a thumbs-up. Danny – overdressed in a wool suit, flushed – smirks to himself.

But he must adopt the proper disguise, so unfolds his sheet of prepared remarks, sweaty hand spreading the page. 'Good to be here in Australia,' he reads. 'Wonderful that so many could make it.' He snorts, a tad hysterically, adding to the elderly couple: 'I'm glad you managed to find a seat!' Ronda gives another patronizing thumbs-up, while the cashier is audibly watching YouTube on her phone – it sounds like skateboarders hurting themselves on purpose; she claps her hand over her mouth every few seconds.

Danny explains to the massed crowd of two plus an employee what he intended artistically with *Babylon Lullaby*, how a version of that opening scene – the spider in the baby carriage – really happened (it didn't, but he vaguely believes this now). He'll give a reading of the first few pages, he warns, and clears his throat, wipes his forehead. Jet-lag sweat? Stop getting nervous. Just read what's on the page.

But spoken aloud, the words seem to smash together without spaces. Danny speaks and listens at once to this linguistic pile-up, noting that the author isn't particularly good at writing. Improvising, he edits his novel as he goes, which proves disastrous, lines ending abruptly, forcing him to track back and explain. He keeps clearing his throat, prompting Ronda to present a glass of water. He sips, and croaks, 'Thank you for your patience, everyone.' Interpreting this as the end, Ronda applauds, and the cashier looks up from YouTube and joins in, while the old couple in the front add theirs, a skin-slapping quartet that peters out.

'Do you think,' Ronda asks, 'that we might have time for Q-and-A?'

A customer enters the store, hurrying over. She asks where the travel section is, stage-whispering apologies.

'If nobody else has a question,' Ronda says, 'let me have the honour. Daniel Levittan – what *is* your writing schedule?'

The schedule of a great artist could, perhaps, be interesting. The schedule of a failure is to peep at a schmuck in private. So he obliges with a falsified version, excising the morning hours devoted to reading sports columns and watching clips of capybaras. No more questions are forthcoming, so the elderly lady and prehistoric husband try to stand. Danny rushes around the lectern to help them up. They thank him, and shuffle toward the signing table, which is piled with copies of *Babylon Lullaby*, along with three black Sharpies.

He sits, accepting the woman's copy, her husband's cloudy eyes looking in different directions, neither at Danny. She, at least, is delighted when the author asks her name, and she recounts how well they know South Africa (she seems to think he's from there), and how the part about the doctor resonated because she herself worked in the medical field for many decades at the office of her husband, a podiatrist.

'Feet!' Danny says. 'Must be great stories there!'

As he signs her copy, he marvels for an instant that the 867 pages beneath this pen are his – misspent time perhaps but meaningful in his life, a novel finalized that day when he flung hand-revised printer pages in the air, and Zoey took photos of them raining down, and she kissed him as he sat. Danny considers the elderly woman's excessive make-up, and he experiences such affection for her, a stranger who wants to read what he wrote. His efforts weren't a waste, even if the book was just for her. And if his new manuscript becomes a hit, readers might even come back and discover *Babylon Lullaby*. It's not over. He presents Edith with her signed copy, inscribed fondly.

'Oh, that's okay,' she says, returning it. 'But wonderful talk!' She directs her husband toward the exit, pausing to return their wine glasses.

Ronda approaches Danny, palms together in apology. 'If it's any consolation, *I* thought you rocked.'

'Each little bit of buzz helps, right?' he says. 'Would it be useful, by the way, if I autograph the leftover copies? I know that signed ones sell better.'

'There's actually this weird thing with publishers over here? They don't accept returns if they're signed. So maybe best to leave it? In case they don't? Sell?' She gathers them fast, as if Danny might autograph against her will. Ronda returns with a credit-card reader, and punches up $29.95.

'What's that?' he asks.

She touches the lone copy of *Babylon Lullaby* left on the signing table.

'What, the copy I signed for her?'

'We can't return it with writing inside.'

The cashier shouts across the store, 'Don't charge full price, Ronda.'

'I could offer you our staff discount?' she says, then calls back to the cashier: 'Junior-staff discount? Or senior?'

'Ten per cent.'

'Junior it is.'

In the taxi back to the hotel, Danny is ready to start his morning, which is regrettable since it's nearly 10 p.m. He enters the lobby to find the festival's welcome-mixer underway, with a blare of authors pretending to be extroverts. A young woman – shaved head, long nose, purple lipstick – holds a copy of *Babylon Lullaby*. This must be Nousha, his publicist from the Australian publishing house. They shake hands, and she thanks him for coming all the way to Oz. 'How'd you feel the reading went tonight?'

'Pretty good! Not the best turnout; not the worst.'

'I just got off the phone with Ronda.'

'So not a huge crowd. But enthused.'

'It's about building until you reach critical mass.'

'Yeah, I was pretty near critical mass tonight,' he jokes, not nearly as sour as he would've been months before. A lousy reading is a reminder: farewell to the former self.

Nousha runs through his activities of the coming days, including a writing workshop he'll teach; the big onstage event, where a major TV journalist interviews him; press appointments TBD; plus, the private dinner with Gavril Osic.

Danny steps back in amazement to hear this final item. The early novels of Gavril Osic are, in his estimation, among *the* greatest works of postwar fiction – perfectly constructed, indelible. Besides his writing, Osic was always a hero to Danny for his defiance of the despot who ran his country. Danny knew that Osic lived in exile in Australia nowadays, but nobody said he'd meet this literary idol. Nousha explains that Osic invites a selected group of festival authors to dine at his home each year. The list is submitted by the publishing houses, which propose writers of note. She put forward Danny.

Effusive with thanks, he invites her to celebrate with him at the open bar. Two proseccos and one confession follow – perhaps from fatigue, perhaps from this manic-depressive evening. 'Honestly, Nousha? I'm considering this trip my goodbye to literary life.'

'Don't say that,' she responds. 'You wrote a wonderful novel, Daniel. *That* is what matters.'

She can't be older than twenty-four but speaks with such confidence, as if it's about art not glory – an ideal that he serviced as an amateur, but surrendered as a pro. 'According to BookScan, *Babylon* sold fifty-seven copies total,' he tells her. 'That's almost hard to do. That's how many you sell from people butt-buying on Amazon.'

'I bet *some* people bought it deliberately.'

He laughs, and she's smiling back, black eyes looking right at his, as if she knows something nobody else does, polite enough to keep her thoughts to herself, to allow others to be the experts.

FADE OUT.

END OF EPISODE TWO

'EPISODE THREE'

```
FADE IN:
INT. HOTEL DINING ROOM - MORNING
DANNY is woozy after much booze and little
sleep the night before. He hovers around the
breakfast buffet, disoriented by noise coming
from the tables, which are louder than
morning should allow.
```

HOW DO ALL THESE authors know each other?

They must've bonded at the welcome-mixer last night, and friend groups have formed. Their varied fashions – oversized heart-shaped sunglasses, sitting beside a grey suit, next to a tongue-piercing – imply recent acquaintance, though the braying suggests they've never encountered humans they loved more.

They're bidding over whether Trump is worse than Bolsonaro is worse than Boris, which morphs into humblebrags about festival schedules, and finishes with admiring citations of obscure writers from poor countries. An ageing Filipino busboy frowns – they've left an ungodly mess where pastry platter meets coffee station. Danny lifts a steel lid: porkish steam clears over mud-brown sausages.

He settles at a solo table, sipping the world's tiniest glass of orange juice, and listens unwillingly.

'Four years since Jaipur? I am *so* fucking old!'

'Wait, didn't I see you in Cartagena?'

'Oh, you're right!'

'Hate to do this, but I gotta love you and leave you. I'm on ABC in a half-hour.'

'Radio or television?'

'Christ – radio, I hope. I look like shit.'

'You look totally quaffable, babes.'

'Hotel bar again tonight?'

'I'll be the one holding the bottle.'

'Kisses, all! And good luck today!'

Constipated in his hotel room, Danny keeps refreshing email, awaiting something decisive from Nell. What would Gavril Osic make of the crass literary scene here? Danny's attention is diverted by a dozen new novels in a festival tote bag – it's a tradition to give each author a range of other invitees' work, as a way to introduce everyone. He dumps the lot into the bathroom bin, and feels cleansed.

In the hotel hallway, three writers around Danny's age are gossiping: a perfumed bald Scot in a tanktop; a jittery playwright from rural Newfoundland in butterfly frock; and a sky-high former WNBA player who switched to short stories. They notice Danny's festival lanyard as he closes the room door after himself.

'And *you* are . . .?' the bald Scot enquires, then widens his eyes at the mention of Danny's book. 'Oh, I've heard of that!' he lies. 'It's doing super-well, I'm told.'

Danny is not above sucking up or selling out; he's eager to do both. Just, he's a talentless whore, more concerned with his dimensions than theirs. But now he finds himself in the very situation that Zoey always tells him to seek. Networking is what art is about, she says. So he memorizes their names, and feigns familiarity with their work, asking about their events, and listening with furrow-browed concern as they perform anxiety about performance anxiety.

'I'm *so* bad onstage,' the Newfoundland playwright says. 'I just go blank.'

'You'll be *great!*'

'Finished,' a maid mumbles, emerging from Danny's room, dragging out the rubbish in a transparent disposal bag.

'Hey hey!' the bald Scot exclaims. 'That's my book in there!'

The former WNBA player sees hers too. 'Did you throw those away?'

Danny turns to the maid. 'I didn't mean for you to take those.'

The Scot – enjoying this – crows: 'He thinks our books are rubbish!'

The three writers fish their works from the disposal bag, flicking away chocolate wrappers and miniature liquor bottles that Danny consumed overnight.

'I rested those books *near* the waste bin, not inside.'

'Sir,' the maid insists. 'They was *in* the rubbish.'

'It's a mystery then. But I really would like those books back, you guys. I was right in the middle of them – and hugely enjoying.'

Danny lugs a dozen soiled books back to his room, bidding farewell to his new frenemies. He flops on the king-sized bed, books hopping in air, crashing to the floor, where he leaves them. According to the bedside clock, he should go downstairs for a coach to the festival site. Those three will be on it. He'll take the next. He lies back, and a wave of exhaustion flows over him. He can't stay awake. Must. He sits up.

For stimulation, he checks and re-checks email, and finds promising news. His highbrow editor at PRH, Craig, has no place on his list for a bestseller – but he loved it, and foresees great things. That opens the field: Nell can officially stoke interest, and already has three commercial imprints on the line, with nine more likely to chime in.

Zoey emailed too. He's afraid to open it because of the subject line: 'What the hell?!'

She was missing him, she explains, so glanced at the printout on his desk of *Gentlelady in the Lighthouse Window*. She only meant to read the opening – but could not stop. 'Holy shit, babe. This is the best thing you've done in YEARS!!!!!'

Yipping with joy, he leaps to his feet, and does karate kicks around the room.

Those three from the hallway went on the previous coach, so he safely boards the next behind Marlin Pratt, a parping English historian who hosts BBC documentaries, stomping around the Parthenon in open-necked safari shirt and red shorts. For those already in the coach, Marlin narrates his own entry with high irony as if for a TV audience, and the seated writers laugh obligingly. Danny is the last to board, and maintains a fake smile, nodding to Marlin, who is stretched across two seats. The man reaches up to snatch Danny's reading copy of *Babylon Lullaby*. 'You did this? Well done,' Marlin says. He flips the book, chortling at the author photo. 'Oh, you're having us on. That is *not* you!'

'It was once.'

'I don't wish to offend,' Marlin says. 'But this photo makes you look ever so slightly mentally impaired.'

'It's from a while back.'

'Like a mentally impaired sex offender.'

As the coach pulls into traffic, Danny takes back his book, and falls into a seat a couple of rows behind, not wanting to situate himself too far away, lest he appears to sulk. Finally, they reach a university campus where the festival chairwoman awaits, greeting all, but granting cheeks-kisses only to Marlin, leading him away to teach his masterclass. The other writers check in with student volunteers at a fold-out table, and are chaperoned to their sessions.

Danny is last, and gives his name and that of the workshop they've assigned him to teach: 'Freaks and Geeks: Creating Characters from Yourself'. They check the list, but his workshop isn't listed. Danny produces his itinerary as evidence, but the student-volunteers just squeeze their faces into pained expressions. He demands someone senior, and such a personage emerges from the green-room tent, eventually finding that the Daniel Levittan workshop was cancelled for low enrolment. 'It does happen, alas.'

'Maybe you should inform the person doing the event!'

'We did.'

Danny contends the opposite, and considers himself the authority on whether he knows something.

'Well,' the senior staffer responds, 'that's your truth.'

Two hours remain until his onstage interview, so he loiters in the green room, a vast tent supplied with bagels, carrot sticks, bottled water. Other writers come and go, high from workshop adulation, chattering volubly, wishing each other luck for upcoming events. Danny watches at one remove, as if in a theatrical production where all parts have been assigned, the cast has mastered its lines, and he is thrust onstage, all the other actors wondering if this guy is even in the play. Danny planned to explain in his workshop that fictional characters need conflict, and respond with transformation. But that's false to life, he thinks. In life, people face conflict, and they respond less with transformation than repetition. Gradually, you become what you were. Which is hungry.

He helps himself to a bagel, though he's still bloated from breakfast, and with a digestive tract that remains on New York. He ambles around the campus quad, and settles on a bench, soothed by exotic tweeting from the branches. Danny still thinks of himself as he was in college – except when he sees undergraduates, who shock him by being teenagers. They haven't yet staggered into everyone else's future. He wants to warn them.

A peacock prances across the empty lawn. 'What's *your* book?' Danny asks.

The animal turns, and stalks closer.

'And your agent? Oh, she's *great*. I've definitely heard of her.'

The peacock keeps advancing. Suddenly uneasy, Danny scooches to the far end of the bench, his foot raised protectively.

The bird's beak rears back, readying to peck. Danny kicks the air between them, looking around, in case he's seen losing a fight to a peacock. Is this a protected species? The fucker wants his bagel. Leaping up, Danny abandons his food, speed-walking back toward the green room, waving hello, for Nousha stands there. 'Thank God you're here,' he tells her. 'I just got assaulted by a peacock.'

'For any reason?'

'A political dispute.'

She has a block of free time, so they wander. 'What,' he asks, 'is *the* worst publicity experience you've had?'

'You want to make sure it's not you?'

'That's exactly why, yes.'

She recalls an American peacenik singer of the 1960s who wrote a

Woodstock-then addiction-then rehab memoir, and visited Australia in a baldness-obscuring orange bandana, doing major promos like an event at a cathedral, where he insisted they black out the stained-glass windows, requiring many floors of scaffolding. His rider also demanded that someone attend with an ironing board. When Nousha arrived, lugging this object, he berated her for standing there with a goddamn ironing board when what he needed was toothpaste. Dutifully, she hurried back up the long nave to go and seek some. Just as she reached the cathedral exit, the singer boomed for her to return. She sprinted all the way back. 'Is it so goddamn hard to find *toothpaste?*' he said. 'Seriously?'

Nousha's parents were immigrants to Australia, her mother a teacher from Bosnia, her father an engineer from Iran. They'd settled in Melbourne, the city where she still resides, now living in a small house with her potter boyfriend, raising chickens in the backyard.

Besides doing publicity, she writes poetry. Danny expresses admiration for that form, mentioning Wordsworth — the only poet who comes to mind. In fact, he scoffs at those who publish poems nowadays, versifying for a world that's not paying the slightest mind. But in her case, he sees a romantic, even if that image is undermined by the amount of time she spends thumbing messages into her phone. Well, that *is* her job, communications. And she must dash — another orphaned writer is wandering lonely as a cloud.

'Before you go, tell me: where do I find your poems? Have any been published?'

'I've done a couple of skinny little volumes.'

'That's not nothing! And you like it, the poeming?'

'I must.'

'You'll know you've made it once you get attacked by a pheasant.'

'Wasn't it a peacock?'

'You of all people should appreciate poetic licence. Anyway, birds evolved from dinosaurs, right? No shame in losing a fight to what was practically a dinosaur.'

A festival staffer with clipboard strides past Nousha, who calls out, 'Melanie, a peacock attacked one of my writers.'

'They're ptarmigans. Fuckin' aggressive, hey?'

Nousha asks to hand over Daniel Levittan, who needs to reach his big onstage interview. Melanie chaperones him through the crowd, and Danny confesses to nerves.

'Whatcha got to lose?' she says. 'If they're rough with ya, tell 'em to fuck right off. You got the mic. You got the power.'

'Except I'm posing as a nice human being.'

She laughs, and he's encouraged. Australians find him witty. What if this is the unexpected turn in his story? That his literary career is *here*, that he isn't finished, just that the Brooklyn in-crowd snubbed him – yet the literati of Australia see something special.

As Melanie leads him toward the outdoor festival stages, the crowd thickens. She narrows her eyes, puzzled, and stops to consult a colleague. 'Well, well, Mr Modesty,' she tells Danny. 'There's a massive bloody line for tickets. Looks like you hit the jackpot.'

FADE OUT.

END OF EPISODE THREE

'EPISODE FOUR'

```
FADE IN:
EXT. COLLEGE CAMPUS - DAY
A festival staffer hustles DANNY past an end-
less queue of people waiting to buy tickets.
He knows people are looking at him, so he
avoids eye contact, attempting a sombre writ-
erly expression.
```

DANNY ONCE READ OF a little-known novelist who turned up for a book event in Japan, only to discover that he was a literary celebrity there. Imagine if that were Danny's fate here. Nousha did mention an important print review this morning, though he hadn't thought newspapers mattered anymore. Where in Australia would he live? Is Melbourne the cool city?

He spent this past year dismantling hope, and salving himself by renouncing bookworld altogether. Now, he's like an incel who finds that someone wants to have sex with him: shockingly in love.

Minutes till he goes up, Danny surveys the crowd, emotional from gratitude. But a worrying thought insinuates itself. His trashy manuscript for *Gentlelady in the Lighthouse Window* is circulating at every New York publishing house. Why didn't he use a pseudonym? Nothing ruins a highbrow reputation like a readable book. What time is it in New York? He fires off an email to Nell: 'something crazy going on here. insane buzz for babylon. mega event. lighthouse was error? talk ASAP pls hold off on taking any offers!!!'

Look at this crowd. He's not finished.

The onstage interviewer is a prominent Australian arts broadcaster, Cleo Kleeber, who joins him in the green room, giving a big smile, then fanning herself to cool down. From a ratty handbag, she produces his hardcover. 'I loved it. Absolutely loved.'

'Wow! I'm so glad to hear that. So, Cleo, do you prefer to discuss our discussion ahead? Or just go with the flow?'

'Let's keep it loose. It's always a hoot interviewing debut novelists.'

'Actually, this is my fourth book.'

'Nah, come on!' she says. 'What, honestly?'

Stage technicians hook up their microphone headsets. 'It's go-time.' The two walk into the festival throng, readers everywhere, milling about with just-purchased books, eating sustainable junk food and calling out Cleo's name, for they recognize her from TV.

'This way,' a festival volunteer tells him, cutting diagonally through the crowd. And there it is: a massive stage with a thousand seats before it. He has never seen anything this size for a book event. But he's puzzled. Only a few dozen seats are occupied, surrounded by an ocean of empty fold-out chairs. Wasn't there a huge queue for tickets? He saw the line.

The tech guy directs him and Cleo to the onstage couch, where they sit, he far lower than she, which forces him to talk skyward.

'Is this everyone who's coming?' he whispers to Cleo, hand covering his microphone.

A roar hits them, cheering and whooping, and he tries to sit up in the couch, looking around to localize the noise.

'Wouldn't you love to hear Malala?' Cleo says.

'She's talking now?'

'You must've seen the queue.'

'That queue wasn't for me?'

Cleo laughs, and thumbs-up the sound guy, offering a welcome to their audience (Danny counts them: nineteen people). 'Having a good time today, guys?!' Cleo asks, and reads verbatim the jacket description of *Babylon Lullaby*, then turns to its author. He's still adjusting to this let-down, and is sweltering too, pit stains on his blue dress shirt.

'Daniel Levittan, welcome to Australia.'

He unbuttons his waistcoat. 'Thank you so much, Cleo.'

'First question: why should the people gathered here today, at this celebration of great writing and great books — why should they buy *you*? Come on. Sell us.'

Sinkingly, he looks at the fourteen people in the audience (five left during the intro), and utters a few wandering sentences, barely audible because of the loudspeakers shaking on the adjacent stage: '. . . youngest person *ever* to win a Nobel Prize, author of *I Am Malala: The Story of the Girl Who Stood Up for Education and was Shot by the Taliban*, and the very first . . .'

'So basically,' Danny says, 'I guess you could dub it a novel about memory and the struggle to . . .'

'. . . couldn't be *more* delighted, *more* proud, more *honoured*, to bring up to the stage, our very special guest! Malala Yousafzai!'

Applause drowns him out, so he closes his lips to wait, a space-holder smile. The onstage sign-language interpreter shakes her head at him, cups a hand behind her ear — *Can't hear you!*

After a moment, Cleo resumes, telling the audience: 'Inside scoop, guys: we moderators get assigned events by the festival, and I only got this one yesterday. It's mayhem, going from cookbooks, to self-help, to YA. But that's part of the fun!'

Did she just imply that *Babylon Lullaby* is young-adult fiction? If anything, it's old-adult fiction – that is, adult fiction. Except 'adult fiction' sounds obscene. 'I'm just wondering, Cleo, could we get a super-quick show of hands to see how many out there have had a chance to read my book, so that I pitch my answers right?'

A huge roar from the next stage. Malala is about to speak.

'Personally,' Cleo answers, 'I'm halfway through, and I consider myself somewhat intrigued.'

He glances at her copy, pristine but for the first few pages, the corner bent around page 9. Cleo supplants his question of the audience by asking everyone to raise their hands if they couldn't get tickets to Malala. Everyone raises their hands. 'Well, you can hear her a bit from here, if you strain.' She turns to Danny. 'Soldier on, shall we?'

Sipping water, he nods.

'So, *I* learned,' Cleo says, as if sharing a confidence, 'that this is *not* your debut, which might surprise people. Tell us, Daniel Levittan, why have we never heard of you? Though I figure that might've changed after the review in *The Australian* this morning! How's it feel for a writer to read something like that?'

'I haven't seen it actually. You're making me worry now!'

'I'll read out a bit.'

'Wait – if it's not great, should we skip it?'

'You'll never improve if you don't listen to your critics, right? Like this part here,' she begins, tapping the screen of her iPad, 'saying you have a writing style that's, and I quote: "a male, quasi-autistic register".'

Danny fakes a smile.

'Shall I read on?' she asks.

'I'm not sure what's coming next! Do they say my author photo shows me as a sex offender!'

'Excuse me?'

'No, it's just that someone was looking at my author photo today, and said it reminded them of a sex person. Ignore that; stupid joke.'

'Kinda weird thing to joke about, sexual abuse.'

'Yes. I thought so.' His takes another nervous sip of water.

'You're not on a registry in America or something, are you?'

'God, no! No, no.'

'Not sure why you're laughing like that, Daniel Levittan. There's nothing funny about rape.' She says nothing for several seconds, the word 'rape' hanging in the air.

He looks to the sign-language interpreter, then back to Cleo. 'I really didn't mean to make light of that. Obviously, I'm not laughing at rape.'

'I don't know about you, audience,' Cleo says, 'but I feel a tiny bit triggered right now.' The few in attendance are paying attention now, leaning forward to hear over the noise from the next stage.

'If I made an inappropriate comment, I'm really sorry.'

Cleo takes a deep breath. 'Let's try and move on. Your research,' she resumes. 'Tell us about your process.' He begins to answer – but she breaks in, 'Because there's clearly masses of research crammed into this, right?'

'Hopefully not too much!' He sniffs and fake-laughs at once, recounting his labours at the New York Public Library, where he pored over archival material.

Cleo is fake-snoring. 'Yes, professor,' she says, and the audience bursts out laughing.

She invites Danny to move to a reading, which is punctuated by roars of approval for Malala, jarring with his scene of a deformed jester in 1730s Vienna whose companion is a one-winged canary that, mysteriously at this early point in the novel, speaks Cantonese. As Danny reads – attempting accents – he's hideously aware of the sentimentality, the devices, the falsity. He's no more an artist than all the other imposters.

A whirring noise distracts him. He looks into the audience, where a woman in a mobility scooter is driving down the aisle. She shouts to her friend, who squeaks in joyful reply. The two chat loudly, oblivious to his reading. At last, they bid farewell, and the woman turns her mobility scooter around, and whirs away. With a complicit smile, Danny tells the audience, 'At last! She's gone!'

Someone yells back, 'She's bloody disabled, mate!'

Another roar for Malala, and the echo of her voice: 'Thank you so much all for coming. I thank Australia! Thank you!'

Wild cheers ensue, over which Malala's onstage interviewer shouts that their special guest will be signing books – but no selfies please.

'You can take selfies,' Malala interjects. 'I don't mind.' More cheers.

Cleo concludes too, telling the gathered few: 'This one'll be in the signing tent too.' She drops her headset on the couch, and walks off without goodbye.

Danny stands, unsure how to exit the stage gracefully, a smattering of audience members watching him. He sees Nousha waving to him, and he descends the stairs, her expression either sympathy or gravity, allowing him to pick.

'Did you see any of that?' he asks.

'I got a taste.'

He decides to put on a good face. 'Why would anyone want to hear a Nobel laureate over me?' he jokes. 'Fuck Malala!'

A technician unclips Danny's microphone, muttering with disgust, 'The Taliban shot her, mate.'

He reaches the signing table, where three copies of *Babylon Lullaby* wait, beside stacks of *I Am Malala*, which volunteers frantically open in readiness for a signature before a lengthening line of admirers. One of her fans leans toward Danny. 'What's she like?'

'Malala? I don't work with her. I'm here for a different book.'

Finally, she arrives and sits beside Danny, smiling to him, shaking his hand. She asks if this is his book, and picks up a copy.

'You read novels?' he asks, shrinking inwardly at how self-important he sounds.

'I will try to read yours.' She glances at the queue of people before her, an apologetic head wobble, and begins signing.

Why should anyone care about his writing? It's mortifying that he wants to foist it on them. Malala's admirers are pretending not to see him, the loser with his three copies. Nousha crouches beside him. 'Act like we're having a very important conversation. Saying significant things.'

'Significant things.'

'Important comments.'

'Amazing opinion.'

'Fascinating comeback.'

'Stunning revelation.'

'Urgently but respectfully grabbing author's arm, leading him to pressing appointment.'

He follows her through the crowd, a body among bodies. The one or two novelists who represent his generation have been chosen. The hundred others who'll sign the next open letter against evil – their number won't include him either. He too wants to take a moral stand with no effect. But nobody CCs him on the emails.

He types a message to Nell, just a subject line: 'Ignore previous.'

Nousha seeks to raise his spirits, reminding him of what's ahead tonight: the dinner with Gavril Osic, whose novels will outlive them all.

FADE OUT.

END OF EPISODE FOUR

'EPISODE FIVE'

```
FADE IN:
INT. HOTEL ROOM - NIGHT
DANNY is lying on the carpeted floor of his
hotel room, murmuring along with a meditation
podcast. Eyes closed, he breathes in through
his nose, out through his mouth, readying
himself for the big dinner party.
```

GAVRIL OSIC DOES NOT suffer fools. Danny suffers fools. It's not that some people are fine with fools. It's that not suffering fools is a way of saying you've made it. Fool-suffering is the lot of the ordinary. Or maybe, Danny thinks, sitting upright on the hotel-room carpet, maybe *I'm* the fool. Maybe they're suffering me.

He vows to shut up at tonight's dinner. As the saying goes, 'Better to keep your mouth shut and have everyone think you a fool than to open it and have them know.' He resumes the meditation podcast, mumbling to himself about a fleck of dust floating through a shaft of sunlight.

A minibus will collect the eight chosen authors from the hotel lobby. Waiting around, some jabber from nerves; others hold silent, considering their shoes. Each author received a list of subjects *not* to discuss – above all, you mustn't speak to Osic about his writing. Past attendees violated the rule; it never turned out well. They came across as fans, and Gavril Osic does not tolerate those.

On the minibus, the loudest voice is Marlin Pratt, the much-gesticulating BBC historian, who is flirting with a buxom millennial chef with face tattoos, who just spent a year on a boat off the coast of New Zealand. Marlin boasts of having met Osic at a previous dinner, and declares, 'The man uses silence as a cudgel.' The face-tattooed millennial – promoting a combined cookbook and eating-disorder memoir – hopes to connect with Osic over veganism.

'You vegans, none of you can fucking cook!' Marlin says. 'You can't have morality and edible food. It's simply not possible.'

The millennial, who hosts a YouTube cooking show, retorts that she finds amazing vegan food around the country. The only problem, she admits as the minibus engine starts, is that restaurateurs recognize her now, and they're always trying to impress her with over-the-top dishes. 'Bourdain calls it getting food-fucked.'

A mousy Peruvian intellectual beside Danny asks with a smirk if he's the man who made the wheelchair person cry at his event. Others overhear, and turn with expectant smiles. 'Nobody was in a wheelchair,' Danny replies. 'A mobility scooter. And she didn't cry.'

They pull up to a stylish home in the suburbs, and everyone struggles to both rush inside yet appear casual. Last to enter, Danny finds himself stranded in the hallway. A servant takes his coat, and directs him to join the others, whereupon he clings to a glass of white wine, and glances around for another outcast, or a conversation to sidle into.

Danny always wondered about meeting a great artist, seeing up-close what differed. He's met plenty of authors in Brooklyn but most were as boring as he, particularly the successful ones. Osic is another level, a man who'll feature in literary history. It's as if this were a dinner party held by Dostoevsky himself, if Dostoevsky refused to eat animals or products derived from animals.

Danny flushes, on the verge of a breakdown in a room of strangers. 'This is vegan, right?' he asks a passing waitress, holding up his wine glass. She offers to find the bottle, and Danny follows her toward the kitchen, only to dart into a toilet to control his breathing.

He keeps refreshing email, needing something to inflate him, and finds one from Nell. She has good news, thank God: she's gone wider with *Lighthouse*, and a dozen commercial-fiction editors are gorging themselves on it. She expects bids soon.

How this crowd would shun him if they knew of his trashy best-seller! This secret transgression gives him courage. Screw them, with their essays in the *NYRB* and artists' residencies in New Hampshire. Someone knocks on the bathroom door. He opens to a finely dressed woman in her sixties, whose inquisitive gaze catches him off-guard. 'How are you coping?' she asks, looking so intently that Danny answers truthfully.

She sympathizes, condemning the rigmarole of book-promotion, which has grown so intrusive in recent years, forcing writers to become the marketing operation for themselves. He's dying to ask who she is; she wasn't in the minibus. They chat with such ease that he becomes terrified she'll leave, and he'll be marooned anew.

'I keep wondering,' he says, 'what would've happened if Dostoevsky had a book tour for *The Brothers Karamazov*.'

'Yes, exactly! Gabe doesn't do events at all.'

He twigs: 'Gabe' is Gavril Osic, and this must be his wife, she who forces the future Nobel laureate in her bed to submit to this annual encounter with the outside world.

'Gabe has a line: "Literature is lying to tell the truth about falsity."
But the job of being a writer nowadays is *itself* so false. Here's my
advice,' she says. 'Pick a few eccentricities, and crank up the volume.
Before you know it, you'll become a parody of yourself, and be
having much more fun. Anyway, we all become exaggerations of
ourselves in old age, so you'll have a head start.'

'I might actually try that.'

'By the way, Gabe is *not* like they say – not silent like a Roman
statue,' she says. 'Have you two met before?'

'Not yet.'

'He'd love to know you.'

She leads Danny toward the dining room, where other guests are
taking seats at a long dining table, and she is drawn away by a waiter's
questions about the meal. One space at the table remains, which others
have avoided: beside Osic. Danny expected his fellow writers to stam-
pede the man. Most (except Marlin Pratt, seated on the other side of
Osic) seem as intimidated as Danny. He has no choice, so sits there.

After a spell, Osic tires of the unctuous television historian to
his right, and Danny feels a Great Author glowering at him. Osic
remains silent, hands on the napkin in his lap. This could be the
only chance Danny will have to speak to one of the most important
writers of his time. So he does.

But the stress is so acute that he can scarcely remember what he
says as he says it, gibbering to a hollow face, blinkless eyes. Danny
yammers about how festivals are not suited to him, and he scrambles
for points of equivalence between them, then retracts, then repeats his
quip about Dostoevsky on a book tour, which seemed witty before,
but sounds pretentious now. Danny emphasizes that he's not equating

himself to Fyodor, and is also unsure why he referred to Dostoevsky on a first-name basis, which they aren't on. Osic stares like a punitive skull, which causes Danny to blab more, both asking questions of Osic and answering them. He blurts that he's changing publishers for his next book, and asks Osic for advice on what to seek in an editor.

After a silent silent silent silence, as if Osic first had to slide off the coffin lid, he replies – but first, a slow spoonful of soup: 'Once. I had an editor. Who told me to put the beginning in the middle. And put the middle at the end. And the end at the beginning.'

'So an editor shouldn't interfere? In your case, I mean. For me, I probably need tons of editing! That's me. Not you. Is that ideal, though? In your case? Or . . .?'

Another spoonful of soup.

Perhaps the conversation just ended, and Danny should look away.

'Once, there was a book,' Osic resumes, 'with a ferry trip.'

'Is that a riddle?'

Osic glares at this fool. 'One of my novels had a ferry scene.'

'Ah, yes – I remember that. I love your stuff, by the way.'

'My editor found schedules for this ferry. The departure that I had put, the time was wrong. He told me this, and I corrected it. That,' Osic concludes, 'that is a good editor.'

'Would this apply to bus schedules too? Or just ferries?'

Eyes storming, Osic fixes on him. 'I've said too much.'

Danny is caught with an ingratiating chuckle halfway from his mouth, looking at the back of a skull.

In his hotel room, Danny punches his thigh repeatedly, mobile phone on speaker, ringing Zoey. She's at work, but agrees to eat her sandwich early. Chewingly, she tells of inept staffers and her idiosyncratic boss. 'You've gone silent,' she says. 'You still there?'

'This might've been the worst day of my career.'

'Maybe I have something to cheer you up.'

After she tells him, he makes his way downstairs to find Nousha as arranged – it's the festival-ending mixer. In the lift, he watches floor numbers descend, the doors parting upon a cackle of off-duty literature. He's expected to attend, and Nousha kindly agreed to act as his wing-woman. A photographer circulates, snapping pictures for festival's social-media feeds. Gently, Danny is asked to step aside – the photographer needs a few of Nousha Papazian alone.

Danny holds her drink, zoning out. Zoey was so disappointed after she told him, and it failed to lift his mood. He takes out his phone – he'll message her to explain. He'll claim to be excited. He finds an email from his agent with the subject line: 'Update on Book Offers.'

The Wi-Fi connection is terrible, the wheel slow-spinning. Even if they're low bids, he's taking one. He can tell Nousha about the sale, act like it's trivial, that none of this matters to him.

The email opens: words and words that he cannot turn into sense. Fifteen editors, Nell reports, have had the pleasure of reading his manuscript. Fifteen turned it down.

FADE OUT.

END OF EPISODE FIVE

'EPISODE SIX'

FADE IN:

INT. AIRPORT BOOKSHOP - DAY

NOUSHA is picking through piles of novels to
see if they have a copy of *Babylon Lullaby*
for an impromptu author signing. DANNY busies
himself seeking a volume of her poems. He
plucks out a thin volume as a BOOKSELLER
hovers behind.

                    BOOKSELLER
    I LOVE her stuff.

                    DANNY
    Well, I happen to have the author right
    here with me.

THE STAFF HURRY AROUND the bookstore, gathering any available
volumes of Nousha's poetry. After she autographs them, Danny
and Nousha walk toward the departure gates – she's flying back to
Melbourne, he to New York, via Dubai. He looks at her askance.
'You,' he says, 'were on the bestseller list on their wall.'
    'I know.'
    'Number one. You realize that, right?'
    'I've been pretty lucky with this book.'
    'Why the hell are you shepherding a putz like me around? I
should've been publicizing you!'

'It's been a surprise. Everything took off. But I'd committed to the publishing house till the end of the season.'

'And after?'

'I'm doing a fellowship thing.'

'What, studying poetry?'

'No, teaching creative writing. Just a thing in Iowa.'

'This is insane, Nousha. You're on the Australian bestseller list! How much poetry pulls that off?'

'Weirdly, it's on the New York one too.'

'The New York what?'

'The *New York Times* bestseller list. I'm on next week's, under "fiction" for some strange reason.'

'So *that* is why my book never made it! Your damn poems stole my spot!'

She smiles.

He is moved, not sure why. 'Seriously. Congratulations.' He takes out his copy, bought at that store. 'You need to sign it for me.'

She borrows his pen, opens the copy, and looks directly at Danny, as when they first met. She inscribes his copy. They bid farewell.

At his departure gate, he rests Nousha's book of poetry on his lap. He can't open it. He's afraid.

He wakes his phone, and googles her, looking at the images first. One photo links to a *New Yorker* article that she seemingly contributed to their website. He clicks the link – but the article isn't *by* her. It's *about* her. Apparently, she's a phenomenon, with a huge online following, massive sales. Danny, who always scorned social media, finds her Twitter account, where she has 97.5K followers. On Instagram, 340,000 people follow her. Throughout his time in

Australia, she has been thumbing stuff into her phone, which he took to be tedious publicity work. He reads a few of her posts now: lines of classic poetry; witty quips; incisive political opinions. Any time she hits SEND, more humans read her than will ever read a word by Daniel Levittan.

He feels no envy. In an unserious way, he's in love with her, as he used to fall in love at age nine, when seeking a goodnight kiss from the fourteen-year-old girl working as camp counsellor. The greats spend years among fools before they needn't suffer them anymore. He must've been one of hers. Danny always thought himself the protagonist, but he was only a character actor in a show about her.

He dreads New York, fears going home, so phones Zoey, either to save what's ahead, or to worsen it. She flares that he's still not excited about the pregnancy. If writing makes you this miserable, she says, you need to find another occupation.

'What if I try one more book? It'll be a flop. But then I can jump out the window in peace.'

'Why, though? Seriously, Danny. Why go through it? Why put *me* through it?'

Previously, when he bemoaned his writing career, she urged him to hang on, that the public would come around, that the endeavour was noble.

'I can't talk about this,' she says. 'I'm at work.'

'I am too.'

'How are *you* at work?'

After they hang up, he looks vacantly at his phone, whose screen is still showing the *New Yorker* profile of Nousha Papazian. He wonders if she found him attractive, and knows the answer.

The cliché of midlife crisis is an accomplished older man pursuing a vivacious younger woman, he buying a sports car, and wrecking everyone who ever supported him. But what if the middle-aged man can't afford his own car, has accomplished nothing, and persuades nobody to have an affair with him?

That's the real midlife crisis: you're irrelevant.

FADE OUT.

END OF EPISODE SIX

'EPISODE SEVEN'

FADE IN:

INT. AIRPORT DEPARTURE GATE - DAY

DANNY recognizes a fellow novelist who attended the Osic dinner, DORA FRENHOFER, a tall woman in her seventies. She sits by the departure gate, rolling her left shoulder, arthritic hands crossed in her lap. She must've forgotten to remove the festival lanyard. He reads her name aloud.

DORA LOOKS UP, SQUINTING at him. He points at her lanyard, then locates a waste bin, and disposes of it for her.

'How did you find it?' she asks.

'The rubbish bin?'

'I meant the festival. But whichever you have opinions on.'

He tries to sound casual, yet admits his trip wasn't a roaring success.

'Literary events are spectacularly dull,' she says. 'I pity anyone who makes the mistake of attending mine.'

For her amusement, he embellishes his bad experiences at the festival. She listens, smiling.

'Tell me something,' Dora says. 'Do you actually *read* novels anymore? I mean, I know that you *have* read novels. But do you still read them?'

'Definitely.'

'Me neither,' she says. 'It's the dark secret of the literary world:

nobody who doesn't have to read this stuff still does. Why would they? My theory is that contemporary fiction is only there to be bought nowadays. Who has time to suffer through it? The funny part is that people – a class of person – still worships literature, so they buy it on Amazon, keep it on their bedside table for a few months, then slot it unread into their bookshelves, perfectly satisfied with themselves.'

'Oh, come on – contemporary fiction is still vibrant,' he counters. 'Tons of people are producing novels; think of all the creative-writing programmes. They're just not reading *ours* – or mine, in any case. So maybe me groaning that "the novel is dead" is just a way of trying to feel better, when what I actually mean is "*my* novels are dead". Could that be it?'

'You're talking about *writing*. Yes, people still want to do that. Everyone under sixty at a book event is a wannabe writer. They're scrambling for the last dregs of literary status before it's gone, the ability to drone about one's sorrows for pennies in profit. But half of those in the audience just want your seat onstage. By the way, I've not heard your name before,' she says, turning stiffly to look at him. 'Should I have?'

He cites his books.

'No. Don't know you.' She goes on: 'We mustn't complain, though. We're on a free trip to Australia, hotel and flight paid for. You realize how many people would kill for a week of our lives?'

He glances around in case other authors lurk, and witness their heresy. He confesses to his late-night habit during this festival, searching online for the words 'retraining' and 'man in his forties'. He mentions some of Google's answers: driving instructor, pet sitter, life coach. 'What even is a life coach?' he asks.

'It's someone who has ruined his life then telling other people how to succeed.'

'What kind of fiction do you write?' he asks.

'The sad kind, where nothing happens, then it ends.'

'I might be one of your characters.'

'Oh, you are. Are you only realizing that now?'

'Maybe you're one of mine.'

'Do you write women?'

'Of course.'

'Do you write them well?'

'Do you write men well?'

'Very well. Men on the verge of a nervous breakdown. Written for women who ended up married to them.'

He suggests a character truce – neither uses the other in fiction. She declines.

'You attend lots of these literary events?' he asks. 'Or you avoid them?'

'They avoid me.'

'*My* problem is,' he says, 'I'm not anyone's idea of The Author.'

'Pardon my directness, but I'm Dutch, so you must accept it. Nothing we're saying matters. If you have great talent, it comes through. But you don't have great talent, I think.'

'I don't.'

'Nor I.'

Elite-club passengers are invited to board. The festival provided business tickets to the well-known writers. They await economy.

Danny almost suggests that they sit together, but she speaks as if with an arm extended. Also, it's a long flight to Dubai, he onward to New

York, she to London. Danny fears spoiling this complicity. But he must stay in touch. When they disembark in Dubai, he'll exchange details.

At last, they approach the ticket-taker. 'Maybe it's time for us to stop, and leave this world to others,' she says.

Once seated, Danny places Nousha's poetry book in the seatback pocket before him, watching it recline into his knees when they reach cruising altitude, then leap upright as the whiff of reheated chicken pasta infuses the cabin. Finally, he opens the book, and steels himself for her dedication – where she'll urge him to keep writing, and not to be discouraged. He flips the opening pages, and finds her handwriting. All she wrote is *Nice to meet you!*

Danny watches everyone in little seats before little screens. Zoey will be in bed by now. A new lifestyle awaits him there. He tries to spot Dora across the far aisle, wondering what she's reading. He gave her a copy of his. Danny stands to see. She's watching an episode of *Succession*.

When the plane touches down, Danny stands fast. He needs more from Dora – he must ask how to resolve his story. On the other side of rumpled passengers, she rises painfully to her feet, brushes down her shirt. Overhead luggage and arms impede Danny. He cranes around, but loses sight of her.

Finally, he pushes past the laggards, approaching the toothy flight attendants saying bye-bye, bye-bye. He hurries past, lugging his bag into the long tunnel to the terminal. But that character is gone. He's on his own.

FADE OUT.

END OF SHOW

DIARY: MARCH 2021

I'm not someone who talks louder when people stop listening. So, if nobody is especially interested, why finish writing this manuscript?

Lately, I've heard this question often, posed most aggressively by the winking cursor. But I have kept poking it along, prodding approximately at my keyboard. (As another old writer remarked of his arthritis, 'If I pointed that hand at you like a pistol and fired at your nose, the bullet would nail you in the left knee.') What was that writer's name? We forget almost everything, but I worry that my blanks are no longer the normal kind.

Before, when something escaped me, I rummaged through my mental archives, flipping its pages, tracking down the wanted slip of paper. Or someone presented the missing fact, and: 'Ah, yes! Of course!' But it's more than just lost names now. I awake in the night, caught between states, frightened. Eventually, daylight seeps around the curtain edges, and I find courage. I'm coping.

I glance at my attic-office window: birds are chattering out there, a wavering tree limb hailing me. I stand, and open the window, hearing words from the street below, a man and a phone. When you can't see the talker, you realize something: speech is rarely about anything, least of all what the person means. Words are to remind someone that you're there.

During lockdowns, this street became hushed, and my eavesdropping migrated online. There, billions had something to disclose. Perhaps humans always wanted to shout their opinions, but now share the ability, so hate it. Anyway, this era of blurting has had the opposite effect on me: I want to shut up. Which is why, some months ago, I abandoned my manuscript altogether.

In the ragged time since, I've monitored what everyone else seems to care about. Gradually, something overcame me. I no longer feared that I might be insignificant; I became convinced of it. I won't matter as I wanted.

When I was small (but big enough to lie in bed until ten), my father once pulled off the covers, and warned me: 'You'll waste your life, sleeping and sleeping, then dead!' In adulthood, I assumed this horror of indolence, that I needed to accomplish, or I'd be humiliated. Most of my life has aimed at this: succeed. Writing is what I tried.

But what if my adolescent self was right? Maybe you should just make the most of your chapter. Laze in bed, and read all the books. Maybe it's my approach that amounts to a squandered life, beholden to that ever-vanishing endpoint, ambition.

So why am I resuming this manuscript today?

I could claim kinship with great artists, those misanthropes of myth who toil away, supposedly indifferent to society. But I'm nothing so brave. I've just missed the bliss of concentration: my efforts, my pages. Also, I want to see how this book turns out. I get to write the second half now.

All morning, I've typed in my dressing gown, only putting on clothing minutes ago, owing to the downpour. (Like snails, I come out in rain.) Now I'm heading outside, down toward the river, these raindrops — old friends tapping me on the head — dampening my white mess of hair.

Who's to notice? I reach the pelted, brimming Thames, which slops onto the pavement. The seas and the skies are closing in. Something has changed, but people can't.

For decades I behaved as if a contestant in this world, everyone trapped together, elbowing for position. Was it all just my imagination? Look around now: nobody anywhere in sight.

I step into the silent roadway, close my eyes, and exhale — only for a bicycle courier to burst around the corner, clipping my elbow, which I clutch.

He halts and swears but never looks back, as if I were a puddle. Setting forth, the man stands high on his pedals, and stamps down, rainwater on the back tyre spitting over my apology.

~~He bikes through London traffic at speed, on a manic high at his recklessness, silver hair rippling, no helmet.~~

Or

~~He swerves around the obstacle, cursing in English and German, standing from the seat to regain full speed, a long and lean figure when pedalling, as if mounting an endless staircase.~~

Or

On a foldable bike, he weaves down deserted London streets.

6

The deliveryman
who stood in the rain

(WILL DE COURCY)

O N A FOLDABLE BIKE, he weaves down deserted London
streets, his grey hair fluttering and arms tensed from holding
up this contraption, bought on eBay and forever trying to collapse
under him. He turns a corner, swerving past an elderly woman who
has stepped distractedly into the street. 'Stay home and save lives,'
Will mutters as he passes. 'You absolute numbskull.'

Dismounting at Westerley Business Park, he rolls his bike through
a complex of buildings on an artificial lake, with trees standing around
like dejected security guards. Trundling past the outdoor meeting
pods, Will glimpses a couple behind tinted glass, passionately latched
together. The country is in another Covid lockdown, with household
mixing banned – in effect, adultery is illegal. But fornicators need
somewhere to sin, and he doesn't object. Will rarely musters outrage.
Anyway, his eyes are smarting from smoke – without processing it,

he rolled and lit a cigarette. Blinking wetly, he perceives movement near his feet, and flinches. Another rat? On closer view, a crow bouncing along the hem of a hedge. 'You lot have the entire sky,' he reprimands it, coughing in a deep rumble. 'This is our bit.'

Will finds Building 6 and, from his cargo shorts, extracts a surgical mask, the same he has used for weeks, its baby-blue front specked with pocket lint. He takes the stairs to the fourth floor, where he finds the closed offices of an accountancy firm, a television-production company, and the destination of this package: RCN Ltd. Behind its locked glass door stands a thick-necked man in black Fred Perry polo shirt with yellow-tipped collar, buttoned up to the top. He leans on a receptionist's desk, yammering to a bald man at a computer whose smile is so false that his cheeks twitch from fatigue. With relief, the bald man notices their visitor, and buzzes him in.

'Devin Doyle?' Will asks.

'You're not off to a flying start,' the thick-necked man responds, and reaches over to shake hands.

Instead, Will presents the package.

'You're just a delivery? For fuck's sake,' the thick-necked man says. Then, to his bald colleague: 'I *want* that bloke to turn up now, just so I can tell him, "You get here *this* late, you can fuck off home!"'

Will extends a digital pad and stylus. 'If you'd sign, that'd be fabulous.'

Noting Will's accent, the thick-necked man smirks, steel braces on his teeth glinting. 'It'd be "fabulous"? What are you, Deliveroo by way of Eton?'

'I'm not with Deliveroo, no.'

'Whoever you're with, you fell a long way.'

'By talking to the likes of you?'

'Ooh – banter from the delivery boy!'

Aged fifty-six, Will is rarely described as any kind of 'boy'. Yet he is youthful for his age, tall and fit, a zigzag nose from rugby at school, creases bracketing his lips. He was always athletic, a low resting heart rate and a low resting expression.

'At least you speak English. Want a job?'

'Not particularly. Who are you lot anyway?'

'Reality Check News.'

'I know nothing about journalism, I'm afraid.'

'We're not proper news. It's fucking spellchecks.'

'You pay well?'

'Give us your name first.' He wipes his nose on a plump hairless forearm, and points Will to his office at the back. Dev flops into his desk chair, googling Will's full name while chewing his fingernails. 'You don't exist, mate.'

'I'm fairly convinced that I do.'

Dev points at him. 'Take off the fucking mask. I'm not hiring someone I can't see. Or are you MI5?'

'Yes, that's right. Undercover with Deliveroo.'

'I thought you wasn't Deliveroo.' Dev notices a packet of Golden Virginia tobacco in Will's cargo-shorts pocket. 'Health-and-safety don't let us smoke up here. Come on.' He makes for the lifts, and they descend in silence to the ground floor. Before exiting into the empty plaza, Dev is already exhaling smoke, a grey cloud trapped in the revolving doors behind him, turning to a slow dissolve. Outside, he shivers and slurps a can of Diet Coke, shaking a packet of Silk Cuts at Will. 'Go on – treat yourself to a big-boy ciggie.'

Will only half-listens as Dev puffs complainingly about two fellow editors who recently quit, and how he's got all the rewrites himself now. RCN does no news-gathering, he explains, just translates foreign blog posts, slaps on clickbait headlines, and puts them out as original content.

'So you're a translator?'

'What, me? I barely speak English! That other bloke.'

'Short on hair?'

'That's the one. It's a fucking nightmare,' Dev says. 'These foreigners I got – they can't barely write. So I'm sat there, trying to make head or tails. We'd be better with Google-fucking-Translate. A proper mare, it is. I can get you four hundred a week, which is more than what Amir, my Arab up there, pulls in.'

'I'm still not clear what my job would be.'

'There's six translators between here and the other bureaus, working twenty-four-seven, giving us shite. We turn it into articles.'

Office jobs never appealed to Will. But he's become irritatingly poor, as may be inferred by close inspection: his collar frayed, its threads tickling his throat, the shorts button above his fly missing. Last night, he perused his bedroom drawers, wondering if he'd manage without shopping for clothes ever again. Twenty years more to go perhaps? Even roll-your-own tobacco is pricey now, and his savings were never saved. 'So it's proofreading?'

'Correct our Latin too, if you like.' Dev takes a last drag of his cigarette, and flicks it to the pavement, the ash starbursting. 'Ten tomorrow. I'll put you through your paces.'

A COUPLE IS COOKING in Will's house. He doesn't know who they are.

'Sausages and baked beans,' the woman explains, three pink dreadlocks swaying to the waist of her sarong. Her green T-shirt says:

Extinction

=

Everything.
Everyone.
Gone.

'Is it supposed to smell like that?' Will asks.

Her companion – a hairy young man in ironic top hat, shirtless under the wool overcoat – replies: 'They're NotDogs. It's the smell of saving the planet.'

'Way too high.'

'Who is?'

Will lowers the heat under their pan. The spit-sizzle subsides.

He has a half-dozen tenants, fervent youths with meaningful tattoos. But Will is unsure if these two belong here. Also, he's distracted by audible scurrying under the floorboards. A pest-control man offered to pull up the hardwood, and cement all entry points. It'd cost twenty thousand, which is many thousands more than Will's bank balance.

The only thing that keeps Will in this house is this house. Which is to say, tenants paying him rent. In the mid-1980s, his gentleman-farmer dad in Somerset had the foresight to buy this terraced home in North West London for his lankiest child, who'd just loafed to a disappointing degree at Cambridge. Yet this place, intended as a safety net, ended up as the foundation of Will's torpor, permitting him to loll for more than three decades now, a typical day incorporating a fleck of household maintenance, a couple of hours' low-wage labour, then carousing till late, and concluding with a soak in the tub and a book. (Will is a rare physical man who reads seriously, and he remembers the contents, though his knowledge is entirely untapped – a fact that has never bothered him.)

He has few house rules and fails to maintain them, offering to whoever he finds lurking a glass of whatever he finds bottled. He provides without expectation, is tolerant without resentment – until, every few months, he's pushed too far, and explodes. But his outbursts are hailstorms: fierce and fast-forgotten.

As a landlord, Will's chief failing is to never record who's in residence, and who is merely in bed with who's in residence. As a consequence, the house has attracted a population of scruffy piercings who affix Extinction Rebellion stickers to the front window, combat American imperialism by frequenting the Iraqi street-food van on Kilburn High Road, and atone for their white privilege by apologizing to people who aren't there. They are easy to ridicule, but Will rather admires them. Most of his friends during young-adulthood expressed political commitment by Blu-tacking posters of The Clash to their bedroom walls, buying the 'Do They Know It's Christmas?' single, and walking into impressive jobs right out of Oxbridge, married and babied and propertied by thirty.

Causes existed then too, of course. Will recalls the Rock against Racism gigs, and he had a girlfriend with a Campaign for Nuclear Disarmament ring. Years later, Will marched in that vast protest of

February 2003, a million fists in the air to oppose the pending war in Iraq, everyone shouting along Whitehall, massing in Hyde Park. How vividly he sees that scene, which he has recounted many times. Yet a muted portion of his brain suspects that he never attended, just saw footage. Anyway, they didn't stop the war, so perhaps not the best demonstration of a demonstration. Will's grandfather – a cad whose life's accomplishment was twice racing at Le Mans – always claimed that humanity's worst prognostications never come to pass because people are so devilishly clever. Never forget the Great Horse-Manure Crisis of 1894, he said: heaps of equine ordure threatened to bury every major city on Earth, the panic spreading far and wide – only for man to invent the automobile, thus saving the planet.

Anyway, catastrophes do feel rather more imminent lately. For this, Will sympathizes with his housemates' lamentation, and is patient about delayed payments, especially during the pandemic. But he can't sustain it much longer.

He himself has been relatively lucky regarding coronavirus. He caught it early, but suffered only a nasty fortnight. Two tenants developed Long Covid, and moved home to their parents. Others had fellowships deferred, once-in-a-life travel deleted from their lives, job offers withdrawn. Cooped up, fed up, and bequeathed a planet in flames, they itch for revolution, and have taken to directing their fury at Will, slandering him as a *rentier* capitalist.

As it happens, he considers himself a working man, never suffering qualms about low-status drudgery. He's taken a fiver to sweep cat droppings from a neighbour's front garden, and spent years washing dishes at a burger bar, and carrying boxes of frozen French fries from a lorry. When lockdown shut that eatery, he became a deliveryman, charmed by the vacancy of sooty old London, deserted for the first time since the Great Plague of 1665.

At first, Will drove a wine-shop van, lugging bottles to the work-from-home bourgeoisie as they embarked on panic alcoholism. Once the weather improved, he bought his second-hand collapsible bike, and took up food delivery, circulating alongside the formerly invisible: Bangladeshis on motor scooters laden with KFC; Nigerian nurses awaiting the next empty double-decker bus; that morose Romanian woman who leapt in and out of her grinning Amazon van. Essential workers served the inessential, who filled their bathrooms with anti-bac soap and hid behind locked doors, shouting through the mailslot: 'Just leave the curry! And step back, please! I'll tip you on the app!' When a few offices reopened, Will upgraded to the courier gig: important documents rather than important kebabs.

Throughout the pandemic, he has cruised through the ambient panic, asking himself if it really would be so tragic if humankind fell to ruin. At times, Will suspects that he may be missing an ingredient, unperturbed by civilizational collapse. He tends to view society as a rickety convoy, directed by rumours as much as maps, most passengers wanting only a comfy seat, while a few shriek at the drivers. But only saints and despots and the middle class believe they can change the world. As for the activist generation in his home, their zeal is close to nihilism, as if – grasping for control of that rickety convoy – they glimpse a horror: the steering wheel doesn't turn. So they overdose on the internet, they self-harm, they gorge on NotDogs.

This couple devours theirs straight from the pan, the top hat boy ashing his joint in a tea cup. They're planning to glue themselves to London monuments in protest against how the world is so depressing. However, they face a conundrum. Should they buy glue that comes off?

'Isn't that the police's problem?' the pink-dreadlocked woman says.

'That depends on the system of governance,' answers Top Hat. 'In a dictatorship, it's your problem if the glue won't come off. In a democracy, it's theirs.'

Will pictures this chap – top hat removed, scrubbed and shaven – as a guest on BBC News in a few years, live from a think tank, talking over everyone.

'The thing *I'm* kinda wondering,' Dreadlocks ventures, 'is whether the—'

'And basically,' Top Hat resumes, 'can we even call this a democracy anymore?'

'There's an easy way to find out,' Will says. 'Glue yourself to something.'

DEVIN DOYLE IS HATE-GOBBLING his breakfast from a Greggs bag, inserting rather than chewing a sausage roll whose crust showers over his gut and keyboard. He arrived late at RCN this morning, although Will was on time, admitted by members of the overnight staff – translators of Turkish, Tagalog and Russian who were kibitzing until the boss walked in. As they packed up their belongings, the Arabic/French translator Amir arrived, taking the desk of a departing Turk, adjusting the chair height with difficulty, thwacking it, then struggling with an uncooperative mouse cable.

Dev commands Will to stand in his doorway, as if to impart a lesson, though he's just watching a Facebook video claiming that George Soros and Hillary Clinton are the secret owners of Facebook, that Jeffrey Epstein isn't dead, that Bill Gates is microchipping bats. 'Why don't we have a story on this?'

'I'm not sure how to respond.'

'By making us a cuppa,' Dev says, sneering but losing his bravado upon eye contact. More sternly, he explains the workflow, how web trawlers at headquarters identify catchy blog posts, translators render them into broken English, and the day staff churns this into quasi-publishable copy, which is amplified by Twitter bots.

Will understands little of this. 'Right. Shall I give it a go?'

'Like I said, first assignment: the kettle.'

Dipping tea bags, Will watches the steaming water turn mahogany. Amir mumbles at him – he's reaching for the Nespresso machine, and asks if Will would mind making space. Up close, Amir resembles an algebra teacher, circa 1983: budget metal-frame glasses, chinstrap beard, razor burn under his chin. Hobbling around on a bad leg, he moves like a man of sixty but is probably half that, his lower lip hanging open, front teeth cracked. Will has a soft spot for the feeble, as when he saw a fox cub wander into traffic on Goldhawk Road, and leapt off his bike, ordering drivers to stop, then escorted the pup from the roadway, whereupon it scurried under a parked car, and Will resumed his journey.

He introduces himself to Amir, whose handshake is a single clammy downstroke. Seeing the two befriending each other, Dev intervenes, shouting, 'What in fuck's a "double-edge *knife*"?'

'That is not a saying?' Amir asks, hobbling over.

'No, you fucking idiot.'

Will says, 'Presumably, "a double-edged sword"?'

Dev – who clearly knew – hears this as if it were a revelation, and Amir confirms that this is what he intended.

'Well, put that *in* then!' Dev says. 'Nobody's heard of a double-edge fucking *knife*.' He rolls his eyes to Will, who places a steaming mug on his desk. 'Cheers, mate.'

As the morning progresses, Will notices that his boss addresses him differently than he does the translators. Above all, Dev berates Amir, whose language errors the boss shouts across the newsroom. He also treats Amir as tech support, ordering him to limp over and recover deleted files, or update the betting app on his phone. When mocked, Amir adopts the servile half-smile of one who needs the job, then enumerates the pieces that he's translating, while Dev feigns incomprehension.

'Don't spill a lung, Amir. It's pronounced with a "haitch". *Hhh-hhhhhaitch.*'

For the next two hours, Will corrects the syntax of bloggers confabulating an inversion of reality: that climate science is a plot against the poor, ethnic cleansing is the fight against terrorism, and human-rights groups are child-abuse rings. Each article concludes with a version of, 'Ask yourself this question: Why aren't the elites talking about this?'

Will is half-entertained to proofread mental illness for its respect to the laws of punctuation. This slop is so ridiculous that nobody could take it seriously. Indeed, nobody even advertises on the website, which raises the question of how RCN funds itself. Dev is vague, ranting about headquarters, how they're asking the impossible. When Will enquires about the location of headquarters, Dev just mutters about 'rich foreigners'. Dev found his way here after telemarketing in Salford, then was an estate agent at Foxtons in West London, next selling property ads for a magazine in Dubai, which is where he came across this job online. 'And the rest is history.' He turns his thumb as if hitchhiking, and jabs toward the lift. Once outside, Will forgoes the cigarette, and fetches his bike.

'Why are you unfolding that thing?'

'It's not for me, this job,' Will says, at which point his fat-necked former boss curses the empty plaza, and turns his back, still swearing as Will rides away.

HE PROBABLY SHOULDN'T HAVE done that.

After biking home, Will finds that his tenants are threatening to halt rent payments because another rat was discovered, this behind the kitchen bin. The pest-control man could lay traps and poison, Will suggests. It won't solve the matter, but it'd be affordable. An assembly is called a few weeks later in his living room, where the tenants agree that nobody should harm any animals, only capture and re-house them.

'Re-house rats?' Will says. 'Where exactly?'

'Isn't there a forest they could go to?'

Another tenant: 'I'm, like, looking around every corner now, expecting a corpse. It's seriously becoming a mental-health issue.'

'We're talking about two rats that left for greener pastures,' Will says. 'Do you have any idea how much the full remedy costs? Twenty grand, minimum. How am I expected to come up with that, if none of you pays rent?'

'Couldn't we get cats?'

'You think cats are gentle?' Will says. 'You think they'd coax our rat friends lovingly into the woods?'

'At least it'd be natural.'

'Look, some of you don't even live here!' They're startled – most haven't seen Will lose his temper. 'All of you! Right now! Write your names on a sheet of paper!'

'What is this, *Nineteen Eighty-Four*?'

'If you're not paying, you're not staying – and certainly not voting. You are, however, welcome to fuck off home. Or find yourself a forest where you can be humanely re-housed.'

'Can you just chill?'

'Absolute numbskulls, the lot of you!'

The outburst is behind him as soon as Will steps into the street. It's empty, bright. His protesters are correct: rats must fall. He really should've kept that desk job.

Will logs onto his courier app, and clicks ON DUTY. A private message awaits – a client requested him. He accepts, and bikes to the address for a pickup. Months back, he delivered a package here during a downpour. He banged on the red front door, needing a signature, then backed away, as per company policy. A tall elderly woman opened, sizing up her bedraggled deliveryman, the dripping grey hair stuck to his forehead, rain rivulets meandering down his zigzag nose. He checked that she was the name on the package: 'Dora Frenhofer?'

She accepted the damp parcel, but hesitated to sign immediately, saying, 'Why don't you come out of the rain?'

Thanking her, he stepped beneath the overhang of her roof.

'Tell me,' she said. 'How's life in the inferno?'

'Which inferno is that?'

'Case numbers soaring. The hospitals in overload. I'm safely in here whereas you're biking through it all. So? Give me a first-hand report.'

'At the moment, the inferno is raining.'

Her eyes laughed, and she retreated a step into her darkened corridor, pressing him to come inside for a coffee.

'Alas, not allowed,' he said. 'But I'll take a smoke break under your eaves, if that's acceptable.'

She encouraged it, and kept him company, speaking to Will with uncommon intensity, as if testing how to use words again. Squinting at him, she cast an appraising gaze over this sopping man, and declared herself terrible for asking what she was about to. But she specified herself to be Dutch, therefore allowed to be blunt. 'Why is a man your age and your class a bicycle deliveryman?'

'For the fresh air.' He needed to tap off the long ash on his cigarette, so stepped toward the pavement, noting her blue recycling bin, piled full of books. 'Is there anything good in there?' He knelt to inspect. 'Balzac and Kundera and Böll.'

'You're a reader?'

'And you're a writer,' he replied, raising a novel with her name on the spine. 'If this weren't waterlogged, I'd ask to take it.'

'Not worth your time! And I'm not a writer anymore. I stopped recently. After which, the funniest thing happened: I had this urge to get rid of *all* my books. I loved them for my whole life, but now? I can't even remember what's in them! Colette and Woolf and de Beauvoir and Nabokov and Gogol and who knows. What were they actually about? I don't expect it matters anymore. But damn them for tricking me!' Half-smile. 'Last chance for coffee?'

But he'd finished his cigarette, and mounted the bike.

'When you go,' she said, 'you know what I'll be doing?'

'What?'

'Staring at my keyboard for two hours, trying to spell the word "lullaby".'

'I thought you'd stopped writing.'

'I thought so too.'

Nearly a year has passed, and he expects to find her greatly aged, confined here in this narrow three-storey house. Instead, she answers in a suit jacket and slacks, lipstick on, perfumed. 'You remember me?' she asks, pleased to see him again. She recalls how they spoke of books, and says she hasn't had such a good chat in ages. Better weather than last time too. She checked the forecast (and the ever-changing Covid rules), and they can speak in her back garden, if seated apart for social-distancing.

'That's very kind of you,' he says. 'But afraid I can't on this occasion.'

'Pity.'

His goodbye is cut by the closing door.

Will has a different plan, to cycle to RCN. Although he worked there only a few hours, they still need to pay him.

Amir buzzes him in. 'You are back.'

'Only briefly. Is Dev around?'

Amir looks down. 'In fact, he is passed. Is this the right word, "passed"?'

'How do you mean? That he passed away? Well, that rather dampens my payment prospects. What happened?'

'A cardiac stop in his office. We are all very shock.'

'The man chain-smoked and ate pies non-stop. His neck was wider than his ears. How was it shocking?'

Amir stifles a laugh. 'Yes, not so healthy.'

Will looks at his watch. 'Fancy a drink? It'll almost be afternoon once we find a place.'

They walk past the fake lake, surly trees, and glass office buildings. Not even adulterers in the meeting pods today. This complex has a ghostly air, as if humans were gone, and only their saddest monuments remained.

'How'd you end up here, Amir?'

They find an empty tapas bar with an outdoor patio. The staff – surprised to have customers – rush out a wine list.

Downing an overfull glass of Malbec, Amir talks, eyes averted, telling of his bedsit in Hounslow, how headquarters pushes material that disgusts him. He hates himself for staying, but needs the money. He grew up mostly in Paris, a French mother and Arab father, both deceased.

'Why London?'

'A bit more wine first.'

Will hails a waiter.

Growing up in Paris, Amir recounts, he cultivated a passion for seedy Americana, and planned to pursue a doctorate in the United States. But Homeland Security turned down the visa application, and his life changed. He ended up at a terrible grad programme in London, and dropped out. For a while, he worked in removals to support himself. Then his father fell seriously ill and died, and Amir flew to the Mideast. While there, something happened.

'You're not saying what,' Will notes. 'Quite a cliffhanger.'

'I can't explain. Maybe I try to write it sometime.'

'Write it how? You mean for yourself? Or for people to read?'

'Who can know. We see.' Amir clutches his thigh, which stops jiggling. 'Everybody wants to say things – why people should read what I say? You know? I'm just one stupid guy.' He raises his chin, lips purpled from wine, and closes both hands around the stem of his glass. 'Maybe,' he jokes, "maybe you can help me with this writing.' Suddenly, Amir is self-conscious, and changes the subject, demanding Will's story.

The life of Will de Courcy has been fine but he isn't terribly interested in rehashing it, so gives a summary in French, Amir's mother tongue – reminiscing in foreign words is more engaging to Will. After university, he dawdled in Vienna before the fall of the Iron Curtain. Did a bit of translating himself, come to think of it, including putting a surrealist Bulgarian novel into English. When hired for the job, Will pointed out that he knew no Bulgarian, but the cheapskate publisher presented him a German-language version, which he was to work from. When the Bulgarian novel proved impenetrable in any language, Will sought clarifications from the author himself, exiled in Bonn. The man was dismissive, so Will just cut and added bits to his liking. 'And thus it came out.'

'Did he learn what you do?'

'The author? Well, no. It was rather disappointing: no scandal whatsoever. My unfaithful translation even won him some obscure award for experimental fiction. They held this event with the author, and an arts critic interviewed him onstage, and kept citing plot points that actually weren't in his plot. I kept waiting for him to object.

Instead, the Bulgarian just soaked up the adulation. I don't know if he didn't care, or if he thought the critic was bonkers, or if he genuinely believed *he'd* come up with those bits.'

'The last one.'

'Yes, that's what I think,' Will says, smiling, appreciating this Amir chap, who's clearly sharp.

Will continues his story: how he grew bored of Vienna, and returned to Britain to his current house. In the subsequent years, he participated in a series of ill-judged businesses: attempting to license broadcast rights for London dog races to a Chinese television network; starting a Nepalese restaurant; selling batteries that recharge from your car's lighter port. He has a daughter in Austria, based in Innsbruck now – an oddly Teutonic child who never connected with him. His ex-wife, Will notes, once described him as 'an enthusiast with a short attention span'. The girl is thirty now.

'Around my age,' Amir remarks.

Later that evening, Will stretches out on his green futon bed, rereading *La Vie Devant Soi* by Romain Gary, which they'd mentioned in passing. The smell of incense leaks up from downstairs, where a political meeting is in session.

Will ponders his daughter, whom he rarely has reason to mention. He rolls a cigarette, shifts to get comfortable, mistakenly sending a half-dozen paperbacks to the floor. He thinks of that elderly woman, the retired writer. The envelope that she called him to collect seemed empty, and was addressed to herself.

His phone beeps with a message from Amir, who reports having logged onto the RCN internal system: Will's payment has gone through, for £1,249.

Will frowns and leans back, reading that again. That much money for four hours work?

A car engine growls outside, then trembles to a stop. He looks from his bedroom window down at the pink Porsche Cabriolet. A petite middle-aged woman steps out, wobbling on high-heels, then brushing a hand down her red-suede skirt, followed by a second middle-aged woman who unfolds her long legs from the driver's side, and struts from view toward his front entrance. The doorbell rings; a tenant answers. Muffled conversation.

Will goes down for coffee, curious about these visitors, whom he finds in the living room, like two pointy sculptures considering the gallery staff. The taller is mother of an Extinction Rebellion activist who lives here; the petite woman is her dear friend. Both call themselves 'massive supporters of the movement'. They've handed out bottled water at eco-rallies, and dropped by today because they wanted to see an XR squat.

'Hardly a squat,' Will corrects her. 'They're paying customers. Or they were until the rent strike. It's like the October Revolution in here lately.' He blows on his coffee, whose surface ripples, then flattens.

'You're the guru then?' the taller woman asks, while her son — he of the top hat — chastises her for something, causing her face to squeeze lemonishly. She thunks toward Will in vertiginous wedge sandals, her black-leather trousers laced at the hip, with a chest and face that have clearly benefited from modern science. In such sandals, she is eye-to-eye with Will, he behind half-moon reading glasses, she behind baby-blue contacts. She's approximately his age, though her hair is shiny blonde and professionally styled. Technically, hairdressers aren't allowed to operate under Covid restrictions. But in today's Britain, rules are optional.

'Hardly a guru, no.'

He departs for more oat milk for his coffee, only to find her alongside him at the fridge. She glances around as if the house were for sale but not *quite* what she's looking for.

He still has the French novel folded over his hand, and she's impressed that he reads in other languages. 'Can I tell you a secret? I've read literally one book in my life,' she confides, pausing. 'Aren't you going to ask *what?*'

He sips.

She continues, 'I'm actually *writing* a book.'

'I haven't met anyone lately who isn't.'

After a few minutes of flirt-chatting, Will excuses himself, for he has something on his mind, that £1,249 payment from RCN. He phones Amir, who laughs, and says he was awaiting this call. They agree on another early-lunch glass at the Spanish place the following day.

Will folds his bike by the window, noting Amir already inside, the young man's face slack as a corpse's – until he looks over, lips parting in a smile, the cracked front teeth disfiguring him.

They speak in French, and Amir tells of changes under his new boss, Shannon, who flew in from the Sydney bureau of RCN. She's worse than Dev – not merely a conspiracist, but a hard-working one.

'If you ever fancy upgrading to deliveryman, you'll always find a bike for sale on eBay.'

'Not possible in my case.' Amir taps his leg meaningfully, the damaged one.

Among the stresses of Shannon is her demand that Amir tweet to 'amplify' RCN pieces. It's one thing to loathe yourself for working on vile material; it's another to become a public voice for it.

'No, you can't be known for that,' Will tells him. 'Especially if you want that memoir published of yours someday.'

'You remembered!' Amir says, palm pressed to his chest. 'I was actually thinking of showing you something I've written.'

Silence falls over them. Amir drinks more, then says how he lies in bed dreaming of quitting his job. But rent is so high. How, he wonders, do people save money? How does anyone have a mortgage?

'A better question,' Will responds, 'is whether one needs to go into RCN at all. I seem to have earned a massive paycheck for quitting after a half-day.'

Amir laughs, and explains. During Will's first shift, Dev registered him as a new employee, then considerately died before updating the system with Will's resignation. So his monthly payment chugged through the system. 'That's the problem with RCN. There's money to be made there. And who files the office accounts?'

'What, you?'

'Listen to this,' Amir says. "A few months ago, I had tons of overtime, so I put it in the system. The next month, I never adjusted my salary back, and waited to see what happened — I could've just claimed it was an oversight. But nobody noticed. Shannon is a problem, though. This morning, she asked who you were. I said a recent hire who took compassionate leave because of Devin.'

'After a half-day on the job, I needed time off? That said, even a half-day there probably merits compassionate leave.'

'If she finds out that you quit, she'll make headquarters rescind your payment.' Amir looks up tentatively. 'But if you come back, you could keep it. And get paid again.'

'What, working for a boss worse than Dev?'

'Here is what I am wanting,' Amir says, reverting to English. 'I like that we work together, me and you. If Shannon is now looking at the money, I cannot anymore do what I want. It's fine; maybe I leave this place. But let me before tell you my idea.' He mentions the Bulgarian novel that Will once translated. 'We can do this at RCN, no? I give to you my translations, and you change them, and we post online like this.'

'I'm not following you.'

'We don't make *better* the stories. We make *worse*.'

His proposal is to concoct lies even more repugnant than those RCN publishes, to slip them into articles, and keep track of how they spread, especially via Shannon's tweets, which will be composed of provable fabrications. 'Then we tell to everyone, and she is destroy.'

'And you'd be out of a job.'

'Why I care?' he says, looking at Will, like a man who wants to be brave with someone watching. 'I can *do* something!'

Neither drinks for a minute. Each is thinking.

'We could make up pandemic-related nonsense?' Will suggests. 'Claiming it's all a plot to vaccinate children, and make them gay?'

'RCN is already doing a version of this.'

'How about microchipping people at the dentist?'

'Microchipping is always nice, but nobody cares of dentists.'

Years earlier, when 'adjusting' that Bulgarian novel, Will sought only to make sense of nonsense – he was never particularly creative. He's a man who can quote a poem, but would struggle to write one.

'We must think more big,' Amir suggests. 'At RCN, they say a crazy thing like it is rumour. Then, they do a second article saying, "According to reports" – with a link to the first story, to the rumour they just made up.'

'She'd figure us out, Amir.'

'Have you work for this people?' He reverts to French: 'You know what I've learned from conspiracy theorists? That real conspiracies are almost impossible. People are too stupid to pull them off; or too distracted; or too self-interested. Usually, all three at once. And *that* is why bad things happen. But a global conspiracy? Come on! Have you met human beings? You think they could keep that together?'

'But aren't you suggesting that *we* carry out a conspiracy?'

Amir laughs. 'Yes, perhaps. So the question becomes: "Who is more stupid – us or them?" I say them.'

Will realizes he's rather fond of this chap, who's not much older than his tenants, but with another world in his head. Something cracked those front teeth; something took out his hair in a strange pattern, as if pulled out in handfuls.

'Shannon has no way of knowing where my translations come from,' Amir continues. 'She doesn't read Arabic. She can't even understand French!'

'So what's my role? Why not make up this rubbish yourself, and ship it directly to her?'

'If it comes from me alone, maybe she'll wonder, and check it. But if it comes from me, through you, they're not going to assume that two of us are duping them. Also,' he admits, 'I want to work with you, my friend!'

They drink more cheap Malbec and they plot, Amir relishing what he calls 'the conspiracy conspiracy'. Soon, he's slurring, seeking the waiter impatiently, before turning foggily to Will, muttering about when he tried to reach his father's funeral. 'But they throw me in prison. And who is there? My brother.'

'You must save this for the memoir, Amir. Which I'm very keen to read.' Will fears that the younger man is tipsy, and about to make a fool of himself.

'Okay, but I want to tell you what happened there. With my brother.' Amir calls the waiter over. 'The more wine, please?'

'Actually, perhaps we should pause there,' Will says. 'Don't you need to get back from lunch?'

They walk to the RCN office, the younger man sucking deep breaths to sober himself. At first, Shannon pretends not to notice Will, play-acting the edgy journalist, shouting across the room to the translators: 'You guys need to see this!' She storms around, slamming her fist on stacks of old newspapers. 'So,' she says finally, turning to Will. 'How was compassionate leave?'

'Full of compassion.'

'Who *are* you exactly? I couldn't find anything on social media. Are you British intel?'

'Your predecessor asked me that too.'

'Then died suddenly.'

'I must say, that's the shortest gap I've ever had between "hello" and a murder rap.'

She's distracted, messaging on her phone. 'Just DMing HQ.' She hits SEND, looks up, face contorted about whatever she just typed. 'Okay, boomer. What've we got for you?' She tells Amir to send Will something for proofing, and she'll review his work.

Will puts on his half-moon reading glasses, tilting his chin up to read Amir's first offering. It's too obviously made-up: anonymous allegations that volunteer rescuers in Syria are secretly NATO agents harvesting children's organs. He approaches Amir's desk, saying softly: 'We need to tone that down, Amir. She'll know.'

'No, that one isn't made up. I mean, it *is* made up. But not made up by me.'

'That's an actual RCN article? What am I supposed to do with it? Check for typos? Or add aliens?'

'Just make sure it makes sense.'

'It doesn't.'

Will's phone vibrates: a message from Allegra. Who in hell's Allegra? He suffers name-blindness, and must read her message five times before remembering. Ah, yes! The woman from the pink Porsche at his house, who put her number in his phone before leaving. She's flying to Spain tomorrow, and has an apartment to use in Almería, and thought she'd suggest something crazy: **u speak spanish, right? come interpret 4 me!!**

Strictly speaking, it's illegal to take holidays during lockdown, but everyone in Her Majesty's Government seems to fuck off on vacation. Will goes down to the plaza for a smoke. He unfolds his bicycle. He leaves this nonsense behind.

DOWN DOWN DOWN, DEEPER into the cold Mediterranean, then slowly back up. Will surfaces at last, the sun dazzling. He turns to locate her, for Allegra is laughing: still on the black boulder that he just leapt from. 'You're mad!' she cries.

This isn't a swimming area, just a promontory off the Paseo Marítimo. But, as soon as he glimpsed the water, he sidestepped the family of stray cats, pulled off his shirt, and jumped, still wearing his cargo shorts, flinging back his Ray-Bans in midflight.

They're staying around the corner at an Airbnb haunted by the ghost of deceased air-freshener, with framed photos of serious Spanish children from decades ago. On arrival, Will and Allegra had sex. But the bed is short, and they are tall, so they copulated diagonally. After, she longed for hash, mentioning that shady Moroccans sell it around the port. Since Will can manage in the local language, she expected him to procure for her. But he has soured on Allegra – he already had on the early-morning flight over, when she was nagging the steward for more prosecco, complaining that it was warm, demanding another mini-bottle for free.

He sun-dries while she buys endless knick-knacks from a shop on the *paseo*, more plastic to fill the sea where he just swam. Will pictures the water infested with silicon phone cases and watermelon inflatable mattresses, so clogged that he could walk across the surface. While she's paying, he grabs his daypack, and steps into a bike-rental shed. An oddball with a 'Brooklyn' cycling cap answers in fast Spanish. Will, in peripheral vision, sees Allegra walking past, scanning for him, only the Botox impeding her scowl.

He asks about bike routes eastward along the coast, and is soon pedalling peacefully. After the paved walkway, he passes an abandoned house on the beach, then agricultural lots with a trillion tomatoes under plastic, waves crashing on his other flank. They rented him a city bike with tyres as thin as a finger and a seat so hard that each time he stands on the pedals, pain surges up his blood-starved perineum. Nevertheless, it's a glorious gashing windy route toward Cabo de Gata.

Halfway up a hill climb, he pulls over, admiring the view. He's not as fit as once – ageing but unbothered. He turns a wide circle in the middle of the blacktop, no sightline around a hairpin turn. If a car were coasting downward, Will's brains – well developed, lightly employed – would be splashed across hot tarmac.

He takes the downhill too fast, with little in the way of brakes, inhaling slowly, meditating on danger. Once the road flattens, he veers onto the sand, allowing the bike to slow and sink, then flop sideways as he leaps off. He kicks away his flip-flops, and yanks off his shirt too, soon engulfed in cold liquid, swimming an athletic crawl, then treading water, wondering how deep it is, and what creatures' wars unfold beneath him.

A sandstone tower, El Torreón de San Miguel, stands abandoned on the beach. A plaque explains that it was built in the eighteenth century to survey the water for Barbary pirates. Fear preserves our species, Will thinks, which is why we need panics, why they'll never cease. The tenants embody this. But they might as well shout at these waves, ordering them to stop. Nothing really stops anything, he thinks.

His daypack vibrates – another message from Amir, wondering where he went. Voicemails keep coming from Allegra too, asking that same question, but not politely. He mutes the phone. Between those two, he knows which side he's on: the damaged. Tomorrow, he'll insist that Amir leave that job, and do something better with his life. Perhaps they can do something together. Then again, why this need to 'do something' with your life? To what end?

Biking back, he squints at the sinking sun till it's gone, and he is lit only by the headlights of oncoming cars, whose beams glint off his pedal reflectors. He passes a perimeter fence, behind which passenger jets rise from the airport where he and Allegra arrived earlier that day. He rests the bike outside, and reads a departure board. A budget flight to London leaves tomorrow at 6:20 a.m. He phones the bike shack, informing the eccentric owner that he won't return, and is leaving the bike at the airport, but the man can keep the two-hundred-euro deposit.

'That bike isn't worth a hundred!'

'I know. I've been riding it.'

BATHING AT HOME THE next afternoon, Will's buttocks sting where chafed from that pitiless Spanish bicycle seat. He's ignoring calls from Allegra and from Shannon. But when Amir messages yet again, Will thumbs a reply: **RCN wasnt for me in the end.** Bathwater beads the glass screen.

Amir replies: **But our plan . . .?**

The doorbell rings yet again downstairs: Extinction Rebellion is holding a seminar in his living room, and its supporters keep arriving. Will stands up in his tub, dripping, and types **Come over for drink, my friend!** Two hours later, deep in a preposterous debate, Will is tapped on the elbow. 'Amir!'

The young man shakes Will's hand in that earnest way of his, and presents a bottle of newsagent wine, as if this were a dinner party. He also holds out a brown package.

'Something to do with the conspiracy conspiracy?' Will asks.

'No, no. It's my memoir. For you to see.'

'Gosh, you certainly wrote a lot!' He slaps Amir's shoulder, and grips it warmly. 'And I get an early read – I'm honoured.'

'Not an early reader. The only reader.' Touchingly, Amir insists on shaking his hand again.

'Come with me.' Will escorts his hobbling friend to the kitchen, uncorking that bottle of South Australian red, filling two pottery mugs. (No wine glasses remain.)

'Is a party allowed?' Amir asks, taking all this in: fervent radicals, yapping disputes, couples kissing. 'Nobody even in masks?'

'It's a political gathering. Which is probably even more illegal. But they're all in their twenties, so presumably Covid safe-ish. Anyway, who fucking knows. It's a free-for-all in this country, isn't it?'

'I must be a bit careful. I have health conditions.' He looks to Will, hoping to be asked.

'I'd introduce you around, Amir. But honestly, I don't know half these people, many of whom probably reside here.' He rolls two cigarettes, offers one.

'Could you maybe read it soon, what I gave you? I'm feeling nervous.'

'All else is put on hold,' Will pledges. 'Tell me, by the way, if you spot a rodent. I've not noticed one in days, and I think we might've got the better of the bastards. My tenants credit their new house cat, Chavez.'

A speech is starting in the living room, and they go to listen. The seminar is 'Decolonizing the Environment', with an anti-ecocide academic explaining how the poorest countries suffer worst from climate breakdown, so white campaigners must overhaul the white-dominated movement to represent the Global South, converting it into an intersectional struggle that recognizes structural racism. Rather than clapping, people waggle their hands in approval. Amir is puzzled by this. Will explains that it's 'jazz hands' – a substitution for applause, to avoid marginalizing the hearing-impaired.

'Are there many deaf people here?'

'None, I don't expect.'

Amir keeps glancing at the brown package, which Will holds in his free hand.

'You're worried about it?' Will asks.

'No, no – I trust you. Just, I don't have a computer at home, and I didn't want this stuff on the RCN system. So I wrote it by hand.'

'Amir, I feel this document is too precious. Make a copy, and I'll read that.'

'It's fine. I want you to have it.'

'At least keep it safe for me till later.' He slides it under Amir's arm.

Cheered, Amir downs his wine – then catches himself grinning, and represses it, lest people see his teeth. Will tops up their mugs, and directs Amir to the concrete back garden. Outside, Will lights another cigarette, introducing himself to a phone-reading smoker of purple haircut and septum ring, who turns out to be associate editor at BreakStuff Books, an indie publisher in Brighton. Will informs her that his friend just completed a manuscript, and she congratulates Amir. He seems mortified, insisting that he's still working on it, and has nothing to show, and anyway this early draft is only in French. Will encourages the two to chat, and departs to tell the seminar to shush before his neighbours phone the imperialist authorities.

When Will returns a few minutes later, Amir is clutching the neck of the wine bottle – almost empty by now – and speaking too close to the associate editor, who leans back, holding a beer bottle across her chest. He's telling her that his life turned out differently than expected. He was planning to finish his doctorate, but something happened, and he's not ready to say it aloud, so he wrote it down. He looks directly at her. She mumbles that you need the right reader. Amir asks if *she* is the right reader. BreakStuff only does political manifestos, she says wearily, as if for the fourth time.

Amir pulls Will's sleeve, and forces a laugh, broken teeth on full display now, as he drags his friend into the conversation. 'Look at her tattoo – she is not telling what it means. Why you don't tell us?'

'I should find my friends,' she says.

Will leads her back inside to her cohort, at whom she bugs her eyes, whispering about the weird bald guy. Will is diverted by a bizarre exchange about how long a person can live without sleep. By the time he returns to the back garden, Amir has gone.

A few tenants are heading out for further drinking, and they want Will to come. The house cat seems to have pacified everyone for now: no more rats, and monthly payments will resume. When bundling out of the house, someone treads on a drunk – Amir, who is slumped in the front walkway, that brown parcel stuffed in the pocket of his windbreaker. Everyone else high-steps over Amir, stifling laughter each time he snores. But Will crouches, arm on his friend's shoulder, which causes the young man to blink awake, see Will, smile slowly.

'We're off for drinks at a car park in Hackney,' Will says. 'Enticing, I know. But do come if you like.'

Wobbling to his feet, Amir asks for a cigarette.

The others know that one person here doesn't fit. But decorum is such that they can't exclude Amir, the only non-white-privilege person in that house all evening.

Normally, Will would bike to Hackney. But if Amir tags along, they'll share a taxi. The others chastise Will for taking private transport, but don't push the matter – they'd probably prefer not to have this drunkard in cheap office attire leaning over them on the Tube. They bound down the street, racing each other, lit under the next street lamp, then dark, then lit by the next, then in darkness again, voices fading.

Will puts his arm around Amir's waist and helps him regain balance, recommending a steady stride till Kilburn High Road. As they walk, Will proposes something more: what if he translates the memoir into English, so that media types (obviously not that woman before, but the right person) could judge it for themselves?

'I *love* this idea!' Amir responds, and insists that Will make any changes he likes, that he fill in the gaps because the writing might not be good. He wants this to be their project together. He grips Will's forearm. 'Hope, yes?'

'Hope what?'

'I feel hope.'

Will reaches into the road, for a black cab passes. 'I do know a few people from university who became important in publishing and such. After we have a translation, I'll show a few of them. See where this goes, shall we?'

The driver rolls down the front window. 'Where to?'

Will climbs in. 'Coming, Amir?'

'I am too drunk,' Amir says gleefully, wavering in the gutter. He prefers to slog home, alone but with happy dreams. They'll talk soon. 'You read fast?'

'Fast as I can.'

The taxi driver: 'I can't drive till you close the door, mate.'

Will to the driver: 'I'm saying goodbye to my friend. Start the meter if you want.' On the plastic divider, he notes a sign that payments are also accepted in Bitcoin.

The driver: 'You said Hackney, but where in Hackney?'

'For fuck's sake. Give me a second – I'm talking to my friend.'

'Bad language now!'

'Amir, I should go.'

He hands Will the manuscript, and the driver pulls out. The passenger door swings shut.

'Steady on!' Will says. 'I'm barely inside. Could've taken my leg off.'

'*Where* in Hackney?'

Will gives an address. 'Why am I even in this taxi? Should've taken my bike.'

'Yeah, you should've.'

'You're a jolly presence.'

A talk show on the radio features a caller ranting about how elites are transfusing blood from trafficked children. Will listens for a minute: was that part of their conspiracy conspiracy? He can't recall. What bizarre animals we humans are, he thinks, and rests his tobacco pouch atop Amir's brown parcel, which sits on the taxi seat beside him.

'No smoking,' the driver says.

'I'm only rolling one. I'm not about to light up in your taxi.'

'You'll get tobacco all over my seats.'

'I won't. I'm being careful.'

The engine thrums in traffic, that Bitcoin logo staring at Will. Each time they stop, a red light on the door clicks, and the driver goes into a diatribe to his radio about how everything is hell now, and they're all paid shills, and you can't trust a word.

Will says, 'Does that red light come on to warn me when you're about to say something absurd?'

'Hey!' The driver spins around. He's alarmingly frail – he looks ill, frightened. 'I don't have to put up with abuse!'

'How was that abuse?' Will's phone is ringing. It's Amir. Will swipes away the call. 'Calm yourself, driver.'

The man slams on the brakes, jolting Will forward. 'Don't have to put up with this!'

'Steady on! I already gave one man a heart attack this year. Not trying to make a habit of it.' Will's silenced phone is flashing on his lap – Amir again. 'You're seriously throwing me out of your taxi?'

'Out! Now!'

Will opens the door. 'I see why Uber are running you lot out of business.'

The taxi roars away.

Will is on a bridge over a railway track. His lips flicker with a smile, recalling the crippling bike in Almería, left unlocked at the airport. Someone in need of a ride will find it, and pedal home.

That Bitcoin nutter wasn't well. He thinks of Amir too, pumping out tripe at that job. He *must* quit. If the only obstacle is paying London rent, Will can offer a bit of empty floorspace. Amir would thrive at the house: comrades, wine, debate.

They can work on the memoir too. Will imagines leafing through a (probably mediocre) piece of writing by Amir in the bath later, taking sleepy drags of a cigarette. But perhaps Amir is a gifted writer. What if it causes Will to leap up in the soapy water, suddenly wary not to splash a dot on what he's holding?

He recalls that beach in Spain where he dried himself after the bike ride and swim. He gazed at the Mediterranean, as if viewing the sea centuries in the past, or centuries in the future. Either side of this chapter of mine, Will thought, I'll amount to less than the specks of sand between my toes. So perhaps Amir was right: 'I can *do* something!' A strange feeling, this stirring sense of mission. Forget drinks at a Hackney car park. He'll march right back home now, and read the memoir.

But wait. Will pats his pockets. 'Fuck's sake.' He can see it there on that taxi seat, driving away into impossibility: his tobacco. Will looks up at the night sky, nearly yowling from irritation. He takes out his half-moon glasses, fumbling to unfold them in the cold, and awakens the contact list on his phone.

So, Amir is going to move into the house. After which, the tenants google his name, and find that he once worked on fake-news rubbish, not least about climate change. They discover that Will himself did a brief stint there. He's liable to end up with no tenants except the rats. Fine! He won't be bullied by revolutionaries barely out of their teens.

On the other hand, Will *has* rather grown accustomed to the right side of history, an exception to his corrupt generation, more youthful in spirit and in physique, admired by women on the premises, some of whose activism has included a week or two in his bed.

His plan had been to read Amir's memoir, then decide if he fancied slaving at it. Now, he must inform Amir that an idiot cabbie drove away with it. He plays this out: causing Amir to rewrite the whole manuscript from scratch, which rather obliges Will to work on the result.

Will scrolls to *Amir* in the contacts list, contemplating the dreary walk home, not a single cigarette for company. 'Fuck it, I'm afraid.' He blocks Amir's number, deletes the name.

Inhaling through flared nostrils, Will pockets his phone, and strides down the sidewalk, raging about that cabbie, who drove off with his tobacco, and caused all this. But with each step, Will's anger dwindles. 'Onwards and upwards,' he mutters, casting forward to what's ahead in life: a bath and a paperback. Really, what more could one want?

DIARY: APRIL 2021

Three chapters left till I reach the end. Previously, when nearing comple-
tion of a manuscript, I grew impatient. I'd revise thirteen hours a day,
short of breath from urgency to be done *with an idea conceived a few*
years earlier by an elapsed version of myself. It felt like I was finishing
someone else's book. Until, at last, I'd submit my manuscript, and leap
to the new idea that I rared to begin — till a few years passed, and I was
once more finishing someone else's book.

What differs this time is that I've resisted any next idea; this manu-
script is the last. I'm apprehensive about what's to follow in my life,
blank pages I'll need to fill.

I look up from the sandy track across Hyde Park: people are shouting.
I never did get those glasses, so proceed toward the commotion in a fuzzed
state, mistrusting the landscape around me, which is half-imaginary —
not particular trees but brown columns with swaying green lids. A pebble
almost trips me. My limbs are so slow to react.

Finally, I'm close enough to identify the shouts. The Household
Cavalry is practising, guardsmen in silver helmets with white plumes,
red tunics and gleaming chest plates, each rider's sword drawn. 'Eyes!'
the commanding officer shrieks. 'Front!'

Another civilian observes too, a blurred man to my flank. I've spoken in person to almost nobody this past year, so I try out my voice again. He's agreeable to an exchange as we walk onward, each of us commenting on those shiny soldiers, prepping for war in the wrong century, playing at battles that this kingdom could no longer win, and so consoles itself with dress-up.

The man is a TV news correspondent, whom I've previously seen gesticulating in war zones. 'Didn't you just win an award?' I ask.

He affirms this, modestly adding nothing more.

'What was it, a report on the far right?' I ask. 'Or something on climate change?'

'Those are my only options?'

'If you tell me the prize-winning message, I'll tell you the subject.'

'That nobody's coming to save you.'

'What, me personally? This is troubling news.'

Laugh lines precede the sound, his rugged face plumped by midlife, or is it the beard?

Before us, a playground roars: little buccaneers rampaging up a pirate-ship fort. The television man sighs, for he has young children himself — yet must hasten back to the studio. I'm left at an empty swing set, much like those where I once pushed Beck. She never cared for kicking back and forth, so I was her propulsion as she watched parkland swing up and down before her. A pit of sadness opens inside me.

I clasp the swing seat, and release it. The empty saddle hops away, crests, and wobbles back toward me.

~~She's an unathletic but game mother, bruised and muscle-strained as she hasn't been since schooldays.~~

Or

~~The kids are squabbling again.~~

Or

She pushes them on the playground swings after dark, her two children swooping away and back slightly out of sync.

7

The novelist's last remaining friend

(MORGAN WILLUMSEN)

S HE PUSHES THEM ON the playground swings after dark, her two children swooping away and back slightly out of sync, for Sofie is braver and kicks higher than her little brother, Casper.

Each time one of them whooshes toward her, Morgan – an unathletic but game mother – leaps aside, sending the kids into hysterics, each trying to flick her with their feet. She tells other mothers that, were it not for these two, she'd get zero exercise. She'd also eat less junk, bought for the little ones as treats and bribes but gobbled after-hours by Morgan in need of reward.

'Swing *yourself*!' she tells Casper. 'How did I make such a lazy boy?'

'You're my servant, Mumma,' the six-year-old replies, knowing this veers toward trouble; a late smile.

'She's not your servant,' nine-year-old Sofie objects, swinging higher and higher. 'She's mine!'

The kids are always bickering, telling each other to die, and slamming their shared-bedroom door, which the other immediately shoulders open. For short spells, they get along, usually playing Lego – until one topples a skyscraper, and war resumes.

Morgan knows each of them so well. Her daughter is imperious from fear of losing control, and hypersensitive to everyone's mood. Her son is too suspicious of peers, too trusting of adults, unpopular at school, gentle with smaller kids, rude to her, and sad at night. Do they know her? Not yet. Later. And, she hopes, kindly.

Before having children, Morgan never thought of dying, but her unexpected death has become a fixation – that they'd be raised without her, would need her, and she'd be absent. She wakes with that terror: Sofie and Casper, abandoned, under threat.

Niels talks about moving away from Denmark, that they should try her birth country, South Africa. He longs for warm weather, and isn't worried about work – he's a chemist, and would be employable down there. Morgan wouldn't return, though. She is still fond of Johannesburg and some of its people, but when she meets fellow white South Africans abroad, they tend to test which side she's on politically. *You moved away because why exactly?* Some make probing remarks to find if she's a liberal and if they'll be judged – comments like: 'It's a tragedy, what's happened to the country,' then watching her response. Morgan keeps emailing her husband articles about quality-of-life indexes, with Copenhagen always in the top three.

They met during her university study-abroad year, when Morgan came here to learn about Scandinavian epics in translation. He was playing bass guitar with friends at a party, flubbing cover songs, everyone getting the giggles. She was drunk enough to approach him, the gentle red-bearded ice-hockey player who only made eye contact when smiling. Morgan had frizzy brown hair, cheeks rugged with the final year of bad skin, and a habit in conversation of tilting back, anxious that she came across as too intense. Since age eleven, she'd considered herself fat (minus three months of a celery-and-popcorn diet in her teens), and kept her nerve only through flares of defiance – telling herself she was smarter than most, and who cared what people thought? Also, Niels found her attractive, although she feared he'd get a full nude view and his desire would evaporate, for which Morgan was always in charge of the lights. After she finished that year abroad, they kept in touch via longing letters. When she did a study programme in London, they flew back and forth to Copenhagen. At last, during his doctoral studies, she moved to Denmark, and found work teaching English. A dozen years later, she's pushing swings.

Before starting a family, Morgan worried that children would drown her own aspirations, but they had another effect. They are the location where Morgan is herself for the first time since her own childhood. Other adults comment on how close the kids are to their mother, but Morgan wonders how much is transactional: she provides sympathy and hot chocolate – who wouldn't cling? This exchange doesn't trouble her. They rank her above anyone, and that suffices.

This evening, she has cans of Coke for them in a shopping bag. Niels would object. He grew up with the food-pyramid poster in his classroom, and still recites it: egg and fish on top, vegetables next, milk and bread as your base. *Coca-Cola?* he'd say. *Why can't they have water?!* This is his country, his culture, so Morgan demarcates a corner for herself by minor infractions like this. Still, the kids become more foreign each year. Once they hit adolescence, will she lose them to their father's culture?

They're trying to kick each other on the swings now, voices rising. Previously, each has told her of hating the other sibling, and swore that this feeling would never change, that when they're grown, they'll have *nothing* to do with each other, and cannot *wait*.

The swings fly back at her, Morgan right in their path. One could hit her at full speed. She turns her back, closes her eyes. The swing seats are empty and still. Nobody is there. Just her. Years since those two died.

IN COURT, THE SUSPECTS accused each other. Conventional wisdom said one must've been more guilty: a psychopath and an accomplice. Morgan could never think this way — her hatred had room for both.

The authorities ran programmes in which survivors of crime confronted the guilty. Even if officials took precautions during those meetings, perhaps she could smuggle in something sharp. But, as Niels pointed out, if they had time to stab a suspect, it'd be only once, and that person likely wouldn't die.

'Better than nothing,' Morgan said.

'But which of them?'

The question of culpability again, whom to loathe more, the man or the woman. At first, Danish news coverage was non-stop. In normal times, you might hear of a deadly street-gang attack, or a husband who'd killed his ex-wife. But this was children. The press decided that the male suspect had been the mastermind; a minority view saw the woman as instigator.

If Morgan stabbed a ballpoint pen into one of the suspect's eyes, mightn't it go into the brain?

'This is getting too much,' Niels said.

Logically, you'd need to grasp the back of the head while plunging it in, she said. You'd never have time, Niels told her, with the person flailing around and corrections staff pulling you off. Anyway, can we stop talking about this?

She couldn't. For society had the pleasure of punishment, with the guilty in a starring role, while victims were excised, told to get on with life. That life had become two lives for Morgan and Niels, who existed in jarring time signatures, one needing dinner when the other needed grief.

Could you pay someone in prison to hurt them? But Morgan and Niels knew no criminals. And such people would just inform the police to their own advantage, or expose the plot afterward. To Morgan, afterward was little concern. To be arrested would be freedom. Plus, this was Denmark: nobody serves long in this shitty, cowardly country, she thought.

'Yes, maybe what happened came about from you in some way,' Niels said. 'But this doesn't make it your responsibility to fix.'

Whenever he made this kind of remark, Morgan erupted in fury so volcanic that she could've scratched his face, saying it was *vile*, fucking *vile*, to blame *her* for what had happened. It was a fact, though: without what she had done, their children would be alive.

THE EVENTS LEADING TO the crime hadn't even been something Morgan wanted. She allowed herself to be nudged into it, tempted by the prospect of higher status than that of schoolteacher.

Niels always encouraged her to write – when working on articles for local English-language publications, he noticed, she was easier to get along with. But her last contribution had been years back, before Casper was born. Since then, she'd done an occasional essay on her blog, which she sheepishly forwarded to Facebook friends, who clicked LIKE without reading to the end, except the retirees, who posted over-the-top praise. Niels, tiring of her dissatisfaction with the school, urged her to write again, and gave her an idea. In a rush, she pitched it to an American magazine, and heard nothing back – then a terse request for more details. The magazine might be interested, provided that she snagged an interview. This hardly seemed realistic because Jukka Arve spoke to nobody.

Arve first gained a following for pseudonymous message-board screeds, most of them taken down after his arrest, then re-posted by fans and translated into a dozen languages. In the extreme-right subculture, Jukka Arve was 'the leader we need'. When he was jailed in his native Finland, supporters compared it to Hitler's incarceration before his rise to power. The charge was terrorist conspiracy, and Finnish prosecutors cited attempts to purchase explosives and military-grade armaments.

The Arve manifesto laid out a strategy to chisel deeper into the fissures in Western culture that, he prophesied, would crack into violent conflict, much like the Second Civil War in America, which he contended was already underway. It was this striking claim that thrust Arve into the spotlight, amplified by leftist US sources via condemning podcasts and think-pieces that, in turn, provoked gleeful ripostes from far-right YouTubers. To such types, Arve was just a troll pressing the buttons of liberals who failed to realize how funny shitposting was, especially when it ended in gunfire.

Morgan sought to contact Arve at the prison. Secretly, she hoped for a definitive rejection from his team, a scattered group of young men, few of whom had actually met their leader. Their hobbies included spreading memes of hook-nosed-Jew cartoons, photoshopping immigrants as rats, and doxxing 'race traitors' by posting their mobile numbers, email addresses, even floorplans of their homes. Communicating with Morgan via encrypted message apps, they assumed a haughty tone, saying their leader was *perhaps* willing to grant her a few minutes – he was curious because she was South African, and he wanted to learn more about apartheid. His proxies went into a brief panic when it occurred to them that South African didn't necessarily mean white. She alleviated this concern, and noted that she'd grown up during the final years of apartheid, so knew plenty about it – not mentioning her leftie parents, who'd attended rallies against the race laws (yet employed an elderly African maid in a shack at the end of the garden who referred to Morgan's dad as 'master', a fact she never told anyone). So, yes, she knew something of apartheid.

When Arve agreed, Niels wanted to celebrate, which wasn't how she felt about the prospect of trekking to a prison outside Helsinki to meet a neo-Nazi. Indeed, she profoundly did *not* want to go. But the magazine had said yes, Arve waited, and Niels would look after the kids. She had to.

A running joke in their marriage was that Niels's job was to save the world (researching how to strip carbon emissions from the atmosphere), so her job was bathtime. But what Morgan most looked forward to about this trip was the hotel. She could sleep late for the first time in years. As for air travel, she'd not flown once without her kids since their births, and nearly had a panic attack when boarding, imagining Sofie and Casper growing up without her. But she reached the prison, conducted the interview, and the new Hitler surprised her: he was a bore.

Back in Copenhagen, she listened to their recorded conversation, and became frantic. She had nothing worth writing. Had she failed to ask the right questions? She was making an idiot of herself, posing as a proper journalist. An editor at the magazine in New York dropped her an email, asking how it had gone. Arve's proxies pestered her too, demanding to approve the article beforehand, which the magazine forbade. So they sought a veto over any quotes. Again, she wasn't allowed to grant that. Finally, they just asked the publication date.

She compensated for her dull interview by filling the article with background. After an all-nighter, and days of overlooking Sofie and Casper, she ran spellcheck, and emailed her piece to New York, wishing as she hit SEND that she could suck it back. Three months of silence followed. Finally, the editor replied with a fake-cheerful note and a massive rewrite. This confirmed her worst self-opinion, so Morgan fought every change, leaving both sides aggrieved. Months later, they ran the piece, buried as a Q&A, her questions rewritten, and Arve's answers condensed, often distorting the meaning, under the headline: 'Little Hitler: Behind Bars, a Notorious Nazi Talks of War and Soup'. They played up his petty whining, how Arve spoke in a high voice, that he was overweight. Also, the magazine paid only for the words published, 800, though they'd commissioned 3,000. Why was *she* penalized because they'd butchered her story? Was that normal?

The article had no apparent impact. Morgan was busy teaching, and embarrassed by her flop, but other duties distracted her. Then she found something on Facebook: strangers saying that she, by interviewing Arve, was promoting racist ideology. The degree of hostility frightened her. At school, a group of pupils complained that she had platformed a Nazi. The school administrators were caught by surprise – Morgan had used vacation time to report the piece, and they'd only been faintly aware of her previous freelancing, a few movie reviews in a local English-language publication. This wasn't that. They cautioned her never to repeat such a stunt.

This scolding incensed Morgan, who'd fallen into a skittish state regarding those personal insults online, checking her social-media mentions whenever in the bathroom. Some people defended her, saying she'd conducted an important interview with a repugnant man whom society should prepare itself against. When criticized, Morgan felt that the article had been twisted into somebody else's; when people approved, the writing felt like hers again. In this nervous state, she searched online for journalism jobs – was that out of the question? She'd studied literature and communications at university, and took adult-education writing courses after. She often contemplated the routes her life hadn't taken.

One night before bed, Morgan did the umpteenth search of her name, and discovered memes featuring her, with an image lifted from the school website, and photoshopped with a bullet hole in her forehead. Apparently, Arve was outraged by her article, which had led to the removal of several prison privileges. His comments had been taken out of context, he said. This was correct; her editors had done so. She never sought to remedy it because the magazine seemed powerful and her subject powerless. Someone known as 'the new Hitler' could hardly sue for defamation. His online supporters flooded her and the magazine with abuse.

Morgan had always been contemptuous when media types bemoaned their social-media shitstorms. But she found that when an accusation was totally unfounded, it lingered – their disgust stamped on the bruises of her introspection. The deluge peaked at nearly a hundred emails one day, some calling for her rape and death. Yet she kept checking, aching for messages of support, though these never cleansed her. Morgan kept this frenzy from everyone. At dinner, she tried to act normally with the kids and Niels, who wasn't on social media. At moments, it felt as if what animated her phone wasn't quite real, a purgatory beneath the screen, like scenes on the walls of medieval churches, with cross-eyed demons spearing the shocked sinners. Throughout each meal, her attention was fractured. His, too. They'd long ago developed a relationship of co-workers – sometimes your colleague turns up in a foul mood, so you hope for a better shift tomorrow.

His best friend turned forty, and the all-male birthday celebrations ended up at their place. They'd already drunk plenty, and those overgrown boys shouted competitive reminiscences from their ice-hockey days. At first, they spoke English in respect of Morgan's presence, but blood-alcohol levels switched the banter to Danish. How differently Niels behaved among male friends, she thought: loud and vulgar – but also a spark he never revealed with her. She checked on the kids, then returned, knowing she'd sound like the nagging spouse but: 'Maybe let's keep it down a bit, guys?'

When Niels collapsed into bed finally, they didn't touch. She fell asleep with her phone on the duvet.

TWO YEARS LATER, MORGAN was reading an article in *Politiken* about science and the justice system, under the headline 'Who Is Guilty Anymore?' The article explained the rising field of neuro-criminology, how breakthroughs in brain imaging would transform the courts. While every human has dark thoughts, the article said, scientists have proven that those who commit violent crime tend to have deficits in the prefrontal cortex. In other words, evil is a physical handicap, one's body unable to stop normal anti-social impulses. If so, love, disappointment, cake – anything that feels like experience or choice – is simply another biomechanical reflex. Whether drinking yourself into homelessness or landing in government, one's machinery is responsible, not the person strapped into it. Even the will is a fiction, the soul redundant. This article cited a notorious murder case, and Morgan realized that they meant her children. Hours passed before she regained her composure. This same plunge happened every morning upon waking, to remember that it had really happened, that this was her life – like a stroke patient whose memory is wiped in sleep, discovering each dawn that everything is over.

In the month after the murders, she and her husband had sex once, desperately, and never again. Morgan fell quiet when people discussed the background of the second culprit, Freja Bækkelund, a hanger-on in neo-Nazi circles who was half-Danish, half-Somali. Journalists recounted her roots, discussing radicalization in the underclass, and psychologizing about internalized racism. The male co-defendant, Jens Uhlén, preened in court, smiling and joking with his lawyers. In the media conception, he had a soul; she was 'a product of'.

Morgan, who had always leaned left in her politics, found comfort from victim-advocacy groups, most of whose members were conservative. She stopped caring if people assumed that she was right-wing. Niels grew dismissive of her fantasies about hurting the culprits, and this retreat contained all that she resented about him, how every step of their lives, from having children, to finding this apartment in Vesterbro, to furnishing it, even the ad for his current job – everything required *her* engine, she the airplane's lone turbine, he the cargo.

An argument. Many. Long into shouting, she didn't recall her original complaint, which had ramified into twenty, all boringly familiar. When they calmed one night, he approached as she sorted through mail. 'I feel like you hate me,' he said.

After a pause, she replied, 'I don't hate you.'

He urged Morgan not to blame herself. 'You are, only in the tiniest way, responsible. But you're not culpable. Nobody can say that you are. Really.'

His distinction between 'responsible' and 'culpable' suggested, not for the first time, that Niels had a more nuanced grasp of English than she'd assumed. She saw herself as the more intellectually nimble spouse, that he had the mechanistic brain of an engineer. Even in his family, they judged Niels the least clever sibling but the best at sports. But really, how could she even assess his mind? Her shorthand was 'Niels cleans the atmosphere', but she had little grasp of what he actually did. This gulf between them seemed important, and sad, as it never had before.

After the killings, she took extended leave from the school, which was a mistake. Morgan had little to do but meet her suffering every day, alone in the apartment, or in this small city where you always bumped into everyone. She came to hate the society, whose bland goodness meant that the guilty would never experience anything close to her torment. All the *hygge* bullshit of Denmark, those endless frothy articles on how this lifestyle was better than anywhere else, accompanied by photographs of cosy-socked feet before a fireplace. She couldn't leave, though – the criminal trial was here, and Niels refused to speak to the press. Once again, it was for her to look out for their kids, to inform reporters that justice required the longest prison terms possible, that these people would do something like this again. (She wasn't concerned about that last part. She just wanted them to suffer.)

At first, a Danish press organization spoke in support of Morgan, whose children had been targeted for her work as a journalist. They invited her to events, and asked her to speak once. She told of how awful it was to be on this side of a news story, especially when the media spun it to favour the mixed-race culprit. She didn't hear from them again.

Meantime, the editor-in-chief of the American magazine phoned her to offer his support, and made clear that she should consider it her home publication, that she could contribute ideas whenever. This didn't amount to a job offer, but they'd consider her future pitches seriously – and pay more per word. Yet in the two years after the murders, Morgan contributed only one more article, a first-person piece that the editor requested about what had happened. This was Morgan's selling-point. However, she wanted to write on anything but that, which meant proposing topics she had no expertise on. Awkward emails flew back and forth. They paid the kill fee on a second article, and she returned to teaching full-time. But she had lost tolerance for kids, these older than hers had been, or would be. Her work felt valueless, teaching adolescents already fluent in colloquial English, picked up from Instagram and Twitch.

Each night, she and Niels decompressed with red wine, calmer after the first glass, passive-aggressive after the second, out-of-control dispute after the third. Following that, she couldn't sleep yet again, and increased her coffee intake the next morning, not to mention the snacking and weight gain. She hadn't been this heavy since her teens, and the fat distribution was even less flattering at her current age.

Awake with insomnia, she searched the web in private mode for how to kill someone quickly, or how to pay someone to kill someone. In her imagination, the two culprits were beaten for years. First, they'd be told what was to happen, that they had no way to stop it.

SIX YEARS PASS AFTER the trial. A parole hearing for Freja Bæk-kelund becomes mandatory, and will take victim statements into account.

Morgan — furious that this is happening so soon — prepares to deliver hers. She stands before her bathroom mirror, wondering whether to avoid make-up, if it's advantageous to show how much she's aged, or if she'll have more sway if well-presented.

Morgan asked that she and Niels speak to the hearing on separate days. The officials couldn't oblige – time was limited in that conference room. They did agree to hold this part in English, until Niels specified that he wanted Danish, which she took as a personal slight. In any case, her Danish is good now, much improved since their divorce.

Morgan has left teaching, and is retraining as a forensic linguist, a field she hadn't heard of before the trial. She's midway through a PhD, her speciality parsing social media for clues to help criminal investigators. Already, she has worked as a consultant to the police when English-language slang is involved – for example, the case of a young American couple visiting Copenhagen on their honeymoon. The bride's parents in Minnesota received a distraught text message from Denmark in which the young woman said the marriage had been a terrible mistake, and that she wanted to die. They tried to reach her, but no answer. Her new husband wasn't picking up either. So they phoned the hotel. The manager visited the room, and discovered her body hanging. The husband was not present. When he returned, he sobbed uncontrollably, explaining that they'd argued, he'd left to cool off, and she must've done something insane – she had a history of depression, he noted. The lead detective was conducting a graduate seminar that week, and asked the students to review a suicidal text message sent to the woman's parents. Later that day, Morgan also pored over the bride's posts on Instagram, as well as tweets by her husband. She determined (and told the detective with greater assurance than she felt) that the husband had faked the suicide note, that its syntax and abbreviations bore his style, not that of the wife. When the pathologist's report came out, it gave the wife's time of death as before her final text message was sent.

Her phone had a face-recognition passcode, meaning that someone in their hotel room must've held the phone before her asphyxiated face to open the messenger app, then falsified a suicide note, and messaged it to her family. In other words, the husband. After this, the police department asked Morgan to participate in a programme to catch Danish men who sought to groom foreign children online, and she taught specialized officers to write English as if kids themselves, to catch paedophiles in stings.

Morgan is alone in the conference room when Niels enters. He avoids eye contact, and sits on the same side of the table, a few chairs away. He's too cowardly to address her, so she stares at the side of his face. He's lost weight and dresses more stylishly, with a hipster jacket his wife must've suggested; or perhaps he just cares again. She knows he has a newborn daughter, with a fellow Dane this time. Niels wears a wedding ring too, though he refused one when they were together, saying his father never wore one, and that he considered jewellery effeminate. Suddenly, Morgan feels old, foreign, bulky, and this collapse of confidence panics her. The officials *know* we're divorced. They said they'd respect the difficulty of this meeting. Then they just leave us here together?

'You got wet on the way,' Niels says.

'Awful Danish weather, as usual.'

'There's no such thing as bad weather. Only bad clothing.'

'No, there's bad weather.'

Niels says he never expected her to be here.

'What's that supposed to mean?'

'Please, Morgan, I'm not trying to offend you. I just guessed you wouldn't stay in Denmark.'

'You want me to leave the country now?' He must've known she was still around. She often glimpsed Niels around the neighbour-hood, at an outside table for a work meeting, or on a family outing down Strøget, his infant daughter in the BabyBjörn. Morgan was always mortified to be seen alone, so hurried away.

'I think it's enough,' Niels says. 'Don't you?'

'What's enough?'

'This woman. Nearly seven years. It's a long time.'

'Are you serious?! She killed our children, Niels! She fucking killed Sofie and Casper!' Normally, Morgan avoids saying their names aloud.

'You can't say *she* killed them. Anything she did was because of the man. That's established now.'

'Bullshit. Bullshit. And it's *six* years. Not seven. Are you men-tally ill?'

'Okay! Calm down.'

'Don't tell me to calm down.'

'Forget it. Forget it.' He wakes his phone.

She's quiet, but only for seconds. 'No fucking way.'

'The man, *he* should stay behind bars. But she was – I don't know. What good is it, keeping someone in a cage forever?'

Morgan is sweating to discover this betrayal. She had assumed each would tell of how their lives had been devastated, how excruciating this remained every day, and what Sofie and Casper had been like. Morgan wasn't sure she could get through that part, but had pledged to her online supporters to be brave. Now, she has the humiliation of explaining how wrecked only *her* life is, and admitting this before her ex-husband, and everyone will think she's defective, that she is shaking with wrath while he is so merciful.

Following the crime, the Danish public was gripped with horror at the murders. After a couple of years, once the guilty were imprisoned, everyone moved on. Then a TV channel produced a two-part documentary on the case, claiming to Morgan when they interviewed her that it'd simply be a retelling of the tragedy. But the documentary hardly troubled itself with her children, instead profiling the female culprit, Freja Bækkelund. The tragedy was her life, and they won an award for it. Morgan had still not watched it – she had to turn it off in the eighth minute, and broke her remote control.

'You have to forgive. At some point, you do,' Niels says, placing his phone face-down on the conference table. 'It destroys one more life to keep this going. She has parents and sisters and brothers too. She probably wants a family someday.'

'You actually don't care about your own children.'

'Come on, Morgan! Come on!'

The officials enter, smiling. It's a three-person panel: two female officials and a chairman.

Before they've sat, Morgan asks to speak first. She struggles with the zip of her backpack, and mistakenly rips her prepared statement. She reads out a first sentence, voice quavering, then clears her throat, and asks to stand.

'Whatever makes you comfortable.'

'I'm not comfortable in any way,' she says in English. 'I just feel like this is fixed.'

The older female official looks confused. 'How do you mean by "fixed"?'

'This is a hearing for the person who did the crime – to find out how she's not that bad, how she's done all sorts of prison programmes. You're looking away from me now. Yes: *I'm* the horrible sight. You want me to hurry up, and get out of the way.'

'Not true. Not true.'

'Don't you realize how *sick* this is, that you're even making me *talk* about letting her out? The mother of the victims, and I have to *plead* with you, *beg* for a minimal punishment?'

Niels, seated beside her, stares at his knees.

'You must say whatever you feel,' the chairman assures her. 'You're allowed.'

'I was trying to. Then you interrupted me.' He didn't. But nobody corrects her. Morgan's mouth is dry.

'We care what is right for society. This means you and the victims' father,' the chairman says. 'But we must also think about her.'

'Why not think about two people who aren't here? Who were *children*.'

'We never forget them. But we have her in our care.'

'Lots of people have a background like hers,' Morgan says. 'They didn't do stuff like this.'

'What do you mean, "her background"?'

Morgan's heart is pumping faster.

The younger female official raises a finger. 'You must agree, Mrs Willumsen, people from different backgrounds have different experiences. You can't blame all the same way.'

'What does that have to do with this situation?' Morgan says. 'You're saying that a person isn't responsible because of her skin colour?'

'*Nobody* is saying that!' the younger official says, offended.

Niels, still looking down, shakes his head.

'Hey, hey,' the chairman says. 'This is getting away from us. Can we please return to the question of you, Mrs Willumsen, and what you have come to say? To speak for the two victims who, you rightly tell us, cannot be here today, and whose voices we want to hear.'

'Their voices?'

The official who blurted '*Nobody* is saying that!' has pursed her lips, and placed her hands on the conference table, thumbs hooked together, as if to restrain her dismay.

Morgan reads her printed statement. After, when pushing the lift button, her hand trembles. She phones a contact at the victims-advocacy group, exaggerating how badly everything went. Her allies initiate a media campaign against parole for Freja Bækkelund. News articles come out in the conservative press. A right-wing party takes up the cause.

Ultimately, the board gives its ruling: too early to release the inmate, given the severity of the crime, and public outrage surrounding the case. The victims-advocacy group throws a party to celebrate, with a dozen activists in a community centre, drinking beneath a slow turning disco ball. Everyone cheers when Morgan enters, and a twitchy man in a Danish-flag waistcoat hurries toward her, his shiny forehead twinkling under the lights. He's smoking a cigarette, and tells her he's so grateful, so admiring of what she's been through. He confides statistics on crime, laments who's running society nowadays, how everyone's seen videos of other countries, and that's not here.

Morgan steps back but the man has hearing difficulties, so keeps moving nearer. She questions his conclusions, mentioning that she grew up during apartheid, and that repulsive evil system showed how every human deserves the dignity of equal treatment. And isn't *that* the point here? He smiles indulgently, not quite hearing, handing her a glass of prosecco, saying he's never met a lady who didn't love bubbly. He smiles wetly, urging her to drink.

When Morgan finds an excuse to leave, a pink-mascara woman with asymmetrical facelift makes pouty sympathy lips, and the Danish-flag-waistcoat man insists – insists! – on driving her home, 'Or would I be a gentleman?'

Outside her building, he switches off the engine of his banged-up Mercedes, slings his arm over the steering wheel, and pops the car lighter, pressing its orange glow into the umpteenth cigarette. He opens his lips to speak – but Morgan has the door open, thanking him too many times. She suppresses her shiver until the building door closes behind her.

THE HANDWRITING IS CHILDISH, and littered with mistakes in English. Above all, the letter is about its author, Freja Bækkelund, explaining that she'd been an immature girl trying to act like a woman at the time, how awful her upbringing was, that she wasn't trying to make excuses.

'Yes, you are!' Morgan shouts at the page, slamming it on the kitchen table, her fingertips pinning it there. '*All* you're doing is making excuses!' She balls the page so tightly that her knuckles go white, and stamps it on the kitchen linoleum, using a napkin to dispose of the letter, as if it were a squashed cockroach, dropped in the kitchen waste. She pours used coffee grounds on top, and washes her hands twice.

The parole review is annual. Morgan could tick a box, and her previous victim-impact statement would apply again. That's what Niels did. But after last year, seeing that the system wants to free this woman, Morgan plans to attend, to make her case even more forcefully.

She's hamstrung, though. You're to consider only the future; the past is bad manners. That's fine for the guilty, but do they not understand that Morgan's future is nothing but the past? Some people prefer to downplay the murder of two children for the embarrassment of its having happened a few years ago – yes, she'll say that.

In a Netto supermarket bag, Morgan brings her son's Spiderman pyjamas and her daughter's nightdress with the emoji motifs. She passes these to the three officials, telling each to take a turn holding the garments. 'That's what they were wearing. When they were suffocated. I've never washed them. That's what Casper and Sofie were in.'

Solemnly, the officials pass the items around, each unsure what degree of scrutiny to undertake, till the chairman holds the items in both hands as if sacred, hesitating to return them. Morgan doesn't intervene, for she is talking, they are listening. And she prevails, entirely in Danish. She planned to change to English if too upset, but she managed.

No party this time; she never flagged this hearing to the victims-advocacy group. On the ride home, it's jarring to resume banality, the routine of bus stops and occupied seats, that Netto bag on her lap, she knowing its contents. Morgan brought earbuds but plays nothing, overhearing pre-teen girls chatting beside her, one perched on the other's lap.

Morgan is trying *not* to consider something. But the matter recurs when she's washing dishes, working down a tower of dirty crockery. (Living alone, she cleans up just once a week; she'd be ashamed if anyone saw. Nobody sees.) She enters her study, surrounded by forensic-linguistic reference works, knowing why she feels wretched: speaking of her kids today was a recital. Down another memory corridor, she still has access to her living children. But she employs them as anecdotes now, parts of her story.

FREJA BÆKKELUND KNOWS MORGAN'S home address on Gasværksvej – the crime took place there – but she is barred from communicating directly with her victims. Only with permission will the prison forward letters. Morgan is preparing to defend her dissertation, and has no time. She puts the letter aside; she'll open this when it suits her. Or burn it, unread.

She resists only a few minutes, then opens the envelope. Freja Bækkelund is claiming to be sorry, saying Morgan was justified to criticize her in the reply. Her first letter, she admits, was inappropriate, a litany of self-pity, as if her victim should care. She wanted to explain herself. But in hindsight, it wasn't her place. Except to say that she is so sorry, also to have troubled Morgan.

Morgan speed-walks across the apartment to her laptop, impatient to type out the lacerating words in her head, a response even more pointed than the first. She has the measure of this cynical piece of shit.

After Morgan's reply, a further apology arrives.

So Morgan writes another ferocious letter, because Freja Bækkelund is now saying that she followed an abusive man into this crime. 'Your pseudo-apologies are pathetic, and you disgust me,' Morgan writes. 'I will do all I can to ensure that you die in prison, that you never have any joy in your life, there or on the outside, and that everyone you ever meet knows what you did and who you are.'

That night, Morgan runs a bath, still agitated. She talked down to that person, as one isn't allowed to do in normal life. But Morgan must tell herself to feel pleased; she feels something else. In recent years, she has developed such low regard for human beings, considering them delusionals who claim their good luck as utterly earned – while their misdeeds, *those* are nothing to do with them!

The next day goes better. Morgan is invited to a linguistics conference, and has a good phone call with her sister. She enjoys a healthful lunch, and a late-night walk, admiring the Danish summer sky, a twilight of noctilucent clouds. Everyone she passes is good-willed, and she notices an elderly gentleman sorting through his wallet, confounded, and she helps him entirely in Danish. He's so thankful. Once home, Morgan replies to Freja Bækkelund, a less eviscerating note this time. She knows that something as petty as her full stomach affects the contents of this letter, so she summons a little anger, mentioning in passing that when she herself is overwhelmed, she does nothing more violent than colouring in – so don't pretend that circumstances 'forced' you.

Freja Bækkelund never disputes anything. She doesn't even write words in response this time. She sends a notepad of her pencil drawings, an offering for Morgan to colour in. Morgan throws the notepad in the waste bin, then writes back to say stop sending shit like that. Freja Bækkelund responds that she has taken Morgan's advice: she loved colouring as a little girl, and it really helps with stress, which is high in prison.

Morgan scoffs at this, for everything is taken care of in a Danish prison. You live better than we do out here! Stress comes from obligations and responsibilities. Morgan enumerates her own, making sure to mention the Facebook group that she administers for survivors of violent crime.

These letters, Morgan realizes, are the sole venue where she can speak openly about her children, whose personalities and troubles and quirky joys she cites at shaming length to Freja. Morgan cannot get through writing another letter without knitting her fingers over her eyes, pressing hard against the bones of her face, as if to push herself back inside. Around the city, she glimpses classmates of her kids – some not far from adulthood, presumably thinking of university, careers, romances, perhaps even contemplating children of their own.

Freja is the only other person in the world who thinks every day of Morgan's children. After refusing it for months, Morgan asks that the criminal explain herself. Cautiously, Freja tries to, specifying that she has broken away from those people. She writes in imprecise English, never asking forgiveness. She knows that Morgan will keep denouncing her to the parole board, and has never sought to change that.

Morgan expresses anger that Freja might someday start a family while her own chance has gone, that she'll probably die stranded abroad without a single person in this country. Freja explains that she cannot have children – she struggles with endometriosis, which developed after her arrest.

Morgan asks more about this, but Freja is wary. She doesn't want to excuse herself. The facts are these: Freja was brought up in Christiania by her mother, who raised her communally, claiming this was on principle. However, it was merely practical, for the woman suffered from manic depression, and self-medicated on whatever drugs were around; often, she was unconscious in the daytime. Even before entering school, Freja had tried illegal drugs – her mother made her eat something to take a nap. By age eleven, she was sniffing glue on her own, which the prison psychiatrists said had probably caused brain damage, although she feels fine in the head. In the streets, she found older friends, adults who treated her as an adult, and she still doesn't quite believe some of those men were predators, as she's been told in counselling. They were her friends. From outside, maybe it'd be considered a violation. But she can't see her life from outside.

She certainly had the wrong companions, though, taking up with a gang of guys who made videos of bare-knuckle fights; several had self-made swastika tattoos. She became their toy, including sexually, and was subjected to constant racial taunts, mocked for her ultra-Nordic name despite the dark skin, dubbed '*Lortebrun*', meant to imply 'shit-skin'. Even she referred to herself by that nickname. As for the night of the crime, she was on heavy drugs, and remembers only her arrest. To be clear, Freja keeps saying, none of this is for sympathy. She's actually stopped petitioning for parole. Previously, she wanted freedom, but she has become low when reflecting in these letters. Thinking about it all, Freja feels that she should not get out.

To check on this, Morgan contacts the parole office. Freja is telling the truth. When the state conducts an annual review, prisoners normally send thick folders, and work for months on their pleas. Freja submitted nothing corroborating her rehabilitation, and she refused to attend her hearing.

Morgan messages Niels, asking whether he's available to drop by their old place: **I want to make peace.**

did not know we r at war! he texts back, **but yes of course . . . :)**

In the apartment doorway, he wears the wrong expression. He's upset to return to where the children won't grow up. Morgan planned to seduce him. Not anymore. Her ex-husband can't even go down the hall – it'd mean passing the kids' room, now her study. 'You *work* in there?'

Fury rushes back, a wave charging up the sand at her, rising to her throat. How fucking out-of-line, to imply that *she* is inappropriate, when it was she who stayed here, who slept on the kids' floor for three years, right by their bunkbeds.

'What did you want to talk about?' he asks.

'Forget it. There's no point.'

'Morgan, I came all the way here.'

'Just get out of my house!'

'Why are you shoving me?! What is wrong with you?!'

'Get out!'

After he leaves, she suffers an extreme drop in mood. The dissertation gripped her earlier that day, but she sees only pages of nonsense now. On the street, any sound of people is evidence that humanity is despicable.

The last time she felt such self-hatred was after Niels moved out. She reached out to a former friend then, her tutor in an earlier life, back when Morgan still harboured hopes for her writing, and did that programme in London. Every student was assigned an external tutor, third-tier authors whom nobody had heard of, people who'd had novels published once, but were now politely starving from indifference. Her tutor was a Dutch novelist, Dora Frenhofer, a jaded but witty fiftysomething then, whose pre-teen daughter had just moved to California to live with her father – a change that Dora mentioned with disregard: 'At last, I get to work uninterrupted again!' Art was what mattered, insofar as nothing really mattered. Morgan – still in her early twenties – wanted to be a European intellectual like that.

They kept in touch now and then, Morgan recounting her ongoing love affair with the cute Danish grad student, Niels. In handwritten letters, Morgan attempted to echo her mentor's style, mistaking amorality and sentence fragments for literary sophistication. But her correspondence was sincere in its way. So Morgan was hurt when Dora didn't come to the wedding. Still, she visited her older friend in London three times before having children. Those were odd trips, with intense talk while crossing parks and down busy streets and suddenly back home, the sharpness of Dora's remarks often funny – all followed by tense silence in her house, worsening when Morgan's departure neared, as if the older woman wanted her gone by now. When it was time to head to the train, Morgan considered an embrace, but realized that goodbye was enough. 'I need to get back to work,' Dora said. Only one of them was truly a writer, and she needed to show which.

But over time, Morgan realized that her friend's career was not as sturdy as presented, that Dora struggled to publish novels anymore, each attracting fewer readers than the last. On inspection, her private life looked different too. She'd characterized her daughter's departure as a blessed absence, yet the ledge behind Dora's writing desk contained various images of Beck: a toothless toddler; then a pudgy girl eating a peach; then an eleven-year-old trying not to smile. When Morgan asked about that girl, the writer closed the subject.

She and Dora spoke by phone only occasionally, wry observations that made them equals, until the day that Morgan offered advice. Dora went silent, so that Morgan – losing confidence to speak into a void – asked, 'Are you still there?' To which Dora said just, 'Mm,' and resumed her silence till Morgan improvised, blending apology and change of subject and farewell.

Something peculiar followed. When next they spoke (and Morgan didn't call back for a year), Dora was far the needier, speaking with such negativity about her writing, as if wanting her younger acolyte to deny this – but becoming scratchy when encouragement came. Morgan had an epiphany: she'd become one of this person's closest friends, perhaps her only friend. That made Morgan value her less. Anyway, with the birth of her children, she had no more time for phone calls.

Only after the crime did Morgan again hear from Dora, a sensitive condolence letter in which the older woman recalled how close they'd been. When Niels moved out, Morgan phoned Dora once, needing the voice of someone bold and far from Copenhagen. But nothing of the friendship remained, just old details, as when bumping into someone from schooldays, where one person cites names the other doesn't recognize anymore. Dora asked prying questions about the murders, and became strident, saying what should and shouldn't happen, and the exchange plunged Morgan even lower. Both put down the phone, knowing they'd not speak again.

The coda was that Morgan learned a few years later that her one-time mentor had actually published a novel with a character whose two children had been murdered. Morgan discovered this long after the book's publication, which showed how irrelevant Dora Frenhofer's work had become – nobody had even associated this novel with its obvious inspiration. Morgan happened across a copy in a remainder basket at Books & Company in Hellerup, and paged through with apprehension. She had to keep searching, finding no character like herself, and realizing: it was the husband. Dora had switched the sexes. Morgan didn't know how to interpret this.

She's recalling this angrily now, for everything feels insulting after her interaction with Niels at the apartment. From spite, she decides to compel Freja to join a restitution programme, where the criminal must meet the survivor in person, and seek forgiveness. Morgan will offer none. She'll do as in their letters: use this criminal to speak at, and she'll have to take it. She'll ask no questions of Freja – and will tell her to shut up if she veers from the subject of Morgan's distress.

At the prison, she is led into a 'family room': brown sofas, old magazines, individually packaged cookies, and (inappropriately, given the crime) children's toys. Weirdly, Freja tries to hug her. Morgan leans away. 'Sorry, sorry,' Freja says.

'It's fine,' Morgan replies, though it was *not* fine.

Their conversation is short. Morgan ends it abruptly.

On the train ride back, she recalls that article in *Politiken*, about how neuroscience today equates the brain to a supercomputer – that everyone is born with hardware, loaded with software, programmed to run algorithms. To explain behaviour, there's no need to cite anything but biomechanics. We are programs, never choosing anything, nobody at the keyboard, nobody moving a mouse. Condemning someone's actions is as preposterous as blaming them for their eye colour.

That can't be. It feels so wrong.

For her doctorate, Morgan must stay up-to-date with social-media apps, those that her own kids would have used, uploading shameless selfies and teen rants they'd never outrun. Technology has ruined humankind, Morgan thinks. Or maybe the internet – freeing us – is the truth about our species.

She visits Skydebanehaven, standing with her back to the playground swings, the two saddles perfectly still. It's already getting dark; Danish winter.

Morgan wakes the next day, well rested for a change. In the mirror, a different person: something of her younger self. She resumes her dissertation, even visits a trendy restaurant for a late lunch, where the attractive Swedish barman pulls up a seat and chats. He mentions a small-batch vodka made in the north of his country, and how it's unlike normal vodka, and he pours her a glass on the house. 'You drink it like that?' Morgan asks. 'On its own?'

'On its own,' he says.

That night, she writes to Freja, explaining that she wants the young woman to apply for parole again. When the letter is finished, she prints it, and rests it on her palm, the paper warm. She never sends it.

But the next day, she phones to talk Freja through this. She speaks of how this just came to her, and how she's felt light since. Freja grows emotional. Morgan declares, more forcefully, that it is the right thing; it *must* happen. She demands that Freja start considering a future outside that place. They even plan a meeting someday, somewhere in the open air – one of those cafés on the Lakes, where they could take a bench and buy hot drinks. Freja is drawn into this image, then bats away the prospect. But at moments, Morgan hears the young woman edging toward the unimaginable: free.

Morgan contacts the parole officials. They're taken aback, but delighted that she has found mercy. This puts her off, as if they were pastors, and she the humbled sinner, accepting a seat in the pew. She acts irritable about the necessary paperwork, partly to remind them who she is. They turn formal, specifying that they'll certainly consider her opinion, but other issues enter into it. First, the children's father deserves his say. Society is a stakeholder too.

A COUPLE OF STRANGE years pass, those of the pandemic. After Morgan's second vaccination, she gets a haircut, shorter than any in her life – for ages, she'd wanted to, but feared doing it. It's a shock in the hairdresser's mirror: her face is so round. She imagined this cut as grimly suited to a woman approaching her fifties. But that isn't the point. It's less bother, just as this stage of life is about fearing less that people can see inside her.

She arrives at the meeting place, ears chilly. Morgan checks what shoes she's wearing, and improves her posture, looking around: a country that was never home, where she has lived almost half her life.

They planned to meet at the outside tables of Original Coffee.

The rain has stopped, the sun meekly out. Morgan – abruptly dry-mouthed, arm over her handbag as if for balance – checks that she brought a hand towel to wipe raindrops from their benches. Anyone in the city could see them together.

She and Freja have spoken only once since her release two weeks ago. They have, however, already decided what to order. This respectful little café, which Morgan chose, sells the biscotti that she's addicted to. She promised they'd try some, along with the ginger-lemon tea that Freja cited as the soothing drink she most missed.

The state is providing Freja with housing and counselling and job opportunities. But Morgan suspects that a decade of institution-alization has made the young woman passive. Before release, Freja worried about how she'd make friends at any job, noting that one must mention the past, and it'd come up in the first conversation: *Where were you before this?* What happens when they search her name online?

She asked if Morgan's ex-husband, Niels, should be present for this meeting. Morgan dismissed that, and never looked too hard at why: that it'd make the encounter about the murders, which perhaps it should be. But Morgan is excited for another reason. This occasion affirms her humanity.

Freja arrives eighteen minutes late, jogging the last stretch down Sortedam Dossering, hand cupped over her mouth in embarrassment, apologizing profusely for her bus. She seeks a hug, which is tight and rocks side to side. Morgan abides this, but wants to push away. Finally, Freja stands back, smiling warmly. Morgan tries to smile back. This is more upsetting than she foresaw.

In prison, Freja always wore sweatpants. Here, skinny jeans

accentuate how slender she is, and a belly-shirt hangs off one angular shoulder, exposing a black bra strap. No jewellery in prison. Here, an ear full of studs, the other bare, and a nose ring, which bothers Morgan. But Freja is young, and this look is how she wants to present herself.

Morgan already bought their herbal teas and biscotti. The drinks have gone cold. Freja insists that's fine, and takes a sip, beaming. But, no – Morgan wants this to be perfect. 'You always talked about having your favourite tea, so it *has* to be hot.'

'Actually, you know what? If you're going back, I might have a cappuccino instead.'

'Really? Not your famous ginger-lemon tea?'

Once they have hot drinks, Morgan opens the bag of biscotti, which Freja expresses much gratitude for, though she takes only one lipstick-preserving bite. 'I need to stay in shape,' she remarks, patting her flat stomach. Freja talks of bureaucracy, the grind of it – it's as if they want to make it harder for ex-prisoners to adjust, she says.

Smiling, Morgan is growing distraught, and diagnoses why. Nothing is mentioned of her children. Nothing. Just filling out forms, waiting in offices.

A man passes with a large shaggy dog, and halts, crouching beside Freja, while the animal looks confusedly at Morgan. 'Is that *you*?' he asks Freja, who leaps to her feet.

'No way!'

They embrace.

'What the hell?!'

'How *are* you?'

The man shows no interest in acknowledging Morgan. Freja is

unsure how to introduce the older woman, so Morgan offers a mild greeting, then looks down to pat the dog, which allows them to resume their chat. This guy wasn't interested in knowing a middle-aged woman anyhow, and their conversation is none of her business. Yet she hears, and cannot help wondering what kind of person would ask so blithely about whether she's going to this club or that later.

Morgan looks at her phone, but is distracted by the invasive sight of her heavy breast and gut, this view downward, and how uncomfortable it was to sleep when pregnant, and neither side felt right. Was that Sofie or Casper? How can she not remember? She's blocking out their conversation, hearing only the fast breaths of the dog.

On the morning after the killings, Niels left for work without noticing that someone had broken in. He didn't check on the kids, and later explained that he hadn't wanted to disturb them. He probably just wanted to get out before anyone was up – to be free for a spell, as if he had nobody but himself, which is how it seemed sometimes.

Morgan enjoyed a late sleep that morning, a rare event, for the two kids normally burst into the master bedroom, arguing over breakfast or turning on the TV, which wasn't allowed before school, or shouting at her to punish some villainy of the other sibling. That morning, glorious silence. Morgan finally called out: 'Guys! Time to get up!'

She heaved herself into flip-flops, and clomped down the hall into their room. The children were on the floor, Sofie holding her younger brother's hand. The little girl must've reached over when they knew what was happening. Freja told them they were about to be killed; that came out in the trial.

Freja's friend is bidding goodbye, and they agree to text later.

'How weird is that? Haven't seen him in *ages*,' she says. 'Yeah, so how are *you* doing?'

'Not too bad. Not too bad.'

'I need to ask you something.' Freja touches her hand, as if to herald something important. 'There was this issue that came up.'

'Go ahead.'

'About you writing to him?'

Morgan is puzzled, thinking of the man with the dog, only to realize whom Freja means.

'Write to *him*?'

'Or he could to you, if that's better to start.'

'Wait, Freja. Sorry, I'm taken aback. You're talking with him?'

'Only recently. Now I'm out, we can. He is *not* like he was. So much was the drugs before, and a lot of mental challenges, lots of which never even got mentioned during our trial.'

'They got into tons of that stuff during the trial.'

'Well, anyway, he's still stuck in there, dealing with that place. Which is kind of like torture.'

'What is like torture?'

'Being in prison. For someone with psychological issues.' She adds, 'And he feels like shit about this.'

Morgan struggles to order her words, her throat hot, hands cold. 'You said before that – sorry, I'm in shock here.'

'No, I get that. But he's like a brother to me. He got me through so much when I was in there.'

'I thought you'd only just got back in touch.'

'We couldn't talk by phone before. Letters were always allowed. And when we got on the phone yesterday, he was *not*

in good shape. I could hear he was suffering. It's not helping to
be locked up.'

'He's not getting out, ever.'

'We don't know that. Who can say?'

Morgan reaches for her tea but takes back her hand, digging the
fingernails into her palm. She stands.

A few people look over.

Morgan cannot identify her own state. Her mind is locked.

Freja stands too, saying, 'I'm so so sorry.' She keeps saying it.

'Stop it.'

People turn away, pretending not to listen.

'It's just . . .' Freya begins.

'Stop talking to me. You're a liar.'

'I want *you* to feel better.'

'Stop talking!'

'Didn't you say that you felt better forgiving?' Freja says. 'We're
in charge of what happens, right? We all get to decide if we're happy
or not, no?'

'Don't touch me!'

But two little hands won't let go of her, squeezing her fingers,
needing her.

DIARY: MAY 2021

I'm tasting insects today.

I proposed this to an American travel magazine. But the senior staffer I once knew there had retired a decade earlier, it turned out, so my emailed proposal meandered among work-from-home journalists, eventually finding a commissioning editor who — desperate for copy after the barren pandemic months — accepted the pitch, somewhat to my alarm. Suddenly, I had to plan an insect-eating expedition in the Cotswolds, obliging me to rent a car (I've not driven in years), and finally buy new glasses.

I'm driving there now, the engine purring down optically sharp country lanes, sun glinting off old puddles. Every few minutes, I pull over to the grassy shoulder, hazard lights blinking, and check Google Maps on my phone. Much as I try to make this little screen comply with the arthritic finger-and-thumb double act, my pinches and pokes either do nothing, or close the app, or spin the route wildly off-track.

A van whooshes past my car, too close, the driver holding down his horn. I turn back into the road (forgetting to stop the hazard lights flashing), and drive onward, lost and late, even though I left home an hour early. At last, I find my destination, turn up a bumpy track, and park in mud.

A cheery Englishwoman — Barbour jacket over heavily pregnant tummy, rubber boots, pink cheeks — greets me at the converted beehives, which her company calls its 'test kitchen'. She's evidently surprised that the journalist is a tall old woman, struggling out of a Nissan Juke.

She offers a steadying arm, then rescinds the offer. 'We probably shouldn't touch,' she says, wrinkling her nose. 'For Covid safety.' Instead, she begins the sales pitch, from growth targets in the edible-insect business, to outlets where their products are sold, to planet-saving corporate principles. 'Sweet or salty?' She opens a packet of Sea Salt 'n' Balsamic Locust Crisps, and readies a Caramel Locust Brownie for after.

'Is everything locust-based?' I ask.

'We're developing some awesome cricket options. But locusts are the go-to. Crazy high protein.'

'These ones taste mostly like the topping flavours,' I say, chewing. 'Not sure I'm getting a strong note of locust.'

'Keep in mind sustainability,' she notes. 'Our ancestors ate insects, by the way. And people even put dried locusts on pizza!'

'In Palaeolithic times?'

'I don't believe they had pizza then, right?'

'No, I was only—'

'Actually, I'm only on the marketing side. I've never even been out here before. I work for a PR firm in London; they're our client.'

'So you drove all the way from London for this too?'

'Actually, off the record, this set-up is mainly for photo ops — pretty much all the products are made at their factory in North London. But they said the journalist wanted something "atmospheric".' She looks around: a farmer's field rising behind the beehives, barbed wire festooned with a puff of sheep's coat, a jagged stone wall up the hill. 'It is lovely here.'

'Peaceful.'

After an hour of chatting as I digest insects, she grows distracted, and apologizes: must rush back to London. She touches her belly meaningfully. 'Doctor's appointment in Peckham.'

I ask when she's due, and allude to my child-bearing, back in Palaeolithic times. She asks which London school my daughter attended, and what it was like, and whether it was hard to get into, and should she put her unborn son's name on a waiting list?

I know some of what's ahead for her. She's right to feel hope.

Driving back along the half-empty motorway, I glance in the rear-view: nobody behind me, only a bespectacled elderly woman peering into the mirror. How did I become her? I remember a green-eyed girl, smiling as I can't anymore. Somewhere, I changed. This person took hold.

Perhaps it was that I'd never matter in any domain, so preferred to retreat to my own. Gorillas do that, quitting the troop once realizing they'll never ascend. But an outcast gorilla doesn't write about other gorillas, imagining apes who aren't present, then presenting her efforts to those she might not respect but whose approval she craves.

Recently, I read about the lottery of your birth year — if it was 1935 in the United States, for example, and you were a middle-class white man, you had every chance of a good life. Born a decade earlier, you'd have survived the Depression, fought in World War Two, perhaps had a son serve in Vietnam, and would approach death just as technology was stealing the known world from you. What, I wonder, will birth in 2021 have meant for that woman's son, when he nears the end of his term?

I picture a future overcrowded, bestormed, flooded — such that a diligent upbringing, designed to prompt kindness and graduate school, leaves him unqualified for the coming hellscape. Though, even long before such fears pervaded society, I myself hesitated to have a child, worrying about what I might propel that possible person into, a world I couldn't affect, where I'd someday abandon them to cope alone.

What's strange about today is how such dread cohabits with such luxury. My insect-eating article will discuss this, how we flip between shamed horror and shameless indulgence. So: a thousand varietals of dark chocolate from exotic locales, but employing ethical cacao farmers, but poor ones, but paid well, but cute packaging, but sugar rush, but great for the immune system, but inclusive, but expensive (or how else to know that it tastes better?).

When I emailed the magazine editor this concept, she hinted that my instincts were off. 'I'd get directly into what it's like to eat insects, and how gross it is,' she wrote back. 'Then maybe a kicker on how caterpillar burritos *could* actually save the planet?'

Now that I'm back home, I email her again to ask my word count. Immediately, she replies: 'Sorry. I didn't have a chance to update you before.' She's moving jobs, and her successor wants to take the magazine in a different direction. They will, of course, pay a kill fee of eighty dollars.

I pass Beck's former bedroom, and look in, as if her six-year-old self might still be there, unable to sleep, as she often was. I'd tell her about my absurd day, driving all the way to the Cotswolds, having mouthfuls of insects, then driving all the way back – and for nothing! She'd laugh and laugh, and I'd be infused with her glee, and she'd leap on her mattress and onto me, though it's really far past her bedtime.

'If you did that today,' she'd ask, delighted, 'what'll you do tomorrow?!'

I'm not sure. I wrote books for a while, but it didn't work out.

'Well, you tried your best,' she'd say. 'Something will happen next.'

~~After decades alive, if you've paid attention, you'll see a few things more clearly.~~

Or

~~The window over the building courtyard is open, and someone down there is shouting about a delivery.~~

Or

Food and drink. Alan wants neither, though his career preys on those appetites.

8

The novelist's former lover

(ALAN ZELIKOV)

FOOD AND DRINK. ALAN wants neither, though his career preys on those appetites. He contributes articles to glossy magazines for Americans who dream of living where he does; he appears on National Public Radio with a whimsical (cynical) 'Letter from Paris'; and he writes non-fiction books that sell moderately: *A Poetical Journey Among the 500 Cheeses of France*; and *Broken Bread: Border Cuisines of Europe from Brittany to Borscht*; and *How Wine Saved the World*, a title foisted on him by a slapdash editor, though the book contains no world-saving, instead dwelling on an irony about the phylloxera outbreak that killed European vines in the 1800s: Old World wines come from new varietals while New World wines come from the old. He's embarrassed by this book, and keeps just one copy, turned backward on a living-room shelf. Otherwise, visitors might ask, 'How *did* wine save the world?' His answer: 'It didn't.'

Some of the above isn't true. Alan Zelikov doesn't write for glossy American magazines or appear on public radio or write books. That stopped. But he still describes himself this way, citing publications that would no longer recognize his name. When he retired, it was due. Yet he's unsure why he ever did. Mentally, he remains lucid. Physically robust too, walking sturdily and far at whatever age he is. (Alan doesn't celebrate birthdays, but is around eighty.) Perfectly bald, he has shed his eyebrows too, a saggy neck narrowing to the collar, like a lightbulb screwed into a sweatshirt.

The real reason for his retirement was the absence of his former editors, who'd died or left, sometimes in the appropriate order. Many of the magazines are themselves defunct. And those periodicals that remain are unrecognizable, led by youngsters who check his social-media footprint, and find nothing. Even before he retired, they had begun ignoring his story pitches, or they magnanimously agreed to consider pieces only for the website, which mysteriously paid a fraction of the print edition, although nobody read the print edition anymore. Those young editors weren't wrong to judge him as past it. Previously, he pursued gastronomic novelty with an ardour to match a chef's. But all his favourite restaurants are, by now, as ratty as ageing movie stars. Experience becomes a weakness: you lack the fizz to engage in another round.

Over the course of his career, he has tasted the rare and the expensive, and struggles to digest either nowadays. His last meal out was – well, he can't recall. In reviewing days, he avoided dining with the talkative because others' opinions affected his palate. His finest eating had nobody on the other side, perhaps an owner-operator in the distance, stealing sidelong glances; maybe a couple feuding in a far booth; or an after-work gathering that roared briefly, then was gone.

Nowadays, he begins each day with an apple, which he preps in slices, wary of cracking that tooth again. His paring knife hits the plastic cutting board with a repeated *clack* that is his son's alarm clock. Alan consumes the apple core and stem last, chased with a small glass of water. Around midday, he dips into a bag of mixed nuts, breaks the shells with a nutcracker, alternating left and right hands to work his grip, flicking away the rubble of almonds and walnuts. Evening is steamed chicken with zucchini, salted to excess. Lastly, a thumb-sized *pâte de fruit* from a boutique on Rue de Turenne, swallowed as if medicinally, the sweet dissolving on his tongue, eyes darting left and right as he determines which flavour: rhubarb or lychee or blood orange.

Besides a daily walk, he fetches groceries, and reads news on his sluggish computer, maddened by the world and responding with a cigarette. He retains that vice but without commitment; sometimes none a day. The purpose of smoking is conversation. His son, Benjamin, takes a break from working too, and they open the apartment windows over Rue Oberkampf, stand side-by-side, a pane apart, inhaling and exhaling in approximate synchrony.

The boy is a sports writer, pumping out thirty online briefs a shift for the news service of a gambling site. His territory is France, meaning Ligue 1, Six Nations rugby, Tour de France, Roland-Garros. He never attends the events themselves. It's quicker and cheaper to watch on TV, which allows him to benefit from his father's input. Alan has a memory for sports, can discuss jockeys who won the Arc, or rivals to Eddy Merckx, or the Yugoslav basketball powerhouse of the 1970s. History pads out a thin article, which is what Benjamin's are: word-scaffolding around an athlete's distracted reply to the post-game interviewer, copied verbatim from television. His writing is earnest in a field that is not. Consequently, his articles are dull. Alan never says this.

Benjamin looks old, a half-eaten doughnut of greying brown hair around a shiny dome. Once a month, Alan gives the kid a haircut. 'Kid' isn't the right word. Frightening to have a son this age. Frightening that Alan's existence is mostly behind him, and lost from view there. The same is true for Benjamin — but that is too rattling to linger over. Alan sits up in bed from his afternoon nap, swivels his legs around and stands, clearing his throat while — from the other side of the door in the living room — the boy clears his throat.

They communicate in English. Benjamin attended French public schools, and keeps friends from those days, corresponding via online messaging. He has no romantic life, and probably never did. Even before the pandemic, they lived a monkish existence in this two-bedroom apartment, within a nineteenth-century building that looks grand from afar, grimy from near, with an exhausted *bar à Cocktails* and a Turkish kebab shop on the street level. They prefer life up here in high-ceilinged rooms that — owing to the shape of the building — narrow into a wedge as one proceeds through the property, ending at a triangular bathroom with specialized bidet, toilet and walk-in bathtub. Neither enters the other's bedroom; they meet in the living room, where Benjamin works because of the TV. Never do they bicker. The closest is misapprehension, as in, 'Oh, I thought you'd said I should have it.'

'Sorry if I wasn't clear. Go ahead.'

'We can share.'

When the boy was around five, he told Alan: 'We do anything together. We're the best of friends.'

ALAN HAS NEVER DELVED into his son's private life, which once took place in school, then via a landline in his room, now the internet. Benjamin applies this same respectful incuriosity to his father. They've never discussed Alan's female friends, not even the boy's mother, a Dutch novelist, Dora Frenhofer, who left here too early to lurk in her child's memory.

Sometimes, Alan wonders what his son contains, plenty or little. The younger man never fights anything, not if the conditions of his job worsen, not if the assignments become preposterous. Where did he develop that? Alan's flaw is the opposite, to shoulder into conflict, something he inherited from his father, a Jewish socialist who wanted to farm without understanding farming, and moved the family constantly, impoverishing them from one American state to another. When Alan recalls childhood lodgings, it's with his three big sisters, who cannot remind him of details, each dead, first the middle, then the younger, lastly the eldest. Alan sees rooms that he struggled to fall asleep in, his father cursing downstairs, perhaps because he'd dropped the can opener, and its disobedience typified the disobedience of the world, and the man's indignation grew hotter, leaping up the staircase, till Alan pushed off his blanket, and came down, preferring flames to the sound of fire. He sees his mother at the kitchen table, smoking, asking why he's up still, and he didn't wake his sisters, did he? (All three at the top of the stairs, having egged him into going down.)

While Alan was at college, his father died of lifelong disappointment. His mother lived years more, well into her son's Paris residence, his sisters caring for her fading face. Nobody reproached him for failing to return. They knew what Alan contended with, raising his son alone. Alan tries not to think of his mother because the sorrow is too sharp, so she is erased, except when he's caught out – for example, watching classic American movies with French subtitles, and Benjamin poses questions of his father as if awaiting search results: 'What *is* a Manhattan cocktail?'

Alan will crack an almond shell, place the result beside his son, who takes it. 'My mother used to drink them.'

Looking back, Alan considers his career as an accomplishment without value. He cured no polio, built no town. He pointed the rich to overpriced food and drink. But who is satisfied at eighty with what lured them at twenty?

Some people of his age calculate how many years they have left, and make plans, and acknowledge their predicted number, as in, 'I don't expect I'll be here more than a decade!' (granting themselves a couple more years than the average lifespan). Others avoid knowing. Alan is that way. In his opinion, a man is not to be frightened in sight of others, least of all his children.

Fetching groceries that afternoon, he bickers with the woman selling roast chickens from a metal skewer, which rotates behind spattered glass. Neither is sure if the other is insolent, she calling him '*monsieur*' emphatically, he responding with an abundance of '*madame*'. When leaving, he swears under his breath, on the false assumption that American profanity remains little-understood in this country, as when he arrived half a century before. Recently, he was buying milk at the Monop', and a small child on a bike (yes, biking around a mini-market) cycled into his shin, and Alan gave a muffled yowl, exclaiming through his mask 'Little fuck!' only for the little fuck's mother to speed-walk over, and berate him in broken English. On such occasions, Alan finds it odd to still live in Paris.

He carries groceries past the courtyard mailboxes to their building, up the stairs, raising and lowering the bags as he climbs, to exercise his arms. In the living room, he's breathless, looking at Eurosport on the muted television: the pole vault.

'I have a sister,' Benjamin says.

'How?'

'She messaged me from America. She's coming to Paris.' The boy looks up from his laptop, fleetingly, then back at the screen.

'Coming here? What for?'

'For me.'

FROM A DISTANCE ACROSS Place Léon-Blum, Alan identifies her. Benjamin's half-sister, Beck Frenhofer, looks to be nearing forty, darker skinned than her mother, bulkier too, with short spiked hair, a men's suit jacket, red dress shirt, and green brogues. To Alan this combination of styles proclaims that she frequents the arts, supports progressive politics, and is open to spinsterhood. A cascade of thoughts: some people broadcast their neuroses, volunteering the stereotypes they'd like to be saddled with; how he's glad to choose clothing only by neatness and what regulates body temperature; how it'd be if people went around nude; that genitals are unaesthetic and it's strange they captivate anyone; how lust and love are genetic programming, nothing more.

Her mother's eyes.

'Can you walk?' he asks.

'Since I was a baby.' But she hastens to keep his pace. 'So. You're the vetting process?'

'Would you be able to go faster? This is my daily exercise.'

'By the way, am I supposed to keep the mask on outside?'

'Depends on your appetite for risk.'

'Purely for my information, should I expect to meet my brother soon?'

'I'll leave you on the Left Bank. That's where you're staying, correct?'

'He's there?'

'It's where you're staying, I understood.'

His daily constitutional is at least two hours, so Alan's plan is to lead her to the Jardin du Luxembourg, do a lap around the perimeter fence, then back here to the *mairie*. This grants him opportunities for an abrupt goodbye if she's awful. He doesn't dislike the young, but tires of their predictability. Above all, he is unsure what she's been told about his son and Dora.

No talking all the way to the park, except when Alan projects his arm before her like a railway barrier, protecting Beck from a turning taxi. 'I saved your life.'

'I'll owe you forever.'

As they walk, she's silent but for audible mouth-breathing – badly out of shape. He diverts them to a sidestreet shop to buy oranges. Beck removes the N95 mask, under which her face is dripping sweat – that suit jacket was a mistake, and her red shirt is untucked now, tails crumpled. She must've dressed to meet her brother.

'I never know how to buy oranges.'

'It's not hard,' he says. 'Or it *should* be hard: don't buy a soft orange.'

'Not like peaches.'

He selects one on her behalf, and they sit on metal chairs in the park. As they peel, their fingernails clog with white pith, a mizzle of citrus, the distant sound of traffic over the iron railings. He bought a bottle of water, and presents it unopened. She glugs, and gasps.

'Yours to keep,' he says. 'I'm fine.' He glances at his watch, calculating how much longer the home aide will be there – one of a public-health team that helps Benjamin bathe and with other sundry tasks. Beck mentions feeling connected to her brother, though they've never met, that she always felt someone missing in her life, and wonders if he does.

'You are in touch with him,' Alan responds. 'You can ask.'

'But what's your opinion?'

'That he can speak for himself. And Dora? She ever talk of us?'

'Only in passing. You were this sophisticated American bachelor in Paris.'

'Sophisticated.'

'Seems strange to think of you two together.'

'Every couple is strange once they're not a couple. Sometimes when they are.'

'I searched online for your last name and "Paris", and found Benjamin's Facebook profile. I figured you guys were related, and it had his birthdate. I calculated he'd been born while my mom was here in Paris and with you. She never mentioned anything like that; always just you as this bachelor. I figured maybe you had a wife, and Dora was the other woman.'

'Did you put all that to Dora?'

'I never get answers out of her. I messaged Benjamin, just to ask about you actually. He said a few things. I pieced it together.'

'So you asked Dora then?'

'She never even told me I *had* a half-brother – why would I tell her I'm going to meet him? It's nothing to do with her.'

'Did you talk to Benjamin about why his mother left?'

'Why? Does he not know?'

'For someone in comedy, you don't say much that's funny.'

'I don't tell jokes. I just write them.'

'If you promise not to tell me jokes, I promise not to laugh.'

She smiles. Against his will, he does too, then finds a way to part company.

Back home, Benjamin is clean and combed.

'She cut your hair?' Alan asks.

'It was Marc – the tall one from Côte d'Ivoire. He forgot to do my neck.'

Alan fetches the electric clippers, stands behind his son, and buzzes fuzzy hairs off his nape.

'Should I message my sister to come over tomorrow?' Benjamin asks. 'I said I'd be in touch.'

'Let me give it some thought.'

'Sleep on it.'

'That's what I thought.'

The following day, Alan fails to mention her. So does Benjamin.

A second day passes. On the third, Alan finds a letter in their mailbox in the communal courtyard. She'd like to chat about something he mentioned, and is going to be in the Jardin du Luxembourg that afternoon – she has returned there daily since he introduced her to it. Same place, about 2 p.m.?

HE CAN'T BANISH THIS woman from Paris. Nor can he stop her from knowing Benjamin. But he needs to understand her motives.

Beck sees Alan approaching, and removes absurdly large headphones. She saved a metal chair for him. He remains standing, and she shades her eyes, looking up. They're walking again.

'I'd like to apologize to your son,' she says. 'I feel it's something to say in person. On behalf of her.'

Alan is irritated. He always tells Benjamin the truth, with one exception. He said that the boy's mother turned against Paris, and that he, Alan, had been impossible to get along with, so she left. The story felt incomplete – that his mother had just gone, never once contacting her son. But which explanations from childhood add up?

The ostensible reason for a second meeting with Beck, as cited in her letter to Alan, was that she wanted advice on expat life in Paris. For now, she's in a short-term place in the 5th arrondissement that's wildly pricey. But she is unsure how to decipher rental ads in French, let alone job postings. Is she legally allowed to work here?

'No such job exists here, writing jokes in English.'

'I could do other things. Though I'm not qualified for anything else. But hey,' she says, 'I actually flew out here because I met a Parisian woman online, and came to surprise her.'

'Why not ask *her* for tips?'

'This is where it gets awkward. I was on this dating app before the vaccines, when California was in lockdown. Basically, I wanted to be anywhere else than LA, so I put my location as Paris, to see what'd happen. The algorithm matched me to Karine, and we started messaging. She wanted to improve her English, and kept telling me that – since we were both in Paris – we could meet up outside. I managed to delay for months.'

'Does she know you don't live here?'

'I fessed up yesterday. Didn't go great. But maybe I *will* live here, right?'

'My son thinks you came to meet him.'

'In part. Also for Karine. She kept saying, "Why you would come ear?" – that's supposed to be a French accent.'

'I realize. They're endemic.'

'She's only willing to see me again, she said, if I actually become the profile she clicked on. Meaning living here, a job, speaking at least basic French. She's not looking for someone needy.'

'Isn't needy what dating websites are for?'

'Maybe she was more, like, "Why you would come *ear*?" She'd actually prefer to live in California. She's into the idea of a big dog, like I used to have, and the beach outside your door, which I never even go to myself.'

'Fly her there, and you're both happy.'

'We only just met. And I haven't seen my brother.'

They cross Pont Neuf, north toward Les Grands Boulevards, Alan giving perfunctory notes on Haussmann's renovation of Paris. They turn toward Marché Bastille, where he does his grocery shopping.

Vendors stopped offering samples because of Covid, but they've known Alan for years, and make exceptions when it's quiet. He takes an extra cube of melon for her, slapping it roughly in Beck's palm, knowing how ripe it is but betraying no appreciation in order to haggle down the price, handing over euros and tipping the man all his change. He also picks up a Crottin de Chavignol, plus a *ficelle*, and a plastic-handled steak knife. Away from the flow of shoppers, he saws the bread. When the nub falls, he lurches for it, his limbs slower than expected, arthritic hand fumbling. The bread lands on the pavement.

'Should we find somewhere to sit?' she asks.

'You digest better standing.'

'Is that true?'

'No. There just aren't any seats.' He finds a statue against whose rail to lean, under a revolutionary less pertinent today than the pigeons on his tricorne. Alan chews, swallows, and his hairless eyebrows rise expectantly. 'Opinion?'

She's distracted, looking around, a visual inhalation, her eyes saying, *After so long indoors, I'm actually in Paris, and nobody knows I'm not from here.* 'Creamy?' she answers.

'Well, yes. It's cheese.'

She sputters a laugh, and he can't help chuckling, so turns away, ready to move on. Alan has the sensation – not felt in years – that this is a friendship, her expression shifting when he speaks, he amused by her snarks, and intrigued by what she says of California nowadays, where he himself spent a year when small, albeit in farmland. She isn't sure of her route back, so he extends their walk, ending before her fourth-floor walk-up by the Panthéon. He reads aloud a blackboard on the wall of Café de la Nouvelle Mairie, listing a dozen wines.

'You have better vision than I do,' she comments.

He doesn't mention his cataract surgery – it's untoward, he thinks, to speak of medical procedures. Also, he notes a second reason: he doesn't want to appear old to her. Restaurants – closed until recently by virus restrictions – are limited to half-capacity. They're lucky to find a table. He orders a glass of Ajaccio white for himself. The waiter asks for Beck's order, and she despairs at replying in French.

'Take a sip,' Alan says, handing her his glass. 'Then decide.'

'Is that Covid-safe?'

'Come on – try.' He's domineering, as if to assert that there's nothing amicable about this. She tastes, approves. 'The glass is yours now,' he says, and calls for a carafe. Bread too. The oysters that she nervously slurps are the first of her life – not an intrepid eater. He tells her to chew. 'Do it the mercy. It's alive.'

'Are you serious right now?'

'The taste comes when you chew. Otherwise, it's just seawater.'

Her mother was Alan's eating partner too, an assertive tall young Dutchwoman with large ears who'd heard that this American food writer took female company when reviewing. She wanted finer dining than she could afford, so invited herself along. Dora ate half of each dish, and he did the same, then they exchanged. Alan wasn't curious for her opinion – another's presence just helped him order more dishes, granting a broader sense of the menu. So she never talked at their meals, shaking his hand beforehand, and reading a paperback between courses. Once, he and Dora split a platter of

Gillardeau oysters and, for a change, she spoke: 'The life of a man is of no greater importance to the universe than that of an oyster.'

Alan was jotting a tasting note, and reached for another shell, emptying it nude into his mouth: fishing nets and barnacles. 'Who said that?'

'Me or David Hume,' she replied. '"The life of a man is of no greater importance to the universe than that of an oyster." Which seems an argument for cannibalism.'

He leaned back.

'If man is no more than an oyster, and we eat oysters,' she went on, 'why not eat a man?'

He deposited his shell on the ice chips, wiped his mouth with a thick-cotton napkin. He invited her elsewhere, resulting in his apartment, which was that of an established man nearing thirty. Everything followed, twisting through the decades until this stout American woman before him, who is so unlike that tall Dutchwoman, except the eyes.

Alan orders Beck the pistachio duck terrine next. He tries it first — a habit from professional days.

'Making sure the food's dead this time?' she asks.

Alan swipes another lump of terrine onto baguette, exhaling hard through his nostrils as he passes it to her, clutched by an unexpected pleasure: a person nearby, this human, here. He didn't think he needed them anymore.

Wine saturates their exchange with permission. She offers quips about her romantic flops, how she's ditching a solid career as a comedy writer to get jilted by a woman who doesn't know they're supposed to be in love; how she's tempted to bribe her prospective girlfriend into bed with the promise of a dog. A few times, she almost makes Alan laugh; he raises his brow, looks down at the food.

Alan jerks the conversation elsewhere, telling of composers and radicals and dipsomaniacs who once inhabited this neighbourhood. There's an unwanted loudness to Alan's delivery, for he misjudges volume in crowds. Remembering this, he sits back – till she comments, whereupon he leans forward to reply, and she says something, and he has an answer. For years, he quenched himself with trips outside Paris when researching a new book, visiting exquisite purveyors, driven around by them, engaging in friendship-flings for a day or two with others who eroticized taste, and whom he recollected as you do a favourite restaurant from vacation – at your peril would you visit again. But 'again' is what he's thinking, that he should re-read the books he mentions to Beck, re-try delicacies cited, listen again to the singer he cannot believe she's never heard of.

Beck jars him with insights into his former lover since Dora left, telling of her mother in London, how she has wilted over the years, gradually shedding all companions. She did this in pursuit of her writing – yet isolation only made her novels barren.

'I never hear of her books anymore; I don't see reviews,' he says.

'She goes from one tiny press to another, costing them all money. Like someone running out on the check.'

'That's unkind.'

'That was the point.'

BENJAMIN LONGS TO MEET his sister, but Alan remains vague. Another letter arrives from her with no postage stamp – Beck must've taken to heart his lament about emails and messaging, so left this envelope by hand in their courtyard mailbox. In the letter, she thanks Alan for the drink the other afternoon, though not for the live oyster, which haunts her dreams. She enjoyed his book on wine saving the world – found a copy at Shakespeare & Company. She listened to Edith Piaf too, and he was right.

Alan drops off his reply at her address but not until days have passed, to avoid seeming eager. On the way there, he exerts himself to witness Paris as she might, the surroundings projected against a screen as in old-movie backdrops, Citroëns streaking through the rain.

More hand-delivered letters pass between them, connecting his days as they've not been connected in some time. He's distracted by thoughts of Beck. It's not lust, just the intoxication from a stranger attending to his opinions, and isn't this what he always sought, why anyone writes anything? Benjamin remarks that, since his sister arrived, she hasn't text-messaged once.

Alan doesn't want them to. At first, this was because he feared that she'd hurt Benjamin, that she knew enough of their mother to say something wounding. But that reasoning has passed. Alan is disturbed by his current motive: their meeting would ruin something of *his*. Because of Benjamin's lack of spark? Or because Alan becomes elderly if presenting a son who is himself old?

'Do we look alike?' Benjamin asks.

'She's dark-skinned. I assume her dad was. Heavy-set too. The same eyes as your mother.'

'What are those like?'

'Green.'

'You're going to bed already?'

'Finish what you were saying, son. No rush.'

'No, just that I'd be curious to see them.'

'See what?'

'Eyes like my mother's.'

Benjamin is always in the living room lately, wanting proximity. He never turns in first. More than before, Alan is away, walking fast as if to stamp on what perturbs him, doubts skittering like spiders from pavement cracks.

'I wonder what I'd tell her if we end up meeting,' Benjamin remarks. 'What do you think I'd say?'

ALAN ROASTS A *poulet de Bresse*, butter and garlic and thyme and lemon zest pushed under the skin, in the oven for ninety minutes, plus Charlotte potatoes in goose fat, and purple-sprouting broccoli. On meeting her brother, Beck asks if they should hug, causing Benjamin to laugh nervously, blush. She narrates aloud her own embarrassment as it happens, and ends up seated in an armchair, with Benjamin on the sofa. They're too far apart for easy conversation, each leaning forward and back, like strangers sharing hummus.

Alan busies himself in the kitchen, but there's little to do besides watch the closed oven, its fan whirring. The conversation in the other room falters, gaps that almost prompt Alan to intervene. He mumbles to himself, to drown them out, then says, 'Five minutes!' Instantly, they join him. When he helps Benjamin into his chair, Beck stands to assist, not sure if it's an intrusion. 'Best if you just sit,' Alan tells her.

The siblings are less tense around Alan, nervous only when he steps away to carve and plate, during which they keep addressing his back. He explains the food and wine, ignoring Beck's excessive praise. Alan wants approval as much as anyone, but he never acquired the grace to accept it. So he shifts to the news, the Taliban retaking Afghanistan, the wildfires in Canada. When Alan talks, they watch. When he stops, they eat.

She knows nothing of sports, and admits this apologetically. To Alan's surprise, Benjamin says he isn't crazy about sports himself, but got into them somehow. 'I used to figure it was envy.'

Alan digs his toes into his insoles.

'Why envy?' she says.

'Just because I couldn't.'

'Oh, right. Sorry. Stupid question.'

Benjamin asks about her French classes, offering tutoring, and she accepts eagerly. Alan knows all the reports from her life – the LA stand-up circuit, her floundering affair with Karine, that overpriced Left Bank apartment. They're versions of answers she already gave him, but lacking the humour. She's unnatural because he is present.

Alan never told Beck not to speak about her mother. But she appears fearful to raise the subject. Benjamin equally so.

'One thing I was going to mention,' Beck says, slowing down, as if looking for a way out of this sentence. 'Actually I wanted to actually to actually mention something. I said to your dad before. To Alan. I said I felt that . . . I don't know.' Rushing: 'Not sure if I'm the one – if *I* should be saying this, Benjamin. If you don't want to discuss it, that's totally fine. Obviously, whatever works. I wasn't sure. Whether to message it. But a message felt wrong. I thought there are things you should say in person. To the person.'

Benjamin glances at his father, then back at his food, knife inadvertently scraping the plate, which causes Beck to close one eye.

Alan sips the Côtes-du-Rhône, stifling anger, for his son is upset. This is why he didn't want her here. Now, Benjamin has a sense of something. The boy avoids further sight of his father, or of their guest, and focuses on the chicken. Alan mentions dessert.

'Dad never eats sweet things. Just these little French jelly candies.' The boy is pleased to possess an insight into his father, and he mentions Alan's nutcracker too, and how he's always working on his grip and lifting groceries to keep up his strength so he can help me, Benjamin explains.

The boy could've died. People with his condition did. They said he'd not survive past his teens. But medicine improved, and his luck held, and Benjamin is middle-aged, though he has endured physical pain so long that he looks sixty. Alan never dwelled on his son's health, in order that the boy become resilient. In private, Alan – after indelible events, his son's agony following yet another operation, his pleas not to have another, though he'd need it – when this happened and Benjamin was still young, Alan went into his room and stuffed a balled-up T-shirt in his mouth. He never allowed grief to escape his bedroom. In the living room, you got on with matters. Honesty, he figured, was worth more than a wheelchair over time. So Alan was always truthful – except about why Benjamin's mother never contacted him: she hadn't wanted their son to exist.

The evening improves, for Beck tells appalling tales of Hollywood featuring the cellphone-throwing beasts who thrive in entertainment.

Benjamin answers her questions on French culture, always saying 'Yes, yes!' when Beck gives an opinion, all of which are misinformed. It's clear to Alan that she feels nothing of the connection with her brother that she feels with him.

He has built a fortress around the boy; Alan cannot watch more suffering. Dora never tried to know Benjamin, and his sister bore no blame. But she links to that past. She pulls him away from here.

The following day, Alan offers his son a passing remark: 'Went fairly well, no?'

'It was my best event pretty much. For as long as I can remember.'

Alan takes out a cigarette, lights one for his son. They open adjacent windows, and look out. Benjamin and Beck have plans to meet again, to work on a project, which Benjamin does not explain further. She wants help with her French too.

A WHITE FLUORESCENT LIGHT blinks above the courtyard mailboxes. You bump into neighbours there, squinting side-by-side at flickering letters. Alan finds one in her handwriting, and replaces it unopened.

'Have you heard from her?' Alan asks his son, unloading groceries. 'Has she texted you?'

'She's super busy, I'm guessing. And probably stuff with that woman she's dating.'

'Karine.'

'Silence is good news on that front, I'm hoping.'

Benjamin, who leaves the apartment only for medical appointments, cannot reach their mailbox in the courtyard. He never sees the letter to him, which Alan leaves unopened, allowing days of advertising fliers to pile atop. A second letter lands there, again unmentioned. 'Weren't you going to help with her French?'

'I'm not sure that'll come together,' Benjamin says, the television selling Gillette, a muscled athlete caressing his cheeks. 'It was nice,' Benjamin recalls, 'that evening.'

'It was.'

'Good to meet her.'

'Yes.'

'To have met her.'

A week later, a neighbour in housecoat scolds Alan for leaving his mailbox so full that fliers fall into the passage, and someone could trip. He removes everything, including the unopened letters from Beck. He dangles these over the recycling bin, pausing – then lets them drop. The most recent letter lands face-up. Alan retrieves it, and climbs to their floor, pausing before the front door to catch his breath. Cowbells from the Tour de France rattle on the other side.

'For you from Beck,' he says, as a yellow shirt pedals across the television, pursued by cameramen on motorcycles. 'Hand-delivered.'

'She didn't want to come in?'

'I didn't see her. It was in our mailbox.'

Benjamin hesitates to open it. 'I'm afraid.'

'Why afraid?'

'Could you look it over, Dad? And see what you think?'

'It's not to me.'

'It won't be anything I mind you seeing.' Benjamin returns to his laptop, pretending to work.

Alan opens the envelope. It's an apology. Her foray to Paris didn't work. The woman she was courting rejected her, and living here without the language or a job wasn't going to work. But it'd be good to say bye before returning to LA. She gives her date of departure, which was two days ago. Why didn't she text-message Benjamin before leaving? Presumably, she wasn't that desperate to see the boy again, Alan thinks.

'I'm sorry she didn't come up and knock,' Benjamin says. 'I would've been here.'

'She probably didn't want to disturb us.'

'I bet that's right. She wouldn't have wanted to.'

'No.'

'It was interesting. To meet her. Didn't you think, Dad?'

'I did.'

'I've got a sister.'

AT THE UNMARKED BORDER before sleep, Alan wavers, his bedroom window open, thin green curtains billowing. He turns and turns, overhot, the sheet twisted into a rope. From the adjacent room, Benjamin coughs, possibly in his sleep, possibly on his laptop.

When Dora was pregnant, they feared the child's condition meant lifelong care. She grew enraged at Alan, who didn't seem to grasp that *she* would end up looking after their child, and what this would mean, and forever. Not forever, Alan said.

'Years. Years!'

'Don't take any role then.'

'What's that supposed to mean?'

'Leave the child here. I'll take care of it.'

'Oh, please! Don't insult me.'

Doctors and teachers were always asking Benjamin where his mother was. Alan dismissed the matter, and his son learned to do the same. Alan's gruffness never hurt the boy – or he hopes it never did.

'We do anything together,' the five-year-old said, looking at his father. 'We're the best of friends.'

After decades alive, if you've paid attention, you see a few things more clearly: the pendulum of politics and culture; that each person has, at best, one chance at any stage of life. You raise your children with those insights, showing them how to ingratiate themselves with superiors, how to hold a fork. You teach *what* to want as much as how. But experience only lights the path behind you. It fails to show if that path was itself a mistake, or if your time – the near-glory and the resentments, the chosen studies and chosen ignorance – if it amounted to a life squandered.

Beck was the end of something. Something just finished for Alan: camaraderie – far less common over his life than he'd expected when a boy, when surrounded by siblings, with new kids in every place his family moved to, shouting and running and tripping and fighting and catching up. As you walk deeper into the woods, the people vanish, more elusive than deer.

Alan looks at his wall. Too few hours of wakefulness left. By statistics, about seven years. You can't say precisely. But you can say.

Benjamin is on the other side of this wall. After his father is gone, the boy will be there still.

DIARY: SEPTEMBER 2021

I'm remembering something from years ago. 'Dora,' my stepmother said, phoning from the Netherlands, 'I don't know how to explain it.'

She'd taken my father to the hospital with a gut problem. The doctors suspected an infection, and wanted to admit him for tests. He rebuffed this, yet was too ill to return home. So he sat on the side of a hospital bed, refusing to swing his legs up, growing more upset, more deranged. Finally, the nurses ordered my stepmother to leave while they sedated him. The next morning, she returned. 'He's not the same,' she told me.

The doctors confirmed that my father — despite recovering from delirium, and under treatment for an infection — was not likely to regain his faculties. How was this possible? Yes, he was into his seventies. But he'd seemed cogent weeks earlier. I couldn't query my father himself, for he refused to get on the phone. So I travelled there.

In the hospital hallway, I hesitated, taking a fortifying breath — then entered his room: a stubbly, emaciated old man. He knew me. Much else escaped him.

I kept our conversation light and fleet, as if outrunning my distress — this dignified medical man, who'd always sought to appear invulnerable (though he hadn't convinced me of that in years), and who detested embarrassment — he couldn't conceal anything anymore. Even the curtain over his door was beyond his control.

I drew it closed as I left, my chest imprinted where I'd given him a goodbye hug, unsure where to place my arms, embracing the hospital bed as much as the flat body within. Days later, orderlies delivered him home on a gurney, and helped him into his preferred armchair, where he'd read the newspaper each weekend of my childhood. Tremulously, he drank a coffee, the cup tinkling in its saucer. He was home, as he'd wanted to be, yet absent.

Later, community health workers arrived, and hoisted him onto his bed. When turned, he cried out because strangers pushed and prodded. His temporary room was on the ground floor beside the kitchen. He wouldn't leave his bed anymore, nor take food. How wretched my stepmother and I felt, eating meals with my father starving away, three steps across the hall. So we gathered around his bed with dishes to tempt him. A morsel of trout and a baby potato proved too abundant for him. 'But,' he said, his wrinkly brow furrowing further, 'is someone passing around beer?'

I rushed to the kitchen for a straw. He took one sip from the Heineken bottle, his gaunt cheeks caving, eyelids crinkling closed. After three long seconds, his eyes opened, with a sheen of pleasure unseen in a long time.

I read aloud from an old volume of Chekhov stories he once loved. I was unsure how much he understood, so tried to animate the dialogue, glancing at him as I did the voices, heartened whenever his jaw twitched in amusement. Long before any story ended, he was asleep. Soon, a half-page became his limit. Later, a paragraph.

The community health workers insisted that he turn over, but he feared falling from the bed. 'What are you doing?!' he shouted, bewildered. They called for my help. My father's dry fingers squeezed my hand, his thin arm trembling. To distract him, I spoke of the latest tales from Chekhov, my gaze locked on his.

For some reason, I recall his expression now, looking out my attic-office window over other night-time London houses, their floating rectangles of windowlight, behind which strangers eat, smile at televisions, slouch toward the stairs.

I'm guilty to describe what I have of my father, those private scenes. What do you owe those who aren't anywhere anymore, except in you?

I draw the curtains shut to obscure myself from view. I'm not what I'd hoped. But I wrote books, and thrived when doing so.

I imagine my daughter after I'm gone, leafing through what I put down on those pages. Or maybe she'll avoid my books because they're painful, and she prefers not to think vividly of me, for I'm unavailable but might be in my novels. Isn't that why I wrote them?

If my writing hurts her, I don't want her to read anything I did, only to keep copies on her shelves (if shelves are still for books in the future). My volumes could stand in the background when she's dozy from too much consumption; or joking with a partner; or looking at a child's plump hand, her own pointing at letters on a page.

The last conversation I had with my father, he spoke with awe that I'd come back to see him. He declared that, once better, he'd return to his desk. He'd write it all down.

~~Dora is travelling abroad.~~

Or

On the window beside Dora's seat on the bus, a wasp climbs up, climbs down, seeking escape — an organism like any machine, with its algorithms of if/then.

Or

She's travelling by bus, a black duffel bag between her feet. She needs little today: an apple, the sandwich wrapped in foil, a bottle of water. For company, she dropped in a tattered copy of Chekhov short stories.

9

The novelist

(DORA FRENHOFER)

SHE'S TRAVELLING BY BUS, a black duffel bag between her feet. She needs little today: an apple, the sandwich wrapped in foil, a bottle of water. For company, she dropped in a tattered copy of Chekhov short stories.

Before leaving London, Dora spoke to a lawyer, designating him the executor of her will, and stating her intentions for any last objects. She donated her remaining clothing to a charity shop on the high road, gave her TV to the cleaning team that emptied her cellar, and submerged her laptop in water, then threw it away with the weekly rubbish.

At dawn this morning, she stripped her bed — just a mattress on a boxspring now — and showered for the last time. Dora was pleased to find an empty shampoo bottle: she'd timed this well. She lathered a soap bar against her head, scrubbing roughly, shorn white hair prickling her fingers. Towelling off, she looked down at sagging contours: me, she thought, and her insides plunged, as when watching someone lean over a cliff's edge. She didn't respect the fear; it only interested her.

Across the bus aisle, a masked couple is speaking loudly in French – they're sharing earbuds, a ticking beat audible. A boy sits with a shopping bag full of old shoes. An Eastern European woman – mask under her chin – scrolls her cracked-screen smartphone, rubs her eyes. All these people will end, their calendar events vanishing, along with toiletries around the basin and socks in drawers, at a date to be defined. Dora's date is today.

When organizing this, she expected they'd have someone at the location to explain how it worked. But for legal reasons, nobody will attend. She expected a psychological evaluation beforehand. That never came either.

You know your own personality, she thinks, in the way that sonar knows distance, by bouncing it off what's around. According to others' reactions, your confidence shrivels or becomes bloated. Over time, this is who you consider yourself to be. Rarely, you stumble into yourself unmediated, brushing your teeth perhaps, or travelling alone.

She was in London this morning, in a black cab headed for St Pancras, not a word exchanged with the taxi driver, even when paying. She found her assigned seat on the Eurostar, which dipped for twenty dark minutes under the sea, surfacing in sunny France, then rolling across an invisible border into Belgium. At a bustling station there, she passed bakery stalls whose iced cinnamon curlicues looked like craft, while young voices commiserated with phones, and rushed to meetings with other phones. A different train took her from the city to a town, then to a smaller town, where Dora entered this bus, from which she now descends, holding to the rail, wondering if her knee will give out and she'll tumble to the pavement. A physiotherapist recommended a knee brace that sits in a cupboard at home; a doctor offered steroid injections and discussed surgical options. She limited herself to leg exercises, puffing on the carpet at home. Something must've helped: her shoes touch down safely on the pavement, paired and pointing like ducks. She holds still as a wave of pain rises from her knee, crests, withdraws.

She has no luggage in the belly of the bus, and its front doors hiss shut behind her. The exhaust pipe coughs hotly. The bus pulls away. Before her are outlet stores fronted by parking lots, not a single human.

She consults the printout of directions, and walks past a long window of sofas, each waiting to be adopted and stained. A golf store next. Dora has never tried that activity, so importantly unimportant. Golf will exist onward, and she'll never have known of it. Anything she hasn't done, she will not.

She finds the correct street, lined with new-build apartments, the kind that estate agents call 'town houses' and residents call 'small'. There's a person, the first since the bus: an old man in a navy tracksuit, plastic tubes from his nostrils to an oxygen cylinder on two wheels. He's muttering, looking around.

Dora adjusts her glasses, and checks the house numbers, seeking her destination. That man is waiting before her door. She didn't expect irritation today – she expected to speak to nobody, and has managed all the way here. Dora has no space for an old man, not for a long-winded complaint, nor to help him find keys or a daughter who has keys.

'Excuse me,' she says, in the local language. 'I need to get in there.'

'What?' he replies in English. 'I don't understand.'

From spite, she persists in the wrong language: 'Come on! You're in the way!'

He prattles about someone called Scott and a lockbox, as if his worries are her worries, that she arrived for his sake, and if he just sticks with English, she'll learn it sooner or later. In short, that *he* is the subject of this story. He is wrong.

'Fuming, to tell the truth,' he says. 'Me, sat here, and Scott driving off like that. Nobody said I'd need a password or – what's it called? – a code thing.'

'I'm not here to help you.'

'You speak English?'

'Evidently, yes. But I need to get past. I'm going in there.' Her stiff hands unfold the printout, and she finds an access number for the lockbox, and prods its buttons. A flap falls, and a key lands in her palm. She opens the front door: the plastic smell of air-freshener. The old man staggers past her, entering first, as if she worked here.

'Excuse me, but *I* arranged to be here,' she says. 'I have an appointment. I can show you the email.'

He's resting against his oxygen canister, wheezing. 'Don't know what your email says,' he responds. 'But I paid good money to be here.'

'You have paperwork proving that?'

'Scott's got it.'

'Should I know who this Scott is?'

'My son-in-law. He drove me all the way over here. He'll be back in a minute.'

'Either way, *I* have the appointment. I'm sorry, but you need to leave.'

He's stammering about a car now. She watches this half-broken machine, whose switch she inadvertently flipped.

Dora has taken pains in her life to avoid arguments with foolish men. Now, her last day, and this. She'll lead him back outside. But then? Proceed to the plan, yet with a doddering man at the front door? 'I'll call the emergency number, and they can explain it to you. Then you need to leave.'

They're in the lounge area of the apartment, with framed doilies on the wall and a boxy old television. The bookshelf contains a Bible and a pink-spined romance. In the wheelchair-accessible toilet, a hanging plant is living out its days, while the 'Peace Room' contains a leatherette couch from the superstore down the road. 'You sit there while I call,' she tells him.

A vase of orange tulips in cloudy water stands on the kitchenette table, with a letter stuck underneath. It welcomes her, including forms to sign, instructions on which order to take the drugs, and whom to call if there's a problem. 'You see,' she shouts toward the Peace Room, holding up the letter. 'This has *my* name on it.' She fails to mention that the three boxes of pharmaceuticals are all stickered with 'Mr Frank H. Ward', presumably him. She needs to prepare for this phone call. *He* must return another day, not she.

A woman answers the emergency number, caught in mid-conversation with a child or a dog: 'No, Karl! Stop eating that!' The woman offers to call back when she gets a moment, but Dora demands attention now. Both she and this old man travelled from overseas – they need this resolved immediately.

'The British person is who we scheduled.'

Dora explains that, though she speaks the local language, she too travelled here from Britain.

'Maybe that explains the mix-up,' the woman says. 'But I don't have access to Birgit's computer.'

'Birgit? I dealt with Gisela.'

'Gisela's on leave. You need Birgit.'

'Put her on the phone then.'

'I'm talking from my house.'

'So where's Birgit?'

'This is just the emergency line.'

'That's why I called with an emergency. Is there a mobile for someone who can take responsibility?'

'I can't give out that number.'

'Do you not have a calendar of who's supposed to turn up? This is unbelievable. Look, you need to get senior staff involved.'

Minutes pass. Nobody calls back.

The old man is muttering to himself in the Peace Room. Dora stays in the lounge, midway between exasperation and amusement that her last hours are this: waiting for customer service. She calls again. The same woman answers, claiming to have just spoken to someone, and that it's for them to decide.

'What, me and him?'

'You two are the ones who turned up at the same time.'

'Because you told us to! Even legally, this can't be right.' But Dora veers away from the legal angle, remembering those medications in his name. She plans to ingest them, and considers deceiving the old man, telling him the office ordered him to leave. But if he phones them to complain, they'd discover her duplicity, and could expel her.

'When is this Scott person getting here? You two can arrange to return tomorrow, alright?'

'What?' he shouts from the other room. 'Can't hear you!' He joins her, complaining between wheezes that he doesn't have anyplace to stay in this country. Scott was planning to head back to London alone tonight – he just popped out to buy something. 'There's a special wine Tina loves. He'll make out that it's from me.'

Dora pushes her duffel bag under the coffee table as if to assert her rights. Old magazines are fanned across the tabletop, their glossy covers torn: a woman presenting brownies; a tattooed sportsman holding an orange ball.

When a rat died in Dora's cellar, the smell forced her to go down, wincing in pain each time her weight shifted on the stepladder. With her bare hand, she cleared cobwebs around the light switch, and illuminated the brick-walled chamber: black droppings on the floor, and a rodent, dead on its side. She avoided the sight of its toothy grimace, and held her breath when sliding a piece of cardboard underneath, the rubbery tail hanging over. With the laden cardboard in one hand, she struggled back up the stepladder, and imagined losing her footing, with nobody knowing that she'd fallen, the cellar bulb fading. In distraction, she nearly missed a step, causing the dead rat to roll down the cardboard into her midriff. She bobbled the corpse and grasped its tail, the body swinging like a pendulum, her lips pursed in revulsion as she flung it up to the ground floor, then climbed after, polluted, her knee throbbing. Absurd shoes, she thought, looking at

hers covered in cellar dust. When young, she coveted elegant foot-
wear. These were nuns' black rectangles – among the concessions
of age, surrendering bits of yourself until you look nothing like you
expect. People whisper to each other, after seeing the empty-eyed
elderly at nursing homes, '*I* wouldn't let myself get to that point.'
But they will. The wheelchair that once seemed degrading becomes
salvation. Yet the question that troubled her that day was: 'Which
recycling bin for a rat?'

Dora reckoned that seventy-five years was enough, and she
had reached that term. Her mother died before fifty, her father at
seventy-three, which seemed old at the time. Hendrik – a country
doctor – was lanky and fit until, a few years after retirement, he
chopped firewood, and missed, and the axe blade severed the flesh
between two toes. Despite medical knowledge, he failed to care for
his worsening wound. It was a clue to dementia, which crept over
him in coming years, slowly, gradually – then in a catastrophic
lurch, after he visited the hospital with a gut infection, and delirium
overcame him. When he regained sense, Hendrik wasn't quite there.
His final months were nightmarish.

The suddenness terrified Dora. When ageing, she thought, you
compromise in small measures until, abruptly, you've lost control;
you're acted upon. She vowed to end her time before that. To monitor
her decline, Dora compiled a list of what had failed in her father –
errors and confusions that should serve as her warning signs. But
if she waited for *all* those hints, she'd likely have lost the capacity
to respond. So, you must act a bit too early. Dignity or time: you
can't have both.

Shortly before the Covid pandemic – in those distant late months of 2019 – Dora attended a concert at Wigmore Hall alone, her bad knee mashed against the seat in front, among a crowd of white-hairs watching the young perform Bach.

Afterward, amid the polite middle-class exodus, an extrovert of Dora's age asked what she'd thought, and Dora expressed appreciation for some of the pieces – though she'd not loved the sympathy. That was wrong. What *was* the word? Other cases too. She asked a shop clerk where to find those round nuts, and he looked askance, and what're those called they're   they're

When spoken aloud, 'symphony' sounded wrong. Anyway, she hadn't loved it. Or the sympathy.

But what *is* so terrible if orderlies deposit you in an armchair, and you rave, and they clean you? Somehow, personal grooming feels fundamental. Since age fourteen, she has dealt with errant hairs, and were she to enter a nursing home, they'd ignore those, she'd grow wisps on her chin, and they'd not mind – then again, nor would she.

To be human, Dora thinks, includes dominion over your hair. But independence also means laundry, and dirty dishes, and falsified enthusiasm for younger lives that rerun the same theatrical productions, oblivious to how commonplace the dramas are. She refuses to believe that what's new today is worse than what was new. But that is how it feels. It's a lack of savour, as when she ate her sandwich earlier. She hardly remembers doing so, the buttery piggish scent of *jamón serrano* on crusty baguette. When did she have it? She unzips her duffel bag. The sandwich is still there, untouched.

Her mind needs an editor – preferably more indulgent than those who've considered her writing lately. Dora's favourite publishing person died a few years back, and a perky replacement at the imprint said she'd 'absolutely love to take a look' at the next manuscript. It wasn't a major publishing house; those had lost interest after consecutive flops. This young stranger was the last chance, lest Dora's past three years die stranded on a computer chip.

She emailed the manuscript, and waited. When she enquired as to the silence, an effusive apology leapt back. The young editor added that it'd be lovely to meet, and discuss 'your new book'. (She'd written 'new book', not 'submitted manuscript'. A promising sign?) A lunch date was set, then delayed and delayed.

Her manuscript – the late-life attempt of Dora Frenhofer to find words, to say something anyone cared about, to not worry what anyone cared about, to figure out what she cared about and hope anyone cared (then make her keyboard cooperate) – was perhaps rubbish. Anyway, the editor reached a verdict, and insisted on sharing it in person, forcing Dora to wait in agony for the woman's protracted Greek vacation to end. At last, a restaurant was selected, and a date set. Dora's literary agent (another younger woman inherited from another deceased book person) dropped out because of an auction for a novel that everyone was wild about. So it'd be just Dora and the editor.

The young woman picked an upmarket Middle Eastern restaurant in Kensington, and generously ordered too much: pomegranate-specked appetizers, spiced meat platters, rose-scented desserts. When drinks arrived, the editor confessed to not having *quite* finished reading, so she'd refrain from giving her thoughts. Dora pinched her thigh, forcing herself to tolerate the pain as long as possible, while appearing composed above the table. She praised the food and, upon parting, they cheek-kissed. The editor would be in touch very very soon.

She was. An hour later, Dora received a call from her agent: the editor had rejected it. She must've known before the meal but hadn't wanted to cancel after so many delays, thus assuaged her guilt by treating the old woman to a grand last meal.

Dora suggested phoning the editor herself, to offer changes that might satisfy her. Dora's agent dissuaded her. 'Don't want to seem like you're begging.'

'I could write an email.'

'Honestly? I'd just leave it.'

The editor and agent were dear friends, and always met for drinks, probably sighing at the mention of Dora Frenhofer – how awkward it was, how you couldn't just drop her. She'd get the message.

Dora knew before the call ended that she'd never again look at that manuscript. Her career had just ended. For the rest of the week, she tidied her house, its three floors long ceded to clutter and dust. How, she wondered, do you retire as a novelist? Do you leave a note on the kitchen table? And if you live alone?

The old man with the oxygen cylinder is talking to her, something so absurd that she listens. 'Whoever goes first,' he says, 'the other can do a spot of shopping.'

'What for?'

'They got excellent prices on golf clubs, Scott tells me. But you know what they say: you can't take it with you!'

Cliché is rough sandpaper to Dora. Yet it's his presumption that bothers her most – something enters his head, so she must kick aside whatever is in hers.

'I took my last fare the other day,' he says. 'Only lasted an hour. Was worried I'd crash, given the state I'm in.'

'Crash what?'

'The taxi. Nearly fifty years I was on the job.' He laments Uber, and says how Scott needed six years of hard work to pass the cabbies' test. 'Anyone getting through The Knowledge is impressive. Especially for him, with that thing he's got.'

'No idea what thing.'

'Where the words aren't the right way up.'

Dora knows, but can't find the word herself.

'Why anyone uses ride apps, I can't say,' he remarks. 'Would you let your granddaughter get in a car with a strange man? How's that even safe?'

'Dyslexia.'

'You what?'

'That's what's wrong with Scott.'

'Nothing's *wrong* with Scott.'

To Dora, this man epitomizes their species: lost for words, so uttering them. If he wants to keep speaking, he wants to keep living.

He brings out a photograph of his grandchildren. Dora declines to see them, explaining that she has resolved to do only what she wants for the remainder of her life. 'You're bothered by that, I see,' she notes. 'Your question was, "Do you want to look?" I said the truth.'

This directness of hers – normal where she'd grown up in the Netherlands – was especially pronounced in her father, who never softened the facts when warning ill patients of what lay ahead. They had every right, he contended, to know what he did. Whether they needed such graphic detail was perhaps arguable. Hendrik – in his unvarnished way – tended a rural patch of Noord-Brabant, a wedge between Belgium and Germany that a Dutch politician once referred to as 'a place of cows, pigs and Catholics'. However, the manners of their village owed more to Protestant modesty, every family's front curtains wide open to prove that they possessed nothing of value.

Dora's mother, Lotte – large-eared and six years older than her husband – hailed from Den Bosch, a provincial city where she grew up watching German expressionist films and reading novels about modern degeneracy, which she would've rather liked to try. She only met Hendrik in her thirties, during the Second World War, when Lotte was taking rural refuge from the fighting. During hardships toward the end of the war, they became each other's company: he, the most educated person she'd met since leaving Den Bosch.

In peacetime, Lotte accepted the role of country-doctor's wife. Privately, she viewed the village with scorn, and took this out on Hendrik. She mocked the peasants' ignorance, especially when she spoke to their young daughter, Dora, who imbibed her mother's snobbery. Lotte also took great pleasure in overexciting little Dora – wild games and late-night tickling – such that the girl forgot herself, streaking with red-faced hilarity into rooms occupied by her father. Dora sees Hendrik's slender back and high collar, his faint bald spot, and the restrained ferocity – he so full of words, and she with few, except to deny guilt (though guilty). Too late, for he'd lost his temper. Indeed, he'd lost it already, because of other frustrations, only to be presented a child-shaped occasion to discharge his outrage. When castigated by her father, Dora grew as frantic as a cat in a bag, and shouted to stop him shouting. Lotte entered her husband's study, and the sobbing girl opened her arms for her mother's comfort. Hendrik glared at his wife in warning. Defiantly, Lotte's forearm brushed her daughter's back, her fingertips dusting Dora's shoulder blades.

When Dora was six, her mother's skin yellowed, and she slept all day, behind a door that nurses sometimes left ajar. Dora peeped in: her mother disrobed and twisted, only the thinning hair on her head and the patch in her crotch identifying which side of this person was up. One morning, the door was wide open, the bed made. Hendrik returned that afternoon, stating that Lotte had been put in the ground, and earth piled atop. He knew how close Dora was to her mother, so had decided the girl ought not attend.

Dora inherited the books that her mother had not burned for heat during the war. These prized volumes became an after-life conversation between them in the form of tattered hardcovers, which she moved to every home of her life, until a removals man walked out her front door recently, lugging cardboard boxes to his van. What would her mother have thought of Dora's writing? Throughout her career, that question preoccupied Dora. Only after someone dies do you realize how different each human is: a particular space remains deserted, quiet where opinions sounded, empty where they'd have marched into the room.

Dora and her father never again shouted at each other. Over the years, Hendrik even had flashes of humour with her, particularly regarding patients. He viewed people as the greatest barrier to their own interests, all the drinking and smoking and eating to excess. So he adopted an adversarial stance, siding with their health over their will. 'I should've taken up veterinary medicine,' he commented, 'as *those* patients listen to reason.'

Hendrik busied his young daughter with activities — always what he wished, and with pedagogical intent: trees and leaves; the constellations; keeping a ledger. He escorted her to bookshops in Utrecht, Rotterdam, Amsterdam and Groningen up north. Dora was allowed to choose any volume, up to a certain price. Hendrik's interest in fiction was slight, extending only to the great Russians: Dostoevsky, for capturing the angst of life among conformists; Tolstoy, for how history shoulders into the passer-by; and, above all, Chekhov, a brother doctor who shared Hendrik's sightline on humanity, glimpsed while opening the medical bag on a farm visit.

Each weekend, Hendrik leafed through *de Volkskrant* in his armchair by the fireplace, and she'd bring in one of her mother's left-behind novels, sitting on the undersized child's rocking chair, pretending to read. He'd glance up from his newspaper, and Dora spoke for the sake of speaking, noting his unrest, and so strived (worry rising) to hold his attention – a writerly instinct years before her first typewriter.

As for moral guidance, Hendrik offered little besides his own behaviour. Dora was free to go where she pleased from early girlhood. He taught her to drive his run-down Opel Kapitän when she was nine. He let her shoot his hunting rifle without supervision.

Hendrik must've been lonely: years unmarried, a disappointment to his patients, who wished for a gentle doctor. When he found a second wife, it was a development Dora had hoped for. The local population was growing, and theirs was now a town, prompting Hendrik to employ a nursing aide. The house filled with plants, and Margriet's heirloom crucifix appeared on their wall. She was a loving woman, though Dora judged her stepmother to be simple, and looked down on her father for his preference.

Margriet often reminded Dora that her father had suffered a difficult war. *Who*, Dora thought, *had an easy war?* Also, Hendrik hadn't seen battle, and was spared the Nazis' worst crimes because of his half-German origins, his father having moved across the border early in the century. According to family lore, when her grandfather Moritz was a young man – moody-romantic son of a doctor in the German spa town of Cleves – he had a habit of sleeping in De Duivelsberg, the Devil's Mountain forest, which lay on the border with the Netherlands, and which both countries claimed. In those woods, he passed hours, smoking a meerschaum pipe under chestnut trees, listening to the creaks of bush and branch, and responding with bad poetry in a leather notebook. Once, he terrified a Dutch girl whom he took to be lost, though she was not, merely unsettled by a German youth leaping from the foliage to help her when no help was required. He must've found a way to charm Willemina, for they married and settled on her side of the border, Moritz eventually obtaining a little-desired position as country doctor – the job that their son, Hendrik, came to inherit.

During the war, Hendrik maintained cordial relations with the occupying German forces, notably by prescribing cures for venereal disease. In parallel, he gave occasional refuge to Dutch members of the resistance – though never longer than a night or two, and not to Jews. Hiding a Jew, he once explained to Dora, could have meant his death. In old age, he said something more: that Jewish colleagues – friends during his medical studies – had been deported, and he'd helped none. 'The shame of my life,' he said.

Hendrik did suffer detention once, when German soldiers and their Dutch collaborators sought locals responsible for slashing the tyres of bicycles that the Nazis had confiscated. The soldiers gathered all village males aged eleven to eighty, and forced them into a single horse stall whose doors they locked, around forty men so compressed that they could hardly breathe. If the prisoners failed to identify any culprits after the weekend, the soldiers would incinerate everyone, and they proved their seriousness by removing the horses from adjacent stalls. Grunting and screaming, the men were left for the next three days. Many died from suffocation. Hendrik survived, albeit with damage to his left shoulder, which he never again moved without pain. His older brother was among those who perished. In adolescence, Dora – casually condemning as the young are – pictured Hendrik betraying his brother. Only later did it occur to her that, if her father had been bolder, perhaps they'd have burned him alive, and she'd never have existed. Everyone owes their life to the cowardice of an ancestor somewhere.

In adolescence, Dora also heard details of her late mother's war. Contrary to the family fib, Lotte hadn't sought refuge in the village alone, but had arrived with her two small children, Sofie and Casper, whose father had been killed early in the war. When tending to her kids' coughs, the local doctor, Hendrik (more cultured than anyone Lotte had met in the area) became her acquaintance.

In 1944, the Allies launched a campaign to drive back German troops occupying the Netherlands, and this cut incoming supplies. Cold struck: the Hunger Winter. Locally, rumours spread of a hidden cow, and that one could procure milk if the farmer appreciated the woman who visited. Lotte dressed as attractively as possible, her clothing and underwear far too large by then. She set out, shivering. But the farmer and his hidden cow seemed to be a myth – or perhaps it was her poor sense of direction in unmarked fields. Crusted with cold mud, shuddering, she returned to find her two children on the floor by their shared bed, each strangled.

This account, which a village gossip told Dora, was so patchy that she sketched in the gaps herself, concocting a German military-police official overseeing investigations in the area, who learned of the murder of two local children. This Nazi, a devout Catholic, believed in law and justice, and doggedly sought the murderer (untroubled by matters just out of view, crimes in which he was complicit). But Dora never wrote detective fiction. Instead, thinking of these deaths changed something: she'd always imagined her missing mother as her closest friend, that they were alike. Now, the woman felt like a stranger.

'So you're from here?' the old man is asking.

'Here? No, not here,' she says. 'Not far, though. But I've lived in London for years.'

'London as well. Small world.'

No, it's a large world, Dora thinks, though she voices faint agreement. She's distracted, calculating how many years since she left these parts. Her father and his new wife had a young son by then, Theo, although Dora took little part in family life. After finishing school, she left, driving with a boyfriend to Paris, which was still gearing up for its student-revolutionary outburst later in the Sixties. Dora spoke French badly, with a strong accent and no fear, perturbing Parisians with her effrontery. Soon, she left the Dutch boy who'd brought her, preferring the company of older men, both for the quality-of-life and for the education. Among these was a dashing short Jewish-American food writer, Alan Zelikov, whose expense account introduced readers (and female friends) to exquisite dining. Those he brought to top eateries had no obligation to sleep with him. But they could. She pictures Alan in a fine restaurant, jaw contorting, nose flaring, jotting copious notes on a reporter's pad. What, she wondered at the time, is there to write about taste?

After one extravagant meal, she took ill, queasy to recall the three-tiered seafood platter, whose former occupants swam around her digestive tract. She convalesced for days, an anti-nausea medicine failing to revive her. Finally, a doctor confirmed that it was simple food poisoning but warned that the anti-nausea medicine was making matters worse, and could have harmed the foetus, which was a strange way to inform her of a pregnancy. She was barely out of her teens.

Alan, learning of his parental responsibility, rapped his knuckles twice on a polished sidetable, shaking the full ashtray, as if this marriage proposal were a far, far better thing than he had ever done. For the first time, Dora detected a nervous need in Alan: she, a dining partner whom he'd previously disregarded, was to determine his future. She never saw him again, but googled 'Alan Zelikov' not long ago, finding the archived obituary of a food writer who'd died of a stroke in 1997, leaving no survivors. All those years ago in Paris, doctors had no reliable way to evaluate the health of a foetus, and the suffering of a handicapped child was more than Dora could contemplate. She visited London, where men still wore bowler hats, everyone carried rolled-up umbrellas, and abortionists could be found. That child would've been past fifty now. Dora can't remain in the same air as that thought, so walks to the front door, which concentrates her on the present, the old man droning.

He's preparing tea, narrating his actions, fumbling in the fridge, spilling a milk carton. She ends up making it for him.

'My wife's gone,' he says, when she places a steaming cup before him. 'You?'

'I'm not married.'

'Pity,' he says, adding, 'Some like it that way, I suppose.'

'It's for the best in my case. Whenever I picture myself with a husband lately, I kill him off.'

'I don't follow.'

'No, nothing. I used to write stories – that was my job, a writer. Every time I wrote a husband in recent years, it didn't end well for him.'

'Whodunnits?'

'No, no. Just novels.'

'Why'd the husbands get bumped off then?'

'In the latest, I had an old woman who walks into her kitchen for lunch, and she finds this grey old fellow at the table, and wonders: How did I end up married to him?'

'What, she doesn't know?'

'She knows. But she . . . It doesn't matter.'

'Then she offs him.'

'No, he starts choking.'

'Poisoned?'

'He's eating a sweet, and it goes down the wrong way, and she sees him suffocating, and leaves him there.'

'Not believable, if you don't mind me saying.'

'You're probably right. But the idea is, her husband is the only person keeping her going, which makes him an obstacle, because she wants to end her life. When this old man – the last character in her last story – is gone, she has nothing holding her to the world. But she's frightened: wanting him there, wanting him gone. Anyway, that was the idea.'

'Here's a better ending,' he suggests. 'This husband, he's playing around on her, and he slaps her once too often, and she's had enough, and wants revenge. So she poisons him for his money.'

'Much better. You should be the writer.'

He smiles, and coughs. 'How's a person get into your line of work?'

In Dora's case, indirect blame lay with Klaus, the bearded German sculptor she lived with in Paris. A brawny man known for vast rusted artworks, Klaus aspired to write important novels someday, and loaded her with German literature that he'd equal. She was attracted to the mercurial moods of Klaus, to the depth of his voice, to his ambition. He never noticed that she had that last trait herself.

Together, they moved to his native Munich. Once, he went lake-swimming with friends, and inadvertently locked Dora in his studio. At first, she banged on the door and shouted, then fiddled with his clay and tools, irritated with Klaus, thus careless if she damaged something. Eventually, she picked up pen and paper.

Klaus flung open the studio door, shaggy hair dripping down his bare chest. She didn't respond, preferring the people on her pages, and needing to hold him back a little longer. When he realized what she was doing, Klaus laughed, as if hearing a child mangle a grown-up word. He assumed she'd be writing in Dutch, but she did so in German, which limited her to clipped prose – a happenstance that became a style.

Dora published before he did, and that ended their relationship, though she didn't realize it at the time. All she saw was how dull his drinking had become. Decades later, she gave a reading at a low-ceilinged restaurant in Nuremberg, attended by nine elderly locals, including a leonine man in brown corduroy jacket, who smiled little brown teeth. Afterward, he shook her long hand with both of his fat ones, fingers soft and warm, his gaze humbly on hers, and he expressed such admiration for what she'd become. His remarks lingered as she returned alone to the budget hotel: 'Yes,' he said, 'we must!' – one of those farewells disguised as a plan.

Her first published story paid a pittance, which was more than enough: when Dora was young, money served only to fund each week. She wanted no objects, except Italian shoes glimpsed in shop windows – but only as one admires a *château*, without expectation of ownership. After moving out of the Klaus apartment, Dora sold colour televisions, then men's ties. But secretarial work was how she earned most, and what quickened her typing. When it came to her writing, Dora preferred longhand. No rush; just a hobby. Yet it was becoming more than that. When composing scenes, Dora experienced the physiological responses of her protagonists, swallowing if they did, clearing her throat, growing upset, shouting (only realizing this when a housemate barged in, asking if everything was alright). After writing, she needed to habituate to people again; their predictability grated.

'Don't you agree?' the old man concludes.

She wasn't listening, so responds: 'Absolutely, yes.'

He nods with satisfaction, knowing they're on the same page. 'You don't say much. But you're good to talk to.'

Once, Dora's father remarked that she could be wonderful company – when she wanted. As a young woman, she did want that, becoming the one who strode up to the jazz-club doormen proposing they admit her whole party for free, and they'd smirk at her gall, and oblige. Yet once inside the club, Dora turned into the quietest, with a running commentary hidden in her head, evaluating everyone. Above all, she identified people's motives, and judged them: the successful as schemers, the failed as fools. Yet despite these judgements (which never spared Dora herself), she wrote tenderly of people in her fiction. The writing contained more humanity than the writer.

Dora sold her first novel at twenty-seven, and decided to pause while awaiting publication. She'd replenish herself among friends and a lover she'd overlooked. She enjoyed only the first day. People spoke so much slower than written dialogue.

'I can't tempt you?' the old man asks, offering that photo of his grandkids again.

Dora regrets turning him down earlier. She's tired of insisting on candour over kindness, and wants to remedy herself. 'You *can* tempt me, yes. I was distracted before – probably just tense about all this,' she says. 'Do show me. Thank you.'

She takes a long look at the grandkids' photo: all grins and missing front teeth and birthday cake. Dora almost asks if they won't miss him – it's the kind of question she'd normally pose. But it'd be cruel. Instead: 'Very sweet, all of them.' She returns the picture.

In Dora's young adulthood, the only child she knew properly was her younger brother, Theo. She'd hardly bothered with him when they were in the same house. But after she left the country, and was writing in Germany, she developed an opinion about her adolescent half-brother, whose difficulties Dora heard in telephone reports from the boy's mother, Margriet. He'd finished school with no plans, and was a mess, convinced that his peers mocked him, and somehow knew his thoughts. The reality was far less: nobody considered him at all. He'd been a minor presence at school, and they'd surpassed him since leaving. He stayed in bed most days, and Hendrik indulged this, as he never would have with his daughter. In annoyance, she decided to fix what her father and stepmother merely flapped at. She was generationally closer to Theo, and considered herself adept at wrangling complicated men.

The plan was to force her brother up and out of this funk. What'd really solve matters, she thought, was for Theo to leave that claustrophobic little town. She had an early success, persuading him to travel with her to Amsterdam. There, she took him to see tour operators selling voyages to the East. A flight was prohibitively expensive, but you could board a bus, and just go.

Theo wore a jean jacket and stinking jeans, his fingernails chewed, pimpled cheeks visible through stringy hair; a long greasy teenager. As they walked through Dam Square, he trickled with sweat at the presence of so many people, more than since school hallways.

You won't achieve anything with your life, she thought of him. You'll stay still, waste away, trying nothing.

At a canal-side café, Dora ordered him a beer, then a coffee. Theo kept gripping his shoulders, as if to protect himself from ambush. She spoke of how the world wasn't like their town, that he'd find situations where you have to manage, and thus return stronger. She mentioned friends who'd visited Indonesia, and hadn't Theo loved eating *kroepoek* when smaller? What if he went there? Other people she knew had trekked across India, seen the base of Mount

Kanchenjunga, leapt nude into a glacial lake across from China, and came home transformed. You needn't be stuck with the second-raters we grew up with, she said.

As they stepped from the café onto the road, Theo was nearly hit by a cyclist, and she grabbed a handful of his jean-jacket collar in anger, supposedly scolding him for his distraction – but secretly because she was vexed by his failure to embrace her proposals. 'Throw yourself into situations, Theo! Not into roads!' She let go of him. 'You *need* difficult times. That's growing up.' Strange, she thinks now, how that which hardened you seems the correct preparation for life, even if you're not particularly happy with how you ended up.

Cockroaches scattered across the carpet of the hippie tour agency, and a frizz-haired freak at the desk looked up from a comic book. An overland bus left weekly, including that night, arriving in New Delhi. She asked the price, and impulsively counted out the guilders from her purse. But how impulsive was it really? She'd brought along Theo's passport.

Dora expected he would be more thrilled, but he remained a musky teenage boy. The tour-company employee promised to show her brother nearby shops where everyone picked up basics for the trip. Dora gave Theo cash for this too, folding bank notes into his breast pocket, as if it were a movie scene. 'You ready?' she asked, and slapped the back of his hand with affection.

His mother spent the rest of her life trying to find Theo, taking repeated trips to India, where he'd last been seen. She hired detectives, and leads emerged over the years, all false.

'So which was it then?' the old man is asking.

'Which was what?'

'Your most famous book.'

'Mine? None is famous.'

'Don't be shy now. Give us a name.'

She mentions one.

'Never heard of it.'

An upstart British publisher bought translation rights to that book, her debut, saying they'd promote her as a Dutch version of Françoise Sagan – a silly comparison that she permitted. Dora gave London a try, and began writing in English, which sheared another layer of artifice from her prose.

The mid-1970s were grim for Britain, still in the thudding hangover of empire, its workers striking, with electricity cuts, and a mood of dejection. Yet Dora's first years there had the opposite tint: glittering book parties; taxi rides with authors of note; 3 a.m. at the electric typewriter in her bedsit, the frisson that this line before her might be superb.

Her first three novels came out too fast. They needed revision, but she resisted. Back then, Dora considered her fiction as akin to her body, and objected to uninvited prodding. Those first books were reviewed favourably, without selling favourably. She contributed occasionally to the *Times Literary Supplement*, had a few pieces in *Partisan Review*, and once in the French edition of *Playboy*. But her dealings with editors often ended bitterly. The term 'difficult', she believed, was what people applied when *they* barge ahead at the butcher's, and *you* stand up for yourself. Dora had a habit of frankness about other writers too, in reviews and in person. 'I'm Dutch,' she said, by way of explanation.

Those times belonged to another person, a character recalled with a pang – a woman who, for a decade, was mistaken for a rising star, pencilled into the family tree of important writers. But, as a fellow novelist once told her: 'A writer can be difficult. A writer can deliver late. A writer can be mediocre at writing itself. But only one at a time.' Dora was two at a time. While never late, she was difficult, and less-than-outstanding. They could pass. They started to.

'What's the word I'm looking for?'

'Is it "hazelnut"?' she tells the old man. 'That's one I can't seem to remember lately. That and "symphony".'

'We're losing it, aren't we.'

Her father's incipient dementia came during Dora's mid-thirties. Hendrik's hard edges wore away; his eyes became vague. She tried not to notice, and visited rarely. Margriet denied any decline, which bothered Dora, for it epitomized what was childish about her step-mother. Once Hendrik's mind betrayed him entirely, Margriet spoke only of prolonging his life, that he must eat well, drink enough water, stare out the window. He lost all sense of his body, and felt safe only if lying flat. When turned in bed, he clenched a bony fist, all knuckles, no threat. When Dora arrived, her voice soothed him.

'I don't know if I could do this for you,' he told her.

'You've done everything for me,' she said.

Dora needed to leave – a small French publisher was flying her to long-scheduled book promotions. Once in Paris, she sat in a hotel room, unable to concentrate on the newspaper, nor savour a croissant. She looked emptily at the *International Herald Tribune*, blinded by flashbulb images of Hendrik in bed, his toenails pointing at the sunless ceiling.

After that lacklustre promotional campaign (no journalists came to interview her), Dora was flying home, when a Brazilian academic – a man she'd chatted with at the departure gate – collapsed in the aisle, miles above northern France. She became his advocate with the cabin crew, and was still playing that role weeks later at a Paris hospital. Doctors there diagnosed a woeful condition whose treatment threatened his fertility. Gustavo was youngish, so banked his sperm for a future family. The form had a box for 'Designated Recipients', and he wrote 'Dora Frenhofer', which offended her. They had no romance, just adhesive circumstances, with Gustavo exploding into terrified rages, she turning cold, he cowering, she indulgent, repeat. His family assumed that she loved their Gustavo. She never even liked the man. Rather, Dora became addicted to virtue, all while neglecting the condition of her father.

Gustavo went faster than anyone warned. When his parents flew from São Paulo to deal with his leftover belongings, they informed Dora that she had their blessing. For? To bear his child. She winced in surprise, having no such wish. Weeks later, she saw Hendrik for the last time. He slept with his lips apart, a black hole between. Only one eye closed, he took her fingers, refusing to let go.

Dora inherited enough money to buy her terraced house, back when London property was still just about affordable. The place was in need of an overhaul that she never got to. Years passed, and Dora (who stole a book from every man she slept with) accumulated many more. She wrote several of her own too. Nearing forty, she needed plot points, so contacted Gustavo's sperm bank to research how such a place works. They had no record of him. But this *was* the place. She contacted his best friend, who revealed that Gustavo had never deposited any sperm. He just needed Dora to nurse him, and lied in order that she stay. This prompted a triple reckoning: (1) a man whose intellect she didn't respect had duped her; (2) she wanted a child now; (3) Gustavo had believed the prospect of his offspring would stir devotion, which misappraised both the qualities of Dora and the qualities of his sperm.

At an LSE public lecture, she met Clive, a Black American political economist visiting London on a fellowship. When she fell pregnant, he offered to move countries to raise their child together. Dora insisted that he stick with his teaching job and family in the Bay Area. She preferred to do this alone.

When the nurse presented a swaddled baby, Dora looked at this gummed-up stranger, experiencing only emptiness, which terrified her. She was over-drugged from her C-section, and kept slumping to sleep, waking in alarm when she nearly dropped Rebecca. This first meeting always haunted her, as if she'd botched matters from the start. Mothers, she'd assumed, instinctively know how to breastfeed, how to cradle a child, how to check a temperature with the back of one's hand – indeed, Dora saw other women doing so with natural mastery. She lacked such facility, and it rattled her. Judging herself a failure, she comforted herself by denigrating motherhood, telling friends that you were vomited on, urinated on, woken in constancy, your essence sucked screamingly from veined nipples, overwhelmed by the relentlessness of an activity that wasn't considered 'activity' but a form of self. Yet she dearly wished herself better at it, and tried, secretly reading instructional manuals that never answered her questions.

For her first post-natal outing, Dora attended a London Book Fair luncheon, standing with a glass of wine among publishing sophisticates, feeling unclean. She sought to embody her previous self, and feigned that woman's brash confidence, claiming that she still found time to write despite the newborn. She dramatized the tale of her Brazilian man on the plane, how she'd cared for him till he'd died. Misery memoirs were in fashion, and a tipsy editor commissioned one – though she seemed to regret the offer once sober the following week, and spent their next conversation enumerating all that the idea lacked. Above all, an epiphany. 'But you'll come up with one!' she informed Dora, with the costless optimism that some editors have for writerly tasks.

Dora needed income, so typed fast, hating the result, waking to the hum of the electric typewriter, or lurching upright at the wail of Rebecca, recently nicknamed Beck. An epiphany? She reverse-engineered the tale of Gustavo to make that relationship a precursor to blissful motherhood. For a change, Dora accepted every editorial suggestion. Just yes yes great yes. She fabricated sections when instructed that the true story needed more [fill in the gap], then she cut the last third, as requested, and added a phoney conclusion, so that the misery memoir ended in the mandatory glow of redemption: daughter in her arms, Dora gazing down, discovering love.

She looks up, an old man jabbering. Then to the door, exhorting the son-in-law Scott to deliver her from this purgatory. Soon, if she plays this right, her two last people will drive away. Dora's mouth goes dry, an animal reflex, programmed to resist extinction, the deletion of everything that happened.

To compose herself, she studies his face. One of us won't see tomorrow while the other swallows breakfast, considers the weather.

More could happen to you. But should it? 'You haven't said what's wrong with you,' she remarks. 'Are you dying of something?'

He answers by rattling the oxygen canister. 'Sick for bloody months. Barely get out of bed now.'

'What is it?'

'A broken heart. Jill went. All's been downhill after that.'

'Jill was your wife?'

'Course. A stroke got her.' That sounded flippant but his gaze loses focus, as if this statement is well worn but still summons her cupboard, the metal hangers tinkling. He's suffering after-effects from a savage bout of Covid, he explains. 'You name a part of my body, it done a job. Sick to the stomach. My heart beating funny – just skips a beat sometimes, and I reckon: Here it is; I'm done for now. My hands shake sometimes. Look at them! Pulling on socks takes a half-hour. When I had the Covid, I'd tell Jill: "You sleep on the sofa. I'm not making you sick too." Exhausted, I was – and still doing my shift.'

'You were driving a taxi with Covid?'

'Hang on, hang on. One of them got *me* sick.'

'You think Covid could've caused your wife's stroke?'

His eyes go black. 'I didn't give it to her, if that's what you're driving at.' He turns with difficulty, arm tangled in the plastic tube running to his nose. He shuffles to the kitchenette, and turns on the electric kettle. Over the next minute, it rises to a rolling boil, and beeps. He makes no more tea, only sits again. 'That's vicious, what you said before. Jill could've got it anywhere. Me and her, we was together since year dot – since she was seventeen and I wasn't nineteen years old. What am I supposed to do now? Sit and watch telly?'

'And your kids?'

'Dave works in Wrexham, but he don't give a monkey's. Tina's the one. Thing is, I never had a proper end with my taxi. That's what bothers me. Years I sat in traffic, looking out the window, thinking: "Wait till my last day! You'll be waving me down in the rain, and I'll drive right past!" Didn't go that way. Still, Scott done me proud. He set me up that last shift, and gave me my cab back for it. Then some posh bloke gets in, abusing me the whole way, trying to roll his tobacco, getting it all over the back seat. Finally, I go, "Get out and walk, mate!" A bitter end, that was.' The old man grimaces, pops an antacid. 'I decided, that's enough. I started talking about going to Europe, and just get it over with, given the state of me. Scott's the one had the idea of a last bash, like we done. Best day of my life. Just having everyone around me.' He's quiet, eyes welling up. He looks down. 'Kids are everything. Aren't they.'

Dora would've died for Beck. So, no: she didn't regret motherhood. But Dora had borne a daughter under a false assumption. She'd expected they would be closest friends, them against the world. Yet they were such different characters, whether it was what they wanted for dinner, or which fashions were laughable, or what humour wasn't laughable in the least. They so rarely aligned.

Beck's father visited once a year. Dora remained fond of Clive, and always planned activities for them all: picnics, board games, the theatre. 'Might feel strange to have your dad back,' she warned Beck, mentioning fathers who returned after the Second World War with thick beards, petrifying the children who knew only a smiling young man in the wall photo. But Clive was a cuddly presence, and the two instantly nestled into each other. Dora recalls her nine-year-old on Clive's lap, just moments after he'd arrived, Beck eating a vast duty-free Toblerone, he with his ear to her jaw. 'Even listening, I can taste the chocolate!' he marvelled.

'Really?' Beck asked, smiling up at him, besotted.

Dora needn't have been there. 'You shouldn't give her so many sweets, Clive.'

After he flew home, Dora tracked down a bar of Toblerone. She promised Beck a special treat after dinner, and invited the girl to sit on her lap, which Beck did with a reluctance that weighed on Dora's thighs. She presented the Toblerone, but Beck claimed not to feel like it. 'Since when do *you* turn down chocolate?' She listened to Beck eating, but only heard herself urging the girl to stop squirming, and what is the reason for that? Beck looked away, swallowing.

At twelve, her daughter visited California for the first time. Clive – when renewing his marriage vows – had confessed to his wife about the dalliance years before during his sabbatical at LSE, and that it had resulted in an English daughter. Clive was sick with guilt that his kids in Oakland didn't know their little sister. Once the shock subsided, his wife was accepting. They'd welcome Beck to visit that summer.

After seeing her off at Heathrow, Dora took the Tube home, and climbed the stairs to her attic office, the house quieter than in more than a decade. From her study window, she looked over the backs of other terraced homes. She listened for the sound of neighbours.

Beck enrolled in an Oakland school, and never again lived with Dora, except during vacations, where she complained about London, all that you couldn't find there. Today, they're hardly in touch. Dora would never reproach Beck for this. Had Dora been any better when her father aged?

'I've been to my share of funerals,' the old man is saying. 'So I didn't want to put anyone through that. Plus, why have people saying all them nice things, if you're not there to hear it? That was Scott's point. Tina, she was dabbing her eyes through all the speeches. Poor girl had to leave early. She's like, "Can't do it, Dad." I was about to pack it in myself. But Scott goes, "Look at the turnout, Frank! All for you, mate!"'

So admiring, the old man is, when referring to Scott. Yet it sounds as if the son-in-law has taken over Frank's black cab, and moved with Tina and the kids into Frank's house, taking over the master bedroom. Scott – via his wife – presumably inherits what's left. He isn't exactly an impartial actor when it comes to Frank's death.

The old man asks about Dora's farewells, and she breezes past this, noting how sparse her family is.

'That girl of yours in Los Angeles – what's she do? A movie star?' he jokes.

'Yes, that's right.'

'What, honest?'

'No, no. She just lives there.'

For a spell, Beck did try the entertainment industry as a stand-up comic. This seemed an awful idea to Dora, who recalled how petrified her daughter was to speak in public. Anyway, Beck never got far, and now earns money doing odd-jobs via an app. Fortunately, her partner, Karine, makes a decent salary at a production company. Dora follows both on Instagram, sharing in her daughter's domesticity through photos of their bull-terrier pup, Rodney, who has grown up via trips to farmers' markets, hikes in the hills, video clips of him fetching a squeaky rubber chicken off the couch. Once, Beck and Karine vacationed in Paris, two hours from Dora by train. She imagined travelling there to meet them. But she was not informed of the trip, so restricted herself to Instagram, admiring pastry close-ups and romantic views, saying aloud what she'd have said in person: how she stood in just that spot a half-century ago. Amazing that it's so long ago.

'How long do you need?' the old man asks.

'For what?'

'Writing a book. A few months?'

'A few years in my case.'

'Years?! You need to write faster!'

'I'm not sure my arthritis would allow it,' she says, slowly clenching her hands, and unclenching.

When twelve-year-old Beck left, and Dora had her work time restored in full, weeks passed without any pages appearing. She'd taken up a new activity, the internet, which she dialled each morning from a squealing modem, pixelated images and text materializing on her monitor. Already, after becoming a mother, Dora had retreated from the London literary world, and now withdrew from the parental world that she'd frequented at the gates of Beck's school, ashamed to explain that her child preferred the father. Anyway, what was there to discuss anymore? Music lessons and uniforms and school trips? A few oddball friends of Dora lingered: gay bachelors and estimable spinsters who scythed through life, some with courage and wit, some with courage and wine.

Dora presented herself as she'd always been: assertive. But she kept finding situations where, unexpectedly, she was the weakest party, the friend invited alone. She prided herself on stating the views in public that she'd utter in private, yet noticed people finding her rude. She fell out with acquaintances, even a few close friends.

Dora started waking with an ache that wasn't digestive, simply solitude, and which she treated each morning with scalding coffee and a newspaper, repressing it further with finger-bruising activity on her laptop, and kicking it along blackberry-brambled paths outside London, where she was visited by images of her mother, of Gustavo, of her father.

Death is ordinary, organizing every news bulletin, with bomb blasts and earthquakes ranked according to their tolls. Yet few understand the act of dying itself, which is wrongly considered an off-switch to life. What Dora thrice witnessed was another process, the rendering of a person to their essence – or perhaps the vulgarization of that essence, for one never knew if the late behaviour meant everything or nothing.

Dora took notes at the bedside of Gustavo, and snapped a photograph of him after he'd fallen into a coma, which felt evil as the shutter clacked – though she later consulted the picture when writing a scene. She saw herself confined to bed someday, strangers converging around, the paid and the unpaid, though she expected no volunteers, and wanted none. Her dying, she imagined, would be subject to whatever the public health system flung out. Except, Dora decided, she wasn't surrendering control. She must obtain a dose of drugs by the age of sixty, to retain her freedom to act when the time came. Sixty passed. Seventy too. She'd never been in the same room as such medications until now, three boxes of pharmaceuticals on the kitchenette table, for him or for her.

'Whereabouts do you live in London?' he asks, and knows her street. 'One of them narrow houses? And just you there, on your own?'

Over the years, Dora considered tenants, especially after her book advances evaporated, and the memoir royalties ceased. Really, she needed to sell her home. But that would have meant leaving the neighbourhood. Or perhaps the whole country. For where? She watched the world from the internet, captivated by deranged blogs and clickbait, asking herself who read such idiocy, all this rubbish, claiming that passenger airliners emitted chemicals to control our brains; that shape-shifting reptilians controlled the world elites; that victims of war atrocities were just actors. What shabby characters sat before laptops much like hers, writing this drivel? She clicked a flashing ad for 'equity release', finding a company that paid a lump sum – approximately half the value of your home – for which she signed away the entire property, to be sold upon her death.

Dora subsisted on this cash infusion, existing as a ghost, haunting the lower rings of literary London. She contributed a couple more pieces to the *TLS*, with few readers and negligible effect, except on the authors reviewed, who wondered who in hell 'Dora Frenhofer' was, and why she had a right to pronounce on their work. Every few years, she completed another novel, published by a smaller press to a smaller print run. Now and then, she had a relationship with an old man, obtaining a few months' stimulation, though the affairs came to seem alike. The problem with wisdom is that the more you gain, the less you have in common with anyone.

She met her remaining acquaintances at galleries and restaurants, and organized her week around each occasion. Most left her worse off. They expected her to talk of writing and her daughter. Dora felt as if she'd fallen into a hole, and they stood at the top, shining flashlights at her. Other friends were stolen by grandkids; a few relocated to damp hamlets hours away; or they fell under a boulder of illness, their age doubling overnight, or ending altogether.

She had troubled sleeps, waking at the unmagic hour of 3:49 a.m., disappointed at how she'd turned out, at how she'd behaved, at what she'd devoted her life to, writing, which once seemed an exalted pursuit but had become a trivial one. Dora didn't know what she was for.

Yet she remained intellectually alert, reading *The Guardian* and *The New York Times*, subscribing to and cancelling the *London Review of Books* every few months, and growing irate about the charlatans who duped enough of the electorate to worsen life for all. She couldn't get over Brexit. She watched the climate crisis worsen.

Dora took pains to keep up with technology, which didn't interest her but whose importance she had registered back in the 1980s, when she bought an Apple II Plus, reading the instruction manual cover-to-cover. Many of her contemporaries had assumed that – as was always true before – running with the crowd meant surrendering your independence. So they skipped the digital world. But this revolution proved so totalizing that it was the resisters who lost independence, imposters in their former world, needing the young to log on, to do everything for them.

Dora refused to need the young. She never travelled without

first ensuring that she could lift her luggage, and she discarded any items that might require a strapping young chap to pity her. She did, however, gain a younger friend, Morgan, a South African whom she'd once tutored in a creative-writing course, and who'd settled in Copenhagen with a Danish husband and two blond kids in Lego-coloured jumpers. Years after that writing course, Morgan discovered a second-hand paperback novel by Dora, and read it, and found the email address of her former tutor. 'Wonderful to hear from you after so long,' Dora replied.

They exchanged further emails, and Morgan happened to be visiting London for work, so they met up, finding an instant connection – the kind that exhilirates you in mid-conversation, having accommodated poor dialogue for so long, thus assuming your best exchanges are all behind you. Never did she and Morgan suffer that plummeting insight at a café: you have nothing in common, and the cakes haven't even arrived. After that meeting, they kept in touch, Dora always adding a PS that her younger friend needn't email back – she knew how busy life was with young children.

Dora persisted with her daily hikes, and worked on her writing week after week, finding companionship on Radio 4, its patter entertainingly irritating, such as a panel discussion on whether you have a duty to leave the world better than you found it. One guest said that artistic people improve the world by showing what it is to be alive, thus expanding human experience, and this was a vast contribution. But that only applied, Dora thought, if people actually know your work.

Still, she considered her life fortunate, conducted in a time of peace, while she had gone decades without grave illness. She also saw how egotistical her pursuits had been, writing how *she* saw people, all those pages now closed darkly on one another. She searched online for her name, finding Amazon links to used copies of her memoir, bibliographic citations in library catalogues, archived book reviews, plus the defunct webpage of an Australian literary festival she'd once attended.

Dora hadn't left the world better than she'd found it, and had little chance to do much about that. But after the rejection of her last manuscript, she volunteered at Oxfam, which deployed her to a local charity shop alongside two elderly women, all competing for shifts, the others chatting insufferably, then transforming into chirpy sales clerks when someone entered, much as Dora had done in her twenties, selling ties to gentlemen in Munich (much the same ties that now came in as 'vintage'). Yet her sales in Munich involved the customer noticing her, which no longer occurred. She contacted another charity, a cause that she valued, supporting girls' education in repressive countries. The charity had a position, they said, that'd be perfect: soliciting donations in the street. One memorable afternoon, Dora urged herself to beg passing strangers but couldn't, finally stuffing £40 into the plastic container, and returning it.

What she hankered for was an extreme act – to donate her eyes, say, if anyone wanted those much-used organs. She fantasized about meeting a needy person, that she'd get it right this time. Dora found an agency seeking volunteers to teach English to refugees, and surprised herself at the rush of hope, becoming impatient to meet her pupils – not to extract details for future characters this time, just to help them. She bought ESL books online, and followed a twelve-part course on YouTube. Then someone encountered a bat, China locked down, and next the world. All classes were cancelled.

During that first Covid lockdown, she emailed Morgan, proposing a catch-up by phone. Hearing nothing after a week, Dora worried, and sent a text message: **sorry I haven't been in touch sooner but who was to know after our last talk that the world was going to implode! How are things in Copenhagen? Stuck at home here. Not ideal to say the least! Hope you and your family are ok. Dora xo.**

An answer came the next day: **Dora! Crazy busy here. Having to teach my students on Zoom. Ugh. Will get back to you when I find a free moment . . .!**

Dora skimmed the message without needing every word. Those you lose touch with during an emergency are gone on the other side. This marked an ending: her last friendship.

As lockdowns dragged on, she managed well at home, albeit picturing an inferno beyond her front door. At first, little changed besides the availability of toilet paper. But everything seemed suddenly precarious, society a weaker barricade than anyone presumed. She tested how little food she could manage on, down to 800 calories a day, and enjoyed the physical emptiness; it clarified her thoughts. Grocery shopping gave her interactions with people, so she bought small portions daily – one large orange, for example, asking the masked cashier about his day, opening her wallet slowly.

'Next customer, please!'

Along her street, delivery drivers kept clattering up the sliding doors of their vans, raising images of giant strawberries and water-splashed salads. She took the name of one company, and placed an order – a sack of basmati rice, one red onion, anti-bacterial hand-wash – and she waited. The driver chatted on her doorstep until Dora noticed that one of his shoes pointed toward her gate: he was trying to escape her. Next time (always a different driver), she had hot coffee ready, which the man declined. She offered coffee to each deliveryman, as if a pot had just brewed, saying they looked in need of a pick-me-up. When the drivers spoke no English, they'd just point at the bags on her doorstep. She responded with a thumbs-up, dragged in her purchases, and told herself not to be silly – still, disappointing, as she'd tracked that delivery all morning on her computer.

Once, a driver arrived in a thunderous downpour, a surprisingly posh-sounding Englishman in his late fifties, his threadbare white dress shirt rain-plastered to his chest. He deposited three bags, and stepped back for social-distancing, placing himself under the deluge again. She summoned him back beneath the overhanging eaves, and noticed a dripping packet of roll-your-own tobacco in his cargo shorts. 'Have a cigarette break,' she urged him. 'Actually, better yet: come in for a coffee. I was just making some.'

He preferred to stay outside, so she propped open her front door, diagonal rain pelting the hallway, his cigarette crackling as he stood on her welcome mat, sipping black coffee and sweating, for it was humid, this rain overdue, they agreed, and so heavy that it made you wonder what was happening up there (Dora growing irritable from urgency to move beyond the weather to proper subjects). She clasped one knobbled hand with the other, as if to restrain it, to shush herself till he'd finished his sentence. He lived off a patchwork of jobs, he said, and had taken up deliveries for the charm of wandering through empty London, all its mice hiding in their holes.

'Mice like me?'

'Like you.'

Baritone voices always appealed to Dora. He made eye contact

and held it, or appeared to behind the rising streamers of his cigarette. She imagined him as a lover. Worth risking death by Covid for
that! She suppressed a smile. But she should've been ridiculous, and
asked him to sleep with her. He would've declined. So what? And
who knew what he'd have said. Anyway, she missed her chance. Her
regret over this festered, and it metastasized, turning into something
like regret for the future: that she was beyond experiencing anything
more of note, merely edging down a narrowing passage. Dora closed
the front door after the deliveryman went, but she remained in place,
two minutes later opening it again: the privet hedge, raindrops plop-
ping into recycling bins, his empty mug on the doorstep.

She culled overrated books from her collection first, dropping
them with satisfaction into the blue recycling bin (cardboard, paper,
novels). Next, outdated works of non-fiction. Then, decent books
that, realistically, she'd never re-read. After more rounds of disposal, only a few hundred volumes remained, fallen editions on
dust-silhouetted shelves, including the tattered Dutch novels that
she'd inherited from her mother, along with editions her father had
bought Dora more than sixty years before, back when you'd still see
handsome young men and know they'd done something in the war,
back when writing still seemed the defiance of bullies, and books
came inscribed to you, with jokes and unexpressed love, a particular
copy evoking a particular person, or a café where you read it, then
closed it over your thumb, and sat inside its pages, incapable of
resuming the present.

Dora hired a removals man, a bald young Syrian named Amir,
who boxed all the remaining books, including every copy of her
eleven novels, plus the two story collections, and the memoir. Her

bookshelves were empty. The next owners could pull them down, and broaden the rooms.

To keep Amir from leaving so fast, she kept adding objects to take away, amused by this farce of jettisoning more and more in exchange for extra minutes with this reticent stranger. He agreed to a free lunch, which surprised her. In her kitchen, Amir acted like a schoolboy with his great-aunt, hurriedly forking in food, leg jiggling under the table. When Dora found that he'd grown up outside Paris, she switched to French, and he became more engaged, telling her that his father – his only close family member who'd not fled Syria – had recently been buried, but Amir was unable to return for the occasion; too dangerous. He wanted her to know that he wasn't just a man with a van, that he'd graduated, and once had a conditional acceptance to an American college, until his life was derailed by a visa denial from Trump's America.

That week, her phone beeped with an NHS message, reminding her that Covid vaccinations were available to her age bracket. When she failed to book an appointment, a social worker phoned to ask why. Dora explained that this disease seemed an acceptable way to go, provided it took you alone and at home. She cited her mistake of eating healthily and exercising – her body threatened to live for many more years, if she wasn't careful.

'Mrs Frenhofer? Let me find someone who can speak to you.'

On the psychological-assessment questionnaire, Dora was candid about thoughts of ending her life. This must've triggered an algorithm, for a counsellor was assigned, a gentle sixtyish man named Barry, who (she googled him) had been a lawyer but had since retrained, and now appeared every two weeks on her Zoom.

Barry could turn on his camera, and Barry could unmute himself, but Barry rarely achieved both feats at once. The opening minutes of each session, this endearing gnome frowned on her monitor while moving his lips in silence; or a black screen appeared to the audio of stammered apologies about technical difficulties. Barry could've slipped into one of her books. But she tried to see him as other people see people: they happen, and you happen, and there's nothing to take.

He began each session by asking Dora how she was managing.

'Managing what, the end of the world? It's lovely and peaceful here. Except for hearing all these terrible things going on everywhere.'

'We *will* be done with this disease. And not long from now!'

'But, Barry, don't you think it's forever? The virus is circulating like mad, evolving, variants upon variants. There'll be other pandemics too, you have to assume.'

'You're feeling a little down today?'

'Not at all. I have no complaint. I *am* sorry for the young, who inherit all this. But I have nothing to moan about. True: I'm here on my own, and that is challenging at times. But not unfair. I left so many people in my life. Friends and weddings and birthday parties and more that I didn't want to attend. But how else could I have been? I was this.'

'You *are* this. Whatever age, we all live in the present tense.'

'Gosh, I hope not.' One should leave the field to others, Dora believes. It's greedy to linger, demanding more. She never mistook life for a children's story, never wrote happy endings. What matters about a story is that it finishes.

'Take your thoughts to court,' Barry said – one of his CBT

mantras, whereby the patient must interrogate their negative ideas, cross-examining them as a lawyer might. 'Have you taken your thoughts to court, Dora?'

'I'm hoping my thoughts come back with a plea bargain, Barry.'

This was their sixth session – the last covered by the NHS. A phrase kept repeating in her head: 'Let's wrap this up.' At the conclusion, she thanked Barry for such kind efforts. 'If we were in person, I'd give you chocolates.'

'And I'd eat them.'

The old man across this table keeps nodding off, head forward, a long strand of hair hanging free, fluttering each time he exhales. This prompts Dora to tidy her own hair, but when she cups the crown of her head, expecting a bun, she finds it shorn, and runs her fingers down to the bone at the top of her neck. When young, she considered her hair among her most attractive features. This last Christmas, she cut it off. Her fingers were uncooperative, joints too swollen for the fabric scissors. The result made her laugh at the bathroom mirror, her hand across her eyes for a second, then looking again, pleased by her own smile. 'Ah well!' When they lifted Covid restrictions on hairdressers, a stylist behind a face visor trimmed Dora to acceptability, mouthing lyrics to a beat issuing from white earbuds. Afterward, Dora stood on the street, and touched her cold ears.

Once, *he* was attractive to someone, Dora thinks, of the dozing old man. We humans live too long. A chimpanzee is dead by forty. But people outlive their teeth and their competence. A few years ago, she and this man could've fit together, and theirs would've been a freighted conversation, he wondering: 'Would she? With me?' Not because Dora was irresistible but because heterosexual men, she believes, are harassed by such thoughts about unrelated females of child-bearing age. She pities men for this narrow view of the opposite sex — such small periscopes.

A memory distracts her: a literary hero, man of the Left, who'd denounced the Stalinists when they were still in fashion, and withstood condemnation for it. When she met him, he dressed in tweed-and-tie, an émigré recusing himself from the hippie era. They sat in flirting distance at a high-table dinner in Oxford, and she ended up in his cold room, where he stripped with such alacrity that Dora hadn't yet unzipped her knee-high leather boots. Rather than shielding himself, he stood impatiently naked, as if preparing to jump in a lake. Were Hungarians nudists? She'd not known that. Normally, Dora relished quickening the breath of an intelligent man, but he had gorged on butter-dipped crevettes. The more aroused, the more garlic. Their sex was normal enough, though Dora was struck to observe that the penis of such an impressive thinker bent to the right, in contrast to his politics. Afterward, he made coffee only for himself, and she was never able to read him again.

'The end of an era,' the old man is saying, awakening.

'What is?'

'I am.' He's telling of his siblings — he's the last of four. 'And you?'

Dora mentions her younger half-brother, adding that he went missing — almost certainly dead, perhaps an accident, or he took his own life. 'We never found out.'

'If he was alive, would you be doing this?'

Immediately, Dora knows the answer. It surprises her.

In the months after Theo went, no letters came home. Dora reassured everyone: he was exploring, breaking away from childhood and home, as he should. After a few years, she accepted that something had happened – the realization came suddenly: an anxiety dream, Theo locked in a room somewhere, tormented. Even today, she has an eerie sense that he is still alive, maybe in an ashram, praying to something that isn't there. In parallel, she knows he's gone.

During the pandemic, Dora marked his birthday – she opened a decent wine in her kitchen, reviewing all that she'd known of Theo: the little boy with white-blond hair, as clumsy as if on stilts, pushing other kids because he didn't know how to get attention, till they pushed back, and he retreated for the next decade, growing ever taller, and more hunched, and she never understood his eyes. To his birthday wine bottle, she spoke in a soft voice, perhaps not speaking aloud, I wonder where you would live now. In Dad's house? I was sure you'd come back after a few months, and Dad would nod at me, and your mother would wipe her eyes in relief, and you'd tell of adventures, and mention names of friends we'd not heard of. Instead, I find you here, looking across the table. You never say anything.

A ringtone – 'Baby Shark' – causes her to jerk upright. The old man locates his device, but can't figure out how to answer the phone, which is designed for the elderly, with huge number keys. Dora responds for him, putting it on speaker: it's Scott from the taxi.

'Nearly here, are you?' the old man says, deepening his voice. He's trying to impress the son-in-law. Dora has a realization: this man doesn't want to go ahead with this. But he's trapped. That farewell party – everyone came to say goodbye. He can't let them down.

'You *can* change your mind,' Dora blurts.

Scott, voice hissing on speakerphone, responds: 'Who's that? Who's there, Frank?'

'There's a lady that let me in.'

'What, from the company?'

Dora says: 'You do *not* have to go through with this. You don't.'

The old man to Scott: 'They're saying we got the wrong day, mate. She's saying it's not my turn. Actually wouldn't mind if—'

'Bollocks!' Scott replies. 'I'm there in like five minutes tops.'

'No worries, Scott. Thanks, mate.' He puts down the phone, not looking at her.

Dora unzips her duffel bag, takes out the sandwich. She walks to the front door, and opens it. She inhales fresh air.

But she isn't hungry after all, so puts the sandwich back. She looks down the road, and walks in that direction. The old man appears behind her at the front door, leaning against his oxygen canister. 'Where you off to?'

She doesn't turn back, just raises her hand goodbye.

Dora walks along the side of the road, which is dusty from road-works that have consumed the pavement. Every few seconds, a car whooshes past.

When she was a writer, a publisher flew her to a literary festival in Australia, and she heard peers proclaim that their fictional characters felt more alive than living people. You must allow fellow professionals a lie now and then, if it's good for business. But characters halt at the end of chapters whereas people won't stop, even once their stories are done. Dora was never the kind of writer who described the sea, just people. They obsessed her because they disappointed her. Yet now, she can scarcely even recall her characters' names.

Dora planned never to attempt another manuscript after that editor rejected her. She had the awkward Soho lunch with her literary agent, and wondered if this was how a writing career ended. Yet she left the meal with a flicker of hope, enough to sit at her laptop again, attempting stories, which expanded and contracted over the lockdowns that followed. What linked those chapters was one character: a minor novelist in a minor crisis. This was a version of herself, but with an opportunity to behave differently somehow, to solve something. Yet Dora failed to make a case for this person, who remained a middling writer, important to nobody but herself. She deleted the novel, deleted the novelist.

Now, it's only Dora Frenhofer, watching dusty black leather shoes stride beneath her, overcome by a longing for experience, a path disappearing through a field, to march into a boastful wind, her toes clutching pebbles, the coldness of water up her feet, and foaming around her ankles.

She stops to wake her phone, scrolling to a name. If she lowers her forefinger a millimetre, and her skin touches glass, signals will rush to satellites, pulses will dart along cables to the other side of this world, buzzing an iPhone on a bedside in Los Angeles.

Whenever she and her daughter speak, Dora expresses too little. Those are blocked conversations, for Beck has adopted her mother's hardness, unaware that Dora is trying so desperately to renounce it. During lockdown, Dora added more old photos to the ledge behind her writing desk, most of her daughter. Beck always hated posing for pictures: it forced her to think how she looked, who she was from outside. Dora added a picture of Morgan too, during a walk on Hampstead Heath. Beside that was a faded Polaroid: Theo holding a glass of beer in Amsterdam; plus, the only photograph of her parents together, squinting in black-and-white.

Dora swept those photos off the ledge this morning, stacking them in the hamper under her desk, among obsolete computer peripherals. Someday, a removals man will sift through the contents, and empty all those faces at the dump.

She checks for missed calls: only three in recent months, all from Beck, who tried to reach Dora during the pandemic, leaving terse voicemails to enquire how her mother was managing. Dora never called back. She always told herself: your children mustn't look after you.

She is not distressed to do this alone. Hers has been a life richly felt, tasted, investigated. This final phase, she hasn't thrived; that is true.

She half-smiles, for a London black cab is speeding down the hill toward her. Dora sticks out her arm. The driver slows to a halt, lowering the passenger-side window. 'Sorry, I'm not from here,' Scott tells her. 'I only speak English.'

'I don't suppose,' she asks, 'that you could take me to Piccadilly Circus?'

'You what?'

Dora repeats herself.

'I'm not supposed to operate in this country,' he says. 'I'm on a private thing. But we can figure out a flat fee. I need an hour first. When you looking to go?'

'I was joking. Only joking.'

'Why'd you wave me over then?' He drives off, muttering, 'Bloody woman.'

Dora passes the outlets selling sofas and golf equipment. Her knee is sore, a dull ache that is not unpleasant. She touches her cold ears, pulls on them as if they were not her, the skin and cartilage of an old woman. A deep inhalation: her chest rises. She looks up at a tower of blue air, molecules to the top of the atmosphere. How much would those weigh? It's among the facts that other people know.

At the bus stop, she eats part of her sandwich, but has no desire for flavour. She plotted this situation, came all the way here, and must find if she's a character who can carry it out.

She returns to the town house, punches in the code on the lockbox, and enters those rooms again, now emptied of the old man she imagined for company. Dora flicks on every light, reads the letter that the organization left on the table, and checks the instructions against the three medications, all labelled with her name.

'I'm a bit scared,' she says. 'Oh, come on. Don't be silly.'

She fills the kettle, listens to its rising boil. A beep. Quiet.

But she doesn't want more hot drinks. She runs a glass of water. She opens the packets.

Dora Frenhofer is falling asleep, faster than expected. Soon, nobody anymore. Not even her.

Acknowledgments

Special thanks to Natasha Fairweather, my agent, such a valued supporter of my work; your encouragement prompted me to write this book. Also, my lasting gratitude to Jon Riley of riverrun – I'm immensely lucky to have had you championing my writing. Thanks also to my American editor, Ben George of Little, Brown, who provided excellent comments and conversation; I look forward to more of both. Everyone at Doubleday Canada is a delight, from Kristin Cochrane at the start, to Kiara Kent and Amy Black – working with you is always a pleasure. Three fellow writers were exceptionally generous with time and thoughts when I researched this book: Iben Albinus, Diederik van Hoogstraten, Leo Mirani. My warmest thanks.

Lastly, I'd like to express something that can't be heard by its subject, my father, Jack, who died while I was writing this book. When I was a sloppy lad who read only magazines, he put great novels before me, and illuminated them with his passion. Mercilessly (and brilliantly), he critiqued my schoolboy essays. Later, he became the most-touching enthusiast for my novels. Finally, he leaves me with the company of Orwell and so many other writers who, like Jack himself, remain faithful guides long after they themselves have no more words.

About the Author

Tom Rachman is the author of three novels: his bestselling debut, *The Imperfectionists*, which was translated into twenty-five languages; the critically acclaimed follow-up, *The Rise & Fall of Great Powers;* and a novel set in the art world, *The Italian Teacher*. Born in London and raised in Vancouver, Rachman studied cinema at the University of Toronto and journalism at Columbia University. He worked at the Associated Press's Manhattan headquarters as a foreign-news editor, then became a correspondent in Rome. He also reported from India, Sri Lanka, Japan, South Korea, Egypt, Turkey, and elsewhere. To write fiction, he left the AP and moved to Paris, supporting himself as an editor at the *International Herald Tribune*. Later, he was managing editor of *Persuasion* and served as a juror for the Giller Prize. His writing has appeared in the *New York Times, The Atlantic,* the *Washington Post,* the *Wall Street Journal,* and *The New Yorker,* among other publications. Tom Rachman lives in London.